AN
OVERSEAS
BOY

PETER LAZARD

AN OVERSEAS BOY

DESERT ♥ HEARTS

First published in 2005
by

Desert♥Hearts

www.deserthearts.com

PO Box 2131
London W1A 5SU
England

© Desert Hearts 2005

Typeset and designed by Desert♥Hearts

ISBN 1 898948 16 X

A CIP catalogue record for this book is available from
the British Library.

Printed and bound by
Newton Printing, London, England

A . M . D . G .

Papa Legba, ouvrez barrière
pou moin passé!

For the Trickster,
and a gentleman from the Basque country
called Iñigo López de Recalde.

ACKNOWLEDGEMENTS

Thank you Titi (for four decades going on five), Nick (three decades), María (one decade), my friends in Havana and Camagüey (fifty decades), and my familiars, Kim and Heidi, for whom time has no meaning.

Additional thanks to Luiza Khitarishvili and Paul Vale for their help on the cover.

PART ONE

*"If we analyze the principles of thought on which magic is based,
they will probably be found to resolve themselves into two:
first, that like produces like, or that an effect resembles its cause;
and, second, that things that have once been in contact with
each other continue to act on each other at a distance
after the physical contact has been severed."*
—Sir James George Frazer, 'The Golden Bough'

In the mid nineties, *MI6's Havana Station was caught in a no-man's land.*

On the one hand, Cuba was an anomaly in the post-Cold War world order. Despite the economic quicksand it was suffocating in, Havana was still the nerve centre of a web of subversion that entangled the whole region. Dr Fidel Castro Ruz, last of the red-blooded Communists, swam stubbornly against the tide of history, determined as never before to export his Revolution to Latin America and the Caribbean. He had been foiled in Grenada and El Salvador and now even the triumph of the Revolution in Nicaragua had been reversed. Those in the know said that 'El Hombre' had set his heart on Colombia and Venezuela. Now that the Soviet paymasters were gone, he had a free hand and he was on the warpath again. For the spymasters in London and Washington all this smacked deliciously of the Golden Age of the Cold War. Cuba should have been fertile ground for spooks of the old school who had grown up haunting the Eastern Bloc and now hankered for a real Communist enemy to spy the living daylights out of.

On the other hand, Cuba was such a tightly controlled police state that any subversion by foreign operatives was doomed to failure. The in-country activities of MI6 were by necessity very low key. At the Embassy, the military attaché's staff and the commercial and cultural officers—the usual cover for intelligence officers—were genuine FCO and not 'Friends'.

It was the unspoken understanding between the British and their hosts that Level 2 activities only were to be conducted out of Havana Station, located at No. 6, Calle Facundo Vázquez—Level 2 being the opportunistic recruitment of non-Cuban diplomats and nationals, whereas Level 1 is activity aimed directly at the host government. This protocol required the Head of Havana Station and his clerk to front as lowly Consular Officers. Level 1 work in Cuba was left exclusively to the handful of gringos who operated out of the US Special Interests building on the Malecón, Havana's oceanfront drive. In fact even their role was minimal; the real effort against Cuba was co-ordinated by US operatives from within the 'mafia terrorista', the exiled Cuban community that infested Miami, not ninety miles away across the shimmering dolphin-haunted straits. There, the 'gusanos'—the worms—as they were called by Castro, pullulated and grew fat off the carcasses of capitalism.

MI6's operations against Cuba were also directed from offshore—in this case from Mexico City Station. The beauty of the Great Game, as played by the British since the days of Walsingham and totally in keeping with the English character, was that

9

indirect attacks through third parties and the setting of enemies against each other are generally the most fruitful forms of subversion. If Cuban officials were to be induced to defect, Level 2 procedure required the transaction to be conducted offshore.

Now that the Contra war was over in Nicaragua and kleptocracy restored, Mexico City Station and its satellites were preoccupied with providing their CIA overlords with intelligence for undermining the Cuban Revolution's subversion of the Andean countries and its infiltration of the exile community in Miami.

Havana Station was rarely asked to participate in an onshore operation against the host. The Station's most sensitive work against Cuba was to obtain third party corroboration, known in the trade as 'collateral', for the claims of defectors and boat people debriefed in Miami. Occasionally the Station would check out information provided by Cuban journalists or diplomats who had been 'turned' or 'burned' in Mexico, or of Africans who had received military training in Cuba and were now more interested in feathering their bank accounts.

Havana Station was also the first screening point for 'walk-ins', defectors who voluntarily approached British Intelligence onshore. This last category was rare and treated with the utmost suspicion.

CUBA, 1994
THE SPOOKHOUSE

THE SPOOKHOUSE

"There are spooks and there are spooks, Morpheus. In Cuba I became a spooky kind of spook."

Morpheus chuckles politely. He always appreciates his friend's attempts at humour.

They are at the crossroads, where they always meet.

"Now close your eyes," Morpheus whispers, as the drug gently tugs Dr George Sinclair back into the past. "I'll be more than happy to guide you back to those days if that's where you want to go this afternoon. Are you comfortable, my friend? Lie back and relax, then, easy does it. Do you see this door? When we step through it together we'll be in another place and another time . . ."

It is the afternoon of December 17th, 1994. Her Majesty's Passport Officer, British Embassy Havana, arrives at a celebration for the patron saint of lepers. Dr Sinclair is accompanied by his thirteen-year-old daughter Ximena and her Haitian nanny Mem'zili.

The event was held in Guanabacoa, at the house of a prominent *santero*, an initiate of St Lazarus—whose other name in Cuba is Babalú-Ayé. It was to be a *toque*. Sacred *batá* drums had been procured and would be played that afternoon to summon the gods. The *santero's* front room was decked in purple banners, the colours of the saint. Some of the cloths covered the tureens that housed the secrets of the warrior *orishas* who guarded the house. Sinclair, Mem'zili and Ximena paid their respects to the saint by pouring libations of white rum at the feet of his statue. The saint of pestilence and sickness was supported by crutches and draped in his characteristic purple robe, which was covered in dollar and *peso* bills. Two ceramic dogs licked his sores. After paying their respects to their host, who received Sinclair's donation gratefully, they stepped into the *solar*, the inner courtyard of the house.

As they entered, it seemed to Sinclair that the crowd had been there for several hours already, waiting for the ceremony to begin. A *rumba* was under way. The assembly was swaying to the steady beat of a *guaguancó* and sporadic dancing had broken out in the corners of the *solar*. The rhythm was beat out by callused hands on three long drums—the high-pitched *quinto*, with its cracking slaps, the sweet sounding *conga*, keeping the beat and the booming bass of a *tumba*. The drums were accompanied by the hollow rattle of the *chekere* gourd, and were all held together by the three-two *clave* which was tapped out on something metallic, perhaps a country sickle or machete, as was the custom in those parts.

The heady mixture of sweat, cigar smoke and rum and the offbeat syncopation of the drums never failed to produce an adrenaline rush in Sinclair, a tingling of the groin. The thrill of anticipation that periodically jolted the crowd like a charge of electricity was the same pulse of energy that he had felt before the many ceremonies he had attended in Haiti, Africa, and Brazil. There was a sense of something coming, of something imminent. The spirits were stirring in their home across the ocean in Africa.

He clasped Ximena's hand tightly. He fancied he felt the girl's pulse racing with the rhythm of the drums. Mem'zili took her leave with a courtly bow and went to join the concelebrants for ritual cleansing before the saint was invoked.

The *toque* opened in an orthodox manner, Sinclair noted. The insults of the *akpwon*, the singer priest, were directed at Elegguá, the God of the Crossroads, to get his attention. They were accompanied by the frenzied ringing of the *iyalocha's* handbell, the *agogo*. This was followed by several rounds of call and response in the *lucumí* language, led by the *santero* and his *iyalocha*, both wizened African pure-bloods immaculately clad in white. The swaying, turbaned women of the chorus, which now included Mem'zili, radiant in her magnificent white dress, blessed the approach and coming of the man-child Elegguá.

"*Agó* . . . *agó* . . . *agó* . . . ," they chanted, begging for the gate to open.

The *batá* were now playing, having replaced the profane drums. The *batá* were a set of three hourglass-shaped, double-headed drums—large *iyá* (the mother drum), middle *itótele* (the slave) and small *okónkole* (the child) which set the pace. It was difficult to tell for how long the *batá* had been playing before events unfolded, but eventually the taunts of the *akpwon* and the rapid-fire code built into the beat of the drums successfully dislodged Elegguá from his parapet in Yoruba heaven.

The 'horse' that the 'gatekeeper' had chosen to mount that afternoon was a boy not yet in his teens. Until then he had sat quietly next to his mother at the edge of the circle. The child leapt up suddenly, and stood staring dumb-founded at the three drummers on the dais. The entry of the gatekeeper is always violent. It was as if someone suddenly whacked the child across the back of the knees with a cricket bat, Sinclair noted, because the child collapsed and fell forward at the same time. After emerging dizzily from the sudden jolt that signalled the physical mounting of the *orisha* onto his body, the boy, who suddenly was no longer a child, turned his dilated eyes on the swaying and chanting assembly. The *santero* rushed to him, helped him stabilize, puffed the smoke of a cigar into his face, and poured rum down his throat. He then thrust a crooked stick—the *garabato*—into the boy's hand and draped a red and black cape, the colours of the saint, around his shoulders.

The boy staggered at first as the *akpwon* released him, regained his balance, and then, with a mischievous smile, began to spin and dance joyfully around the edges of the candle-lit circle. Playfully he taunted members of the con-gregation with his stick, which he intermittently slashed and jabbed before him, his eyeballs rolling back in their sockets, to clear the path through the undergrowth and into the complicated sub-lunar world of humanity. His but-tocks jutted unnaturally high as he bent double and strutted to the offbeat crack and thump of the drums. He then sprang backwards around the circle in a manic one-legged dance.

This behaviour corresponded, Sinclair observed with academic satisfaction, to the classic characteristics of the God of the Crossroads—a childish disposi-tion and a teasing, puckish approach to the denizens of the world into which he had just parachuted. But don't be taken in by his boyish charm, Sinclair noted, Elegguá is not to be crossed. Yes, he is a prankster at heart, but his sense of humour tends to be black and cruel, and it can turn on a dime.

The doors to the Yoruba spirit world were now open. Elegguá had descended, mounted his horse, and now the other deities, which that night were to be led by Babalú-Ayé himself, could descend in a dignified manner. As if on cue, the boy ran towards the back door and stood behind it, then smart-ly collapsed into the waiting arms of the *iyalocha*. He was carted off to recov-er in the back room, repeating the unerring sequence of a ceremony thou-sands of years old. So far so good.

Under the fussy direction of the *babalocha*, the sacred drums now began to tap out carefully and with respect the proprietary rhythm of Babalú-Ayé. The *iyalocha* was readying the purple cloak and the walking stick for the next 'horse' to be mounted. As was the invariable sequence of events established in the tradition of the *regla de ochá*, Babalú-Ayé would soon manifest himself as a crippled dancer, barely able to hobble around the room on his crutch. And then, as his healing dance wore on, his back would straighten and his limbs would become filled with the vigour and rhythm of the stronger *orishas*, until he also became warrior-like in his manifestation, drawing on the same energy as Kabiosele Changó, the God-King of Thunder and lover of rum, women and the drum.

The rhythm commenced slowly and gradually built up in tempo and intensity. The three drummers sweated profusely but otherwise showed no sign of emotion, their faces impassive. These drummers had trained for months and years in the magic rhythms before being initiated and allowed to handle the sacred drums, for the drums were inhabited by spirits called *aña* and had their own names. *Iyá*, *itótele* and *okónkole* conversed among themselves in a complex interplay of pre-ordained beat and counterbeat . . .

And then, to Sinclair's alarm, it all started to go wrong.

The first sign that something was amiss was that the deep thump of the mother drum developed a curious lag. One of the drummers had missed the beat. And then another.

At first Sinclair suspected that it might be a case of one of the women in the congregation getting too close to the drums. Tradition holds that the *batá* are allergic to women and can fall out of tune at the approach of a woman, particularly a menstruating one.

But then the drummer holding *iyá*, which was draped in bronze bells and cowry shells, appeared to swoon and then collapsed. The sacred drum fell from the dais to the floor with a thunderous crash and rolled into the candlelit circle. Something as dreadful as this had never been seen in Guanabacoa before, and it was surely a sign that the intervention of the saints had taken a decidedly wrong turn. It could only herald the coming of something evil. A collective gasp seized the crowd.

Something made Sinclair turn.

It was then that he saw her.

His daughter stood quite, quite still in the centre of the magic circle, her brown skin honeyed by the light of the votive candles that surrounded her. She looked small and alone. She was stooping slightly, and was staring intently at a spot on the ground, her head cocked to one side as if listening intently to secret instructions on a wavelength from another dimension. The expression on her face was curious, reminiscent of the mildly surprised look of those suffering from epilepsy in the moments just before they are taken by a fit.

The *babalocha* and *iyalocha* stepped back out of the circle nervously and held Mem'zili back when she tried to rush into the circle of light where the girl stood. The *solar* fell silent.

The sweet soft English-rose voice of Helen Henshaw reached Sinclair's ears. He realized that it was coming from his daughter's mouth.

"... I'm in here George I can see you I'm afraid of the woman with the dark eyes she is here with me she hurt me very badly this place is dark George can you come to me George I can see you from in here I remember our first dance and the cricket flats I remember Pendle in the moonlight I remember what happened to me in India I remember Oxford and what happened in the museum and then what they did to me afterwards George I can see you but I'm afraid of the woman she hurt me I once did love you you know it's cold here and I want you here beside me just like old times in Gran's flat in Goodge Street when I knelt before you come and be with me I beg you bring me warmth protect me from them from the darkness . . ."

Everyone looked at the foreigner.

Even those in the congregation who understood English were confused by the curious words and names emanating from the dead girl.

"*Una muerta! Una muerta!*" someone in the crowd shouted: the dead were present.

Others moaned in anguish and confusion, because this *toque* had been dedicated to honouring the *orishas* and not to summoning the dead—a *toque* for the dead would have required a very different rite.

But the horrors of the hijacked seance were not yet over for George Sinclair. The crowd gasped again as it sensed a darker and stronger presence enter the circle. The candles flickered and almost blew out. Ximena's slight frame straightened and the girl seemed to grow more robust and literally several inches taller. Her face took on an air of defiant self-confidence as she set her dead gaze directly upon her father.

"*Es Oyá! Es Oyá!*" a woman from the chorus shrieked in panic, thinking that she had identified the coming of Oyá, the *orisha* of the cemetery.

A scent of almonds suddenly wafted through the *solar*, stronger even than the smell of sweat and smoke and rum and fear. A strident Australian voice replaced the gentle whisper of the convent girl.

"Your bitch Helen is here with me George Sinclair you bastard with her dimples the ones you loved so much dimples to die for ha ha and the good

Doctor Aggarwal is here too without his head ha ha and so is that stupid cow Jane Redskin or whatever her name is . . . ," and after a pause, as if in doubt, the disembodied voice spoke again but this time with less confidence, ". . . there's someone else here too George but I'm not prepared to say who never mind ah that daughter of ours was too strong for me George what a way to be dispatched eh ha ha sport like your worst nightmare what a way to be . . . *to be* . . ."

Then, with a meaner, spiteful tone, she continued: ". . . he was right about you George my father was I can see that now ah it's easier to see things as they are from here always good for a fuck on the sly that Sinclair boy father said clever sod but with the morals of an alley cat he said not to be trusted he said still it was my choice to take you and what goes around comes around ha ha as your girlfriend Helen liked to say George eh enough said . . ."

And that was that.

Sinclair wondered whether his grandmother—Grannyjee—would be the next to participate in the chorus of the dead.

It was then that Ximena collapsed where she stood and all hell broke loose in the congregation.

"*Dos muertas! Dos muertas!*" they cried, terrified that the two dead women would follow them home.

"*Dos muertas!*" they screamed, in a paroxysm of fear.

"*Dos muertas ASESINADAS!*" someone groaned, as men and women alike stampeded out of the *solar*, because it was clear that the women who had spoken from the other side that afternoon had both been murdered.

"Let me set the scene for you, George," Morpheus resumes, as Sinclair starts to go under again. "Havana—a city cut off from the world, stressed out and inert in the hot Caribbean sun and inching deeper and deeper into decrepitude, waiting for doomsday. Do you see it? Do you feel it? It's early 1994. You've just arrived from Port au Prince, because SNAPPER has surfaced at last, just as he said he would. You've landed right in the middle of the Special Period. That's the euphemism that Castro uses for the catastrophic nosedive of the Cuban economy. The Socialist Bloc has gone up in smoke overnight and the Revolution is adrift and friendless in the world—no more subsidies and oil-for-sugar deals with the Soviet Union. The Cubans are poor as church mice; they've never had it so bad. There have even been food riots in Havana and there are rumours that Fidel is on the ropes at last. There is talk that the End of Days is at hand."

"Yes," Sinclair replies, "I remember. The End of Days . . ."

That's how the spooks referred to the inevitable last days of Castro's regime—never mind that it was already thirty-five years too late. The End of Days—the Apocalypse of the Revolution, when it was assumed the whole shit-house would collapse in flames following mass starvation, the overdue US invasion or the popular uprising that was bound to come after *El Hombre's* death.

"Things are difficult, even for the diplomats and the spies," Morpheus resumes. "It is a tense and fretful season, and not just for the Cubans. Back in London, the Service is in turmoil. The long knives have come out at last and there is blood on the floor. Many of the old hands are gone. They are shutting down Stations left right and centre. The new Head Boys are turning the Secret Intelligence Service into a glorified drug interdiction operation now that the bogeymen of the Cold War have disappeared."

"Yes, it's a grim, nasty time. There's fear everywhere, you can smell it," George agrees, a gentle wave of euphoria washing through his veins.

"Now then, where were we, my friend? HM British Embassy, Consular Section. It is located in the diplomatic quarter of Miramar, a couple of blocks from the waterfront. Number 6, Calle Facundo Vázquez. Are you still with me, George? Your cover is Passport Officer, unless I'm quite mistaken."

"Yes, but remember," Sinclair insists, his eyelids heavy now, his voice drowsy, "that by then I was a Grade 3 in the Service, and the youngest Head of Station in a generation. Probably since the War, for that matter, even as the heads were rolling in Vauxhall Cross. You can check the records if you don't believe me . . ."

Morpheus waves this away. He would never dream of checking up on a friend. He knows very well that Sinclair's problem is common to all ambitious intelligence officers—how to deal with success in the shadows while to the outside world you may appear to be a serious under-achiever.

It was true. Certain British expats in Havana sometimes asked themselves why Dr George Sinclair was so spectacularly unsuccessful. Why hadn't he prospered in the FCO despite a doctorate from Oxford? The man's stunted career was in Her Majesty's Diplomatic List for all to see: Magdalen College, Oxford, Archaeology and Anthropology, First Class (1981-1985); DPhil, Oxon (1985-1988); Civil Service Selection Board (1988); Third Secretary (Commercial), Managua, Nicaragua (1989-1992); Leave of Absence (Sabbatical), Port au Prince, Haiti (1993); Passport Officer, Consular Section, Havana, Cuba (1994-present).

"Rumour has it," Morpheus resumes, "that you are an academic who has joined the Diplomatic Service—it might just as well have been the British Council, for that matter—for an easy ride travelling the world at the taxpayer's expense. It doesn't occur to most of them that you are a spook."

Some of the expats who had met Sinclair felt that there was something troubling about him. On the surface, the fact that he was an Anglo-Indian, an accident of colonialism, was not held against him. But he was not one hundred percent British and that could not be ignored, they agreed with knowing looks over their gin and tonics—just look at the man's bizarre domestic arrangements.

And then there were the other rumours, about how somewhere along the way he had strayed from the true path and gone native.

As has become their custom, Sinclair lays quite still, pulse minimal, eyes closed, while Morpheus speaks of days gone by. With his mesmerist's voice, Sinclair's friend and guide conjures up the images and words and feelings of the past.

Ah, the past, the other country, the minefield of my history, Sinclair sighs with contentment, sinking deeper into the warmth, because the past is the past and it can't hurt him now. The past, which in his mind's eye George Sinclair now sees coming back to life before him in glorious Technicolor.

He sees a townhouse that serves as an annex to the Embassy. The bone-coloured building has a dilapidated look about it due to the latest Foreign Office budget crisis. It is 1994, the year that MI6 moved from Century House in Lambeth to its new space-age headquarters at Vauxhall Cross, known as Legoland. The move has almost bankrupted the FCO, which controls the secret budget, and the embassies are feeling the pinch. There is a certain resentment in the air against the Friends.

The annex is set back from the street, the Calle Facundo Vázquez, behind a forlorn garden. It stands in the shadow of the monstrous concrete tower of the Russian—once Soviet—Embassy that dominates the western reaches of the city like a bad memory. Two royal palms surrounded by bougainvillea cast the garden of the annex into shade and stand guard over the gatehouse. The iron gate is corroded with the salt of the ocean air that comes off the Florida Straits. Sinclair can smell it as sharply as if it were yesterday.

The MI6 spookhouse in Havana, the nest of imperialist British spies, consisted of two windowless ground-floor rooms cocooned in the middle of the Consular annex. It was your typical MI6 Station in hostile territory. There was an ante-chamber lined with box files stuffed with mock visa applications, where Alison Wiggins, Sinclair's cipher clerk on her first overseas posting, sat at her keyboard. Under her desk was the burn-box, where the one-time code-pads and their secrets were incinerated. Behind Alison Wiggin's room there was a bomb-proof steel door and a smaller office belonging to the Head of Station. Sinclair's room was spartan, more of a cell than an office. It contained a gunmetal desk, two telephones, the ATHS/OATS communications termi-nal, and a safe, where the sensitive files and the Station handgun resided. Inside the safe, next to the Beretta (standard issue) sat Sinclair's stash of mor-phine with syringes and tourniquet, in a red velvet bag. Next to the bag there was a locked casket containing a shrunken head.

One wall of Sinclair's cockpit was covered with an oversized satellite map of the island, dotted with red and blue tacks for his Joes, and a street map of Havana for the dead-letter boxes. According to the standing operating proce-dures of the Station the numbered tacks, cross-referenced to certain incrimi-nating files in the safe, were the locations of dead-letter boxes containing fab-ricated evidence against a cadre of highly placed *apparatchiks* loyal to Castro. It was all intended to confuse State Security's Counter Intelligence burglars who, it was assumed, would break into the Station at the End of Days, when chaos would reign and diplomatic etiquette would be thrown out of the window.

The real locations of SIS's assets on the island had been committed to memory and were locked inside Head of Station's skull.

The wall behind the desk was dedicated to several framed vignettes of Holbein's *Danse Macabre*, in memory of Sinclair's friendship with a man named Guy Underhill.

These were the inner rooms from where Sinclair and his assistant executed the stratagems of Her Majesty's Secret Intelligence Service in Cuba. They were soundproofed and airless. They were swept daily for bugs by the third person in this small circle, the Embassy Security Officer, Sergeant Warren. Warren was a furtive Liverpudlian who spent his spare time preying on under-age pros-titutes, the poorer the better, as far as he was concerned, because hunger made them more desperate and therefore more willing to accept his bizarre propos-als. These girls, known as *jineteras*—jockeys—were the spawn of the Special Period. They patrolled the Malecón, looking for hard currency and a square meal from the invasion of sexual tourists from Europe and Canada.

Nothing could get rid of the reek of stale tobacco, the legacy of the previous Head of Station, who had become addicted to *habano* cigars during his posting. The Consular Section's air-conditioning system failed with infuriating regular-ity, as did the water supply. Sinclair suspected that this happened a little more frequently for the British spies than for the long suffering inhabitants of West Havana—courtesy of Colonel Adalberto Bermúdez, Head of the Counter Intelligence Department of State Security, known as G-2. Bermúdez was well respected in the business because he had been trained the Czechs and East Germans, who had been known to run rings around their Soviet patrons when it came to the surveillance and harassment of foreign spies.

In London, soundproofed behind the thick smoked glass of their new offices high above the Thames, Sinclair's masters had to assume that Bermúdez had fingered Sinclair and his clerk as the resident British spooks from their first day in Cuba. At the end of the day the Head Boys in London had to admit that Havana Station's attempts to subvert the tidal wave of the Cuban Revolution from the modest spookhouse in Miramar were token and very indirect in nature.

The marginal role of Havana Station made it a sure candidate for closure in the global restructuring of MI6 in 1994. You might well conclude that George Sinclair was a second-tier resource of Her Majesty's Secret Intelligence Service in its prosecution of the Great Game—a member of the Second Eleven, or the B Team as the 'Cousins' would have put it. Perhaps not quite as dispensable as his colleagues languishing in Africa, but fairly low down in the food chain of the secret world nevertheless. And not long for this world, professionally speaking.

You would have been correct in this assessment, were it not for the fact that Sinclair's *raison d'être* in Havana, and the reason behind the inexplicable survival of Havana Station, was the running and servicing of a single agent called Carlos Maxwell, codename SNAPPER.

SNAPPER was a Sandinista and a super-agent. SNAPPER was the goose that laid the golden egg for MI6 in the region. And it was George Sinclair who had discovered the Holy Grail of the Latin America Controllerate, recruiting Maxwell in Nicaragua in 1990 during his first overseas posting. That stunning success had made Sinclair's name in the Service and had earned him Head of Station in Havana.

Servicing a single Joe involves long periods of waiting in between contact. It is during these hours of dangerous inactivity that you start to speculate and imagine the worst. You create phantoms of paranoia in your mind, and all this can lead to serious errors of judgment unless you can find a productive way to fill the downtime.

Running SNAPPER left Sinclair with a lot of time on his hands—and this is where the spooky stuff comes in—time which to devote to his academic interests, which since Oxford had revolved around the phenomenon of syncretism in the West Indies.

"Syncretism?" Morpheus asks.

"Syncretism, my dear Morpheus, is the fusion of disparate religious traditions into hybrid manifestations. Are you with me? In the West Indies, syncretism results from an unlikely combination of two imported belief systems: the spirit cults of the slaves from West Africa and the Catholicism of the Spanish and French colonists. The result is more commonly known as *santería* in Cuba, and in Haiti and the French islands as *vodoun*—'voodoo' to the ignorant. In Brazil, it is known as the *candomblé* or *macumba*."

"And what about the English?" Morpheus asks, fascinated.

"Well, the manifestation in the English islands is called *obeah*, although *obeah* is more like bush magic or shamanism than religion. The English were Protestants, you see. They rejected the magico-mystical aspects of Catholicism. You find *obeah* mainly in the Bahamas and in Jamaica. Then there is *shango* in Trinidad, but that's another story . . ."

"Do go on," Morpheus prompts, because Sinclair is beginning to drift away.

"The important thing to know, I suppose, is that the process of syncretization was not voluntary," Sinclair resumes, drowsily, "that is, it was not a natural process. It was born in a crucible of violence and oppression. The West African deities acquired the characteristics of the Catholic saints not because of any love by the slaves for the religion of the masters. They took little or no comfort in it at all. The fusion was not a friendly one. It was essentially an act of deception, of camouflage. Only by pretending to worship St Antony of Padua or the Christ Child of Atocha, for example, could a Yoruba slave, exiled from the warmth of home and family, pay homage to Elegguá, the God of the Crossroads . . ."

Those dead hours at the spookhouse gave him the opportunity to deepen his expertise in *vodoun* and *santería* and the affiliated cults of *rada*, *petro*, *palo mayombe*, *arará*, and *abakuá*. Sinclair was composing what he hoped would one day become a seminal work on the fusion of these cults with Catholicism. He had started his research at Magdalen before his recruitment into MI6. He had added to it during the sabbatical in Haiti before coming to Cuba. During his home leaves Sinclair had been back to England only to transit through to places like Benin and Togo, from where he had explored the Yoruba, Fon,

Nago and Bantu rites in neighbouring Nigeria and Congo. In the New World he had been to the spiritist temples in the *favelas* of Rio and São Paulo and Salvador de Bahía. And now that he was living in the cradle of the phenomenon in the West Indies and he fully intended to take advantage of the fact.

On slow afternoons when the languid torpor of the tropics invaded the spookhouse through the corridors of the Consular annex, the Passport Officer would add a few meticulous annotations and footnotes to his draft of *A Comparative Analysis of Afro-Antillean Syncretism*. He wrote in longhand, mistrusting the computer, under the slow spin of the ceiling fan and Holbein's millennial visions of the end of the world. The 16th-century artist's allegories of rotting corpses and their extravagant vistas of death were the same ones that he and Guy Underhill had first come across as schoolboys in the Arundell Library at the College.

Sinclair was determined that his celebration of syncretism would one day make his name. The book would be the definitive story of the tectonic collision of religious cultures and their inevitable reconciliation in the New World.

Sinclair was an Anglo-Indian, remember. His project would also justify his obsession with the no-man's land of the half-breed, of the half-caste, of the mestizo and the mulatto. It would satisfy that vague shiftless itch of dissatisfaction that he had carried within his own divided self ever since they had sent him away from home.

But by that stage in his career, Sinclair had also acquired an eminently practical outlook. Critical acclaim and therapy were all very well, but he knew that his book was also his passport back into academia should his career fail to prosper in the secret world.

THE RETURN OF SNAPPER

SNAPPER had eventually resurfaced in Havana towards the end of 1993. Almost a year earlier, in Nicaragua, MI6's top asset in Latin America had disappeared off the face of the earth to the near panic of the Head Boys in London. Back then there had been anxious moments in certain fifth-floor offices in Century House and much hand-wringing and gnashing of teeth in the Latin America Controllerate.

Sinclair remembered the frantic cable traffic of those days—you could almost smell the fear encoded into the insistent demands for updates and estimates. But now there was a buzz of excitement as SNAPPER was picked up simultaneously by the monitors at the US Interests building on the Malecón and by the CIA's huge Caribbean Station near Miami airport.

As had been agreed, Sinclair left Haiti shortly after the confirmation of SNAPPER's resurrection. Sinclair arrived in Havana with his daughter Ximena and her nanny in tow. Dr Sinclair took up his post in the Consular Section with a modest cocktail reception given by HM Consul Tony Prufrock, an old stick-in-the-mud who resented having to feed and water the Friends under the guise of Consular cover and made no bones about it.

"You're to keep that inquisitive nose of yours clean while you suffer my hospitality, young Dr Sinclair. There is to be no scandal on my watch, remember that. Not a breath of scandal—understand? There will be no trouble *here*."

It was obvious that things had been said about the New Boy before he arrived in Havana. The business in Managua had made the newspapers, and even though he had not been named in the scandal, those in the know knew that Sinclair had been involved somehow.

But it was when they saw his daughter Ximena and the nanny that they knew for sure that he was nothing but trouble.

After Maxwell had re-established contact with his handler, Sinclair drafted the first of his bi-weekly SNAPPER updates to Mackie, his boss. Mackie had survived the latest bloodletting in London thanks to his success with SNAPPER, and he was desperate for news of his golden boy. Mackie and his crew had barely survived those dark days of corporate restructuring on repeated assurances that SNAPPER would return, as he had promised, and that the flood of high quality CX would resume.

In his first message Sinclair speculated that their prize agent must have taken a detour through Beirut, because when he saw him again in a safe house in East Havana, SNAPPER had the look of a well-fed and well-sexed feline. He was wearing a Palestinian *kefeeyeh* and his eyes were unusually bright and alert. What Sinclair failed to mention in his cable to Mackie was that the name Jamila had come up several times in the conversation and that whenever he mentioned her, Maxwell's eyes would glaze over as he relived the carnal paradise of his Palestinian lover's thighs.

It turned out that SNAPPER had been given a position in the DGI, Cuba's overseas intelligence service. He had been nominated as Chief Advisor *in situ* to the Nicaragua Desk. The Nicaragua Desk had been the most active in DGI's Americas Department in the late seventies and eighties, but it was now less so after the defeat of the Sandinistas in the US-sponsored elections. MI6 now had a high-quality, underemployed Joe sitting at the very centre of Castro's spider's web, and that happy combination of circumstances made SNAPPER's 'access' and potential even greater. SNAPPER, once a remarkable spy, was now set to become devastatingly effective. Mackie and the Head Boys on the Twelfth Floor of Legoland were ecstatic, and Sinclair's star continued to rise.

The domestic arrangements that worried Prufrock and the expats were that Sinclair was wifeless and was accompanied only by his strange daughter and her Haitian nanny. The girl was darker than her father and had insolent eyes that stared at you with intent. The servant, who was called Mem'zili, they whispered, very likely 'worked nights'.

The three of them lived in a bungalow a few miles west of Havana, on the road to Pinar del Río. The gardens around the house reminded Sinclair of his childhood in Goa before he had been sent away to school. The property was vast by Cuban standards. The garden was full of royal palms and tropical ferns and orchids which Wycliffe, Sinclair's predecessor in Nicaragua, would have killed for. At the bottom of the garden stood a massive ceiba tree.

They had given Sinclair a chauffeur, a friendly mulatto called Gumercindo López. Gumercindo's job was to drive his boss to the Consular annex every morning, dropping Ximena off at the French school on the way. Gumercindo liked to drive with the radio tuned full blast to Radio Havana's dance music programme.

Two or three times a week they were tailed by the black Cadillacs of Colonel Bermúdez's watchers, which didn't matter, because Sinclair already knew that Gumercindo was in their pay. By the time Gumercindo drove the Passport Officer back home from the Consular annex in the late afternoon, he had already collected Ximena from school. Sinclair would often find his daughter in the twilit garden sitting under the ceiba, deep in conversation with Mem'zili and their familiars—two lizards and two feral cats.

SANTO

It was not the first time that foreigners had taken to dabbling in *santería*. It would all start innocently enough but more often than not it ended in tears. Unsuspecting tourists and would-be voodooists, an easy source of hard currency, were routinely fleeced of their money and belongings by charlatan *babalochas* and fake *iyalochas* in Havana. These manoeuvres often included drugging the victims with *hierba* or with cheap country rum, followed by mock initiations into the *regla de ochá* and demands for exorbitant fees.

Castro's secret police tolerated the practice of the religion well before the Catholic rites were opened up to the public. Castro himself was rumoured to have his own *santeros* who watched over him, keeping him safe from the never-ending assault of *palo* sorcery that reached Cuba from the sunlit shores of south Florida. They said that *El Hombre* was an initiate of Elegguá, the Trickster God, and that he was bathed in a tub filled with goat's blood every week by his *babalocha*. They said that Celia, Castro's longtime *compañera* from his first days the Sierra Maestra, now dead, had been his *iyalocha*.

The *babalochas* and *iyalochas* were licensed to practise the Yoruba religion. Each and every *casa de santo* was sanctioned and monitored by the neighbourhood CDRs, the *Comités de la Defensa de la Revolución*. The CDRs, Sinclair had been told by his government minders soon after his arrival, were not intended to control the people, as was widely put about by the Imperialist press, but to keep vigil. The CDRs safeguarded the people and their precious Revolution from the attacks of infiltrators from *la mafia terrorista* in Miami. And from foreign agitators like Her Majesty's Passport Officer.

Before the Triumph of the Revolution, Guanabacoa had been a lower working class sector of East Havana. Apart from housing a shrine for Havana's patron Virgin—*La Virgen de Regla*—this nondescript quarter, with its decrepit buildings and dusty sidestreets was, and still is, the spiritual epicentre of *santería* in Havana. It was there that Sinclair and Mem'zili regularly attended *toques*, *asientos* and other rituals of the Yoruba religion.

Sinclair, as always, took along his researcher's notebook. Mem'zili attended for her own spiritual sustenance. Sinclair was fascinated by the living anthropological experiment unfolding in front of him, as he witnessed Mem'zili, a Haitian, immerse herself in the rituals of Cuban *santería* in her own private experience of syncretism. Before and after these rituals he would question Mem'zili closely about the comparative attributes of the *orishas* of *santería* and the *loas* of *vodoun*. Academically, these were the most fulfilling days of Sinclair's life and they yielded much innovative research for his *Comparative Analysis of Afro-Antillean Syncretism*.

Their attendance at each of these events was noted and duly registered in G-2's log of the movements of Dr Sinclair, who was known in the records by his codename, SPINNER. The logbooks were devilled by Bermúdez's Counter Intelligence analysts in the basement of the Interior Ministry. The details of the latest sightings of SPINNER would then be fed into the old Soviet computer, which would calculate and map out the likely location of the British spy's dead-letter drops.

Because of Ximena's unearthly nature, Sinclair and Mem'zili had agreed back in Haiti to limit the girl's access to the spirit world to the most harmless events of *vodoun*. She would be allowed to attend only those rituals not involving spirit possession.

But it was not to be, not in Cuba.

Ximena now insisted, threatened, cajoled and insisted again. Eventually it was agreed that she could accompany her father and nanny to a ceremony in honour of Babalú-Ayé, otherwise known as St Lazarus, on his feast day. It was to be a *toque* ritual, when the sacred *bata* drums would play. Christmas was just around the corner and this kindly old *santo*—Sinclair and Mem'zili convinced each other—was unlikely to harm children.

NGANGA MPUNGO

Sinclair fretted the night away in the tortuous half-sleep that plagued him whenever he was in trouble. The *toque* had been an absolute disaster. He still couldn't believe what had happened there.

What would Colonel Bermúdez make of the reports that landed on his desk tomorrow? How would that old killjoy bastard Prufrock the Consul react? Was this the excuse he was always looking for to throw out one of the Friends? What would Mackie and the Head Boys at Vauxhall Cross think? Would they take his pension away? What would become of Ximena? Would they take her from him and put her into care? And what about Mem'zili? Would they let her into Britain or deport her back to the slums of Port au Prince? Would his role in the deaths of Xancha Bergsma, Helen Henshaw, Jane Redfern and Doctor Aggarwal be uncovered at last?

At first the Colonel might think that it was some practical joke by his underlings, but the more Sinclair thought about it he found it unlikely. Humour was in short supply in Cuba these days. The daily effort to survive in a devastated economy left most people exhausted and bad-tempered. Perhaps G-2's agent at the *toque*, Nacho Alvarado, had hallucinated it all after ingesting the plentiful *hierba* that was passed around these sessions? Not likely either—G-2 was draconian when it came to drugs.

In fact nothing surprised Colonel Bermúdez anymore. He had seen things in Angola and during his tour in Mozambique that no one would have believed if he had the inclination to talk about them. And he had long since failed to be impressed by anything or anyone other than Fidel himself. Bermúdez was a wily old fox and had raided too many chicken coops in his day to be impressed by the antics of a diplomat at a *tambor*, even if the diplomat was a well-known spook.

What would he make of it, then? In the secret world, every piece of information, however bizarre, has its place in the grand jigsaw puzzle of intelligence. It's just a question of timing. The Colonel would wait, Sinclair concluded, as dawn broke over the gardens around the house, for the right moment to leverage this curious piece of information.

Weakened and slightly feverish after the sleepless night, Sinclair worked half-heartedly on an old case at the spookhouse, waiting for Alison to knock the inevitable emergency code on his door. It was like waiting for the priest Spock to tap him on the shoulder during one of the witch hunts at the College. Sinclair seemed to have spent half his life figuring out how to get out of tight corners and awkward situations. All day long, pacing shiftlessly between his office and the anteroom, he scrutinized his cipher clerk from the corner of his eye. On his way in and out of the annex he searched the faces of the Consular staff for any hint that the events at Guanabacoa had been reported to Prufrock, but he could detect nothing out of the ordinary.

Since his days in Haiti, Sinclair considered himself to be under the protection of Papa Legba (or Elegguá as he is also known in Cuba) but he knew only too well that his guardian was capricious, particularly if he had been neglected. As morning passed into noon without incident, he concluded that the gatekeeper was on his side this time, and had left the door of fate ajar for his wayward child to escape through. The offerings must have helped.

Before Gumercindo had driven him to work, Sinclair had gone down with Mem'zili into the basement. There they had joined hands in prayer before the candle-lit shrine that they kept on the floor behind the cellar door—for Elegguá lives behind doors. Mem'zili had ripped the head off a black rooster and had anointed the Elegguá head with its blood, chanting the required salutations and then asking the god if he approved of the sacrifice. After casting her seashells, Mem'zili beseeched the gatekeeper in *lucumí* to open the gate for his child George Sinclair, and to keep the paths clear for him and his loved ones.

That morning, as the code in Mem'zili's cowry shells had demanded, Sinclair placed a miniature shrine to Elegguá in the Station safe, next to his stash of morphine and the shrunken head of Doctor Aggarwal. The shrine consisted of a small cement head with cowry shells for eyes, ears, nose and mouth, set in a small clay dish surrounded by fish meal, a sweet, half a *cohiba* and a tiny bottle of white rum, all provided by Mem'zili. God bless her, she had even rummaged around in Ximena's bedroom and emerged with a tiny rubber ball. Elegguá, she had reminded Sinclair, requires a toy at his shrine, to keep him amused when he is not up to his usual tricks complicating the lives of his initiates.

At the house Mem'zili nursed Ximena back to consciousness. The girl had taken a nasty knock on her chin when she had fallen to the ground at the *toque*, but otherwise she was completely oblivious of the events of the previous evening. All she could remember, she told her nanny, was walking into the *santero's* house past the statue of Babalú-Ayé and his dogs.

From that day on, Ximena was plagued by nightmares of her dead mother. In her dreams her livid mother would chase her down the endless secret passages of the College where Ximena used to hide and play as a child, or rise vampire-like from her tomb, hell-bent on revenge. These nightmares she confided to Mem'zili, who was always there in the middle of the night when the child awoke screaming. Mem'zili mopped her brow and comforted her back to sleep with Haitian lullabies.

Then things took a turn for the worse. It was no longer just a question of nightmares. As Mem'zili suspected would inevitably happen, the phantoms in Ximena's mind became real, and one evening during a thunderstorm, the girl appeared in her nanny's quarters and said matter-of-factly that her mother had just appeared to her in the bathroom and had threatened to drown her in the bathtub.

Sinclair was troubled. In his research he had come across these vengeful female wraiths before. Such an angry spirit is called a *lamia* or *succubus*. To his daughter, who was particularly vulnerable to attacks from the spirit world, the spiteful manifestation of her dead mother was extremely dangerous and potentially murderous.

From then on the ghost of Xancha Bergsma began to prowl around the house and to haunt Ximena with increasing regularity. The house became infested with cold spots and poltergeist activity. One night Sinclair himself witnessed the entire collection of porcelain in the dining room shatter and spin its way across the room, as Ximena fled in tears.

Sinclair never saw Xancha Bergsma's shade in Cuba, but he did not doubt for a minute that her ghost was mercilessly hounding his daughter. Her fury knew no bounds, least of all the bounds of a cold English crypt. For weeks Ximena reported sightings in the living room, in the bathroom again, and even in the gardens under the ceiba tree, which she had always regarded as her refuge. There in the garden, Ximena's cats had arched their backs and hissed and spat at the spectre and the lizards were nowhere to be seen. Each episode seemed to increase in intensity and menace, and Sinclair and Mem'zili began to fear for Ximena's safety.

And then Ximena took to waking in the night to see her mother's shadow standing at the foot of her bed, oblivious to the strands of garlic and dried serpent skin that her nanny had draped over the bedstead.

"Desperate times call for desperate measures," Mem'zili declared in Creole, shaking her head. She had just finished serving them their favourite dinner of curried goat and candied yams. She left the dining room. She returned a minute later with an empty gourd in her hands.

"It is time to confront your mother, *ma 'ti cherie*."

Mem'zili said that it would take time. The arrangements had to be planned meticulously, because they could not afford to make a mistake with the ingredients. These included certain parts of a freshly buried cadaver, as well as dirt from newly dug graves in three different cemeteries, the locations of which had been revealed by the cowry shells. In addition, the carcasses of various small animals and the specific organs of others were required.

It took Mem'zili several visits to the *paleros* of Guanabacoa to confirm the instructions and for certain expensive and hard-to-find ingredients, which Sinclair financed without a second thought. His only desire, when he was lucid in the evenings between doubled doses of morphine, was to free his terrified daughter from the clutches of the undead.

The most effective way to deal with hostile ghosts, Mem'zili had advised, was to work with the rites of the *palo monte* which, Sinclair knew, was Congolese sorcery that resembled that of the Haitian *zobop*. Like the Haitian sorcerers—the *bokors*—the *paleros* worked with the dead rather than with the *orishas* or *loas*. The *regla de monte*, Sinclair knew, has very little in common with the benevolent and mainstream *lucumí* ways of the *regla de ochá*, the religion of the Yoruba in Cuba.

Mem'zili and Ximena summoned their familiars—the lizards Nemo and Spock and the two feral cats that inhabited the overgrown garden, who Ximena had christened Mischief and La Negra. Before the emergency,

Ximena and her nanny had spent hours under the ceiba tree communing with these animals and training the cats not to attack the lizards. Soon it would be time to put them to the test.

In the meantime, with Mem'zili riding shotgun, Ximena fought a brave rearguard action against the menacing blue apparitions of her furious, suffocated mother. When the time came, one sultry evening in early January, Sinclair watched from the house as Mem'zili led Ximena three times around the ceiba tree, holding a black candle, and then three times in the reverse direction. He then spied them burying something at the foot of the gigantic tree.

Two days later on a moonlit night they dug up whatever they had buried under the ceiba and proceeded to summon the restless shade of the girl's mother. They raised the haggard and reluctant spectre of Xancha Bergsma at midnight at a crossroads in the countryside not far from the house, under the full moon.

Mem'zili was reluctant to provide details to Sinclair, only going only so far as to say that the dead woman had been furious and had put up a fight that had left them exhausted. And that, after all was said and done, the undead were to be pitied. Xancha Bergsma become a *mpungo*, an enslaved spirit.

They had returned to the house in the early hours of the morning, as Sinclair dreamed his old dream of black crabs, viciously sharp monstrances and of monkey judges masturbating in the Old Bailey. While Sinclair slept his fitful sleep, the strange little procession had returned to the house; Mem'zili, exhausted and almost undone by the titanic struggle with Xancha Bergsma, but dignified and solemn as usual. She was followed by only one of the cats, the one called Mischief, because by then the black La Negra had gone missing. The cat was followed by the lizards Nemo and Spock, and finally there came Ximena, proudly holding the gourd before her. This was the *nganga* where they had trapped her mother's spirit.

"Within the *nganga* dwells the *mpungo*, whose only purpose from now on is to do your daughter's bidding," Mem'zili explained.

Ximena's bidding, for good or evil, 'til death us do part.

CREEPER

Some of the Brits who worked in the Consular annex affected to wear crêpe-soled desert boots, otherwise known as brothel creepers. This allowed them to wander silently along the corridors of the annex, which, they were taught to assume, State Security had bugged deluxe from floor to ceiling. As you approached the rooms of the Friends, large notices placed every few yards along the corridor requested you to observe absolute silence.

Three weeks after the disaster at Guanabacoa, Sinclair was tidying up the third chapter of his book. It was just before the weekend. He was aroused by someone tapping on his door. It was Alison. This was not the emergency code that they had rehearsed in advance but it indicated an in-house visitor. This is it, Sinclair thought, tensing, they've finally found out about the *toque*. Get ready, steel yourself, deal with it. Deal with it, boy, he heard his father intoning in his head. This is just one more Predicament of many. You've been in worse holes before, in tighter corners, so get a grip.

Sinclair cleared his desk and then flicked the 'all clear' switch under his desk. The armoured door sighed as it swung inwards on its hydraulic hinges, to reveal the smug shiny face of Robin Ruskin looking over Alison's shoulder into the inner sanctum. Ruskin was Head of Personnel at the Embassy. Sinclair knew him casually but he had never had the pleasure of a visit. It must be bad news for Ruskin to have dared to venture into the realm of the Friends. In the Embassy Ruskin was known as 'Creeper' because he crept around silently on his rubber soles delivering official edicts, usually of the nasty variety like early retirement notices, official reprimands or one-way tickets back to Heathrow. The presence of this bird of ill omen lurking at Sinclair's door that Friday afternoon, in his tight-fitting suit and brothel creepers, could only mean bad news.

The first thing that struck you about Ruskin was his eczema, which had made him raw around the collar. The second was his hands—nervous little things that clutched and fidgeted with the manila folder he was holding and reminded Sinclair of those delicate pink sand crabs that scuttle among the rock pools on the seashore.

Ruskin was a Protestant from a minor Public School near the Welsh border, which had the happy name of Giggleswick. The College regularly trounced Giggleswick at cricket, Sinclair remembered with satisfaction. As Ruskin stood there in his doorway, rubbing the scaly skin of his chin, it occurred to Sinclair for the first time that he had seen that face before somewhere. Certainly not on the cricket pitch, for Ruskin's posture wasn't that of a sportsman.

That was it. It had been at Darby House, after his first interview with Mr Holiday in 1988. Ruskin was the boy in the tight suit under the stairs, rubbing himself raw as he waited for his interview with the Secret Intelligence Service.

Sinclair himself had become a master of the lie. His training in the arts of deception had started long before the new intelligence officers' training course at Fort Monckton. He had first picked up these skills at home in Goa. It was there that he had learned to lead a double life as Major Sinclair's son, the English-speaking Masterjee, and as the Marathi-speaking cricket chum of the garden-wallahs. Not to mention the double-dealing with the Catholic *Bom Jesus* and Grannyjee's Hindu gods and *devis*. Then there were the counterfeit reports of happiness in his letters home from Prep School in Surrey, followed by the interrogations under the Jesuits' lamps at the College. It was there that deviousness had become a way of life as he learned to feed his drug habit and prosecuted his schoolboy *'affaire'* with Matron. All this had led to the business with Guy Underhill in 1979, which he had officially decided to forget.

But what had happened at the end of that disastrous summer term at the College was not the end of it. It had gone on. During his year abroad from Oxford he had gone on to take advantage of certain individuals in Martinique. And then back in Oxford came his manipulations of Helen Henshaw, poor Jane Redfern and the hapless Doctor Aggarwal. And still it had gone on as he progressed through SIS. His deviousness had found its crowning glory in his victory over the bitch Spedding in Managua during his first overseas posting.

And now, thanks to the annual training refreshers at Fort Monckton, Sinclair had honed his skills to near perfection. The instructors had once complimented him on his unusually steady heartbeat and on the fluency of his lies. Such a talent for lying and for beating the polygraph, which was much in vogue those days, thanks to the Cousins.

"After nine years at a Jesuit school, anything else is a breeze, even a Stasi grilling," he had joked. He then regaled the trainers with the story about now Himmler's SS had modelled its organization on the Society of Jesus. This made them laugh. They liked him. That George Sinclair, they said after he left the mock interrogation room, was truly a 'natural'. Without batting an eyelid. A natural. A master of the porkie pie. They liked a man who could look you straight in the eye and convince you that he had never set foot east of Docklands, even though something in his accent and the slight wobble of his head suggested otherwise.

But back to Ruskin. Sinclair steeled himself for disaster by mentally chanting his private mantra while counting backwards to control his heartbeat. This routine was followed by a quick invocation in *lucumí* to his guardian—*agó, agó,* open the gate, keep the way open—as the smiling Ruskin, scratching eagerly at the pink scales on his hand, stepped into Head of Station's cockpit to deliver the *coûp de grace*.

"Good news, I hope?" Sinclair murmured casually as his pulse dropped.

"Actually, yes, *sahib*," replied Ruskin with an insolent a wag of his greasy blond head, mimicking Sinclair, "in fact, perhaps a career enhancing move if catch my drift, and if you act on my recommendation."

"Which is?"

"Before I start, let me say that I expect full credit and a special mention in my personnel review in December, mind you, and consideration for my application to join the Service . . . a good word, you know," he simpered grotesquely.

"Shoot," Sinclair growled. Now that he was in the clear, Sinclair was growing impatient in the imbecile's presence.

"To cut a long story short," continued Ruskin smugly, "a friend of a friend of a friend has pointed in my, I mean, in *our*, direction a well-placed Major in Dr Raul Castro's Ministry of the Armed Forces, Diplomatic Liaison. Said Major wishes to provide privileged information to Her Majesty's secret servants in return for certain emoluments to be deposited into the Crédit Suisse, Geneva, Switzerland".

"Cut the crap, Ruskin," Sinclair snapped, as the hard-nosed professional in him took over. Here was the walk-in they had all been waiting for. "What I want is names, facts, places, exact times and collateral before I fall for that kind of bullshit."

Sinclair spent the rest of the afternoon carefully debriefing Creeper. Sinclair despised the man. He was just a scabby wannabe spy in desert boots. Sinclair methodically set out to wheedle any inconsistency out of Ruskin's story, probing for weak spots and making him repeat it again and again, in the text-book style of the Fort's instructors, looking for the tell-tale signs of the plant. Eventually even Ruskin got bored with this drill, but Sinclair kept at it, finally drafting his encounter report well after close of business.

All of which Alison Wiggins, exhilarated to be working overtime on a real case for a change, duly encrypted. The report was then transmitted through ATHS/OATS in a compressed blip disguised as static within the normal diplomatic traffic that pulsed from the Embassy's antenna. Instantaneously the microburst bounced off a satellite hovering miles above the Florida Straits and was logged into a computer terminal in Mexico City Station. There it stayed over the weekend, because the message was classified Level 2, until it was downloaded the following Monday morning by the duty officer.

On Monday afternoon, Alison, eagerly anticipating her first operation since arriving in Cuba, decoded the ATHS/OATS encryption with a one-time pad which she then disposed of in the burn-box. The message was finally delivered to Sinclair just as he was putting away his manuscript for the day. The terse reply from London, c.c.-ed to CA/MX/1, a.k.a. Head, Mexico Station, read:

> *Proceed with extreme caution. Validate and verify source only, repeat validate and verify source only. Moscow Rules apply.*

Sinclair was not surprised. Validate and verify. This was textbook procedure for dealing with walk-ins. It meant that he was simply to verify the identity of the subject through conventional, above-board means. Moscow Rules were tradecraft tactics that were applicable in the most hostile of host countries. In the context of Castro's Cuba, Moscow Rules were the norm rather than the exception. Typical of those lazy bastards in London to remind him of the obvious.

London and Mexico Station were paranoid of walk-ins. Any walk-in, they immediately assumed, was an *agent provocateur* on a mission to misinform, disrupt and derail. And SNAPPER, of all Her Majesty's secret assets, could not, and should not, be derailed. He was to be protected at any cost, Mackie had insisted again and again, on pain of death or worse.

It was in this fashion that the business of Major Alvaro Mendieta and his wife started.

Major Mendieta's official codename was selected in London and would never be revealed to him. For his own purposes, however, Sinclair named the Major LAZARITO in honour of Ruskin's scabrous skin and in thanksgiving to Babalú-Ayé for granting him a narrow escape following his disastrous *toque*.

LAZARITO

From the very first time Sinclair laid eyes on LAZARITO at a cocktail party thrown by the Italian Embassy, he had disliked him. The Major was a small, tidy, sleek-headed man with a pencil-thin moustache worn in the manner of some Hollywood star from the 1930s. Unlike the saint he was code-named after, he was smooth-skinned and well groomed, and fastidiously neat in his pressed khakis and over-polished boots. There was something coiled and compressed about LAZARITO, however, a nasty, latent violence. He was the kind of man who beats his wife.

It was the small men who caused all the trouble in the world, thought Sinclair as he appraised his new Joe. The Major affected not to recognize Sinclair as he shook his hand. LAZARITO's handshake was dry and limp and quickly withdrawn. Quite a pro, thought Sinclair. LAZARITO's manner with Sinclair was frankly, well, condescending. And in Sinclair's book, that made him a martinet. Bonding with this Joe would be a challenge. Well, you should never assume that you would like your Joes—after all they are by nature disloyal people, who would be quite prepared to betray you, their handler, in order to save their own skins.

From the far corner of the room, Creeper winked at him and puckered his ladylike mouth as he chatted up a young Asian male diplomat.

Mendieta's wife, whom the Major introduced offhandedly to Sinclair as "*la Compañera* Martina de Mendieta", was a brunette and had the dead Helen's venerean strabismus. The dazed look in her eyes endeared her to Sinclair immediately. When LAZARITO moved on she came closer to Sinclair and soon he was standing in the radius of her scent. Unlike her husband's, *her* handshake was firm and warm and lingered for that meaningful split second. She was wearing a well-worn dress with a floral print, probably from Eastern Europe or a hand-me-down from some relative in Miami. This endeared her to Sinclair even more. In Cuba, cardiologists and Central Bankers depended on bicycles these days, and smart girls like Martina Mendieta had to dress like paupers.

She addressed him in Spanish. Sinclair watched the straight parting in her chestnut hair, the bridge of her nose and the sunburn under her brown eyes as she spoke.

"Do you like astrology, Dr Sinclair?" she smiled, sipping her wine, when her husband was out of earshot. Her eyes lazily scanned the room over the brim of her glass. My God, how she reminds me of Helen, thrilled Sinclair, even the same sweet voice. I have found a tropical Helen, the love of my life.

"I know a bit about the subject, *Compañera* . . . ," he replied, trying to keep his composure.

"Call me Martina, please." Something had come alive in her eyes. "I can see that you are a Gemini, born in the second quartile of the month, most definitely," she said, studying Sinclair's face for a reaction.

"But how could you possibly . . . ?"

She tapped her nose, winked, and smiled, creating deep dimples in her love-ly, Helenish cheeks. She moved closer, almost imperceptibly, a fraction of an inch. There was a warm animal smell under the scent that she exuded. Sinclair experienced a stab of lust.

"And a Cancer Rising . . . hmmm . . . how interesting . . ." But then she frowned. "And that would put Aquarius in your Seventh House . . . how curi-ous . . . and Gemini in the Twelfth . . ."

"That I cannot say—" stuttered Sinclair, trying desperately to remember the astrology lessons that Grannyjee had given him in Goa, as he absorbed the revelation that he was standing on the precipice of obsession again.

"Yes, Cancer Rising makes you a very protective individual, almost mater-nal, I would say . . . I would not be at all surprised if there is someone very close to you, a child perhaps, that you love dearly. *Do* you have children, Dr Sinclair?"

"A daughter," he croaked. Then there was silence as he lost himself in her eyes. His mouth had gone dry and his heart pounded in his chest. All of his pulse-calming mantras could not save him now. She seemed amused by his discomfort.

"Are you feeling unwell, Dr Sinclair?"

"Perfectly well, thank you . . ."

"I can cast it for you, your birth chart, you know. Just give me the exact time and place of your birth."

"Around 7.30 in the morning. Goa, India, June 11th, 1962."

She noted the details with an old ballpoint on her paper napkin.

"Until next time, then?" she said, with a hint of urgency in her voice, and a sudden, pleading look in her eyes. There was just enough time for another lin-gering handshake before LAZARITO appeared beside her from out of nowhere and led her away by the elbow to show her off to another group of foreigners.

The next time they met it was at a reception hosted by the Ministry of the Armed Forces in honour of the independence of Algeria, one of Cuba's oldest revolutionary allies. As LAZARITO strutted among the diplomats, Martina stood with her back to the crowd and pressed a folded sheet of paper into Sinclair's hand. It had a wheel with astrological signs drawn on it in blue ink.

"I would like to explain it to you," she whispered.

She asked him to meet her on Saturday at three o'clock at the gatehouse of the Morro, the colonial citadel that overlooks Havana Bay.

And that is how Sinclair began his *affaire* with Martina Mendieta.

JERKING THE LEASH

In orthodox tradecraft, control is key. If you don't control your Joe, he will end up controlling you, make no mistake about it. That was one of the cardinal principles that they drummed into the new boys and girls at Fort Monckton, especially those expecting a first posting to the Third World. An illustration of the principle at work was the case study of a compassionate handler, let's call him 'Softie', who was too easy on his Joe and ended up creating a Frankenstein.

Softie's Joe persuades him to raid the petty cash every now and then, because Joe's family is in dire straits. Softie simply can't wait for the next cash imprest from London. And then Softie ends up lending Joe his own money, because it's heartbreaking to see a Joe in so much trouble. Heartbreaking but also of professional concern, because the quality of Joe's product suffers as his economic situation worsens. Joe's so worried about feeding his children and his long-suffering wife that his pilfering of the wastepaper baskets at the Ministry is no longer his top priority. How can you concentrate on betraying your employer if you don't know how you will be able to feed the kids *and* buy medicine for your sainted mother? Soon it's become too tedious for Softie to get Head Office approval for every minor disbursement from the reptile fund.

The next thing Softie knows is that Joe has used the cash to buy a one-way ticket on a raft to Miami or to pay some coyote to smuggle him across the Rio Grande and into a new life as a crack dealer in L.A. Needless to say that Joe's family has been left behind. And who is left carrying the can back at the ranch but Softie, poor old bleeding heart. He is hauled up by Housekeeping for petty theft and is forced to retire from the Service in disgrace. As a consequence Softie is now enjoying the delights of middle management in the City, God bless his philanthropic soul.

They teach you at the Fort that a good agent runner is a puppet master, a kind of god. Every so often a good handler has to twitch his puppet's thread, even if it's not entirely necessary—just to keep his hand in and to remind Joe who is in control and who is feeding him and his nasty little sprogs.

Major Alvaro Mendieta, codename LAZARITO, made many demands on his handler. Sinclair deflected these artfully, hiding behind the excuses of policy and protocol and Head Office authorization and delegated authority. The latter, LAZARITO noted, seemed to be entirely lacking, and he told Sinclair as much.

LAZARITO had many complaints about the way he was being treated by the British. Little if anything in the way of assurances, remuneration delayed and insufficient, no respect for his rank, and where were the exfiltration plan and the resettlement terms that he had been demanding from day one? He threatened periodically to go over to the French, who were gentlemen and treated their spies generously and with the respect they deserved. Especially, he added, when the agents were officers of rank and were risking their lives in the furtherance of Democracy.

And risking the virtue of their wives while they're at it, smirked Sinclair into his cup of tea, as he savoured the latest memory of Martina Mendieta's inner thigh.

LAZARITO was undoubtedly a Frankenstein in the making—nothing but trouble. Sinclair had suspected as much the very first time he had met him at the Italian Embassy. A Frankenstein with *attitude*. Case Officer Sinclair did not have to consult his training manual to know that he had to jerk the little arsehole's leash, give him a good slapping down, and good and hard while we're about it, teach him a lesson before *attitude* became *problem*.

Everything about the man had grated on Sinclair's teeth and had set them on edge from their first meeting. His instincts had been spot on.

For a start, LAZARITO hated his codename. Accordingly, Sinclair insisted on addressing him as LAZARITO at every conceivable opportunity. Just for the pleasure of seeing the ambitious little martinet squirm in his chair and scowl and whine about the negative connotations of the name. In Cuba, he lectured Dr Sinclair, San Lázaro is the patron saint of lepers and paupers. Mendieta wanted nothing to do with any of that mumbo-jumbo bush-magic crap, Catholic or Yoruba, it was all the same. And why LAZARITO and not LAZARO? Sinclair assured him that it was Head Office policy and that code-names were set in stone. Furthermore, he had personally had nothing to do with codename selection: some nameless desk monkey in London pulled them off a list.

At Fort Monckton they had spent many hours learning how to role-play and how to shed and reinvent their personalities in various operational contexts. Sinclair felt pleased with the character he had created—the harried, timid, fearful bureaucrat—a creature all too familiar to someone like LAZARITO who had grown up in the Communist machine. On the other hand, he should be careful not to overplay it. LAZARITO wasn't as stupid as he looked.

Now that Sinclair had established the persona, it was time to move on to the next stage. At their next meeting, after listening to the little man's complaints and repeating the stock excuses, Sinclair said with just the right amount of craft mixed with reluctance:

"However, LAZARITO, as you know, everything in life has a price," Sinclair sighed, shifting his weight on his buttocks, consciously imitating Dr Tantum in his study, his interrogator at the College. "Even in the inflexible world of British Intelligence, LAZARITO," he went on, "rules are made to be bent, but they can only be bent in return for something, for a very good reason. I would need to expend much political capital with Head Office to change your codename. To do that, to use up my bullets, so to speak, I must persuade my masters that you are no ordinary asset, that you have *special* access, and *value to add* . . ."

Sinclair said this in parody of the Management Consultant jargon that the Service had adopted in recent months. On the agent management refreshers at the Fort, consultants from Industry strove to enlighten SIS's fieldmen with concepts such as value-added, the productivity matrix, incentive management and other motivational gimmicks.

Management consultancy had become the latest fetish at Legoland. Its terminology had infested every department and its jargon found its way into every bulletin from the Head Boys upstairs. For fuck's sake—as those who fancied themselves as hardened fieldmen used to moan in the Over Thirties Mess at Vauxhall Cross—those paper-pushing fuckwits upstairs are turning the Service into a fucking High Street bank, give us a fucking break.

ABAKUA

Of all the missions that Sinclair could dream up for his Joe, what did he task LAZARITO with? Again, he had followed the tried and tested principle of killing two birds with one stone.

"*Abakuá?* You're not serious, Dr Sinclair, surely . . ."

The *abakuá* are the most notorious and secretive of the secret societies in Cuba and are rumoured to be a very sinister lot indeed. Some Cuba watchers went so far as to say that they controlled all organized crime on the island, and that they even had a hold over *El Hombre* himself.

The cult had been brought to Cuba in the early 19th century by Negbe slaves from the Calabar region of West Africa, where it was known as the Leopard Society or *efik*. The *abakuá* were the Afro-Cuban equivalent of the

Freemasons but with the twist that their black magic was said to be peerless and drastically effective. It did not do to cross a member of the *abakuá*.

The society was a subject that Sinclair had long been obsessing over, and the time had now come for the *abakuá* to be written up in his *Comparative Analysis of Afro-Antillean Syncretism*. The problem was that the Leopard Society was impenetrable and membership was never disclosed. They met in their *cabildos* at night under the strictest of security. Ordinary Cubans refused to talk about the *abakuá*, crossing themselves and spitting on the ground whenever the word was uttered. They were like the sandman or the bogeyman. Exasperated Cuban parents regularly threatened their naughty children with the *negros carabalís*, the black devils from the Calabar. They'll come and take you off into the night and melt you down into bars of soap if you didn't belt up. And to prove the point, on the special feast days of the *abakuá* the children would be taken out into the street and shown the devil dance of the bogeymen—the dance of the *iremes*, otherwise known as *diablitos*—spinning around frantically in their straw costumes and nightmarish African masks.

"Yes, LAZARITO, *abakuá*. Head Office insists that the *abakuá* hold some sort of hidden influence in the armed forces, G-2 and even the DGI intelligence service. It is imperative that we find a way in to them, gain a foothold, an insider, an informer. That is your task, LAZARITO. You are hereby tasked by Her Britannic Majesty to find a way in to the *abakuá*. Not that you have to do it yourself, because even we stupid Imperialists know," said Sinclair tapping his forearm with two fingers in the Cuban gesture for black, "that you have to be a *prieto*, a black man, to be admitted into the society. But, LAZARITO, come back with some decent intelligence, and I give you my word of honour that I'll do my best to get your codename changed. But I must have product, *good, solid* product, to pass on to my masters in London. As proof of your *productivity*. And of your *bona fides* . . ."

"You have a Malefic Saturn in your Twelfth House, Dr Sinclair. That is the house of enemies and of the subconscious. It is the house of secrets. Has anyone ever mentioned that to you before?"

Something from the distant past rang a bell in Sinclair's mind. For an instant, in his mind's eye he saw Grannyjee's face and himself as a boy seated at her feet in Goa, surrounded by candles and icons and crucifixes and Hindu gods and goddesses. The old girl was reading from a piece of paper with a wheel drawn on it.

Martina Mendieta sat beside him now, very close, so close that he could feel her body heat. They were sitting on a bench in the fortress of the Morro over-looking the city and the afternoon sea.

The Morro is the Spanish fort that has guarded Havana Bay since the 16th century. It had served as Che's headquarters shortly after the triumph of the Revolution, and then as Castro's bunker. Rumour had it that even now certain sections that were cordoned off from the public housed the dungeons for top security political prisoners.

Sinclair had met Martina at the gatehouse the Saturday after their second meeting, as planned. They had spent the afternoon in the Che Guevara muse-um, admiring his favourite submachine pistols, lovingly preserved in glass cases, and the exhibition of fake documents with which he had infiltrated Bolivia prior to his death. Their hands had brushed together several times and she had let Sinclair lean against her casually as he stood behind her at the exhibits, looking over her shoulder and listening carefully to her commentary on the contributions of Che to the Revolution. She poo-pooed Sinclair's pointed questions about the role of Fidel in Che's death in Bolivia. Her inter-pretation of Cuban history was entirely orthodox.

Now as they sat on the bench high above the bay, Martina's finger traced a loop through the Twelve Houses of the Zodiac. It ran along the lines which showed the oppositions and angles between the planets in Sinclair's birth chart. Sinclair leaned into her closely as he followed her interpretation.

Having an *affaire* with the wife of one of your Joes is a 'no-no' and breaks every rule in the book. Sinclair conducted his relationship with Martina Mendieta with a heightened sense of pleasure, completely forgetting the res-olution that he had made in Nicaragua—to play with a straight bat. He had learned from his relationship with Brenda van Kempen in Nicaragua that the straight bat is all very well but that it lacks, well, the *frisson* of something total-ly illegal and inappropriate. Like the feeling you get when you hook a bounc-er for six off your back foot with a cheeky cross bat.

In the mornings after Alison had cleared the dead-letter boxes in Old Havana, Sinclair would sit waiting in his office at the spookhouse as she decoded LAZARITO's messages. Sinclair smiled inwardly as his assistant read out the CX, in the knowledge that in the evening he would be pleasuring his Joe's wife in the safe house.

The real challenge was not hiding his activities from LAZARITO or even from Alison Wiggins, who in her blissful ignorance never suspected a thing. The challenge was not even in training Martina to evade the suspicions of the

Major. At every meeting he would train her in the basics of tradecraft, the objective being for her to dodge any surveillance from her pathetic little husband. She took to it like a fish to water, as most unfaithful wives do. She was a natural, and her talents for deception further endeared her to Sinclair, because there is nothing more gratifying than seeing yourself reflected in your lover.

No, the hard part was making sure that Gumercindo, Mem'zili and, most importantly, Ximena never suspected a thing. For the deception of his family he applied Moscow Rules, scrupulously observing the principles of tradecraft for hostile territories. On the days when he met Martina, he created diversions, surveillance traps and wild goose chases for his family, while he artfully dodged his way in and out of Martina's bed.

There was one person that he did let into his secret, at the next of their weekly debriefings. What he did not share with SNAPPER, though, was his interest in the *abakuá*. That was, well, purely academic.

"Apart from astrology, what else are you interested in, Dr Sinclair?" Martina whispered in his ear after they had finished the tour of his birth chart.

"I am very interested in the Leopard Society of the Calabar—the *efik*—otherwise known as the *abakuá*. Tell me about the *abakuá*, *Compañera.*"

He felt her go tense next to him and withdraw.

"Yes, I know you are interested in them," she said, "because Alvaro has told me how you have forced him to penetrate them . . . he's terrified."

"Does Alvaro tell you everything that I tell him?"

"Most things. He trusts me absolutely. We have been together since we were Young Communists—'Pioneers'—on the Isla de la Juventud."

"So what about our friends the *abakuá*, then?"

Her Helen-eyes were suddenly alive with worry and she looked earnestly at him and said: "You must be very careful with the *abakuá*, George, very careful indeed. It's not a game. They don't like people, especially white people, snooping around and sticking their noses into their business. They wouldn't hesitate to kill you, or me, or even Alvaro, for that matter."

"Is that so?" he asked, trying to keep the tone light.

"Yes, George. I wish you hadn't tasked Alvaro with that. He may get hurt."

"That seems to worry you, his getting hurt."

She turned on him, her eyes lazy but resentful. "I am not a monster. Even though I am betraying my husband."

That's the spirit, thought Sinclair, relieved that she had the courage to

challenge him. But the word 'monster' made him uneasy. It always brought
back bad memories of Helen Henshaw.

"Yes, I understand you very well, *Compañera* Martina Mendieta. Even
though you are betraying him, you've been together since you were Pioneers
on La Isla de la Juventud . . ."

"I may not love him, but I *do* admire him and what he is doing. Alvaro needs
us to be his friends. He is risking his life for you. And for me. For a better
Cuba. He wants to save his country. He *needs* to."

About as much as I need a bullet in the head, thought Sinclair. As if the little
Major had not just last Friday increased his demands to $5,000 US dollars to be
deposited monthly into Crédit Suisse, Geneva. As he has no doubt neglected to
inform you, my dear Martina, he carried on in his head. As he has no doubt neglected to inform you, further, of the exfiltration plan that he has been developing with his handler, and the resettlement terms that do not make provisions for
anyone other than himself. There is no room for you, you see, *Compañera*, in
the viper's nest which he is feathering at everyone's expense but his own.

But he could not bring himself to say these cruel things to her. Instead he
decided to test her.

"When was the last time you slept with him?"

She stiffened and pulled away from him. She gave him a sour look out of
the corner of her eye and refused to answer.

It was then that he knew that the stupid bitch was still with LAZARITO.
You stupid, silly bitch, he thought, how could you do this to me?

Sinclair restrained the growing sense of outrage and jealousy that he recognized welling up inside him again, like the return of an unwelcome friend
from the past. Instead of lashing out, as he felt like doing, he apologized. She
let him slide back close to her on the bench.

After a while, she said: "You know, at first I thought that you were a son of
Changó, the God of Thunder. He loves drums, women and rum."

"And whose daughter are you, my dear?"

"I belong to Oshún, the Goddess of Love."

"But of course you do. I can see that. So whose son am I, then? And how
would you know, anyway? I thought you were an astrologer, not a *santera*."

"The stars are accurate. But the *caracoles*—the cowry shells—are more accurate still. And unlike the Zodiac, they provide solutions to our problems."

"I suspect they are the same, in any case, the *caracoles* and the Zodiac. All
systems of divination are based on the same principles." He sounded vaguely
ridiculous and pompous to himself.

"You are *omo Elegguá*, a child of Elegguá. You are a tricky customer. But you are often too clever for your own good, Dr George Sinclair . . ."

LAZARITO was in good spirits. He looked extremely pleased with himself the next time they met at the safe house in Old Havana. Sinclair wished he could say something to wipe the smirk off the little man's face. But what LAZARITO revealed next surprised even Sinclair.

"Your driver, the one called Gumercindo López, is *abakuá*."

"And would you be so kind as to tell me how you have come to that conclusion, agent LAZARITO?"

The little man shrugged off the deliberate slight and tapped his forearm with his index and middle finger. "I have certain *prietos* under my command in the barracks. They know him."

"Have you approached Gumercindo?"

"Absolutely not. I consider that I have delivered. You asked for a way in. I have given you the way in. There was no commitment to go any further than that. And now, Dr Sinclair," he said, with a triumphant smile, "it is time to deliver your side of the bargain."

"Congratulations, Major Mendieta, the dividend has come through."

It was two days later and they were sitting on a park bench in Guanabacoa.

"Dividend?"

Sinclair then had to explain in some depth and at some length the capitalist concept of the dividend, which is totally alien in Socialist Cuba.

"You see, Major, when you start investing the many thousands of dollars that are accumulating in your Swiss bank account, you will eventually receive a return on your investment. If you invest the money in a bank deposit or a bond—the debt of a company—you will receive interest. If you invest your hard-earned funds in the capital of a company, you become a part owner of that company and you will be entitled to receive dividends."

And so it went on. The Major seemed unimpressed. "So after all that, Dr Sinclair, what is the point?"

"The point, Major," said Sinclair with his best smile, even though he felt like snapping the little cunt's neck like a twig as he had been taught at Fort Monckton, "is that your new codename has come through, and I hope you like it—it is MARTINET."

The Major blinked but he seemed pleased with the result, even though he didn't understand what it meant. "What is the meaning of MARTINET?"

"Well, in England, it is in fact an aristocratic title, like the title 'baronet'. You may have heard the title 'baron' perhaps?"

"Like '*Esnoopy and the Red Baron*'?"

"Precisely. Now, the baronet is a step below the full-blown baron, but that's another story."

"You mean, then, that the 'martinet' is junior in rank to the, ah, 'martin'?" he asked, putting two and two together with a frown.

"Yes, now that you mention it, that's quite correct. But look, Major, it's the best I could do. And it does reflect your importance as an agent of Her Majesty. You *are* royalty." It was the most Sinclair could do to keep himself from slapping the little martinet about his insolent little face.

The Major nodded and gave grudging thanks to his controller for sticking his neck out on his behalf.

"Really, Alvaro, it's the least I could do for you. I feel as if you are a brother. A brother in arms."

It was then that an elegantly Solomonic solution occurred to Sinclair.

LAMIA

The day that Major Alvaro Mendieta, codename MARTINET, disappeared off the face of the earth, Havana was battening down the hatches for the arrival of Hurricane Gigi.

That morning when Gumercindo had taken Sinclair's bags out to the car, the breeze was rising and playing with the palm fronds in the garden. Sinclair had told Ximena and Mem'zili that he would be away for two days on a trip to Mexico City to visit his business associates.

As the hurricane bore down on the island he planned his next move. He would call Mem'zili from the safe house in Old Havana, where he would be 'debriefing' MARTINET's wife, to say that the storm had delayed the return flight to Cuba.

He then gave the ever watchful Gumercindo the slip, after he had been driven to the airport. Sinclair outwitted his chauffeur with deft footwork. Gumercindo promptly reported to the Ministry that *el Doctor* was safely on Cubana's Tupolev, flight 109, bound for Mexico City—after Sinclair had smartly bribed the Cubana station manager to falsify the passenger manifest and to let him out of the airport through the cargo bay and into a waiting taxi.

During his phantom trip to Mexico, Sinclair was woken by the wind crashing through the trees of a nearby park and the drumming of rain on the roof. The outer winds of Hurricane Gigi were descending on the island. The walls of the safe house, he noticed as he awoke, were blue.

The ancient Soviet-made air-conditioner had been turned off in anticipation of the inevitable power cut. He and Martina had gone to sleep with the windows open, but now the sheets were damp with their sweat. Through the windows Sinclair could see the frenzied palmtops of the park caught in the wind which came in off the coast after flattening the vegetation of the tropical keys that protected the northern coast of the island.

He lay there in the darkness listening to the storm settle over the city. He heard a sigh in the darkness and turned to look at Martina's profile against the blue wall. As if sensing his gaze, she opened her eyes and turned to him. She moved closer to him and he felt the apple-scent of shampoo in her hair as she lay her head on his shoulder. She looked at him with her slightly cross-eyed gaze, which created in him a doom-laden sense a sense of *déjà vu*. Her sleepy brown eyes were dull in the twilight.

She spoke in Spanish, in a small voice. "I was dreaming about you, Dr Sinclair."

In the corner of the bedroom something scuttled into its hole.

After they made love, he dreamt of the Infirmary at the College and of Matron, Xancha Bergsma, who was dead.

In the dream he was standing at the entrance to the Dispensary, in front of the painting of the Darwinian explorer riding his crocodile into the rainforest. In a taxidermist's glass box beneath the painting he saw a movement in the feathers of a bird, then saw its head cock to one side and its bright pin-prick eyes peering at him. The thing was alive. A movement in the corner of his eye made him turn and he saw her standing next to him. With the logic of dreams, the fact that she was dead did not frighten him.

He walked with her from the Infirmary. She led him by the hand through the deserted corridors and galleries of the College and eventually down into an underground boiler room known as the Pit. From there they kept heading underground, entering a doorway and descending into the subterranean passage beyond the Jesuit wine cellars towards a crypt that Sinclair had explored with Guy Underhill when they were schoolboys. Above them, in the church, Benediction was in progress and the *Tantum Ergo* was being sung, but in a different way, a very different way indeed.

For the second time that night he awoke. Now he was woken by chanting, which seemed to be coming from within the room, but in fact came from the room next door. It sounded like a coven of witches celebrating its Sabbat. This was not *santería*, because the chants were not in *lucumí*—they seemed to be a mixture of Spanish and Latin and a language that was much older and was vaguely familiar to Sinclair. Among the voices of the keening women he heard the French-Creole inflections of Mem'zili. High above these incantations floated the lovely pitch of Ximena's angelic song. His daughter was taking the lead in invoking whatever or whoever it was that they were raising up next door . . .

Sinclair was sure that he was dreaming, because he could not move, or speak out. He could sense the warmth of Martina's presence asleep beside him, her breathing calm and regular, undisturbed by the chanting. Later, he would be unable to remember for how long he lay in the dark listening to the invocations before falling asleep again.

It was the flapping of the curtains in the breeze after the passage of the hurricane that woke him for the third time. It must have been hours later, because Martina was already stiff with rigor mortis, her eyes wide open and staring at the ceiling, two tiny blue puncture marks on her throat. A dead scorpion lay curled on the pillow beside the beautiful chestnut curls of her hair.

He heard a girl's voice. It was his daughter talking to someone who he could not see. He still could not move anything but his eyes.

". . . just like his *putas* in Oxford."

Even if he had been able to, he could not bring himself to turn and look at Ximena. He felt a mixture of fury, grief, shame and guilt. His latest betrayal had been discovered. The *lamia* had struck.

His daughter spoke again, from somewhere in the room.

"Later you will thank me, father. That woman was not what she seemed to be. In time, you will be grateful."

From the corner of his eye he *did* see Mem'zili walk through the door with a meat cleaver and set to work methodically on the evidence.

Sinclair's nerves were shot. For the second time in his posting to Cuba he expected a visit from G-2 at any moment, followed by the one-way ticket back to Heathrow. He could imagine how the Head Boys in London and Colonel Bermúdez would react if they found about his dalliance with the wife of a recently vanished Cuban defector. He had broken every rule in the book. But when this sin was combined with murder, no one could predict which way the ball would turn.

Later on, he would barely be able to remember the frenzied all-night drive from Havana to the coast beyond Varadero, where they had disposed of Martina Mendieta's body.

It was in the twitchy days that followed that he first noticed a deterioration in his eyesight.

To start with, he would see a shadow in his periphery vision. The shadow would take the blurred shape of a man who moved sideways and silently and seemed to live only in the corner of his eye. And then people and objects would move in an out of his blind spot, as if eluding him, as if playing a game of hide and seek with his optic nerve.

It was all stress related, his daughter assured him, as she flicked his vein and tested the syringe.

As inevitably happened after the various crises that fate had laid in store for him (and which invariably involved his daughter), it was Ximena who put him back on an even keel. She listened patiently to his fears and complaints, the latest of which was this insistence that he was being followed. In the evenings she would encourage him as she prepared his morphine shot before putting him to sleep.

And it was Ximena again, acting as usual way beyond her years, who sorted out the practical issues raised by the disappearance of Martina Mendieta. A week after the disaster she told her father, as he was going under to meet with Morpheus, not to worry because she had spoken to Uncle Carlos. She had told Maxwell how her father had been deceived and abandoned by his friend Martina Mendieta. It seemed that she had done a moonlight flit with that horrible little husband of hers. They had both vanished off the face of the earth. They were probably in Miami by now, Maxwell had said. Father was not to worry about what happened ever again. Uncle Carlos would see to that, and she had Uncle Carlos promise her that he would never, ever bring the subject up again in the future.

LA CABEZA DEL CAIMAN

Cuba is a long crocodile-shaped island. On its tail, almost touching the tip of Florida and within spitting distance of the Revolution's arch enemies in Miami, rides Havana. Its head points away from the Imperialist Norte as it flees southeast towards Hispaniola, Puerto Rico and the Leeward Islands. Oriente Province and the Sierra Maestra are in the head of the crocodile—*la* *cabeza del caimán*—and the provincial capital, Santiago de Cuba, is its glittering eye.

Whenever Sinclair looked at the map of Cuba on the wall of his cockpit at the spookhouse, he thought of the country as a crocodile. He was reminded of the painting at the entrance of the College Infirmary—the Old Boy, mad as a hatter, riding into the rainforest on the back of a cayman. Sometimes he fancied himself as the rider in the painting, and Cuba the beast.

Sinclair was beginning to recover from Martina's death and was now enjoying a long ride down the spine of the crocodile. The road would take them through Camagüey, on the way to their final destination. Gumercindo was driving him down the national highway past endless fields of sugar cane and tobacco and unforgettable vistas of palm trees and rolling hills. Their imported air-conditioned jeep with its black diplomatic plates sped past clapped-out Ladas, reconditioned Caddies from the 1950s, and old Soviet trucks and buses stuffed to overcapacity with hitchhikers. These vehicles would require many more hours and stops to complete their journey to Oriente. As was their custom whenever Gumercindo drove, they listened to the latest *son montuno* and *songo* hits at full blast on Radio Havana, Gumercindo's head nodding enthusiastically with the pulse of the music, Sinclair's hands tapping out the conga beat or the *clave* on his thighs.

Sinclair made this journey twice a month on the pretext of compiling trade data for the commercial department of the Consular Section. The real purpose of the expeditions was to debrief SNAPPER away from Havana, which was never one hundred percent secure.

Sinclair felt the sense of joy and well-being that grips you when you drive along the highway past the miles upon miles of royal palms that grace the Cuban countryside. These are the trees of Changó, the God of Storms, because they act as lighting rods. The hypnotic repetition of these immensely tall and majestic trees along the road has a calming influence on you. It induces a sense of satisfaction as you benignly contemplate the future, as the miles fall away and Havana becomes a memory. The sun rides its arc high above you and you project yourself into the future that is waiting for you in *la cabeza del caimán*.

The crocodile's head is very different from its tail, for in its prosperous days Santiago once welcomed Haitian and Jamaican immigrants looking for a better life. Santiago is the other face of Cuba, truly Caribbean and more African than sophisticated Hispanic Havana.

The road links the croc's head to its tail, like a spine, or rather attempts to, because the national highway, a symbol of Cuba's arrested development, was never finished. You can get as far as Holguín in Oriente Province but then you have to take country backroads before you arrive in Santiago de Cuba. The city nestles between the sea and the foothills of the Sierra Maestra, the cradle of the Revolution. The road passes through the town of El Cobre, in the copper mining region where Cuba's patron virgin, La Virgen de la Caridad del Cobre (otherwise known as Oshún, the Goddess of Love) holds court in her basilica, surrounded by sunflowers brought by her pilgrims.

Halfway down the spine lies the town of Ciego de Avila, surrounded by a sea of sugar cane and tobacco plantations. It was here that Sinclair decided to make his move. He did not relish the idea of putting pressure on Gumercindo, who was a gentle soul, but the success of his research depended on it. No serious study of Afro-Cuban cults could be complete without an in-depth and hopefully groundbreaking evaluation of the *abakuá*, the ultra-secretive Leopard Society of the Calabar. Other scholars' attempts to uncover its secrets had repeatedly met with disappointment and the cult remained tantalizingly and infuriatingly inaccessible to outsiders. If he played his cards right with Gumercindo, Sinclair's *Comparative Analysis* could well become *the* definitive study, even a textbook, required reading on every Arch and Anth course.

Sinclair had decided to be blunt with Gumercindo; a prolonged and tedious courtship in the manner taught at Fort Monckton was not on the cards. Sinclair would get what he wanted by hitting Gumercindo where it really mattered.

Sinclair turned down the volume of the radio and turned in his seat to observe the smiling profile of his chauffeur.

He had it on good authority, he told Gumercindo casually as the driver negotiated the heavy traffic down the main street of Ciego de Avila, that he was a fully paid up member of the *abakuá*. He also assumed that this type of affiliation would not go down well with his bosses at G-2.

He saw the smile collapse and the tendons on Gumercindo's forearms stiffen as he clutched the steering wheel in near panic. The cheeky grin that usually lit up Gumercindo's face was extinguished like a candle flame in a gale.

Abakuá.

It never ceased to amaze Sinclair how a single word could evoke so much fear and suspicion among the Cubans, who are generally not lacking in self-confidence.

The Special Period was well and truly upon them and now, half a decade since the collapse of the Socialist Bloc. A few extra pesos a month could make all the difference between sending your kids to bed hungry (Gumercindo had three, *and* a mother-in-law) or getting through the week, and that went even for the salaried pavement artists of State Security and part-time watchers like Gumercindo.

When Gumercindo had finally negotiated the amount of his stipend, for which he would deliver certain information on the initiation rites of the Leopard Society, his face closed up again, as he realized what he had just agreed to do.

BELÉN

Sinclair had just concluded that when you start feeling at home in safe houses, you're really in trouble. These drab but secure meeting places were his 'homes away from home' and he felt safer in them than at the house with Mem'zili and Ximena.

He particularly liked the little back room in Santiago, which was rented for a pittance from a pensioner. After the successful 'burning' of Gumercindo, Sinclair was pottering around preparing for his next debriefing. He had set out the rum and snacks on the coffee table when the door opened and SNAP-PER slouched in, his usual scruffy self. But this time it was obvious that something or someone had upset him. Sometimes Sinclair worried that the constant commuting from Managua to Havana on those dodgy Tupolevs was taking its toll on SNAPPER. He was pretty much running the DGI's Nicaraguan Desk singlehandedly these days. He spent his time equally between the two countries, and it showed.

That evening Sinclair could see that Maxwell had already been drinking before their session began. There were smudges of fatigue under his eyes.

Perhaps Maxwell had not been able to cover up the business of Martina Mendieta's murder, as he had promised Ximena he would. George started counting backwards again to regain control over his heartbeat. Here we go again. The Predicament.

It turned out that one of Maxwell's agents had just been arrested in Washington. Sinclair breathed easy, off the hook again. He noticed a tremor in SNAPPER's hand as he took the glass of rum that Sinclair had ready for him.

"You may have heard about it already on CNN. It was Belén—

Belén Flores—remember you saw her with me last year at the Hotel Nacional. She was one of my Joes. A Joanne. My top Joanne. I was very fond of her. Very fond indeed."

Sinclair had never seen Maxwell close to tears before.

Yes, he remembered a thin woman with sad eyes and a shy smile, and a handshake that was light and hesitant. Sinclair had stumbled across them in the air-conditioned darkness of the bar at the Nacional. It was after one of Sinclair's own debriefings with LAZARITO and he had decided to stop at the bar for a *mojito* on his way home. Maxwell had jumped up out of the shadows to embrace him, declaring in a loud voice to the woman sitting next to him that Sinclair was his brother in arms and a true hero of the Revolution. As heads turned in the gloom of the bar she had appeared to be as embarrassed as Sinclair over Maxwell's indiscretion.

Carlos Maxwell was never one for respecting the rules of 'need to know' and tradecraft. For him, the business of spying was a very human and intimate endeavour, that's what made it interesting. After all, as he had once told Sinclair back in Nicaragua, the only institutions that Carlos Maxwell was loyal to were Friendship and Loyalty itself.

Now, as Sinclair plied Maxwell with rum in the safe house, he told Sinclair the sad story of Belén Flores.

"I was put on to her by DGI's New York Station."

It was common knowledge that most of the people at Cuba's mission to the UN on Lexington Avenue work for DGI, its overseas intelligence directorate, in one form or another.

Back in the summer of 1989, Maxwell had been summoned from Managua to New York through the usual channels, with the approval of Comandante Tomás Verga, his boss. It had all been above-board, by the book, Maxwell assured Sinclair with a suspicious glance.

"It was just before you arrived in Nicaragua," Maxwell said, "on your first overseas posting with MI6."

Maxwell had been instructed to meet a DGI officer, codename RUFINO. RUFINO was overweight and full of himself, but not lacking a certain charm. They met at a Cuban diner called La Cachita in Union City, a bus ride across the river from Manhattan. Union City is another world, Maxwell said, gulping his rum. You might as well be in Santo Domingo or Guayaquil. Anyway, in between mouthfuls of *congrí* and fried plantains and yucca and boiled pork, RUFINO, who took his perks seriously and had atrocious table manners, briefed Maxwell. They had been watching her for months, in Washington and whenever she came to New York. They had already codenamed her in advance of her recruitment, in the same way that MI6 had christened Carlos Maxwell SNAPPER before Sinclair had recruited him in Managua. RUFINO referred to Belén Flores by her codename—SABRINA. RUFINO's patch included secretaries and junior staff at the UN and his specialty was the honey trap. Arranging honey traps, rather than *acting as*, that is, because his own corpulence ruled him out operationally. He tended to recruit his boys and girls by following the successful guidelines and formulas employed by the Stasi in East Germany for identifying and recruiting lonely secretaries in the West German ministries. After weeks of evaluation, RUFINO had decided to register Belén formally as a target with Centro Havana. The thing was, however, that it turned out she was far more than just a lonely secretary. She was the DIA's top analyst on Cuba and Nicaragua and she had access to top level intelligence. And here was the icing on the cake, said RUFINO, in his enthusiasm spraying Carlos with flecks of food and saliva, it wasn't just intelligence on Cuba and Nicaragua but, because her security clearance was so high, she was on the distribution list for the bulletin on National Security, the daily digest of global intelligence that makes the rounds of the great and the good of Washington, DC. This ancillary catch would have immense tradeable value to the Soviets.

Belén was Puerto Rican. She had been born in West Germany, where her father, an army psychiatrist, was posted. She had lived the life of your typical army brat, growing up on a series of bases in the US and abroad. Because she was smart girl she had had a smart education including a degree in international studies at John Hopkins University. She was also a graduate of the School for Foreign Service in Washington. Ironically, she had started her career in government service at the Freedom of Information Office, and had then secured a transfer as a junior analyst to the DIA. It was there that in her own quiet way, and thanks to her language skills, she had advanced nicely through the ranks of analysts and was establishing a reputation for hard-hitting analysis first on Nicaragua and then on Cuba.

RUFINO said that Centro Havana doubted she could ever become a genuine traitor. Someone in Havana smelled a rat, he said. She was considered too American, too clean. Not really susceptible to blackmail. He told Maxwell that Centro was considering instructing him to drop the case—"overtaken by an excess of caution", as Maxwell explained, helping himself to another dose of the safe house rum.

"You see, it was almost too good to be true—it would probably be the top intelligence coup of the century, as far as DGI were concerned. For fuck's sake, the woman was right there inside the nest of vipers and she even had a hand in formulating US policy towards Cuba—so naturally they were being careful."

Maxwell told Sinclair that some of the divisional *Jefes* in Havana had insisted that SABRINA was a plant. That suspicion was to dog RUFINO and Maxwell throughout the entire recruitment and running of SABRINA. At lunch that day RUFINO had called his controllers in Centro Havana *maricones* and cowards, "*políticos*, technocrats, bureau-trash."

RUFINO could afford to be offhand about his colleagues and superiors in front of Maxwell, because he knew that Maxwell was not Cuban and therefore not one hundred percent DGI. And, RUFINO surmised correctly, Maxwell would never have entertained the slightest notion of informing on him. That would have been an unwise move because RUFINO had picked up certain bad habits involving bush magic in Angola and Mozambique, his previous postings as a spook.

RUFINO had now moved on to dessert. His brow was moist with the sheen of a serious eater. He spooned the flan into his churning orifice, speaking with his mouth full. He continued to spray the table with food and spittle in the process. RUFINO insisted that he, and only he, to whom all future honours and credits and ensuing promotions would be due, was the one who had taken the initiative of saving the operation. He had insisted to his flaky superiors in Centro that there was something genuinely pathetic about SABRINA that was susceptible to attack.

"The bitch is a gold mine," he had preached between mouthfuls, "and in this game, only the bold make a difference, *Compañero*."

She was after all a lonely woman—surveillance had confirmed and reconfirmed time after time her lack of friends or lovers. The friends she had were few and not close, more acquaintances than anything else, while she lived an entirely quiet and discreet existence, commuting in her red Toyota from her Georgetown apartment to work at the Quantico air base, and back again.

Her father was dead, and contact with her family was minimal. She was an Americanized Puerto Rican and appeared to treat her mother, like most Americans, with disinterest. She was totally dedicated to her work and so her life outside the office was empty and desolate. The extent of her social interaction was the occasional minor activism against her condominium association. She had recently started a campaign against the board's latest effort to impose additional fees on the residents.

"And I liked the Nicaraguan angle," RUFINO had told Maxwell with a wink of his bloodshot eyes. "Remember, she had specialized in Nicaragua before moving to the Cuban desk at DIA. So after checking back with Centro, we came up with you. And you're not too bad looking either—a bit scruffy perhaps—but good enough bait to honey-trap a mouse like Belén Flores . . ."

RUFINO was the type of man who could say things like this without the least hint of self-consciousness.

"With Belén," Maxwell recalled, "it wasn't just a case of loneliness and emotional starvation; she also had a social conscience. Not like those sad creatures in Bonn who the Stasi recruited and who agreed to spy in return for six inches of Russian beef, and for that I truly admired her. Belén was—still is, let's hope—a decent, intelligent, human being. When I first met her she really did believe that the embargo against Cuba was immoral and she was almost already there in terms of her readiness to betray the United States. It wouldn't take much to make her do it. That's why I argued against the 'false flag' approach," he said, referring to the technique of making a target believe that he or she was being recruited by a different country.

"It was on our secret trip to Cuba together that I took her over the edge. She took the plunge wholeheartedly and without reservation. That was when you met her, in the Nacional. We had just made love for the first time."

"Tell me, Carlos," Sinclair asked, intrigued, "how did you do it? How did you manage to get her to Cuba in the first place? What was your hook? How did you reel her in?"

"Heidi."

Heidi was Maxwell's boxer dog.

"Did I hear you correctly, *Compadre*?"

"Yes, you did. Heidi is probably the dog that has contributed the most to the Revolution. There will be special place for her in the annals of canine heroism. She has contributed far more than many humans I could name, in fact. I used Heidi and she performed her Socialist duty beautifully and without complaint. She deserves a medal of some sort. The Order of Lenin perhaps, not that it exists anymore . . ."

Maxwell was tired. He was in danger of becoming emotional again as he remembered his dog.

As he lunched with the unbearable RUFINO in Union City, Maxwell was told that SABRINA was in New York attending a UN conference on the latest Salvadorean peace initiatives. She was staying at the Salisbury Hotel on West 57th Street. The day after that heavy lunch with RUFINO Maxwell tailed her from the hotel to the UN building, and watched her enter the complex with a wave of her plastic badge.

"She is a slight woman, remember, George. She has no great presence I'm sure you will also remember. She wore her hair short in those days—she didn't want her male colleagues at DIA attributing any of her success to her gender."

As an accredited Cuban diplomat, RUFINO was already inside the UN building and monitored SABRINA's movements throughout the day, shadowing her between conference rooms, sitting in the back row at her meetings and keeping his eye on her in the canteen, where she lunched on her own. He phoned Carlos on his mobile when she was ready to emerge that evening after the conference wrapped up for the day. Carlos picked up her tail outside the UN complex by the river on East 41st Street.

"I remember it was a lovely evening, the kind of evening that single women should not spend alone. The summer heat was starting to cool and it was a pleasure to be out and about in the city. She took a long detour back, down through 23rd Street and into Madison Square Park, in front of the Flatiron building, where Broadway intersects with Fifth. She stopped at the fence of the dog run, and stood there for what must have been almost an hour, staring at the dogs. After the dog run I followed her back to 57th Street where she went up to her room at the Salisbury and did not emerge again until the next morning. There was something definitely sad about this. That evening I arranged for Heidi to be flown up in her kennel from Managua. I picked her up at JFK the following morning."

The next day Maxwell followed the same routine, except that the hunter now had a boxer in tow. "Excellent cover, a dog, and great company too, for all those hours of waiting that take up most of a spy's life."

Sinclair remembered the cocked head and protruding eyes of Maxwell's familiar watching him as he snooped around Maxwell's bedroom in Nicaragua.

"First contact went like clockwork. I followed her to the UN and then kept in touch with RUFINO all day by cell phone. As she was leaving for the day, I set out with Heidi and arrived at the dog run on 23rd Street a few minutes before she arrived. Heidi was having fun socializing with the capitalist dogs of Manhattan, and I had to deal with their masters. I managed to strike up a conversation with the owner of a male boxer—the dog was called Maximilian, I remember, and he was very interested in my Heidi. Out of the corner of my eye I saw Belén's lonely figure drift up to the fence and look in. I pretended

not to see her for a few minutes, and continued chatting with the fat bugger—
a flabby investment banker—who owned Maximilian."

Maxwell had let more time pass by before he ambled up to where the
woman was standing at the fence. Heidi followed him and sat down in front
of the fence, looking up at Belén. "Heidi can be jealous, you know. At first I
think she spotted some kind of threat from Belén."

"She—Heidi, that is—could probably smell the testosterone or the
pheromones or whatever men emit when we are on the prowl," offered
Sinclair.

"I don't think so, not at that stage, anyway," said Carlos, thoughtfully.
"Believe me, at that stage there was zero physical attraction. Anyway, I had my
hands full with Jamila back in Nicaragua. She was more than enough for any
man, I can assure you."

Sinclair nodded in agreement, letting his mind's eye wander over Jamila's
buttocks and legs.

"You see, unlike Jamila, Belén was thin and not at all curvaceous. She exuded timidity. She did eventually turn her eyes on me, instinctively turning her
face downwards and looking up from under her fringe—you know, the Lady
Di look—shy and simpering but definitely interested."

"Do you like dogs?" he had asked her, in English, and then, when she hesitated, he asked: "Do you speak Spanish?"

"I do. I mean, I do like dogs and I do speak Spanish," she blushed.

"This is Heidi," he said.

Heidi looked up at Belén, her head cocked to one side, still not sure what
to make of the woman. She certainly didn't emit much of a scent. Maxwell was
to learn later that Belén was obsessed with personal hygiene.

"*Hola*, Heidi," she said shyly, looking down at the dog, the ghost of a smile
on her thin lips.

Smiling was an effort for her. He could tell that it cost her a lot and that she
didn't do it often. There were no crow's feet around the eyes, no laughter lines
around the mouth.

They continued in Spanish. Her own Spanish was a little stilted and
Americanized, like that of many second and third generation Puerto Ricans
who live in the US.

"Let me guess then . . . by the sounds of it you are a *boricua*," he ventured,
gently, using the colloquial word for Puerto Rican. "Or possibly Cuban?"

"Puerto Rican. That is, Puerto Rican parents. Where are *you* from?" she
replied, a little stiffly, as if embarrassed by her own forwardness.

"Nicaragua."

He looked for some flicker of interest or suspicion in her eyes, but none came. She was an intelligence pro, after all.

"But you speak English like an Englishman . . . ," she said with a slightly raised eyebrow.

"I do."

Her lips twitched with her almost-smile again.

Maximilian came up to the fence, sniffed Heidi's derriere, rubbed up against her and then attempted to mount her. Heidi sprinted off jauntily, enjoying the flirtation, with the bigger dog kicking up a cloud of dust as he ramped up after her in hot pursuit.

"I have to be careful. She's only an adolescent," he joked, watching the dogs chase each other around the pen. It was true, Heidi cannot have been more than two years old back then in 1989.

"Do you have a dog?" he asked her, watching as Maximilian closed in on Heidi.

He didn't want to be too forward, not at that stage, anyway. He was adopting a shy attitude and avoiding eye contact, grateful for the distraction of the gallivanting boxers. "I didn't want to appear over-confident. I knew she wasn't the type to go for the Latin lover option, so I didn't want to go down that road. I had never had to perform a honey trap myself, so I was pretty damned nervous. I was ready to call it off for the day. I had already gone a little too far."

But Belén had taken the bait. "I love dogs, but I can't have one. I live in an apartment."

What she really meant was that she lived in an apartment *alone*, and didn't have a partner to help her with a dog.

"Oh, I see."

Luckily, a commotion at the other end of the dog run gave Maxwell the excuse to back off for the day. Maximilian had succeeded in mounting Heidi and was starting to do the honours. Maxwell was disappointed to see, from the glazed look of contentment in Heidi's bulging eyes, that she seemed to be enjoying Maximilian's full attention.

"You'll have to excuse me," he said to Belén as Maximilian began thrusting in earnest, "but I have to go and rescue my girl. It's been very nice talking to you."

"*Hasta luego*," she replied. There was a wistful look in her eye, which was promising.

When Maxwell turned to look, after forcing Maximilian to disengage, she had gone.

"And the rest is history," sighed Maxwell.

Compañero Maxwell must have got his money's worth with that one. It's always the serious, saintly ones that are the most passionate. But it's never easy losing a Joe, let alone a Joanne. Shopping your own Joe—as Sinclair had done with LAZARITO—was one thing, especially if the Joe had become a liability and a threat. But losing a Joe or a Joanne who you respect, and especially a Joanne who you have personally honey-trapped must be the worst feeling in the world. Sinclair could not imagine the shitstorm of guilt that was going on inside Carlos Maxwell.

"How was she caught?"

Maxwell's face contorted into something ugly and hateful. "You won't believe it. Guess who shopped her? It was that flabby *coño* RUFINO himself. He defected just yesterday, the motherfucker, when he found out that his posting to New York was up and he was going back to his bedsit in East Havana. No more freebies and *congrí* and roast pork in Union City courtesy of the long-suffering Cuban people, thank you very much. I should never have trusted the fat bastard, with his appalling table manners."

Maxwell took a furious gulp of neat rum and lit up his cigar. There was a look of deep worry in his eyes, as if he knew that things might be about to take a turn for the worse. It was the look of a Highlander watching the massed horse and pike of the invading English army assembling on the horizon.

THE TOWER

To outsiders, the secret world has its own *Alice in Wonderland* logic and operates by its own set of distorted rules. In the world beyond the looking glass, good deeds are punished and treachery or incompetence are regularly rewarded. It is a place where malefactors prosper and imbeciles thrive.

And there are outsiders even within the intelligence services.

So the time eventually came when it was decided by the Counter Intelligence Committee of State Security that the plug should be pulled on Dr Sinclair, chief resident spook of British Intelligence.

"*Compañeros*, the time has come to light a fire under our philandering friend Dr George Sinclair."

These were the words that opened the weekly meeting of the Committee, and they were uttered by Colonel Adalberto Bermúdez himself.

It was a Friday afternoon at the end of October. Sinclair's betrayal of the pathetic *cabrón* Mendieta, alias LAZARITO, was being discussed by the Committee.

"*Coño*," someone said, with genuine admiration, probably that sad fart from Personnel, Eugenio Irigoyen, who was secretly addicted to spy movies, "what a way to stiff someone . . . you not only betray him but you also make his wife betray him at the same time. Poor old Mendieta, he thought he was so smart, then along comes an English gent, stiffs him, then puts the horns on him, poor *cabrón*. Fantastically evil, these English gents are—just like 007, no? Is that what they teach them at their exclusive private schools? And by the way, did they ever find Mendieta's wife?"

Bermúdez' glowering look across the table in Irigoyen's direction made it plain that questions about the whereabouts of Martina Mendieta were not welcome. That subject was more than classified.

"The morals of an alley cat, they have, the English, behind all their good manners . . . ," piped in that sanctimonious git Miraflores from Finance, having already calculated the savings in expenses from one less informant to service.

"We could do with more of his ilk," growled General Mazariegos from his seat at the head of the table, sucking on his *cohiba*, to much sycophantic laughter from the company. Mazariegos was G-2's figurehead and Bermúdez's nominal boss, and a master of the art of delegation. He had fought alongside Fidel in the Sierra Maestra and was the successor of Alarcón, the legendary founder of the security service, so he could afford to rest on his laurels while Bermúdez did the running.

Via a Byzantine series of interlocking and often contradictory arguments, the Counter Intelligence Committee voted unanimously (how else?) that it was time to blow Dr George Sinclair's cover. The Foreign Ministry would be instructed to PNG Her Majesty's Passport Officer back to the rain and the fog of London.

All committee decisions in Cuba are determined in advance. That morning, after a meeting in Mazariegos' office at the crack of dawn, it had not taken Colonel Bermúdez long to persuade the Committee of the wisdom of his 'recommendation'. He had called the senior members by telephone to brief them before the meeting. Yes it was true, the Colonel admitted, Sinclair—SPINNER—definitely had potential as a traitor. Yes, just look at his behaviour. There was not an ounce of conviction in the man. Look at how he had denounced our own Major Mendieta for purely carnal motives—just so he could pork his wife. He is the kind of man who thinks with his penis, and that is often a problem, as we all know, *Compañeros*, don't we. They had all laughed. Yes, he continued, the higher-ups do not discard the possibility that SPINNER could be recruited to betray his country. In fact, it is our assessment that it would be very easy to do so. But—*and ours is not to question why*—at the end of the day it is better to deal with hardened professionals than with spectacularly corrupt or perverse agents. Dealing with incompetents like SPINNER always brings trouble in the end. How often have we not seen it ourselves, *Compañeros*?

"But it is his addiction to drugs," Bermúdez announced to the assembled committee that afternoon, "that makes SPINNER truly dangerous. Even if you did manage to recruit him, you would never know what he would say during one of his trips. You could never *control* him, that's for sure."

Mazariegos raised an eyebrow at this last comment.

"Oh yes, we have known for a while about Sinclair's substance abuse—I believe that is the politically correct term for it these days in the United States," Bermúdez added this as his closing remark to general sniggering and back-slapping around the table.

The conclusion to the meeting had been dictated to Mazariegos in the early hours of the morning by Fidel himself. *El Hombre*, who never slept, had summoned the General to his office at three a.m. There are to be no questions, Fidel had said, jabbing Mazariegos in the chest with his finger. Just get Sinclair out of Cuba, and *pronto*.

General Mazariegos had also made up his mind not to mention to anybody that he had spotted DGI's resident Sandinista—Carlos Maxwell—lurking in the hallway outside Fidel's office before the meeting.

The Committee voted unanimously. It was a wise decision.

As usual, the last word was given to the General, who closed the Committee's deliberations with his legendary nod of approval followed by that wonderful Cuban expletive, "*coño!*"

It was, after all, Friday afternoon and time for a *mojito*.

On Sunday night, Ximena spread the Tarot for her father on the dining room table, as her mother used to do. While Mem'zili stood in the background and watched quietly, Sinclair went through the ritual shuffling and splitting of the pack into three neat piles. He picked the cards out of the pack, and handed them to her.

She proceeded to lay the cards out in the Celtic Cross pattern. First the questioning card, which embodies the Querent, the subject of the reading, crossed by the second. Then a series representing past, present, future, and finally several cards tracing the influences that shape the outcome.

Like her mother, she was po-faced whenever she read the cards. Sinclair struggled to watch her down-turned eyes for clues. It was at these moments that the girl most resembled her dead mother. When she would recite the meaning of the cards, her eyes would be inward looking and take on that dead look that meant she was in trance, half in the spirit world and half in our world. But this time, immediately the cross had been laid—question, past, present and future—a frown darkened her face.

"The Chariot, reversed—a man comes, an enemy . . . The Tower, reversed—there may be disaster, father, the end of our home. See the destruction of the tower. We must be strong to survive."

He saw a man falling from a tower struck by lightning, by the Finger of God. He saw Magdalen tower in flames. He saw himself standing at the top of the tower many years ago, deciding whether to jump or not. *Le Prince d'Aquitaine à la Tour Abolie.*

Ximena seemed profoundly troubled by the message she saw on the table.

"*Contra Mundum*, you and I. Remember our pact, my love?" Sinclair said gently, trying to comfort his daughter, more worried for her than for himself. He had already been told what was looming on the horizon and he had already seen the shadows closing in on him again.

She ignored him, as usual, and continued her analysis of the spread. She swallowed hard. "Father, this is a difficult reading."

Mem'zili grunted in agreement. She had now come up to the table, drawn by the troubled expression on Ximena's face, and was hovering behind the girl, looking down at the cards with a frown of her own. Respectfully, she did not intervene but continued to watch and hover.

Ximena breathed in deeply. Her eyes were blank again, focused inwards. Sinclair knew that he must remain silent. Then she spoke at last.

"Many difficulties to come—look at the dead man, stabbed in the back by ten swords, look, father."

"How do we deal with the man from London?" he asked.

"Here is a man who will help you," she said, matter-of-factly, pointing now to the King of Cups, who was not reversed.

"Could that be Uncle Carlos?"

"Perhaps. But we must be prepared for a big change. There is much danger. It could mean the loss of our home, of all this . . ."

Mem'zili laid her hand on Ximena's shoulder, and whispered something in her ear. The girl kept her eyes on the cards, her face expressionless again, and nodded at the secret advice.

"We'll be alright, my love, you'll see," Sinclair said, "don't worry your pretty little head about it."

He didn't sound convincing, not even to himself.

That night after the reading Sinclair met with Carlos Maxwell briefly in the Old Havana safe house and then made his own way back home. From there, he asked Gumercindo to drive him to the spookhouse. While Gumercindo waited in the car in front of the annex, the radio full blast playing Afro-Cuban jazz, Sinclair went inside as if he hadn't a care in the world. He emerged five minutes later carrying a small box which contained the shrunken head of Doctor Aggarwal. They drove back home. Again, Gumercindo was asked to wait outside. After Sinclair had hidden the head in the cellar, they continued their itinerary.

Their next stop was the dead-letter drop halfway down the Malecón. It was there that Colonel Bermúdez and his goons were waiting to arrest him up in front of a handful of well-picked witnesses and several press photographers.

It was in the newspapers and even made it on to CNN and the evening news of the BBC World Service: *BRITISH DIPLOMAT CAUGHT SPYING IN CUBA*.

The story, about which there was maddeningly little detail, was based on the following note which was delivered to the British Ambassador by the Foreign Minister himself on Monday morning. The contents of the note later found their way into the wider world through the good offices of the Prensa Latina news agency:

Ministry of Foreign Relations
La Habana, October 14th, 1999

Dr George Sinclair, Passport Officer of the British Embassy in La Habana is hereby declared Persona Non Grata because of activities incompatible with his status. Dr Sinclair is required to leave the Republic of Cuba within 48 hours.

On Tuesday morning Sinclair, now well and truly PNG'ed, arrived at the spookhouse to find it unnaturally quiet. As he approached the Station through the corridors of the annex he heard his grandmother chanting in his head:

> *By the pricking*
> *of my thumbs,*
> *something wicked*
> *this way comes*

Approaching the Friends' lair he missed the comforting clackety-clack of Alison Wiggins' keyboard. Missing too was Sergeant Warren's chitchat as he performed his morning sweep for bugs and boasted about his latest conquest on the Malecón. Alison and Warren had no doubt been sent home and told to take the day off.

The door was open.

He heard someone talking in his office.

Robin Ruskin stood there with another man.

Ruskin's face was no longer pink and shining, but had acquired a sickly, leprous look in the artificial light of Sinclair's office. He must have been up all night by the look of his greasy, plastered-down hair. Ruskin was picking at his face nervously, eyes averted as he concentrated fiercely on one of the Holbeins on the wall.

The other man was Simon Cavendish. Despite the tropical heat he was wearing a heavy City pinstripe and was showing a lot of cuff. As a schoolboy, the cuffs of Cavendish's shirt had always protruded a good two inches below the sleeves of his jacket, and that had always irritated the living daylights out of Sinclair.

Sinclair had not laid eyes on Cavendish since he had left the College in 1980, and it was unsettling how little he had changed. The same Captain of Cricket's smirk of satisfaction, the smile of belonging, the same double Windsor knot. And still showing a lot of cuff, damn his eyes.

The Station safe lay open and empty and on Sinclair's gunmetal desk they had laid out the evidence—the little Elegguá shrine, Sinclair's syringes, a tourniquet and several vials of morphine. The Station firearm, the Beretta, swung casually in Cavendish's hand.

"I always knew," Cavendish drawled, "that you were a sick bastard, George Xavier *Gupta* Sinclair. A voodooist and a drug-addict. I don't know how the Service ever hired someone like you. It's no wonder you fucked up and got yourself PNG'ed. But then again, you *were* never quite one of us, were you?"

Fee fi fo fum,
I smell the blood
of an Englishman!

Ruskin looked down at his nails, his feminine mouth pursed with regret. Sinclair could feel Cavendish's triumphant eyes on him and could almost hear the word *"wog"* which he knew Cavendish was sneering in his head. He had steeled himself for this. He avoided looking at Cavendish, just as Maxwell had coached him to do the night before. Like Ruskin, he kept his eyes down.

What a way to end the millennium, he thought bitterly. Cunting Tony Prufrock the Consul can celebrate now that his Friend had fucked up and is being sent home. "Told you so, just as I predicted would happen," Sinclair could hear him gloating over his G&T, "when I first laid eyes on that Sinclair character."

He grasped the talisman in his pocket and begged Elegguá to open the gate as he watched the gun in Cavendish's hand.

Fee fi fo fum,
I smell the blood
of an Englishman!

For an instant he felt like grabbing the Beretta and gunning them both down where they stood. But Maxwell had warned him about losing control. Cavendish was bound to provoke him.

Cavendish would have to be dealt with later. By uttering the secret of Sinclair's middle names, MI6's new man in Havana had unwittingly singled himself out for very special treatment.

1971
SATURN IN GEMINI

MASTERJEE

The trouble with Master George Sinclair was that despite his name, he was foreign—an overseas boy. An overseas boy touched by the tar brush.

"You see, Morpheus, Anglo-Indians are the product of two very unlikely bloodlines. I was a creature caught between two worlds, but I didn't realize it until much later. I wasn't always so uncomfortable in my own skin, not at home, at least, not before they sent me to England."

"It's true," Morpheus says, "you *were* quite an awkward specimen, now that you mention it."

When you looked at George Sinclair you could almost see his Highlander and Dravidian ancestors standing behind him in two converging ranks emerging from the mists of time—pale-eyed, blue-faced wild men from the Highlands on one side and delicately-boned marsh dwellers from the Subcontinent on the other.

"The two bloodlines did finally meet in 20th-century Goa, George. You arrived on a monsoon Monday in the second week of June, 1962, under an uncertain star. Yes, it *was* a complicated time," sighs Morpheus, remembering. "You arrived at a very interesting point in the Cold War. On the other side of the world, your friends the Cubans were up to their usual mischief, stirring it up with Soviets. You were born between the Bay of Pigs fiasco and the Missile Crisis. Back in those fraught apocalyptic days all we could look forward to was the mushroom cloud. And then you come along . . ."

Morpheus apologizes for the interruption, and begs Sinclair to continue before the lights go out.

"But was I really a British boy—a Kim touched by the tar brush—or was I really a Portuguese-speaking Indian boy whose genes had been interfered with by the colonial overlords? In the end, I suppose, my name said it all."

Morpheus agrees, as always. "George Xavier Gupta Sinclair," he intones, imitating the chorus of the Fates, "you are hereby condemned to be an only

66

child, divided within yourself and uncomfortable in your own skin. And on your travels abroad you are destined to expend much effort on the concealment of your middle names."

"So why don't we begin at the beginning?" Sinclair suggests, addressing his friend Morpheus at the crossroads, where they always meet. "At the beginning of memory, that is. It's as good a place to start as any. So what *are* my earliest memories, you ask? Well, my first memory is of my grandmother, Grannyjee, sitting with me in her purple sari in the garden, in the shade of the giant rubber plants. I can see her now, Morpheus. She is whisking away the flies as I play with the lizards. I see her sitting there with me in the tropical vegetation, reading me fairytales set in snow-clad pine forests or reciting the plots of Jacobean Revenger tragedies which are delightfully full of sudden death and buckets of blood."

These dark stories took root easily in the child's imagination. George believed passionately that little people inhabited the trees at the end of the garden and from an early age he would surprise and embarrass his parents and their visitors by creeping around the house looking for sprites and child-eating wolves and chanting:

Fee fi fo fum,
I smell the blood
of an Englishman!

"This type of behaviour didn't go down at all well with my father, not at all. He was a military man, you see. He had somehow managed to stay on, making Goa his home after turning his attention to trade, like so many Scots who had administered the Raj in their previous lives."

Major Sinclair was a man of few words and lupine grey eyes which George had inherited and which he would fix on you with the baleful stare of the Ghost in *Hamlet*. He had no living relatives except a great-aunt in Aberdeen, and he was hard as nails. He was the kind of man who could speak without moving his lips, which were very thin.

"He had converted to marry my mother. She was a quiet middle-class Indian Catholic lady, family name Fernandes, who like most Indian wives came with an extended family that included a live-in mother-in-law known in the household as Granny Fernandes, or Grannyjee."

Sinclair explains to Morpheus that Grandfather Gupta Fernandes had died three years before Major Sinclair swept Anudartha Fernandes off her feet at the Goa Chamber of Commerce Christmas party in 1960. And that despite the years, the old man's influence made itself felt from beyond the grave in the form of his grandson's middle name. Gupta, that dark uninvited travelling companion that George was destined to carry with him, along with his trusty tuckbox and cricket bat, on his adventures abroad.

But it is Grannyjee that Sinclair wants to tell Morpheus about.

"I adored her, Morpheus. She doted on me. Because my birth had exhausted my mother, Grannyjee took over the daily administration of my life so that Mother could rest."

At home the Major insisted that only English be spoken but Grannyjee and the garden-wallahs taught George Portuguese and Marathi. Grannyjee encouraged his talents, which were cricket and drawing. In the gardens around the house in Goa, when Grannyjee wasn't telling him stories about wolves and chicken bones and chocolate houses in the forest or poison-tipped poignards, little George would make her bowl to him as he sharpened his batting skills. The garden-wallahs were recruited as fielders. They would laugh and clap in delight as the old woman in her sari bowled and then scampered maniacally around the lawn after the ball that funny looking little Masterjee wearing miniature pads would dispatch with his tiny cricket bat, practising his late cuts and off drives and leg-side glances off the front foot in the manner of the princely Rajah cricketers. Old Ajay, the Sinclairs' chief garden-wallah, did duty as the umpire. He was a bit stiff on his pins but always up to presiding over a good match. It was Ajay who taught George (among other things, of which more later) how to bowl leg spin—one of the most difficult things to do in cricket—how to wedge the ball between your middle and index fingers and how to deliver it with a backward flick of the wrist. This is the most devious kind of bowling known to man because the ball cuts in on the right-handed batsman from his leg side—having to deal with leg spin is like being made to write with your left hand when you are right-handed.

After cricket, there would be the ritual of tea and biscuits on the verandah with the garden-wallahs and then George would spend hours on his belly under Grannyjee's supervision drawing pirates and Jolly Rogers and Spanish treasure galleons. Blackbeard the pirate appeared in all his drawings. Major and Mrs Sinclair speculated that their son must have picked up this curious obsession with Caribbean pirates (in *Goa*, of all places) at primary school.

Grannyjee had another theory, which she kept to herself and later shared with George.

"You see, Morpheus, the old girl was an odd kind of Catholic. Her line descended from the tribes of what eventually became Goa. They were a marsh-dwelling people, Untouchables for the most part. In the 16th century they had fallen under the spell of the Portuguese colonizers, and then of Xavier's bright-eyed Jesuits—the Soldiers for Christ of the Company of Jesus—following hot on the heels of the invaders. Years later, when I looked into my ancestry, I read about how the Jesuits placed the communion wafer on the tongues of the Untouchables with the help of a ruler—not necessarily to avoid contamination but, being master politicians, to please the local Brahmin overlords who were their real targets."

Major Sinclair suspected, to his wife's embarrassment, that Grannyjee Fernandes' loyalties were divided. She seemed devoted in equal measure to the chaste saints and anaemic virgins of the Portuguese Baroque and to the lustful swarm of gods and *devis* of Hinduism. In her cluttered bedroom, if you looked closely enough, you could see the garish pinks, blues and saffron of Hindu deities lurking beside the icons of Catholicism and the images of dead and living Popes. The votive candles that warmed the morbid flesh of the Redeemer and lit up the face of His weeping mother the Blessed Virgin Mary, whom Grannyjee referred to as the BVM, also illuminated the blue of Vishnu's face and the Elephant God Ganesha's pink trunk and distended belly and the puckish face of Hanuman the Monkey God and the crimson tongue of an aggressive dark-faced goddess with many arms called Kali.

George's induction into this divided world took place whenever the Sinclairs were out at one of their cocktail parties or Chamber of Commerce luncheons, or during late-night sessions in Grannyjee's room. Grannyjee instructed George in the intricate rules and interlocking wheels of reincarnation and Vedic astrology. She made him swear not to reveal this arcane knowledge to his parents or to his teachers at school. George willingly became Grannyjee's disciple, and revelled in the marvellous complexity of his grandmother's secret world.

At some stage the question of George's previous incarnations must have come up, because he remembered having a notion, from a very early age, that he was the 20th-century incarnation of Mr Edward Teach, the scourge of the Caribbean, also known as Blackbeard the Pirate.

BLACK SEPTEMBER

By the pricking of my thumbs,
Something wicked this way comes . . .

Eventually there came that time which is dreaded by overseas boys the
world over. Looking back, Sinclair found it all so predictable, but at the time
he had the sense of something creeping up on him in the undergrowth with
the stealth of one of Grannyjee's boy-eating wolves.

It all happened gradually.

For a start, there were hushed discussions in the drawing room. Mother, as
usual, did not participate in these, for Grannyjee was George's only advocate.
It seemed that the Public School imitations of the Subcontinent were not
good enough for the Major, despite Grannyjee's suggestions and subtle
recommendations. These institutions might do for the *arrivistes* and *nouveaux
riches* of Goa like that car salesman Wally dos Santos or Aloysius Ferreira
and their nasty sprogs, sniffed the Major, but any notion of George going on
to any of these pseudo-Public Schools was dismissed as totally out of hand.
The debate did not last long. The Major, it seems, had other plans for
Masterjee.

One Sunday after Mass in early May, George saw his father whispering in
the ear of a priest. It was a European, one of those who wore black robes. Ever
since he could remember, George had spied those hungry-faced men in
soutanes and false sleeves hovering around his father like shadows. Both men
watched George carefully as they spoke at the church door. George felt that
he was being sized up for something. He heard the phrase 'registered at birth',
which meant nothing to him.

The following Sunday after Mass the priest had been invited back to the
house, and after hours holed up in his study with his guest, the Major had
emerged and taken a long cool look down at his boy with those dead grey eyes
of his.

Just after his ninth birthday the announcement was made and it became
official. The servants, Sinclair remembered, were clearing up after curry tiffin
and the family was still seated at the table. With the zeal of the converted, to
the unspoken relief of his wife, and to a deep sigh from Grannyjee, the Major
declared to the household that before the end of the third quarter young
George was to be shipped off to the Jesuits in England. The Jesuits, the Major
informed his family, were the best educators the Church had to offer and,

furthermore, they were a *military* breed. And, he went on, looking hard at Grannyjee, a good dose of discipline never did anyone any harm.

To the Major, who would himself never countenance the idea of returning, the idea of sending his son to Great Britain, into the arms of the soldier priests, had a certain appeal. Being a military man, Major Sinclair had found an affinity with the Founder, Ignatius, and his Soldiers for Christ, otherwise known as the Company, or Society, of Jesus.

For Major Sinclair the act of conversion had been no mere formality to facilitate his marriage. He observed the rites of his new affiliation with rigour and discipline. He was a regular at Retreats and performed the Society's Spiritual Exercises under the supervision of the Father Provincial of the Jesuits of Goa, who had agreed to be his Spiritual Director. These urbane Europeans were the descendants of the original missionaries who had brought the light to Grannyjee's benighted ancestors. They were the guardians of Xavier's tomb at the church of the *Bom Jesus* where the Sinclair-Fernandes family attended Sunday Mass. They had now found a generous benefactor in the Major and they had been very pleased when the Major honoured them with his son's middle name.

After the barber-wallah had been called in for a short-back-and-sides George was dispatched with trunk, tuckbox, cricket bat and a firm no-non-sense handshake from his father. There was a letter of recommendation from Father Provincial to the Headmaster of the school in England, to be hand-delivered by George personally.

For a minute in the car, as Major Sinclair pressed the letter into his son's hand, George thought of what happened to the bearers of sealed letters in Grannyjee's Jacobean tragedies, but this thought was quickly overtaken in the excitement as they approached the chaos of the airport.

If you had asked him, George wouldn't have remembered what his mother had to say about it all.

George wasn't scared—the only things that scared him those days were trolls and malicious sprites—the little people gone to bad—but he *was* apprehensive. If you had asked him what was going through his mind on the evening before his departure, as he sat at Grannyjee's feet and let the old woman stroke his hair, he would probably have told you that he was more intrigued and excited than sad. Banishment and exile and the slow passage of time were concepts that he was not yet familiar with.

The person who suffered most in those days was Grannyjee. George's departure went ahead on schedule despite her protests and Portuguese lamentations, which included an embarrassing scene in front of the servants. Grannyjee's tears had emboldened the garden-wallahs, who had grown fond of Masterjee, to send a delegation headed by Old Ajay to the Major to beg for mercy.

Old Ajay stood before the Major, eyes down, and begged him, concentrating fiercely on his grammar: "Please, not to be sending away our dear Masterjee, of which we have become very fond."

Outraged by this insolence, Major Sinclair gave the old gardener a public dressing-down. Then he made the old lady pay dearly for her outburst, because it was she who had encouraged the servants. The tears continued to flow behind closed doors well after George's departure had left the house empty and the gardens desolate. Ajay had been sent back out to his quarters in disgrace and was threatened with docked wages. The garden-wallahs were close to being dismissed en masse and, for the next few weeks, as Grannyjee wept in her room, they lurked about the gardens muttering darkly and avoiding the Major at all costs.

What had most distressed Grannyjee, who had had George's horoscope cast by a Hindu astrologer when he was born, were certain sinister planetary aspects and alignments in his birth chart. These made her failure to prevent George's banishment very difficult to deal with. She hadn't wanted to alarm him, but in the end she did decide to warn him to "beware among the English".

Of course, George had agreed, the English *are* a dangerous breed, that was well known. You only had to think of the famous pirates with whom he felt a special affinity, like Messrs Henry Morgan, Francis Drake, Walter Raleigh, Calico Jack and then the prince of them all and George's favourite outlaw, Edward Teach, who was Blackbeard.

Through the rear window of the car he saw Grannyjee saying: "Bye bye my love . . ." There was something resigned in her look as she waved at the car that was taking Masterjee away to his uncertain future.

It was September, 1971. In June, Saturn had entered the sign of Gemini. In the astrological chart that Grannyjee wept over, surrounded by her icons and *durgas*, Gemini ruled George's Twelfth House. To complicate matters, George's Ascendant happened to be Cancer, the sign that immediately follows Gemini in the wheel of the Zodiac. The Twelfth House is the house of secret enemies, self-undoing and incarceration. Saturn, the Great Malefic and a severe taskmaster, was to harass those born under Gemini for the next two and a half years and then, for good measure, would move into the sign of Cancer for another three. The Ascendant is in many ways more influential than the birth sign because it governs the house of your personality. George's prospects in England for the next six years or so, from an astrological point of view, were not good.

After completing its visit to your sign, which invariably leaves devastation of various sorts in its path, Saturn goes on to complete its orbit around the sun, working its malevolent way through each of the Houses and Signs of the Zodiac every two to three years. Saturn then returns to hound the natives of each sign some twenty-nine years later.

In 1971 Saturn was also wreaking havoc on a grander scale, by subjecting the civilized world to the double scourge of terrorism and immigration.

September 1971 was George Sinclair's Black September—exactly twelve months after the bloody expulsion of the PLO from Jordan gave rise to the spectacularly successful terrorist movement of the same name.

It was also around that time that what seemed like an endless stream of brown humanity invaded God's own British Isles, courtesy of a Sandhurst graduate, one Field Marshall Dr Idi Amin Dada. The expelled Asians of Uganda had come home to England, expecting a warm welcome from the Mother of the Commonwealth. Before their arrival, the word 'Paki' was relatively unknown in the British Isles.

There couldn't have been a worse time for someone of George's ilk—or for anyone touched by the tar brush, for that matter—to arrive in England.

WOG

"There are wogs and there are wogs," one of the senior boys had said out loud at supper, eyeing the dark little New Boy from India.

At Prep School in Surrey 'George' became 'Sinclair'. 'Masterjee' became an 'Overseas Boy'. An Overseas Boy touched by the tar brush.

In other words: a Wog.

His skin, once supple and tanned, froze and turned a dirty crusty yellow in the mild English winter. He developed chilblains and his knuckles and knees dried, cracked, pussed up and bled and eventually he had to be fitted with plastic surgical gloves to keep the moisture in and to prevent him from picking at the scabs and scratching himself raw.

Many things about him made George—Sinclair, that is—stand out: his jolly

Goan accent, an incipient moustache, the awkward combination of a sallow skin and his father's blue-grey eyes. And then there was the funny way he wagged and wobbled and shook his head when he meant yes or when he was excited and enthusiastic, because in those early days Sinclair was still open to the world and eager to please.

"Being a half-breed wasn't really that bad in Goa," he puzzled, struggling to get warm in his cubicle between the clammy damp of the sheets as outside the endless rain pelted down, drenching the rugby fields, "but here it has made me an outsider among the English boys."

The rain persisted and gradually warmth returned to his extremities. In the safety of his private world under the blankets Sinclair dwelt on the origins of the word wog, which a weasel-faced boy named Crilly had been kind enough to acquaint him with that afternoon after rugby.

"The word wog stands for Wily Oriental Gentleman. W-O-G, see? Geddit? Wog as in Golly Wog, yes, just like the one on the jam jar. But you see, Sinclair, there are wogs and there are wogs. A wog like you is a brown *sahib*, Sinclair, a black who would like to think he is British. Pakis like you are wogs, whereas dagos, you see, are greasy Spaniards, or spics . . . and then there are wops, who are greasers, not to be mistaken with wogs . . . you are not a nigger, or a tar baby, or a *kaffir*, for that matter, because they are Africans or West Indians, nor are you a wop, but you are a . . . wog. Now, is that quite clear, Sinclair?"

Under the blankets, with his inner eye Sinclair could see himself standing in the middle of a circle of boys in the playground. He could see Crilly's snout pronouncing this indisputable truth as the lecture continued. He saw also the fair heads and bright eyes of Crilly's disciples, nodding at his wisdom and sniggering as they relished the humiliation of their victim, who stood encircled in his crêpe-soled sandals, picking at the scabs on his knuckles, a puzzled frown on his awkward little face.

"So what *are* you, then, Sinclair?"

"Yes, speak up, Sinclair," went the chorus.

"Cat got your tongue, eh, Golly?" someone said.

"What *are* you, pakboy?" they insisted.

"Well, then, what are you?" Crilly insisted.

"A wog, I suppose."

"A *wog*, exactly, well *done*, *that's* what you are. Is that understood?"

"I suppose so, Crilly," he had replied with a wobble of the head and to more laughter from the chorus.

And so it was that he took his place in the ranks of the pariahs, in the particular cage reserved for half-castes, next to the dagos from Gibraltar (at least they stuck together and were all related), the two Nigerian niggers (they were good at rugby), and the handful of solitary Vietnamese or Hong Kong Chinese slant-eyes who lived in their own (inscrutably) hermetic worlds and were brilliant at maths.

It's not surprising then that Sinclair withdrew into *his* own secret world. Already in his first term, his naturally sunny disposition was transforming itself into a misshapen, inward-looking sullenness that made him appear shifty and eventually earned him the mistrust of masters and boys alike. He promised himself to protect the secret of his middle names at any expense—especially the name Gupta which lurked there in the middle of his identity, ticking away like a little black time-bomb. Xavier he might be able to explain away, but Gupta was a killer. The only way to guarantee the secret was to prevent anyone from getting close enough to find out.

He almost stopped drawing, which, apart from cricket (for which he still had to wait two terms), was his only talent. And when he drew, he only drew pictures of Crilly and the other English boys being massacred by his Caribbean pirates under the supervision of Blackbeard, or agonizing on crucifixes or with their heads on pikes, or impaled on sharp sticks like fish kebabs, in the manner favoured by Vlad the Impaler, otherwise known as Dracula. He kept these sketches stashed in his tuckbox and would take them out periodically and gloat over them when he was feeling put upon.

In the safety of the half-world under the blankets in his cubicle after lights out Sinclair turned his back on the *Bom Jesus* and instead would summon the images of his grandmother's idols and beg them to assist him in punishing the wicked, comforting himself to sleep with images of Crilly and his acolytes being torn limb from limb by righteous Vishnu and furious Shiva the Destroyer, assisted in his cosmic dance of destruction by the bloodthirsty devil goddess Kali with her black face and four arms and her necklace of skulls. In these flights of fancy Sinclair became a thug, a follower of Kali Maa who was quite prepared to kill to satisfy the bloodlust of his black mother.

The interval between breakfast and Sunday Mass was dedicated to Letter Writing. The boys' letters home were screened by the Jesuits and Sinclair soon learned to report only his successes, which in those days were limited to the classroom, because he was too slight to be a good rugby player. News of his social failure, of the relentless cold, and of his chronic homesickness never made it back to Goa. He lived for his mother's letters, hungrily looking for references to his beloved Grannyjee, because Grannyjee could not write English and the Jesuits had forbidden the parents of the overseas boys to write to their boys in any language other than English. He would take the thin blue airmail envelopes and holding them to his face, breathe in deeply what he imagined were the scents of home and the seaside heat and sandalwood spices of Goa, the few atoms of India that had been trapped between the wafer-thin blue of the airmail. The extent of Major Sinclair's affection was a brief scrawl at the bottom of his mother's letters.

The second Friday of term a letter addressed to "Master G.X.G. Sinclair" arrived. That Sunday after breakfast, when it was time to write back, he informed his mother that there was really no need to use middle initials in addressing letters to boys in England. He buried this advice in the middle of news about his classes and the weather and how the First Fifteen had trounced Sunningdale 21 to 3, and about how he had passed the first practice trials in the indoor cricket nets for the Under Elevens next summer.

That Sunday the censor was their maths teacher, a Jesuit who they called Tic because that was the sound his false teeth made as he champed mercilessly on his gums while he scanned the boys' letters for subversive messages or disguised appeals for help.

Sinclair had learned to watch people's eyes for the first hint of trouble. He saw an evil light come on in Tic's watery eyes and then, as the chewing and the clicking of his gnashers stopped, he watched the priest's mouth twist in the self-satisfied smirk of a hunter cornering a small animal. Tic had picked up the offending sentence and was now peering down over his half-moon specs at the awkward Anglo-Indian specimen sitting there at the desk picking at his knuckles.

Sinclair's hands and feet went cold. He had been rumbled, and his secret world was about to be stormed. The secret of what the X and the G stood for was going to be revealed to the world. He stiffened, steeling himself as Tic opened his mouth to reveal the secret to the other boys, who were busy, heads down, tongues curled around their lips in concentration as they scraped away at their letter writing. Sinclair watched the priest's lips with horrid fascination, waiting for the inevitable disaster.

But incredibly no sound came from the grim orifice. Instead, peering down at Sinclair over his specs with an amused look in his eyes, the priest silently mouthed the word *"GUPTA"* with an exaggerated, obscene contortion of the lips followed by the death's head rictus.

Sinclair was beginning to find out that the Jesuits had subtle ways of getting messages across to their boys. The message that had been delivered to him that Sunday morning was more disturbing than if the Jesuit had shouted out his middle names to the whole class. The message was that he was totally at their mercy, and that if there was anything to be known about him, they knew it. Watch your step, Master Sinclair, you sly little wog, we know all about you, and we are on to you . . .

EGG

"It has come to my attention that one of you has been indulging in ungentlemanly behaviour."

The speaker addressing the assembled school was Anatole Gollifer, S.J., the rotund Headmaster; the place, the Refectory; the occasion, after supper on a winter's evening in Sinclair's first term. It was after an afternoon of exertion on the frozen mud of the rugby flats and the boys were pink from prolonged exercise followed by the scrubbing away of caked mud in the showerplace. The pudding of spotted dick with custard had just slid down 190 still-hungry throats and the plates had been cleared away. Gollifer's usually jovial features were now serious and the knot of anger that darkened his brow spelled trouble.

"Since the beginning of term, which makes me suspect that it is a *New Boy*, one of you has been systematically squashing your *uneaten* eggs in the stack."

He was referring to the practice of stacking. When the meal was done, the empty plates were stacked and sent to the head of the table. From there they would be handed to the boys whose turn it was to serve the others and return the soiled crockery and utensils to the trogs in the kitchen for scrubbing.

"The kitchen staff have complained to me that whenever fried eggs are served, there is always one plate that is returned stuck to another with a squashed, *uneaten* egg. As you can imagine, gentlemen, this creates a grisly task for the washer-uppers. It is most ungentlemanly to subject our menial staff to this ordeal and, frankly, it is the height of ingratitude for food to be sent back . . . *uneaten*."

Sinclair sat frozen on his bench. He heard Fr Gollifer's proposal: that if the culprit owned up, *immediately*, he would be given prolonged kitchen duty and be spared the ferula—the ferula was a twelve-inch length of flexible whalebone which was used to whack the hands of naughty boys in Jesuit schools. If not, severe corporal punishment, and perhaps worse, was the only sanction available.

"Well, then, Gentlemen, I am waiting . . ." Gollifer leaned back on his heels, arms crossed, double chin quivering on his chest and lower lip jutting out, bearing an uncanny resemblance to Mussolini.

Silence. The clock ticked, and snowflakes drifted down soundlessly outside the windows.

Gollifer then delivered threats of mass punishment, designed to encourage the innocent majority to denounce the lone malefactor in their midst.

The miracle was that not a single boy suspected it was Paki Sinclair who was responsible for this outrage. He had become skilled at dispatching the congealed gluten by distracting those next to him as he squashed the runny yellow bird turd under the stack.

Still nothing.

"Very well, Gentlemen, consider that the gravity of the situation has now escalated. It is one thing to own up, another thing to be discovered, and discovered you will be, believe you me. And when you are, there will be no mercy. None at all. The practice of mutilating food with contempt for one's servants is one thing, but to subject your fellows to punishment on your behalf, is quite another. So God help you, whoever you are, when you are exposed—and exposed you shall be . . ."

And finally, using a word that Sinclair had never heard before, Gollifer intoned: "Whoever you are, consider yourself as of now to be in a state of physical, moral and spiritual *jeopardy*."

With that unusual word Gollifer had conjured up the horrific spectre of Mortal Sin and Sinclair could almost feel the tongues of hellfire licking at his feet under the bench.

If you were to ask George Sinclair what he remembered most vividly from those early days in England, it would be that word and the visions of eternal torment that it evoked.

After delivering that terrible *fatwa*, Gollifer dismissed the school and all the boys—no one was spared, not even the Head Boy and his Committee of monitors—were sent upstairs for an extra hour of prep. And to make things worse, that night prep was endured by candlelight because the English coal miners, who the older boys referred to as trouble-making Northern proles and trogs, were on strike that winter.

Such was Sinclair's skill at dispatching the eggs that it took them two more fried egg dinners before they were able to move in for the kill. Each time the plates showed up, stuck together by the glutinous mess, each time the protests of the kitchen staff increased and there was even talk of industrial action by certain of the servants, taking their cue from the miners. With each incident the hysteria of Gollifer's menaces, and the resulting punishments, increased exponentially. Soon the school was languishing under a prolonged regime of extra prep and severely curtailed tuckshop, and eventually a total ban on television, which was then replaced by extra Benediction and Religious Doctrine supplemented by mandatory cross-country runs across the mud flats after Letter Writing on Sundays instead of telly.

Feelings were therefore running high and the whole school was gripped by one mania and one mania only—hunting down the phantom egg squasher, and in short order. It had to be done to end the debilitating deprivation of no tuck, no free time. Telly privileges had been withdrawn. Gone were the comforting family substitutes of Cilla Black, Bruce Forsyth and his Generation Game, and Top of the Pops. For once, the interests of the Jesuits and of 189 out of 190 of their victims were totally aligned. With the full co-operation of several quislings among the boys, and of the kitchen staff, who had agreed to the cunning idea of marking each plate with a number in order to trace the egg squasher, it was only a matter of time before the Jesuits sprung their trap.

The evening of the third fried egg dinner, the cold yellow eye stared up at Sinclair from his plate, swimming in its sickly film of grease. But even before the meal had been served, Gollifer had positioned himself and was standing directly behind Sinclair. A frisson of anticipation electrified the Refectory, as it would a crowd under the gallows at a public execution. The Day of Reckoning was at hand, the culprit had been identified at last, the punishments would be lifted imminently, and now, the boys noted with glee, the authorities were poised to strike and mete out justice to the wicked fellow who had ruined the last few weeks of their existence. Not to mention that George Sinclair, that dirty little paki wog, we should have known it was him all along, fucking dirty little bastard-paki-shit-wog-cunt, would be dealt with separately by the boys later, in their own way. Negotiations would begin shortly among the ringleaders of the various tribes as to the sequence of beatings and humiliations that lay in store for young Sinclair, May God Have Mercy on His Black Paki Soul . . .

The rest of the meal—a 'treat' of soggy bread pudding—was eaten in record time and in silence, so compelling was the promise of the post-prandial entertainment. Supper was over, all except, that is, for Sinclair's lone congealed egg. Sinclair sat immobilized, hypnotized by the disembodied cyclops beneath him. Gollifer said nothing. He just stood there silently behind Sinclair in his black soutane, like a hangman, with infinite patience. The boys on either side of Sinclair, snot-eating O'Reilly and skull-faced Batchelor

Minor, who Sinclair had deceived for so long with his sleight of hand as he had, unnoticed, squashed his egg under their noses, now sat slack-jawed and mesmerized by the events unfolding before their ringside seats.

The minutes ticked by, an eternity passed, silence reigned, the plates were stacked and ready to be sent to the kitchens. Simon Cavendish sat at the head of the table, an oily smirk on his face. He was tugging at his shirt cuffs, which always seemed longer than his jacket or pullover sleeves. Cavendish was fly half in the Under Eleven rugby team and was rumoured to have been chosen to be the captain of the Under Eleven cricket team next summer. The kitchen staff had also assembled at the doorway leading from the Refectory to the kitchens.

The school and its servants held their collective breath and Sinclair repeatedly failed to spoon up the cold mess before him.

As Gollifer hovered above him, Sinclair suddenly felt caught up in one of his improbable nightmares. He pinched himself hard to make himself wake up, but he failed to leave the dream. He watched himself from the out-of-body vantage point of an astral traveller. It was then that he realized that he was actually trapped in reality. For the first time in his life he felt the dangerous but intoxicating surge of adrenaline that jolts you in to action when you know that your mind is made up and you realize that all along there was ever only really one inevitable course of action ever available to you: sheer, hopeless, in-your-face 'Fuck You' defiance.

Sinclair watched himself exhale in resignation, then calmly lift the waiting stack beside him and let it drop smartly on the yolk. The squelching fart-like sound, as several pounds of crockery squeezed the breath out of the egg, was loud and memorable. A chorus of sniggers broke out, and then applause followed by cheering and the pounding of 189 dessert spoons on the tabletops. Sinclair heard applause coming from the direction of the kitchens. Whether it was in old-fashioned English appreciation of the underdog's defiance in the face of utter defeat, or in celebration, relief, catharsis or congratulation of the victory of the English authorities over the paki troublemaker, he would never really know.

"*Shhh, shhh, shhh* . . ." replaced the pandemonium, as the older boys reined in their excitable wards. Gollifer was about to speak. Sentence was about to be passed.

"Well, thank you so very much, Master Sinclair. Now be so kind as to remove the plates and—*eat—your—EGG*. No one leaves the Refectory until you have done so."

What happened next was a classic case of memory block, because Sinclair could never, ever really remember the ghastly horror of what followed that evening in the Refectory for as long as he lived.

BLACK AND BLUE

After the ordeal in the Refectory Sinclair received his official punishment—six of the best strokes of Gollifer's ferula.

Then came the unofficial punishment at the hands of his peers.

The day after his 'cracks', Sinclair joined in the playground cricket at First Rec. Each boy had his own tennis ball which he was allowed to bowl at a batsman in the asphalt yard. When his turn came to bowl, he delivered a poor line outside the leg stump and the batsman knocked Sinclair's ball firmly against the walls of the gym for four. The fielders were under standing instructions. George Sinclair's tennis ball was scooped up by a fat boy who always smelled of mothballs and whose name was Meridew, who promptly threw it over the roof of the gym and into the woods, to the cheers of the assembled playground. Fuming, his eyes pricking with hot tears, Sinclair told the sniggering boys to fuck off, wished them all slow lingering deaths, and sulked off behind the gym to search for his tennis ball among the nettles.

Where he was promptly set upon by a crack unit of ambushers wearing school-issue balaclavas who threw a potato sack from the kitchens over him and kicked and punched the shit out of the brown little cunt-sodomite-bastard-paki-wog-fuckinbastard-black-piece-of-shite until his screams stopped and the squirming sack convulsed silently in the mud and then lay quite still.

He heard the commandos congratulating themselves and the word 'wog' several more times and the plummy tones of Simon Cavendish's voice as he stood in the background, supervising the proceedings.

"I'll have you, Simon Cavendish, I'll have you," were the last words he heard himself say before he passed out.

There followed a spell in the Infirmary, which smelt of iodine and stale piss and disinfectant. He was black and blue, beaten to a pulp, beaten to within an inch of his life, as they like to say in England—a miserable brown life at that, but his bones were intact. The search for his assailants was brief and half-hearted and came to nothing, the consensus being that Sinclair had done more damage tripping over and landing on his sour little face than from being beaten. And anyway, they agreed in the Staff Common Room, if anyone had deserved to be taught a lesson at the hands of his peers, it was that sly little shit George Sinclair.

He missed the next practice session in the indoor cricket nets in the gym. Looking back on it, Sinclair realized that this was precisely what had been intended by Cavendish's squad of hit men. In the Infirmary, reports reached him of a brilliant bowling performance in the indoor nets by Jerome O'Reilly, his snot-eating neighbour at the dinner table. O'Reilly was one of Cavendish's protegés, and a pretty mediocre fast bowler in Sinclair's opinion. Cavendish was pushing for O'Reilly to replace Paki Sinclair on the Under Eleven practice squad. Sinclair's place on the team was being called into question. And to make things worse, leg spin was becoming passé. The current vogue favoured fast bowling, bodyliners and bouncers, not spin. Spin had become associated with those devious paki bowlers who lacked the strength to deliver decent pace bowling, due most probably to malnutrition from that smelly greasy muck they called curry, the debilitating effects of the tropical heat of their countries, but more likely, well, let's face it, the sheer indolence and moral lassitude of black and brown people.

"I wouldn't give tuppence for Karachi. My Pa says it's all shit and beggars and flies. And the stench, my God, the stench."

The boys in the sick-bay cots next to his in the Infirmary made sure that Sinclair, who it seems had taken a rather nasty fall in the playground, overheard this. In loud voices they discussed O'Reilly's brilliance in the indoor nets and the latest Test Match results from the Subcontinent. England was being routed by the Pakis, no doubt as a result of trickery and deviousness and food poisoning by the hosts.

From then on, Sinclair gave up any pretense of supporting England at cricket or rugby. His allegiance in rugby was now with the All Blacks, the Scots and even the devious French, but never with England or Ireland, and in Test Matches he backed the Indians or the pakis or the Sri Lankans, and yes, he even favoured the West Indians, who by then he had discovered were blacks and not really Indians like him at all.

TUCK

In Goa, Masterjee had learned a trick or two about lock-picking from Ajay, Major Sinclair's senior garden-wallah. The old geezer's hobby in between umpiring and gardening duty was to repair, disassemble and then reassemble old padlocks and rusty locks from old gates and doors. George would stand and watch the old boy's gnarled fingers crack open the mechanisms, close them up again and then delicately stroke and pincer the levers open with a safety pin. The old boy would squint through the smoke of his *beedi* as he muttered and cursed his arthritis and passed on his lock-picking wisdom to Masterjee for future reference.

"You never know when it might be becoming useful, young Masterjee," the old boy had prophesized.

Indeed, this arcane skill was to prove very useful to George Sinclair in England, and, afterwards, many years later, on his travels abroad.

As he warmed himself under the blankets in his secret world in Surrey, in his mind's eye Sinclair was no longer a black and blue victim rolling around in the mud in a potato sack, refusing to cry out. He had denied the English their satisfaction. Now he was transforming himself into a Jacobean Revenger, or better still, one of those cut-throat pirates that he used to draw for Grannyjee in Goa, a disciple of Blackbeard (more like his direct descendant or reincarnation), or a secret agent. All these manifestations of revenge were hell-bent on a single purpose; teaching Simon Cavendish a lesson in respect.

Sinclair hatched his Revenger's plot over the next few days. In the meantime he practised picking the lock of his own tuckbox and then graduated onto those of his unsuspecting dormitory mates. Their tuckboxes were kept under the bed in their cubicles, and this is where the Revenger slithered on his belly like a viper when the boys were absent or asleep. His pickings were slim and modest: he would generally pilfer only a biscuit or two hoping that the theft would go unnoticed. More than the food (which was invariably dry or stale and tended to stick in his gullet), what drove him was the pleasure of knowing that he had the power to intrude unseen into the lives of the English boys and uncover their pathetic little secrets, such as forbidden teddy bears or security blankets of various types or illicit hot water-bottles or transistor radios. And all the while, the sad little cunts thought that their secrets were safe and protected behind their trusty Chubs ("Made in Britain") which had proved to be no match for the nimble fingers of Paki locksmiths and leg-spin bowlers.

What the Revenger had in mind for Simon Cavendish had something to do with Stilton cheese—about ten pounds of it, to be precise. This was the amount that Sinclair stole from the school larder and planted in Simon Cavendish's tuckbox during afternoon games. He had exempted himself from rugby with a fake fainting spell the day after being discharged from the Infirmary following his thrashing behind the gym.

He had never seen cheese like this before. Its blue-veined greasy whiteness and stench reminded him of the decomposing flesh of the corpses in the Hammer Horror films that he would watch with Grannyjee at home in Goa.

He kept half a pound for himself, which he gnawed on furtively in the half-world under the blankets. He surprised himself by how much he liked the filthy dirty-sock taste, wolfing down the last crumbs before the theft was reported by the kitchen trogs the following morning and the alarum bells rang.

The school authorities were just as shocked as Simon Cavendish when the surprise dormitory inspection revealed the greenish block of rancid cheese suppurating in the cricket god's tuckbox. But there was nothing to be done. Evidence was evidence, and the padlock was intact. Even though they desperately wanted to believe that Cavendish had been framed, the cricket god was sentenced to six of the best and duly beaten the next day.

The memory of Cavendish's gaping mouth and his indignant protests as he was led away was a prized trophy that Sinclair tucked away in one of the happier rooms in the vaults of his memory. So much for Cavendish's smart, protruding cuffs and his expensive shoes. In later years Sinclair would periodically take this trophy out, dust it off, and relish his victory.

They said later that eventually Cavendish had to throw away his tuckbox. This was because however hard he or the school servants scrubbed and disinfected and perfumed, the stench of the cheese had impregnated the wood and would not be washed away—like the blood on Lady Macbeth's hands.

The night of Cavendish's humiliation, Sinclair laughed himself to sleep.

MAKTUB

"Master Sinclair has exhibited nothing but contempt for his fellows and for the *esprit de corps* of this institution."

George's first report card was being read out to him aloud by his father at the breakfast table. It was the day after his return to Goa for his first school holiday. His mother would not look at him, and sat twisting her serviette in agonized embarrassment. As for Grannyjee, she had been silenced in advance with whispered threats.

The affair of the squashed eggs, George's near expulsion for his show of open defiance, and his anti-social behaviour in general, were being described in excruciating detail. George had been forced to hand-deliver the report card himself and now Major Sinclair was reading it aloud for all to hear. His father intoned the shameful verdict while Mother started to sob quietly and Grannyjee watched the cutlery in silence. Her grandson squirmed in his chair as if he had ants in his pants and stared sullenly at his curried breakfast.

The report concluded that Master Sinclair was "solitary, sly and wilful," and "unwilling to participate in the social discourse of the school".

And so George Sinclair came to see himself as he was seen by his masters and his peers in England, and by now by his father: as a Wily Oriental Gentleman, a nasty version of the jam jar Golly Wog, someone who was unreliable, malicious and skulked around in the shadows with that angry, puzzled frown of his, dirty little foreign fox that he was.

On Christmas day after Mass at the church of the *Bom Jesus*, George made a half-hearted and pathetic attempt to prevent his return to Surrey in the New Year. It was half-hearted because he knew that to bend his father's will was a hopeless undertaking. His tearful whimperings were shrugged off by his father, whose furious silence was worrying, and his mother made herself scarce whenever the subject of school came up. Grannyjee had learned her lesson about open shows of emotion and would now, in public at least, only tell her grandson that there was little she could do, except help him pack up his tuckbox for the return trip.

The night before his return to England was many times worse than their original parting in September. Back then it had seemed more like setting out on an adventure among the pirates of England and young Masterjee had never imagined the miseries that lay in store for him. But now he knew full well and was crushed by the knowledge of what was waiting for him back there among the shadows and the rain.

"It is written in the stars," Grannyjee murmured, caressing his head, "that you should be undergoing these trials and tribulations. But they will pass, in time, my dear boy, they will pass. In the meantime, we must be being brave, mustn't we?" Squeezing his hand, she continued: "I will always be near you. Your Grannyjee will always be there to watch over you, even if we are being separated by the oceans and the deserts."

And then she made him a promise, which he quickly forgot as he wallowed in his misery: "And when your Grannyjee is gone, as one day she must go, she will return to you and continue to watch over you. It is written so—as our Muslim brothers like to say—*maktub.*"

LEG SPIN

"At least I can teach them a lesson on the cricket pitch."

It was the summer term at last, and that meant the smell of freshly cut grass and long shadows on the cricket green in the evenings, and cricket, glorious cricket. During the excruciatingly slow classes before afternoon games Sinclair would daydream of taking hat-tricks with the devious leg-spin bowling that Old Ajay had coached him in and of hooking O'Reilly's bouncers for six off the back foot.

"That," he said to himself in his cubicle as he secretly caressed his Slazenger cricket bat with a rag soaked in linseed oil after lights-out, "they cannot take away from me, even if they call me a wog and a paki."

And later still into the night, because it was still light well after the boys had been put to bed, he would lull himself to sleep with fantasies of scoring centuries and hitting six sixes in a row like Gary Sobers, off the fast bowling of Simon Cavendish and Jerome O'Reilly and their apostles.

And then, to the delight of certain members of the staff who took a perverse pleasure in the success of the foreign boys, George Sinclair was the first New Boy to be awarded his half-colours. He made his colours ahead even of Simon Cavendish, who sure enough was now captain of the Under Elevens. Sinclair had dispatched the school's arch rivals Caldicott almost singlehandedly with his tricky leg-spin bowling, taking seven wickets for less than a dozen runs.

That evening in the Refectory after pudding he was handed his multi-coloured cap and patted on the shoulder by Fr Gollifer to begrudging and thinly scattered applause from the boys. It was the same Refectory where he had been humiliated in public when Gollifer had forced him to eat the squashed egg in his first term. Now it was the stage for his triumph.

But when Sinclair returned to his table after collecting his prize, instead of receiving the traditional handshakes from his peers, he was ignored. Sinclair noticed Cavendish looking at him as he whispered something into Crilly's ear. Crilly nodded darkly as he eyed Sinclair, like a hitman sizing up his contract. Crilly was the same weasel-faced gentleman who had kindly taken the time to enlighten Sinclair that what he was technically, in fact, a wog, rather than a dago or a nigger or a wop, thank-you-very-much.

Cavendish had indeed been confirmed as captain of the Under Eleven cricket team in which Sinclair now served despite the reluctance of his team mates. Cavendish had retained his place of honour at the head of the table, in

86

spite of the puzzling business with the Stilton cheese a couple of terms before. But all that had been quickly forgotten and such youthful high jinks should not be held against good chaps like Cavendish—such are the forgiving ways of the British Establishment when it comes to dealing with their own kind— the same forgiving ways that had permitted Kim Philby to be defended to the last by the club at MI6, and Sir Anthony Blunt, the Fourth Man and bastard son of King George, to remain as a favourite in the Royal household for years after he had been caught betraying his country. The business with the eggs, however, would always be held against George Sinclair. The business of the eggs just confirmed that darkies could not be trusted and were not team players.

There was no getting away from it. Although Sinclair had hoped against hope that his flair for cricket (it was *their* game, after all) would earn him a modicum of acceptance, George Sinclair was, and would always remain, a wog and a paki. He might be good for a few runs and useful at leg spin, but he was still fair game for merciless treatment on and off the field at the hands of Cavendish and his Establishment mafia.

OF TAIL-ENDERS, BODYLINERS AND BOUNCERS

They were out to get him, it was obvious. The method Cavendish and his cronies had settled for was to smash his dirty paki cranium in with a cricket ball. It would all be above board and purely accidental—no one would be charged with murder, it would just be a case of Paki Sinclair not having been able to deal with pace bowling. It happened all the time at Public Schools back then, when helmets were unheard of. Furthermore, they told themselves, Sinclair was a 'tail-ender'—that is, he batted at number 9, in the tail end, where the bowlers, who were usually weak batsmen, languished and were expected to live short lives at the crease and be mopped up by the fast bowlers after the middle order had collapsed. It would be no surprise that he could be easily outpaced and mistime a shot.

It didn't take Sinclair long to figure out what their game was. It started in the nets, and then they tried it again on the pitch during a practice match. Dolly Beamish, physics master and umpire that afternoon, was unable to stop the bodyliners and bouncers, delivered in the style of Jeff Thomson and Dennis Lillee and other Test Match speed-merchants, which were consistent-ly aimed at Sinclair's head by Cavendish and O'Reilly (the very same O'Reilly who used to eat his snot and had almost taken Sinclair's place on the team).

He managed to survive two more practice matches, including the final trials for the Under Elevens, dodging, ducking, weaving and gyrating repeatedly as the bodyliners and bouncers which were aimed at him and not at the wicket buzzed past him. His nerves were frayed and at night, in his dreams, the unending attack of cricket balls aimed at his head and at his heart continued until the waking bell.

In the outdoor nets again, the evening before their second match against archrivals Caldecott, Sinclair threw the balls back at the bowlers with contempt. Cavendish swaggered back to his mark, furiously polishing the ball in his groin, and began his run up again, murder in his eyes.

Sinclair squared up bravely to the bowling. The ball was a half volley outside the off stump. Sinclair drove it smartly off the front foot, easily and very hard, into the netting.

He hooked a short ball off O'Reilly and got a jagged bottom edge.

"Keep your eye on the ball, Sinclair," someone muttered from behind the netting. It was Poof Parker, history master of the swollen bee-sting lips, who was keeping a desultory watch over the proceedings.

Another short ball. This time he kept his eye on it and pulled it hard but far too high, clean out of the net.

Then he badly mistimed a square cut.

On O'Reilly's next delivery, instead of dealing with the ball with a simple forward defensive, Sinclair played too far forward and snicked what would have been an easy catch in the slips.

"They'll kick me out of the Under Elevens," he worried, "if I keep this up."

Sinclair cut the next ball very late and fine. "That's more like it," he told himself, getting into the swing of it.

"That's more like it, Sinclair, that's a fine stroke." This time it was Gollifer, who had appeared at Poof Parker's side behind the net.

Sinclair tapped the bat firmly into the crease on the matting, his confidence growing. He glowed through his whole body. Gollifer's praise was like nectar, because every scrap of praise for Sinclair, or so Sinclair construed, was a criticism of Cavendish and his cohorts.

He glanced O'Reilly's next ball to left off the front foot, right off the leg stump in the manner of the princely Rajah cricketers. Grannyjee, who was George's most devoted fan in Goa, would have clapped wildly and Old Ajay would have led the garden-wallahs in a celebratory jig. Even Major Sinclair would have approved of such an elegant stroke with a dour nod. Poof Parker and Gollifer applauded from behind the net. Dolly Beamish had now ambled up to watch the fireworks and joined in with ladylike applause.

Cavendish's next delivery was an appetizing half volley and Sinclair could not resist, and he duly dispatched it with a solid blow off the meat of the bat, driving it for what would have been a sure six, far above and beyond the disdainful bowlers. It was a delicious feeling, almost as good as ejaculating. Sinclair felt a tingling sensation in his groin at his latest victory over the fast-paced assault. What made it especially tasty was the sour look on Cavendish's face as he turned, muttering, to start the long trudge to collect his ball at the edge of the green. Sinclair could tell that his Nemesis was getting frustrated.

O'Reilly commenced his run up again. This time his face had the impassive hardness of an Aztec warrior.

"*Wog* . . . ," someone whispered from the side of the net. Sinclair turned, taking his eye off the ball for a split second, and saw Cavendish grinning at him.

O'Reilly's delivery was the bodyliner they had all been waiting for.

They said you could hear the crack of ball on bone all the way back in the pavilion.

He didn't feel the impact. The sizzling buzz of the cricket ball approaching his temple at a good seventy miles an hour had simply turned into the hum and vibration of several hundred thousand disembodied voices that hailed him as he was whisked off past them, sucked in towards some kind of vacuum by a spinning centrifugal force. Looking backwards down an immensely long well, he could see, rapidly receding at the bottom of the pit, a group of boys and masters standing around a boy in whites and pads who was lying on the green, his limbs arranged awkwardly like a downed scarecrow.

Looking forward now, he sped along a very fine thread of light through the noisy rotating tunnel and into a far greater light, where someone familiar was waiting for him at what looked like a fork in the road.

ALMOST TO SHIVA

"But Grannyjee, unless I am mistaken, you are not dead yet . . ."

They were in an antechamber, some kind of waiting room, before they could move on to the next stage if their cosmic journey. Grannyjee cradled his shattered head in her arms, as she used to do in her room in Goa, whispering her soothing words to him ". . . no, not yet, not yet, my dear boy . . ." and he

slipped off into a deep sleep, safe and cosy in his Grannyjee's arms and surrounded by the ineffable light of the Afterlife. She told him a familiar story as
they set off again on their journey, towards someone who was waiting for
them, Shiva perhaps.

The journey through the spinning vortex was familiar. Sinclair had the feeling that this search had happened before many different times over the ages.
And that the person he was searching for was just around the corner. He was
just behind the door. He was always just around the corner, always just behind
the veil.

The golden thread twitched, pulling them in. They were almost there . . .
almost there . . . almost . . .

They say that the disappointment of those returning from the dead is
unspeakable. George Sinclair's return from the bliss of the 'undiscovered
country' was no exception. When he opened his eyes in the Infirmary in
Surrey, God only knows how many hours since plunging into the coma, he
immediately knew where he was and he cursed the cold and the grey.

He would never be able to forget the awful sense of banishment that overwhelmed him that morning—or was it afternoon when he awoke (to the silent
relief of the Jesuits). What an immense sense of loss, totally inexpressible in
words. This, he thought, is how the rebel angels which the Js tell us about in
R.D. must have felt when they were expelled from the loving light of heaven
and had crashlanded in hell in crumpled, smoking heaps of devilry.

He longed to be in the light and the warmth again and for his Grannyjee's
arms. He longed for the murmur of the voice that had cradled him in a cocoon
and the talisman of her words protecting him on his journey homewards to
Shiva. Now the journey had been broken; someone had cut the thread and had
given it a hefty tug, and now there he was, a crumpled heap of despair, after
crashlanding into his English cot like a failed kite. And what a headache, what
a headache he had.

Something had woken him up.

It was the words "*Gupta Gupta Gupta*" being repeated softly into his ear.

When he opened his eyes he turned and saw a Jesuitical dog-collar and
Tic's false teeth clicking away not six inches from his face, as he intoned the
awful secret of his middle name into his ear, like the murderer pouring poison
into the sleeping king's ear. The priest was wearing a purple stole and was
looking at him over his specs with that amused look that always chilled
Sinclair to the bone.

Sinclair saw the priest's kit spread out on the Infirmary night table—the little crucifix, the little snuffbox containing the ointments of the Sacrament of Extreme Unction, otherwise known as the Last Rites. He saw Dr Ponsonby, who had been called in from Windsor, standing behind Tic. Matron was lurking next to the doctor with a tape measure in her hands. She tried to hide it behind her back as Sinclair opened his eyes. Sinclair realized that his measurements had just been taken for the undertaker in Egham.

The cunning old Jesuit had been right. The sense of panic that this secret produced in Sinclair was sure to wake him even from the deepest coma. To bring him back from hell itself, the priest must have thought, as he chuckled evilly to himself, champing on his gums with relish.

Sinclair closed his eyes again and wished devoutly to be dead again.

Sinclair's howling was mistakenly assumed by Matron and Dr Ponsonby to be from physical pain. And such was the pain that it was clear that only morphine could help him and stop the awful caterwauling. Back in the early seventies the drug was in plentiful supply in school infirmaries and the good doctor did not think twice before giving Matron the nod.

Soon enough the feral wailing that could be heard throughout the galleries and dorms and classrooms, and which made your hair stand on end and set your teeth on edge, died down to a whimper and then silence as for the first time the drug wended its kindly way through Sinclair's grateful veins.

He was beginning to get used to the easy passage between this world and that other intermediate half-world.

For a while, Sinclair thought that he was reapproaching the light of the godhead, from which he had just been so cruelly shot down.

He heard the familiar strains of a hymn from the Chapel float through the galleries and into the Infirmary. Perhaps they are saying a special Mass for my speedy recovery, he thought, feeling a little lightheaded and disorientated, or perhaps I am already approaching the massed choir of angels that guards the godhead . . .

Lead kindly light,
Amid th' encircling gloom!

Soon he was standing again in the dark of the *th' encircling gloom*, because the light was no longer visible or attainable; and he was quite alone. Grannyjee was nowhere to be seen. He seemed to be standing at some kind of crossroads in the middle of desolate fields and someone had appeared beside him, not quite the godhead or Shiva, and definitely not Grannyjee this time.

The person was a man with kind face and he held out his hand to George Sinclair in friendship. It was his first meeting with his lifelong friend and confidant Morpheus.

1984
TWITCHING THE THREAD

THE LOTUS EATERS

"My first encounter with black magic, Morpheus, happened in 1984. It was after my second year at Oxford. Because I was a rising star in the School of Archaeology and Anthropology I was given the opportunity to spend my third year abroad doing fieldwork in my special subject."

Under the direction of David Blantyre his tutor at Magdalen, he had elected to specialize in syncretism in the West Indies.

With the ever-obliging Morpheus as his guide, Sinclair sees himself arriving in Martinique on a steamy afternoon in late 1983, towards the end of the hurricane season. It is a few days before his formal start date at the Université des Antilles. A Force Five storm called Victor has just brushed past the island. The sky is white and the sweet stench of rotten fruit hangs thickly over the island in a mephitic pall. Victor's winds have clipped the island and have torn the mangoes and the guavas off the trees, and they now lay like tiny casualties all over the island, rotting in the tropical heat.

He had booked himself in to the Hotel Malmaison, a gingerbread monstrosity that nestles in the tropical foliage of Didier, high in the hill above Fort de France. After a few days of finding his bearings and acclimatizing to the cadences of Creole and *zouk* music, he reported to the campus of the university, where he had to find a place in the student dormitory.

He came across a small group of modern languages undergraduates from England inhabiting a wing of the student quarters. Like Sinclair, they were spending their year abroad, in their case to practise their French. They were known as *stagiaires*, English teachers at the university for a year.

There were three of them. There was Rupert, from Cambridge, a charming, well-dressed smiler; there was Lucy Kennedy, an East Ender from London University; and there was Fred, a white boy with dreadlocks from Nottingham. In Sinclair's book Lucy and Fred were 'crusties'.

The three of them had already settled into an indolent routine of doping when they weren't teaching. In Fred's room they had set up a row of bottles containing tropical fruits—mangos, guavas, tamarinds and passion fruit—fermenting into potent alcoholic brews. After lessons in the afternoon, when the rain had stopped, they would sit on a terrace near the dormitory high above the pewter of the West Indian sea. By five o'clock they would be thoroughly intoxicated with homemade rum followed by Fred's ganja. Watching the sunset they would plan the next weekend's activities or congratulate themselves for having escaped the lot of their less fortunate contemporaries, *stagiaires* who languished in the godforsaken industrial backwaters of France.

> *In the afternoon they came unto a land*
> *In which it seemed always afternoon.*
> *All round the coast the languid air did swoon,*
> *Breathing like one that hath a weary dream.*

Sinclair had come across a real live case of Tennyson's Lotus Eaters. When he mentioned this to them one balmy, golden afternoon, Rupert had smiled knowingly. Fred and Lucy had looked back at him vacantly.

Rupert pulled on his joint and surprised Sinclair by reciting the same poem. For Sinclair, the verses and the memory of Rupert's drugged voice that afternoon, would always evoke the tenor of those times:

> *A land where all things always seem'd the same!*
> *And round about the keel with faces pale,*
> *Dark faces pale against that rosy flame,*
> *The mild-eyed melancholy Lotus-eaters came.*

*

The weekends were dedicated to the beaches and to serious intoxication. The proceedings usually ended up with Rupert and Lucy lying unconscious in the sea gorse under some palm tree as Fred swung on his hammock, bug-eyed with ganja, humming some Rasta lullaby to himself.

Sinclair watched these goings-on from the sidelines with wry amusement. He remembered Simon Cavendish and his gang at school talking about how lazy *brown* and *black* people were.

Sinclair knew as soon as he set eyes on them that Fred and Lucy were lovers, although what they did to each other could hardly be called love. In the afternoons and evenings and weekends they went at each other openly, wrestling ferociously with youthful exuberance. Rupert called Lucy 'Dirty Luce' behind her back. Lucy wanted Rupert to join in and teased him when he refused. As Fred pumped away Lucy had once cried out that she wanted to jump Rupert's bones. "I close my eyes, Rupie baby, and it's you I see on top of me, not Freddiekins . . ." Fred didn't seem to care, and Rupert was flattered and egged the two crusties on as the headboards slammed through the dormitory.

Rupert saw that Sinclair was not fitting in. It was true—he felt uncomfortable having to watch Lucy and Fred snogging in front of him. Rupert propositioned him one Sunday at the beach at St Anne as Fred and Lucy copulated in the bushes. Rupert was only hoping to provide some comfort, he said, preferably of the carnal kind. But he stepped back like a gentleman after Sinclair's firm rejection of the offer.

Soon after his futile run at Sinclair, Rupert took up with one of his students, a willowy mulatto called Crispin. They would disappear for days into the interior of the island, Crispin riding pillion behind Rupert on his Vespa, the pair grinning from ear to ear.

When it came to Helen, though, Sinclair wasn't able to become a Lotus Eater and forget his past like his new friends. He fantasized about persuading her to visit him in Martinique. Here, on a New World beach before the turquoise sea, or in the rainforest, he would make it all up to her. But it was a hopeless, doomed fantasy. His letters were returned unopened and by his third month on the island he had given up writing to her.

Sinclair knew that it was hopeless. His world had stopped turning on its axis in his second term at Magdalen when Helen Henshaw's letters from London University suddenly stopped. All of a sudden she would no longer take his telephone calls. The curtain had finally fallen between them, and Sinclair knew why. She had found out what had really happened to her cousin Guy Underhill, as inevitably she had to, and that was that, for the time being, at least.

Instead he managed to distract himself from Helen by fixating on Lucy Kennedy. She was a grubby specimen and had filthy fingernails but under the grime and the expletives Sinclair felt that she might prove to be an appetizing morsel. She was the type of English girl that tans well. As the weeks progressed the sunburn on her shoulders and nose turned to a warm baked brown and her hair lightened several shades. There was something about her crudity—a sluttishness, a dirtiness—that attracted Sinclair: she was the antithesis of Helen, and this is perhaps what motivated Sinclair. It was time that he had a bad girl in his life.

At night while the cicadas roared in the trees outside the dormitory, after he had given up on the latest chapter of *The Golden Bough*, he would lie awake plotting while Lucy and Fred banged away against the headboards next door in celebration of their mindless coupling. The more he saw of Lucy's vulgarity—the vomiting, the hangovers—and the brutish copulation with Fred, the more he desired her.

But for the time being he decided to lay in wait. Patience was everything, he was learning as he grew older. Something was bound to happen, time would take its toll. There would be a quarrel, a lovers' tiff, or she would get bored of Fred's mindless thrusting or his body odour, and that was when Sinclair would move in for the kill.

BERNABEU

While all this was going on, another web was being spun. Its thread led to Sinclair's host on the island, Professor Celestin Bernabeu.

The Professor was a Creole elder, an acknowledged expert in syncretism and a widely respected French West Indian scholar. They said he was a close friend of Aimé Césaire, the famous Martiniquais poet. David Blantyre had written a letter to Bernabeu recommending his star pupil. Sinclair had delivered it personally. Handing it over to the elderly black gentleman, Sinclair remembered a morning in 1971 when he had handed over another letter of recommendation—to the Father Provincial of the English Jesuits—and he remembered the priest's sceptical look over his spectacles after reading its contents.

Unlike the Jesuits of Surrey, the Professor proved to be a gentle and helpful soul. He was a touch otherworldly perhaps, but he was very kind to Sinclair, just as he had been to Sinclair's predecessors.

They were sitting in the Professor's office on the second floor of the Bibliothèque Schoelcher in front of the Savane, as Fort de France's park is known. Professor Bernabeu folded Blantyre's note, put it in his jacket pocket and gave Sinclair some considered words of advice.

"Here in the French Antilles you will hear much about *Negritude*, a concept which my friend Césaire has invented, and you will encounter open hostility against colonialism. Among the intelligentsia you will not fail to see a desire to tear away from the Métropole, as we call France here. It's all noise. It's more than just about the *békés*, as we call the whites, and the blacks. Don't be taken in, young man, things are much more complicated beneath the surface. And the whole business of syncretism and *vodoun* and the relationship between Haiti and the French Antilles is more complicated still—and that's why you are here, to help us look into the complexity. A lot lies hidden beneath the surface. But I'll let you discover that for yourself as you conduct your research. In the meantime, my friend David Blantyre speaks very well of you. I have a little tradition. Before we start our professional relationship, I would like to invite you to my home; it is something I have done with all your predecessors. They find the climate agreeable up there. You gain a different perspective on the island and all its problems from my house."

'Up there' was the slope of a hillside facing the Pelée, the volcano that had erupted spectacularly in the 19th century. Pelée had wiped out the entire city of St Pierre, which had been known as the Paris of the Antilles and then became another Pompeii. Everyone had died in the doomed city, except a single prisoner in chains in the dungeon, or so the story went.

The Professor lived in a whitewashed plantation house with his wife. The property still had a functioning sugar cane press. Sinclair reached it on his Vespa the Sunday after the Professor's invitation. It was a good forty-five minute ride from the heat and the stench of dead fish and diesel of Fort de France.

Sinclair had woken late that morning, with the conviction that it was going to be a special day. He could feel it in his bones. He felt totally energized and ready for anything after a full night's sleep in Morpheus' kingdom.

It rains every day in Martinique.

That afternoon, before lunch, Sinclair sat on the verandah and watched the rain drench the tropical vegetation of the Bernabeus' garden. The Professor went into the cool dark interior of the house to announce Sinclair's arrival to his wife. The *'ti punch* that Professor Bernabeu had pressed into his hand was already doing its good work in Sinclair's bloodstream as he sat waiting there for luncheon to be called, safe from the tropical downpour.

It's 'anything can happen time' thought Sinclair, watching the big fat raindrops roll off the ferns and palm fronds. Time seemed to have slowed down. The Pelée loomed beyond the trees.

Here on the plantation, he told himself, I have reached another fork in the road.

A strange but pleasant feeling came over him as the rain stopped abruptly and sunlight flashed brilliantly on the gleaming wet foliage of the garden. It was one of those mythical interludes, one of those once-in-a-lifetime sensations where time, place and event converge in a three dimensional crossroads, like a cosmic accident pregnant with meaning—when the present already feels like the past. As if what was about to happen, as Grannyjee used to say, was *maktub*—already written in the heavens. He had only to wait for the page to be turned.

He had read about moments like these. It was like the feeling that might come upon you as you walk through some ancient grove on an island in the Saronic Gulf, just before you see the half-goat half-god Pan emerge from among the whispering pines and beckon you into the undergrowth.

For Sinclair, the thrill of anticipation that he felt there on the verandah that afternoon would forever inhabit one of the happier rooms of his memory.

QUADROON

"Haiti is the heart, the beating heart of our experience in the New World. Forget Martinique, forget Guadeloupe. We are minor satellites of Haiti, a weak reflection. Yes, you will find *vodoun* here, but not as in Haiti. You will eventually have to go to Haiti to fully understand the phenomenon of syncretism, George."

These prophetic words were uttered not by the Professor, but by Madame Bernabeu, his nut-brown wife.

Madame Bernabeu sat across the table from Sinclair and spoke confidently and with authority even though she was considerably younger than the Professor. As she spoke Sinclair watched her mouth. Her lips were purplish and her skin was highly polished and fragrant. She was doe-eyed and slightly overweight—a Rubenesque odalisque, Sinclair thought. He had heard about these voluptuous Haitian women before but had never met one in the flesh. At lunch they had discussed Madame's several bloodlines. After enquiring into Sinclair's background, the Professor had proudly announced that his wife was a quadroon.

"I don't believe I've ever met a quadroon before," said Sinclair somewhat at a loss.

"But how charming," she laughed, with a glance at her husband, who looked on kindly.

She had pretty teeth and her mouth was irresistible. The Professor seemed to be amused too, and nodded in encouragement.

"I am a quarter black, of course, as are all quadroons, but in addition I am a quarter French, a quarter Chinese and . . . perhaps you can guess the fourth bloodline?" she looked at Sinclair directly in the eye. An almost imperceptible wobble of her head gave Sinclair a clue.

"Indian. Not West Indian, but East Indian, I mean, like me, perhaps, Madame?"

"Bravo!" clapped the Professor, taken by the *'ti punch*.

His wife nodded with satisfaction and looked across the table at her husband, as if confirming something that she suspected about the visitor and had warned the Professor about beforehand. It was as if Sinclair had passed some arcane test. It occurred to him that the whole thing might be some kind of set up. That the conversation had been rehearsed in some way. That the lunch had been staged and that his visit to the plantation had the mark of some kind of rite, a rite of initiation.

As the maid cleared up, Madame Bernabeu watched Sinclair across the expanse of white tablecloth. The enigmatic smile of a Cretan statue caressed her lips as she listened to the Professor methodically analyzing and elucidating his wife's complicated family tree. Madame Bernabeu would interrupt her husband occasionally but gently, interjecting some detail about her grandparents or great-grandparents which she felt should not be left out and which would somehow benefit Sinclair to know.

After lunch the Professor had excused himself. For some reason this did not surprise Sinclair.

"It is my custom to retire for a couple of hours after lunch. I leave you in the capable hands of Madame. Perhaps she can show you around the grounds of the plantation. There is a lot of history here, you know. Much has happened here, in the shadow of the Pelée."

She took Sinclair by the elbow and then, as they walked through the garden, she slid her arm through the crook of his arm quite naturally and without asking. The overbearing musk of her presence soon had him in its thrall. In the wet heat of the garden, which was still drenched and steaming in the sun from the recent downpour, among the ferns and fronds and giant rubber plants, she spoke of his predecessor.

"Martin was a weak fellow, scared to death of life. He lived only for his books, for his studies—he was terrified of failing his Finals, poor boy. But I think that between me and the Professor we taught him a thing or two . . ."

She said this with a stolen sideways glance at Sinclair.

Sinclair vaguely remembered a pale young Englishman named Martin Brookmyre, a couple of years his senior, silently haunting the Faculty library next to the Taylorian on St Giles, quiet and furtive as a mouse.

She then showed him the cane press and described in grisly detail some of the more spectacular accidents that had befallen the workers. She calmly described mangled hands, the severing of feet and the effects of haemorrhaging. Sinclair was beginning to feel faint.

"You don't look at all well," she said, looking into his face with her amused quadroon eyes. "Perhaps it is the heat. You are not used to it, *peut-être? Mon Dieu*, but you are looking a little, well, *vert* . . ."

Then she did something unusual. She made him sit down and fanned him with the folds of her skirt, sending a peculiar musky scent wafting over him.

While he was busy being squeamish, outside a cloud had blotted out the sun and the downpour had started again, as suddenly as it had stopped before lunch. She sat next to him on a pipe by the press and made him put his head between his knees to prevent him from fainting. When he felt he was recovering, it occurred to him to ask Madame Bernabeu what her name was.

It was Guadalupe.

And you could see all the way to Africa, to the end of the world, when you looked into those laughing eyes.

She was now sitting very close to him.

Her mouth tasted of something tangy and sweet. When he kissed her neck he felt Africa in her sweat. For Sinclair, who had grown up in India and England, Africa was still an unknown quantity. In his mind Africa was like the blank area in ancient mariners' maps that said *Here Be Dragons!* It scared him yet drew him relentlessly in and, before he knew it, he had her up against the machinery and was pumping with mad urgency deep into her as if his life depended on it.

It was still raining when they finished. They sat panting in the straw under the cane press.

She surprised him with what she said next.

"I am a *mambo*, you know." She was looking directly into his eyes to gauge his reaction. "Perhaps I can help you," she insisted, as he stared back at her stupidly.

Something stirred within Sinclair. He was suddenly excited again and felt a stab of lust.

"What's it like being possessed?" he asked aggressively.

"I was possessed, as you say, only yesterday," she replied, matter-of-factly, straightening her blouse and brushing off the straw, "at the *hounfor* in Morne Diab'."

Sinclair watched her hungrily as she passed a comb through her gleaming black hair. He could barely resist the impulse to bury his face in that fragrant mane again.

"Although I believe the Professor would insist on the word 'mounted' rather than 'possessed'," she continued, with a crafty smile on her swollen lips. "The word possession has a very westernized sensibility associated with it. In *vodoun* the concept of mounting is more appropriate and reflects the temporary nature of the phenomenon. And the fact that the *loas* see us as horses. Yes, that's how the Professor would put it to you. As for the mounting, well, the symptom is as follows: your mouth goes dry, you feel lightheaded, your scalp tingles, you are carried on the beat of the drums, and before you know it you are waking up. But when you come out of it, you are utterly exhausted. You remember nothing of the experience. And sometimes, if you were told— which is forbidden—about the things you did while mounted, you might be very surprised. And embarrassed . . ."

These words, and the image of her that they conjured up in his mind, had an unexpectedly priapic effect on Sinclair. Inflamed, he took Guadalupe Bernabeu again, this time from behind, efficiently and without apology. He felt godlike in the knowledge that some Congo deity had only a few hours earlier also mounted her, penetrating the warm moist sanctum of her delicious coffee-coloured body.

"You have been taught well, I can see that," she panted with satisfaction, turning on him, "but you need to learn to use your tongue like a Frenchman. Like this . . ."

SCRUBBER

As dirty bitches go, Sinclair concluded, Lucy Kennedy was top grade, hot shit, a scrubber deluxe, and he just had to have her.

When he had come back to the university that evening, his hair stiff with dust from his ride down from the plantation, the taste of Guadalupe Bernabeu still lingering on his tongue, Lucy Kennedy had stood there leaning against the doorway, blocking his entry into the dormitory. A tin of beer swung lazily in her hand. She was bug-eyed, probably been shagged silly, poor bitch, thought Sinclair as he dismounted his Vespa. She had been drinking, that was obvious. Her blonde hair was greasy and unwashed, and she scratched her armpits, a rollie stuck to her bottom lip. She had an insolent "in your face" look in her bloodshot eyes as she watched him approach, blocking the doorway, without so much as a "wotcha" or "hi, there, George baby". Any self-respecting person would have given him a wide berth. Instead, he had to squeeze past her in the doorway and breathed in her close smell, a blend of sweat and alcohol and ganja and semen and unwashed cunt, and that was then that he decided that he had to have her. At any price.

On the other hand, Sinclair also decided that as oily, unwashed, sybaritic, dreadlocked drug-dealing creeps went, Fred took the biscuit. He simply had to go, him and his fucking fake white man's dreadlocks.

Sinclair was determined to make these things happen as he stared at the rotating ceiling fan through his mosquito net that Sunday night after his visit to the Bernabeus. Next door, Fred was knocking Lucy up in their usual drunken stupor and the headboard banged shamelessly and repeatedly long into the night. Outside, the cicadas had gone wild, as if cheering Lucy and Fred on in a paroxysm of noise.

Later, Sinclair heard some porcine snuffling and then he heard Fred burp with satisfaction as he padded back to his room. When there wasn't much in the way of movement or sound coming from Lucy's room, except the gentle rustle of snoring, he made his move as he had been instructed.

"Madame, you said something about helping me."

"Yes, I did. Because I can see in your eyes that there is something, or could it be someone, that you want and can't have. A girl perhaps. Don't worry, I am not a jealous woman. I believe in honouring the goddess Erzulie freely. When she demands love, she is not to be refused. I can help you. It is something I can arrange. Tell me. I won't be offended."

"The girl I love hates me. She lives in England. I can't have her, that I know."

"Nothing is beyond the reach of the *loas*. But it would take time if she is not here."

"But there is someone else I desire. Someone I must have. Someone here in Martinique." He hesitated, embarrassed. "Although, on second thoughts, having had the privilege of your . . ."

"Nonsense, young man, I insist. The *bokor* at Morne Diab' is one of the best. He can help you. You will see."

She closed his mouth gently with her lips. He returned her spicy kiss gratefully.

"Bring me something of hers. Some hair, nail clippings, a handkerchief, perhaps."

Sinclair did better than that. On his next visit to the Bernabeus, he handed over to Guadalupe Bernabeu an unwashed pair of knickers. He had found them on the floor next to Lucy's bed when she was sleeping the dreamless, animalistic sleep of the recently fucked. Fred had left behind a couple of bum-sucked fag-ends and a few pubic hairs on the pillow next to Lucy's sunburned, snoring face. These had also been collected and handed over.

Night had fallen, as suddenly and as inevitably as a heavy velvet curtain, as it does in the tropics. It was very dark, and they were still climbing steadily in Madame's Citroën. She had asked Sinclair to drive. The headlights swept over palm trees and thick vegetation whenever they came to a bend in the road that runs along the spine of the island. If it had been light they could have been able to see through clearings in the forest the rough surf of the Atlantic on one side and the placid pool of the Caribbean on the other.

"Does it involve selling one's soul?" he asked, cheekily.

Sinclair already knew enough about Afro-Antillean spirit cults to ask such a silly question, but he had decided to play the naive and to see where it would take him. Until now everything he knew was from books. Now she had agreed to take him to a ritual in the *hounfor* at Morne Diab'—the Devil's Fell. It would be his first taste of the spirit world and he knew that he was truly standing on the edge of the precipice of experience. He felt a tingling of the groin that is the first symptom of vertigo.

As he drove Madame Bernabeu's car up to Morne Diab', she ignored his question and adopted a stubborn silence. Somewhere in Sinclair's unconscious, and despite all the books he had read which told him otherwise, the images of *Live and Let Die* had created an expectation of what the world of voodoo would be like. He fantasized about the sweating Jane Seymour tied up to a post and danced around by a lascivious savage wielding a python. He saw the laughing Baron Samedi rise vertiginously from his grave on a hydraulic elevator to claim his victims after the witchdoctor had tapped three times on his tombstone with a machete.

"And does it involve human sacrifice, Madame?" he insisted.

"Don't be ridiculous," she laughed, at last. And then, in a more serious tone, she explained: "*Vodoun* is not Devil worship, you know. And as you also know full well, the soul does not exist, at least not as an individual phenomenon, so we cannot sell it. It is not ours to sell. We are but reflections of the *loas* and anyway our heads are all owned by the *loas*, whether we like it or not, whether we know it or not."

"Which of the *loas* owns your head, Madame?"

"Who do you think?"

"Erzulie, the Goddess of Love?"

Her answer was the Cretan smile. Then there was silence for a while as Sinclair concentrated on the winding road that uncoiled before them under headlights, as they kept climbing into the mountain.

"And who would you say owns mine?"

She refused to answer, for some reason. All he could get out of her was a cryptic "In good time you will know."

He stopped insisting and changed tack. "Would you be able to teach me? I mean, perhaps just how to, well, you know, what you did to Lucy . . ."
Again, all he got was another "All in good time."

Sinclair was startled as the headlights briefly illuminated two ghosts draped in white walking along the road,. The car swerved dangerously but he managed to regain control and looked at her for reassurance.

"It is the celebrants, walking to the *hounfor*. They come on foot from miles around, up here to Morne Diab'. You must approach the *loas* on foot."

"And why is this place called Morne Diab'?"

"The old folk say that the Devil lives up here."

"So *do* they perform human sacrifice up here, Madame?"

She laughed again, her teeth glowing weirdly in the lights of the dashboard.

THE DEVIL'S FELL

The hounfor was a low-slung building, more of a peasant's shack really, and was set well back from the road, surrounded by thick vegetation. Chickens and goats could be seen in pens between the trees as they approached. A scrawny dog emerged from the bushes, crossed their path, and ran busily and with intent on some secret errand back into the undergrowth. Comely lights glowed from the windows of the building, reminding Sinclair of those cosy cottages in the woods that contained nasty surprises in the fairy tales that Grannyjee used to read to him. But here the trees were tropical and the leaves were thick and lush and dangerous looking. God only knows what animals or *loupgarous*—werewolves—or other animistic beings imported from Africa prowled around the spirit house in the darkness.

Inside, the congregation had already gathered and there was a lively buzz of conversation. By the time Sinclair and Madame Bernabeu arrived the atmosphere inside the house was heavy and electric. The air under the thatched ceiling seemed to be thick with swarms of African spirits congregating for the event. The atmosphere was also dense with the heady spice of sacred perfumes and cigar smoke. Sinclair saw sequinned flags and painted calabashes and crudely fashioned heads with cowry shells for eyes lurking in candle-lit alcoves. They were already singing in a mixture of Patois and some ancient African language that Sinclair knew from his books to be Kikongo, and there was clapping and drumming. In the years to come Sinclair would learn to recognize the words of the call and response and the name and the properties of each rhythm and the significance of each beat of the drum, but for now it was all new.

On the floor in front of the *poto mitan*, which is the pole that acts as the lightning rod to the spirits and takes centrestage in every *peristyle* or altar area, a white robed initiate, a young girl, was on her knees. She was tracing a *vévé* on the floor, a pattern of sacred symbols in a white and red powder of ground corn meal. She was supervised by the *houngan*, who was chewing on a cigar.

Sinclair and Madame Bernabeu watched as the girl's hand distributed the powders, to the approving grunts of the *houngan*. She was creating serpents and triangles and the intertwining lines of an arabesque, which represented the intersecting threads of fate, perhaps, or the elaborate grille work of a gate.

In the French Antilles, unlike Haiti or Cuba, the long drums are laid down on the ground and the drummers sit on them and add to the beat by kicking their heels on the skins, while another initiate punctuates the beat with a hypnotic rhythm tapped out aggressively with sticks on a hollow log. The beat was fast and furious and was growing in intensity and had the congregation swaying. Sweat streamed down the faces of the three drummers. Dramatically, it stopped. All of a sudden the silence was truly deafening.

Guadalupe Bernabeu was dressed in a frilled white smock and a bombéed colonial skirt, and the white turban set off her peanut-brown face and hands exquisitely. Her face gleamed in the candlelight and the base of her neck was damp with perspiration. Stooping slightly, her rump raised high in the African style, her right hand hitching up her skirt, she held a bronze *agogo* bell in her left, and was ringing it furiously, an intent look in her eye, to call the confusion of the gathering to order, and to attract the attention of the *loas*.

As the *mambo*, it fell to her to call out the incantation in that odd half-language that was to haunt Sinclair's life from then on, in a surprisingly resonant voice that seemed to emanate from deep within her chest.

> *Papa Legba ouvrez barrière pou moin passé!*
> *Papa Legba ouvrez barrière pou moin, pou moin passé!*
> *Papa Legba ouvrez barrière pou moin passé!*

The eager response came from the *houncis*, a chorus of swaying white-turbaned novices. When the *houngan* strutted arrogantly on to centrestage with his long staff, the drums erupted again, maniacally, in clap of thunder—Sinclair would never have suspected how loud these drums could sound—and the proceedings began.

After the ritual, when the girls had cleared up and the celebrants had vanished into the shadows to sleep or to start the long trek home down off the fell, Madame Bernabeu led Sinclair by the hand down a dirt path behind the building, to a back room.

The *houngan*, the priest, had now become a *bokor*, a sorcerer, and he was waiting for them. A pipe had replaced the cigar, and he held it clenched firmly between his teeth, the taut muscles of his jaw gleaming in the candle light. He was a crabby little man with a face of gnarled mahogany that showed little humour. She spoke first, and respectfully, in Creole peppered with the odd African word with repeated use of the word *blanc*, and *'ti fem*. Twice Sinclair heard the word *fwed*. He realized that the subjects of the conversation were himself, Lucy and Fred. *M'sié le bokor* nodded, yawned, because it was getting very late, and intoned a series of instructions, which included the word *ouanga* several times. Madame Bernabeu nodded politely. She did him reverence in an old-fashioned curtsy. Sinclair watched from the shadows. She then brought something out of her voluminous white skirt and passed the black plastic bag that contained Lucy Kennedy's soiled knickers and Fred's pubic hair to the *bokor*. He snatched the bag from her and looked inside. He looked deeper, sticking his nose in and breathing in deeply the heady bouquet of its contents. He then looked up at Madame Bernabeu, and then at Sinclair, and for the first time that evening he smiled, a wicked gleam in his prune-like eye. He stuck out his hand towards

the *blanc*. Madame Bernabeu nodded at Sinclair and mouthed the word
'*cent*'—Sinclair dutifully placed a hundred franc note in the palm of the *bokor's*
outstretched hand.

"What did he say to you?"
   "That first you must be cleansed."
   "And what does the word *ouanga* mean?"
   This she did not answer.
   "Is he a *bokor* or a *houngan*?"
   She continued to ignore him as she made her preparations.
   They were now alone in the back room. Her face had acquired a ritual
stoniness and her eyes avoided his. She made him strip and walked around his
naked body three times, anti-clockwise, intoning an African prayer. Standing
naked before her he felt none of the Indian embarrassment that had plagued
him in the past. She then lit a fat cigar, puffed on it several times to get it
going, and blew a mouthful of smoke into Sinclair's face. His eyes smarted and
he saw that she was now holding a bottle of white rum. She took a deep pull
from it, turned on Sinclair and blew out from her mouth, dousing him with a
fine spray of alcohol.
   He was beginning to feel peculiar by then, powerless and totally under her
control. She took him by his arms and spun him around and around, beating
him with the leafy branch of some pungent-smelling bush.
   Half awake by now, he felt a flutter of wings brushing against his skin. He
could hardly open his eyelids, but when he did, he saw that she held a
struggling white dove by its claws and was wiping his body down with it,
anointing him as if with a censer. Suddenly the wings were not flapping any
more and the bird went limp, and the next thing he saw was a jet of purple
blood drawing a circle in the dust around where he stood. When he did
manage to look up, he saw Madame Bernabeu's lips smeared with bright
arterial blood.
   The eyes he was staring into were not those of Guadalupe Bernabeu.

And sure enough, two days after Fred's unfortunate accident—which had
resulted in his being shipped him back on a stretcher with a neck brace to
London via Paris on the next Air France jumbo—Lucy Kennedy delivered
herself, or depending on what you choose to believe, was delivered, to George
Sinclair.
   On Saturday afternoon after the daily downpour, he was emerging, totally

refreshed, from a deep sleep courtesy of Morpheus, when he heard something scratching on the door and then the sound of a girl panting.

"So how was it, George?"

He pretended to misunderstand.

"How was it with your *'ti fem*?"

"Oh, you mean with Lucy?"

He saw that coquettish grin again. He felt Madame Bernabeu's brown hand travelling up his thigh, like a warm fat friendly spider. They were in her car again. They were on their way up to Morne Diab', and night was about to fall. The *bokor* had demanded to see them, to collect his success fee.

"It was disappointing, really. And now she won't leave me alone; in fact, she's become a bit of a pest . . ."

What he didn't say though, was that it had got so bad now that Lucy would stand outside his bedroom, masturbating like a monkey, rubbing herself against the door, begging him to let her in.

Rupert couldn't help but notice the unnatural appetite and the otherworldly lust that Lucy Kennedy was demonstrating for Sinclair.

"Bloody hell, George baby," Rupert had ribbed him, "talk about crushes and pashes, but what on earth did you put in Dirty Luce's gin? Whatever it was, have you got any left? I could do with some of that for old Crispin . . ."

"I expect she's missing Fred."

"Be careful you don't get what you pray for . . . ," warned Guadalupe Bernabeu, as if reading his mind, her hand now where she wanted it, as they came to a bend in the road.

HEXED

After the events at the *hounfor*, Madame Bernabeu's demands on Sinclair's time became onerous, and he took to avoiding her. This was Sinclair's first lesson in the African religions in the Americas—that nothing comes for free.

It was raining again outside the Bibliothèque Schoelcher. The water dripped off the leaves of the trees of the Savane in large, ponderous, oily drops. Sinclair's research was progressing painfully and very, very slowly, and he had trouble concentrating. The image of a pirate ship becalmed on the dark Sargasso Sea, its Jolly Roger and its sails hanging limp from its masts, drifted across Sinclair's mind. He watched the raindrops slide reluctantly down the window pane.

Someone had once told him that the Chinese will even bet on which of two raindrops will reach the bottom of a window first. He thought of Helen and imagined what she might be doing at that very moment. He thought of other things and places and events—of the garden-wallahs, of his dead Grannyjee, of what had happened at the College, of Helen again—of anything but his research, which was slow, very slow. He had never felt this type of listlessness before.

Professor Bernabeu emerged from his office and appeared at Sinclair's side. His voice as kind and soothing as usual and there was a look of earnest concern in his eyes.

"Madame asked me to inquire as to your health. It has been a while since your last visit. Madame has grown very fond of you, you know, in fact we both have, and we are worried about your health. You are always welcome at the plantation, you know . . ."

The Professor laid his hand on Sinclair's forearm and added: "*Soyez le bien-venu*, George. We are waiting for you."

After the Professor had disappeared into his office, Sinclair had trouble remembering what the Professor had said after laying his hand on his arm. There was a tiny lacuna of time that he could not account for.

Something mulish inside Sinclair decided that he should remain marooned in his inertia and ignore the Professor's nudge. He would not permit himself to be manipulated by older women any longer, and least of all by their ponces, and that was that, fuck them one and all.

Those who knew Sinclair during those days say that he appeared exhausted and hollow-eyed and that he moved slowly and with great effort, like a ghost walking underwater. Rupert thought that he had contracted malaria or some other tropical disease. There had been an outbreak of dengue fever and the foreign students had been advised to get vaccinated. Rupert had suggested that Sinclair visit the student doctor, suspecting that Lucy had infected him with something. Sinclair was irritated by all this attention and had rebuffed Rupert with a display of bad manners.

"Suit yourself, old boy," Rupert had sniffed.

Lucy Kennedy continued to pine for him like an abandoned puppy and took to confronting him in public. There were several ugly scenes that he would rather soon forget. She would simply not leave him alone. She stalked him around the university and around the island as he went on his errands. She'd follow me to the ends of the earth for one more poke, thought Sinclair in desperation.

One day Sinclair had emerged exhausted from the dormitory toilet to find her slouching against the wall a *louche* grin on her face and a rollie hanging from her lower lip.

One night she threatened suicide when he did not let her in to sate her lust, which, like a hidden itch, would just not go away.

Sinclair was plagued by nightmares. The macacqs from his schooldays returned with their enormous hypodermics and plastic bags of brown blood, tormenting him with threatened transfusions. One night a simian version of the priest Spock in a soutane ambushed him and gave him six of the best with the ferula, and when he looked down at his hands, they had again turned blue from the burst veins, but they were not his hands—they were old and atrophied, like the hands of the green-faced witch in *The Wizard of Oz*. And there was a shadow at the edge of his vision, a shade that moved away sideways whenever he tried to fix his sight on it.

And then there were the nights when he stood in a dock at the Old Bailey. He would look up to the spectators' gallery and see the pale faces of dead people, people whose faces he recognized but whose names he could not remember, looking down at him from the gods with the baleful stare of his father.

One night he saw Guy Underhill standing among the dearly departed but that was ridiculous because Guy Underhill was still alive.

Another night the blue goddess Kali appeared. She had the face of Xancha Bergsma and gave detailed and damning evidence against him in a combination of his childhood Portuguese and Hindi and Aboriginal as he stood in the dock, her four arms gesticulating to make her various points. With one of her many hands she jabbed a bone in his direction, sentencing him to death in the Aboriginal manner, as her black eyes bore into the back of his skull.

In that nightmarish courtroom he prayed for Grannyjee to appear in the spectators' gallery to witness the trial, and to look down at him with her sad loving eyes and a wistful smile, but she never showed up.

And on the judge's bench, where those ridiculous chimps in their barristers' wigs and scarlet gowns used to sit, there now sat Guadalupe Bernabeu in her white frock and turban, with her Mona Lisa smile, her amused quadroon eyes mocking him, the cosmic serpent Damballah coiled lazily around her bronze neck, her swollen lips about to speak, always about to pass sentence.

George Xavier Gupta Sinclair Fernandes, you are hereby sentenced . . . and what goes around comes around.

But the worst of it was that at night, after he awoke sweating and panicky, he would try to calm himself and distract himself to sleep by summoning the memory of his last wrestle with Lucy Kennedy under the mosquito net, and when that did not work, by recreating in his mind's eye the friendly mouth and aroused brown eyes of Helen Henshaw, the warmth of her freshly bathed body, the apple-scent of shampoo in her hair . . . but to no avail. It was as if a curtain had been drawn between him and the memory of Helen or of Lucy, for that matter. It felt as if a switch was pulled each time he tried to evoke her face, or that a thread was twitched in the opposite direction to distract him, as if these carnal thoughts were deliberately being cross-circuited and diverted to their rightful and inevitable destination, which was Guadalupe Bernabeu's creamy brown body, redolent with coconut oil, *maracuja* and musk.

ALL SOULS' DAY

A morbid fascination with death came over him. He remembered Grannyjee often and in his dreams he invoked her repeatedly, but she failed to heed his call. In his waking loneliness he tried repeatedly to summon her spirit from beyond the grave. Again, as in his dreams, his efforts were unsuccessful. He tried to track down his old friend Doris, hoping for some advice on how to summon the dead, but no one answered his letters.

To console himself he started writing letters full of self-pity to Helen Henshaw, but these were sent back to sender, unopened, mercifully, because when Sinclair reread them, he immediately tore them up and thanked God that she had never read their pathetic drivel. He even wrote to Guy Underhill, 'care of' Hull University and, not surprisingly, no reply came, not even the envelopes marked 'return to sender'.

In this orgy of solitude and self-pity, Sinclair read and reread and then memorized and finally recited to himself Nerval's haunting verses, which seemed to sum up his latest Predicament:

> *Je suis le Ténébreux—le Veuf—l'Inconsolé,*
> *Le Prince d'Aquitaine à la Tour abolie.:*
> *Ma seule Étoile est morte—et mon luth constellé*
> *Porte le Soleil noir de la Mélancolie.*

*

All Souls' Day came around and he lay paralyzed and sweating in his bed that morning. He had woken with that awful phrase repeating itself in his head over and over like a scratched record, inducing a nauseous vertigo that made him afraid to get out of bed:

> *What goes around comes around*
> *What goes around comes around*
> *What goes around comes around*

Towards noon he found himself lingering by the whitewashed sepulchres of the cemetery near the bus station in Fort de France. The sun and the glare of the white walls and the dusty heat made him nostalgic for the gothic gloom of Highgate Cemetery and its mournful, wet English vegetation.

As midday approached he watched a horse-drawn funeral roll past him on its way up the hill. The baroque cortege with its ornate casket was pulled by four huge black horses sweating in the sun, bearing the purple plumes of death and clanking in their chains. The hollow sound of their hoofs grating on the cobblestones was a *memento mori*. The bald heads of the fat men gleamed in the sun and were wiped down with handkerchiefs while the matrons all clad in black wailed and fanned each other to prevent fainting.

He joined the procession for a while and then sat on an unattended tomb to watch as families unpacked their picnics and toasted their dead with rum and Coca-Cola and coffee from thermos flasks, surrounded by garish flowers and macabre garlands. All around the West Indies and Latin America the dead were being feted—it was their day.

On the tomb where he sat there were two black and white photographs of the occupants enamelled into the stone. They were two light-skinned Creoles who had died many years apart, because one was a young woman wearing an old-fashioned frock, the other an elderly gentleman with specs. Sinclair translated the epitaph and shivered in the sun.

> *We Are*
> *Together Again*
> *You Are*
> *What We Were*
> *We Are*
> *What You Will Become*

He stayed in the cemetery until late to experience the sight of hundreds of votive candles illuminating the hillside like fairy lights as dusk fell. The *zouk* music from the teenagers' radios blared into the night so that the dead would not feel alone in their crypts on their special night.

What goes around comes around . . .

ZOMBI

It was getting late in the cemetery and Sinclair looked down to check the time. His wristwatch was missing. Instead of its familiar black face all he saw was the pale band across his tanned wrist where it had been.

That night, his door locked to keep Lucy out, he lay in bed wondering when and where he had lost the watch. He couldn't for the life of him remember the last time he had seen it on his wrist. He began to suspect that it might be one of Lucy's tricks. She had been in a nasty mood lately and he feared that she had finally turned vengeful. She just wouldn't accept that he wanted nothing more to do with her. And *hell hath no fury . . .*

To keep panic at bay he decided to read. What he read, though, did not help. *The Golden Bough* fell open precisely at the page where Frazer analyzes the different types of magic and explains how sorcery works. Horrified, Sinclair read about the mechanics of sympathetic magic and how it operates through the stolen possessions of the victim. But of course, he had already seen proof of this in the *bokor's* witching of Lucy Kennedy. Now he started to really worry as he realized the implications. If a nasty, stubborn girl like Lucy Kennedy could be made to do things, then what about him? He was still fretting, wondering how the invisible thread of magic really works, as he injected himself between his toes. He would ask Morpheus.

When he finally did fall into the deep warm bottomless vault of the Sleep God, his last thought was of Lucy. He would confront her tomorrow, hoping against hope that it was she who had stolen the watch.

Of course she denied it and the accusation triggered another episode of hysteria and recrimination.

For days Sinclair fretted about the watch. He simply could not remember where he had put it last. Whenever he closed his eyes he could see Frazer's disturbing words swimming before him.

Eventually the loss of the watch and the dread that had been building up in him tripped a panic wire somewhere in his mind and he was once again in the territory of the would-be suicide, the territory he had discovered at the College during his Predicament.

Deep down he knew what had to be done to undo the torment, but the mule in him was determined to resist.

What finally pushed him over the edge was what he read in another book. He had put Frazer aside and had started a new book about Haiti, *The Serpent and the Rainbow*. Reading about the secret powders of the Haitian *bokors* made him realize the danger he was in—he was now gripped by the fear that he would be turned into a *zombi*.

If he didn't heed Madame Bernabeu's summons, he was convinced, *Monsieur le Bokor* at Morne Diab' would be receiving another of her visits. The old man would be commissioned to procure a puffer fish and would then proceed to distil certain deadly powders from its liver in a process that was described in detail in the book. The powder might be laid on the floor of his room to be absorbed by the soles of his bare feet, or it could be blown into his face by someone passing him in the street. The next thing he knew he would become seriously ill and fall into a catatonic paralysis while his senses remained acutely awake. In a matter of days he would be declared dead, buried alive in a pauper's grave in the outer edges of the cemetery in Fort de France. All the while he would be acutely aware of what was happening to him.

Three midnights later he would hear three sharp taps on the lid of his coffin. He would be dug up and pulled up out the grave by *Monsieur le Bokor*, who would administer a partial antidote. He would see Madame Bernabeu standing behind the witch doctor, under the full moon, watching the proceedings with her enigmatic Leonardo smile. Then, with severe brain damage, he would be put to work in the fields of the Bernabeu plantation, and probably in the cane press, and time would have no longer have any meaning for him because he had joined the ranks of the undead.

It was no use hiding from her. He realized that he had been extremely foolish to disrespect the demands of a *mambo* priestess. He was lucky not to have been zombified by now. He had been hexed, witched, bewitched deluxe.

For the whole of the next day, an ominous Friday, he avoided human contact, refusing to even shake hands with another soul. Now he gave everyone, not just crazy Lucy, a wide berth, because now everyone was a potential agent of Madame and the *bokor* and a potential delivery system of the *zombi* powder. Fear of the powder compelled him to wear socks and to wipe the floor of his room with disinfectant and to wash his plate and knife and fork in boiling water before he ate, like a demented, hygiene-obsessed housewife.

Finally it was Saturday. The panicky Vespa ride up the hill seemed to take forever. Finally after what seemed like hours he stood outside her bedroom in the old plantation house. The Professor was nowhere to be seen. Sinclair saw himself panting with fear, the prodigal son about to knock and ask forgiveness, hoping beyond hope that it was not too late.

Just as he was about to knock the door swung inwards, as if on cue.

She stood there, radiant, all smiles and light.

"Ah, George, my dear, I knew you would be back."

It was she that seemed relieved. Relieved of having to make him pay the price for his discourtesy.

She took his face in her fragrant hands and kissed him tenderly. So she had already forgiven him. She drew him onto her bed under the mosquito net and without uttering another word she anointed his face with her lips, before taking him in her mouth.

That afternoon her skin was shiny with lotion and perspiration and smelt of *maracuja*, the Martiniquais version of passion fruit. When he buried his face in the humidity between her thighs, to do the honours in the old French way as she had taught him, he breathed in the sweet musk of coconut oil. And then, like an old comforting memory, he tasted the unique spice of African sweat of her orgasms.

He lay back on her pillows like a pasha after a sumptuous meal, his confidence restored. "I thought you said that you were not a jealous woman, Madame," he said. "And you said you believed in feeding the Goddess of Love?"

"I am not a jealous woman. And I do feed *Erzulie* freely. But you cannot just walk out on me without paying your dues. Nothing is free under the sun. And especially not after what I have given you. I gave you something and you were not grateful. If anything, this has been a lesson in curing bad manners, George Sinclair. You have been very rude to me. But you have been punished, and now you must make amends. Equilibrium must be restored."

"I will do my best, Madame."

"You are leaving us soon. What I want you to do for me, after you have shown me your linguistic skills again, is to introduce me to your replacement."

GRIS GRIS

It was true, Sinclair's year in Martinique was drawing to a close. He would soon be leaving the land of the Lotus Eaters and returning to England.

Persuading young Andrew Fowler to ride pillion with him up to the plantation was not difficult. Fowler was an anaemic English boy from Sheffield University. He was studying Creole literature and he was eager to meet interesting people. After being pointed out by Sinclair, Fowler had been befriended by the Professor and had received an invitation to lunch.

There was a long meal at the plantation. The food had been accompanied by the usual *'ti punches*. After lunch they left Fowler fast asleep on the hammock on the verandah.

"He is not used to the heat nor to so much alcohol, and he still has jet lag," the Professor said. He was always so accommodating, so kind.

Fowler was now drooling in his sleep. The Professor as usual retired into the dark interior of the house for his afternoon siesta.

In the sugar-cane press Sinclair and Madame Bernabeu made their farewells. She kissed him deeply and left him breathless. She then pressed something into his hand. It was a tiny little red bag—a *gris gris*—stuffed with God knows what, she wouldn't tell him.

"This amulet will help you in the future." But he was never to look inside, she insisted, or it would lose its potency.

He mounted his Vespa for his last ride down into Fort de France. He saw Madame Bernabeu eyeing the snoring young Englishman on the hammock sceptically. A thread of spittle was leaking from his pinched mouth. Thin pickings, she must be thinking, thought Sinclair, extremely pleased with himself.

One down, one to go—now he had only to deal with crazy Lucy. He had the presentiment that things would turn out alright, suspecting that Madame Bernabeu had already twitched the required thread. He congratulated himself for his elegant escape from a tricky situation. It could so easily have got out of hand. In the meantime he had learned much—he had experienced the secret world of magic at last and now he relished his return to Oxford. And he felt comforted by Madame Bernabeu's *gris gris* in his pocket. It would protect him in his future adventures, he was sure. And, she had whispered into his ear during their last embrace, it might well one day deliver to him what he most craved—Helen Henshaw.

He patted his pocket to reassure himself that the *gris gris* was still there. It was then that he felt something warm and metallic in his pocket. He pulled out his wristwatch.

The Professor waved cheerfully from the veranda, refreshed after his siesta.

"Fuck you George fucking Sinclair I'm done with you you sad paki fart I can do a lot better than you in fact I don't fucking well know what I ever saw in you what the fuck made me take up with you in the first place . . ."

He was on the Air France jumbo on his way back to London via Paris. The awful farewell scene played itself out repeatedly in his mind's eye and Lucy's hysterical voice looped around and around in his brain.

The stewardess handed him his peanuts. She had Lucy's sunburned nose.

There had been tears, and then maniacal cackling as Lucy had let rip with an insult that still made him cringe in his seat. "Go on fuck off with you then you nasty brown turd you're nuffink but a braan turd on two legs . . ." Her eyes had been bright with something. She had been smoking again and her voice was shrill and full of more than its fair share of East End glottal stops. People always betray their origins when they are upset. "Yeah that's wot you are George paki fucking Sinclair a turd on two legs a turd wiv eyes . . ."

After her deranged laughter had subsided she had locked herself in her room in the dormitory and he heard her tears again from behind closed doors. Later that night, as he was packing his tuckbox for the return to England, he overheard her talking to her new friend. It was Monique, a sly white girl from Nottingham University who had recently arrived on the island as part of the next shift of *stagiaires*. Monique had latched on to Lucy.

He heard the crack of a beer can being opened and smelled the sweet scent of a spliff being lit up. Pressing his ear to the wall of her room, the last he heard Lucy Kennedy say to Monique was that she was through with fucking Asian wogs like George fucking Sinclair and swaggering white nigger trash like Fred with those fucking ridiculous dreadlocks and that her new mission in life was to take up with a Real Englishman, someone who wasn't a half-breed or who pretended to be black because it was cool.

The problem was, she went on, with a slight belch, then quaffing her beer greedily, that the only Englishman she fancied was a poof. Monique might have seen him, a pretty little blond-haired thing called Rupert. It was a shame, Lucy continued drunkenly, because Rupert was a nice-looking bloke and she had always liked the look of him and had wanted to jump his bones ever since she first laid eyes on him. When they got back to

England, she promised Monique, she would have him, just watch her, she would 'ave 'im.

There was a pause in the conversation, as the two girls ruminated silently on the possibilities.

1975
WITCH COUNTRY

WITCH COUNTRY

"The early years of a boy's life, Morpheus, can seem interminable, especially when you are unhappy and far away from home. Especially when you are an overseas boy and have something to hide. But at last, in 1975, all of a sudden, after a long summer term of cricket, exams and more exams, Prep School was over."

The end of Prep School coincided with the departure of Saturn from the signs of Gemini and Cancer, and for a while, at least, the worst was over and, back in Goa, Grannyjee breathed easy once again. Sinclair had survived his trials at the hands of the English, as had his ancestors the Picts and the lower caste Dravidians. And as the Revenger he had even managed to score a satisfying point or two against overwhelming odds.

"Whenever I look back on those years in Surrey," Sinclair tells Morpheus one afternoon many years later, before he goes under and the lights dim in his palace of memories, "I attribute my survival to the bizarre cocktail of my genes."

He speculates, as Morpheus nods solicitously, about the blended genetic memories that he carries within himself. There is the Pictish highlander, on the one hand, with his dreams of frenzied, blue-faced war dances around the fire. On the other hand, you have the quiet but determined stealth of the Untouchable food thief struggling to make it through the day. Young George Sinclair had, like these two ancestors, resisted defeat with a combination of defiance and deviousness.

"You could say, Morpheus, that by the time Prep School was over, I was beginning to understand my Predicament and was almost at peace with it. You see, by then I had resigned myself to inhabiting the no-man's land of my half-status. I had declared myself an exile from the warmth."

To his friends the garden-wallahs, led as ever by Old Ajay, Masterjee was a hero. That was how they always welcomed him back from England—as a conquering hero returning from an impossible commando mission overseas.

At thirteen, after a long sunlit holiday of cricket on the lawn in Goa with Grannyjee and the wallahs, Sinclair felt fortified and ready to go back to England and face the next stage in his education. It was time for him and many of his contemporaries, which included his tormentors and of course Simon Cavendish, to be transported up North to the College, a Public School which was referred to by some as the 'Catholic Eton'.

The process started in mid-September on platform twelve at Euston Station in North London, where the boys were herded onto the three o'clock northbound train. Some three hours later, as night fell, there was a draughty bus ride from British Rail Preston through the most forbidding countryside that Sinclair had ever laid eyes on.

After what seemed like an eternity, the boys felt the buses make a sharp right turn and speed down a long avenue along half-glimpsed fields and trees and bodies of water glinting in the moonlight. Finally the buses disgorged the boys in the dark. The New Boys were disoriented and nauseous from the combination of motion sickness and the stifling cigarette smoke of the older boys. Others, in particular those who had not been to Prep School and who were leaving home for the first time, were sick with fear.

There they stood in the glacial blast, the New Boys, their eyes pricking from the cold, with their trunks and tuckboxes, outside the main entrance of the building, which was guarded by two immense stone lions. They looked up the façade of the building at two cupolaed towers where stone eagles perched.

It was a cold place set in a river valley in the depths of witch country, at the foot of Pendle Hill in Lancashire. Miles and miles of dry walls and grim fields dotted with wind-stunted trees surrounded the place, which lay in the gloaming under a leaden sky like a monster squatting obediently at the foot of Pendle. It was a monster that had lain in wait for centuries to ingest the sons of the Catholic aristocracy.

The countryside was truly fit only for witches.

Pendle Hill, with its distinctively curved slope, was famous for a witches' holocaust in the 17th century, when scores of local women had been dragged to the gallows. The buildings that now housed the College were said to have played a sinister role in the persecution.

The College was a gigantic complex in grey stone. Above its towers and buttresses you could see cupolas that time had turned green with verdigris.

The towers stood guard above immense long galleries and cobbled courtyards and a warren of corridors, dormitories and inner chapels. The building had been bequeathed to the Society of Jesus by a Recusant family in the 18th century after the order had been expelled from the Continent, where they had been educating the spawn of the Catholic elite since the 16th century. The building was said to be riddled with priest-holes. Inside, the vast galleries and their war memorials were connected by huge staircases and were lined with hunting trophies—all manner of horns and heads and glass eyes gleaming in the twilight and African spears and shields and artifacts from the Empire. There were acres of polished, panelled wood, stained-glass windows and stone floors worn smooth over the centuries by the tread of boys and priests.

Yellow and white flags of the Vatican and the IHS pennant of the Society of Jesus snapped in the glacial northern wind, over the turrets and cupolas. They were a testament to the stubborn survival of the Recusant families that had ensured a steady supply of Catholic Gentlemen into British society—Men for Others, as they liked to be known. *Ad Majore Dei Gloriam*—To the Greater Glory of God—was their motto. As proof of this, apart from a handful of well-known eccentrics, the best known old alumni of the College were thirteen English martyrs (including several saints) and a handful of VCs from both world wars. The school cutlery (and, they found out later, certain antique chamber pots) was stamped with another of the school's mottos, *Quant Je Puis*—As Much As I Can.

The College was surrounded by woods and was accessible to the outside world via a mile-long Avenue, at the head of which stood a statue of the Blessed Virgin Mary, standing guard since 1593 over the community of five hundred-odd boys and their warders. On either side of the Avenue were the playing fields which were the proving grounds that separated the real men from the weaklings, and two icy rectangular ponds, referred to as 'canals', that reflected the granite façade of the edifice.

TENEBRAE

They would not easily forget their first day the College in 1975, because Term started with a funeral Mass. The Requiem was for a boy called Martin Weld who had died during the holidays. No one knew what he had died of. There were rumours among the New Boys that the dead boy had gone missing the term before.

Many years later, Sinclair could still see in his mind's eye the tall figure and hooded eyes of Gervase Morguer, S.J., Headmaster, magnificently enrobed in thick black gem-encrusted vestments. He was surrounded by acolytes clad in black and white instead of the normal scarlet and white. Morguer's languid manner and his funereal bearing had earned him the nickname 'the Nosferatu'.

He hovered over an impossibly small brown casket on a trolley. The dead boy's coffin looked insignificant and seemed to float in mid-air beneath the vampire wings of the priest, a small offering surrounded by garish flowers, laid out under the immense gilt-laden monstrosity of the baroque altar. Blue clouds of suffocating incense wafted from a censer which was periodically swung high into the air by the thurifer. High up behind the congregation, the school choir was chanting the *Tenebrae* in Latin.

When the plainchant stopped, there was a minute of awful silence followed by a tidal wave of sound as the organ let rip. The shuddering subsonic vibration of the organ's bass made the vaults of the church tremble, putting the Fear of God into the New Boys.

Thus are the Mortal Remains of Dead Boys Dispatched from the Kingdom of this World to Kingdom Come, and God Help You if You had Died in a State of Moral and Spiritual Jeopardy.

UNDERHILL

There are overseas boys and there are overseas boys.

There was a boy called Guy Underhill.

At first Underhill seemed to be an unlikely ally. He was blond, blue-eyed, patrician in bearing. He came from a solid Anglo-Catholic family with long ties to the College, and had cousins in almost every Catholic school in the country. Outwardly Underhill had all the attributes of a classic English Catholic Gentleman in the making.

They said that he was a caricaturist. This alerted Sinclair to something, some undefined possibility. And sure enough, as George Sinclair observed Underhill more closely, he noticed that there was something about the way he carried himself, a casual indifference that smacked of corruption. It was more like a profound disinterest in those around him. It was this something that set him apart as a troublemaker from the start, as if he had disqualified himself on purpose and had chosen to live his life 'out of bounds'.

Underhill seemed old before his time, and he had the most un-English habit of looking at you in the eye when he spoke to you, whether you were boy or master or priest. This directness, complemented at times by extreme politeness, was taken as impertinence and insolence by the Jesuits and their acolytes.

Underhill was also an overseas boy, but a different type of overseas boy. For a start, *both* of Underhill's parents were English. His Catholic pedigree was long and well-established, unlike Sinclair's, which was dubious to say the least—for Sinclair was a half-caste in religion as well as breeding. Underhill was, as they like to say in England, Cut from a Different Cloth.

Underhill was secretive about his family, even with Sinclair. The most he gave away was that his parents were expatriates who lived in Africa. His guardian in London was Gran, a formidable hawk-nosed grandmother who held court in a cavernous flat in Goodge Street in London.

They had been at different Prep Schools. Underhill had a head start at the College. He was already streetwise about the place when he crossed Sinclair's path, because he had already done time at the Hall, a satellite preparatory establishment in the grounds of the College, separated from the senior school by the woods. Underhill had been there since before his seventh birthday— for half of his life, he liked to say. He was already familiar with the ways of the 'big' school, and somehow, mysteriously, seemed to know some of the older boys. He knew which way the wind was blowing and the way things were likely to turn out in the College. There was a sense that things had happened to Underhill at the Hall, that he had a history.

They say that Sinclair and Underhill did not hit it off immediately. At first they stuck to their own crowd, outsiders within their own tribes, the omegas of the wolf pack. As they were the only two boys in their year with a talent for drawing, they were assumed to be rivals by the two camps from the opposing Prep Schools. For the first term or so the two bands engaged in a competition to see which of the Prep Schools had produced the best rugby players, crick-eters, scholars, artists, criminals, idiots and outcasts.

Underhill and Sinclair felt compelled to avoid direct contact for a term or two, treading in wary circles around each other but always keeping an eye out. Eventually, they recognized in each other the things that they shared—a fond-ness for being alone, for cruel caricatures, and a subversive cast of mind. Underhill and Sinclair broke ranks and became friends, aware somehow that their paths had been fated to intersect. Their caricatures of boys, priests and masters would appear on the bulletin boards around the school, and they were then passed around by the boys, confiscated and eventually found their way around the Staff Common Room, where they were enjoyed by some, and noted for future reference by others.

UNDERGROUND

When you thought of Sinclair, you thought of Underhill. It was that type of friendship.

They elevated malingering into an art form. They became specialists at avoiding rugby and cross-country runs and took to skulking in the Pit, the underground boiler room behind the kitchens. You reached the Pit through a broken door hidden behind the rubbish skips in the kitchen yard. In a corner behind the tangle of dirty pipes and valves and pumps and pressure gauges, the Pit had an inner door, rotting on its hinges. The door led further down into the entrails of the building, but no one quite knew where to. Being in the Pit was like being in an antechamber, an intermediary place—a hot and stifling waiting room for darker places further underground.

Above ground, on the mud flats of the rugby pitches, freezing rain pelted the sodden masses of boys who languished in their scrums. Above ground, Underhill and Sinclair's relationship developed into one of those silent and undemonstrative friendships that the English are famous for. They reserved their conversations for when they were smoking in the woods or underground.

In the Pit, Sinclair and Underhill discussed the latest albums of Yes and King Crimson and Genesis and Frank Zappa and Pink Floyd, the more difficult and obscure the music the better. They despised pop and heavy metal, latin rock, the abomination of disco and the recent phenomenon of jazz funk.

In an uncharacteristic dropping of his guard, Underhill had admitted one day to being fond of Supertramp's sugary ballads. Not to be outdone, Sinclair had reciprocated with a confession of his own. He adored Blondie—but was she really new wave or punk, or just a pop goddess, they argued. Anyway who gave a toss where she stood in the musical spectrum? Blondie posters were displayed prominently in the boys' cubicles and dormitory rooms, where her comforting presence, next to Farrah Fawcett-Majors and the other big-haired Angels, watched over the motherless and loveless adolescents of the College.

Blondie's Debbie Harry was alright for the odd handjob but when it came to true love and devotion, Sinclair confessed to Underhill how he was a hope-less follower of Stevie Nicks of Fleetwood Mac, with her sleepy brown eyes and her witchy, Gypsy ways.

As time passed, Underhill and Sinclair discovered a common interest in conspiracy theories. Underhill was the more sceptical of the two and believed in the malign influence of secret societies, of which the Jesuits were the paragon, followed closely by the sinister fascists of the Opus Dei. Underhill was uncommonly well versed in the history and traditions of the Jesuits. Sinclair suspected that he had a grudging admiration for the formidable cabal of sinister priests—the Company of Jesus, the elite Stormtroopers of Mother Church—that fate had pitted against him. Underhill lived up to the maxim that to understand your enemy is the battle half-won.

"My greatest ambition," Underhill once told Sinclair, "is to enter the Society as a scholastic and infiltrate the top ranks of the order. I will learn its darkest secrets. I will mine its foundations and bring about its destruction from within in a great implosion. It will be a spectacular betrayal—my destruction of the Jesuits will expose the Society's corrupt worldly ambition once and for all, as well as its manipulative methods. Wasn't it the Jesuits, after all," he continued, taken by his vision, "who said that the ends justify the means?"

Underhill would often quote other Jesuitical gems such as "Our weapons are fear, surprise, and an almost fanatical devotion to the Pope" or "Give me a boy until he is seven and I will show you the man".

Underhill's bible was a book that had just been published in 1975, entitled *The Secret History of the Jesuits*. It was by a French writer and it traced the nefarious activities and insidious skulduggery of the Society of Jesus through the ages. The cover of the book showed a crucifix spinning on the axis of a swastika and one of its more compelling arguments laid out the link between the crypto-fascist Society and the Nazis and the hidden hand of the Jesuits in the destruction of the Jews. The book was explosive and had been blacklisted by the school authorities. Anyone caught reading it would be subject to immediate expulsion. This banned book lived in a pocket of Underhill's jacket and was well thumbed and referred to often in those sessions in the Pit. Sinclair would listen patiently while Underhill expostulat-ed on the obvious involvement of the Jesuits in the assassination of JFK, the Black Pope's control over the Vatican and over the CIA and the United States' military-industrial complex. Before the decade was out, Guy Underhill's theories were to be vindicated when Pope John Paul I was murdered by the combined forces of the Black Pope and an Italian Masonic lodge called P2.

Sinclair was attracted to more sensational secrets. He preferred the glamorous, apocalyptical end of the conspiracy spectrum. He was a disciple of von Däniken and would try to convince Underhill to read his own bible, *Chariots of the Gods?*, as well as Berlitz on the Bermuda Triangle. They would debate for hours, Underhill playing Devil's Advocate as Sinclair defended the existence of UFOs, ancient astronauts, the Loch Ness Monster, astrology, fortune telling, ghosts, witchcraft, shamanism, the Devil, vampires, werewolves, *zombis*, exorcism, Nostradamus and the End of the World. Reincarnation in particular was his speciality, being half Indian and having been trained in the rules of *karma* and *dharma* by Grannyjee.

Sinclair was already predisposed to the secret world thanks to Grannyjee. Now, under Underhill's influence, he was turning into one of those people who sees a bat or a dragon or a winged demon in an ink blot when others see a butterfly.

It was during these subterranean meetings that Sinclair introduced Underhill to illicit drugs. Sinclair imported pot from Goa in a hidden compartment of his tuckbox, along with pink bundles of *beedis*, which he purchased from the garden-wallahs for pennies.

Smoking pot helped them appreciate their Art Rock, heightening their senses and letting them see and feel the shapes and colours of the complicated music they were addicted to. But the mild narcosis of cannabis was only an aperitif. Eventually Sinclair served Guy Underhill a more potent menu. It was a gradual process, and Sinclair was careful to wait for the right moment to show his hand and initiate Underhill into the mysteries of the Sleep God.

"And what do we think of oblivion?" Sinclair said, one night after supper in the Pit.

"A condition devoutly to be wished for, surely," Underhill had replied, intrigued.

"And what do we think of the Lotus Eaters?"

"You mean Odysseus's sailors who were shipwrecked on the island that time forgot? Where it was always afternoon?" Underhill's interest had been piqued.

"Yes. And would you like to forget your own past, Guy Underhill?"

"I would."

Underhill looked down as he said this. It was the closest he had ever come to admitting that he was an unhappy person. Sinclair had always felt that

Underhill was the victim of bad memories. There was a lacuna in Underhill's history. He refused to talk about what had happened to him at the Hall, even with Sinclair.

But now it was time for Sinclair to reveal his secret to Underhill. It was a secret that Sinclair had not even revealed to Grannyjee. That night he revealed to Underhill what had happened to him at his own Prep School—and that ever since his near death experience in Surrey he had become a follower of the Sleep God.

Underhill listened intently as Sinclair described how they had tried to kill him with a cricket ball and how he had fallen into a deep coma and how they had given him up for dead, even ordering his coffin at the local undertaker. And how in his morphine trance he had been rescued from despair by a gentle friend who stood at the crossroads in the half-world between waking reality and the ultimate bliss of oblivion. And that in Goa, his lock-picking skills helped him feed his craving. He explained how he would pilfer minute quantities from the stock of morphine that Dr Muckerjee would replenish from his black bag whenever he attended to George's mother, who was becoming sicker and weaker and paler each time he saw her during the school holidays. He told Underhill how Mrs Sinclair seemed to be wasting away and turning into a ghost before Major Sinclair's wolfish eyes. Sometimes Sinclair wondered whether mother even got out of bed in the months between the holidays. It never occurred to him that each milligram of stolen morphine was one milligram less of relief for his dying mother.

Sinclair completed his recruitment of Guy Underhill by showing him how he injected the drug between his toes. That way, he said, they can't see the pin pricks. Finally he persuaded him to help him steal the little vials of morphine from the drug cabinet in the Dispensary. Like Dr Muckerjee's black bag and Simon Cavendish's tuckbox, Matron's drug cabinet was no match for Old Ajay's lock-picking tricks. Whenever the galleries of the school fell silent— after lights out, or during games, or on free afternoons—Sinclair would stroke the locks of the cabinet open with his pin, as the old gardener had taught him. Underhill's job was to stand watch—keeping 'cave'—at the corner of the corridor that led to the Dispensary.

The take was always modest and unobtrusive. Each operation was planned carefully in advance. Sinclair had learned to replace the stolen vials with the used ones—filled with water and resealed hermetically with the help of a bunsen burner in the chemistry labs.

It all seemed so easy. Easier still was stashing the loot under the bushes and hedges of the gardens that surrounded the College.

It was towards the end of term in their second year at the College. It must have been the end of the winter term because Sinclair remembered that there was still snow on the ground outside. It had blanketed the fields and flats around the College, giving the witch-haunted countryside a strange, muted quality.

They had decided to skip Benediction and they headed down into the Pit, where it was always warm among the pipes and valves and pressure meters.

They lit up. They discussed their plans for the holidays. Underhill quoted a passage from *The Secret History of the Jesuits*. Sinclair spoke about ancient astronauts in Peru and about a new band called Brand X. It was the usual routine and they were beginning to get bored.

The end of term was approaching. This is usually a dangerous time in boarding schools, because you become 'de-mob' happy. End of term induces a sense of euphoria and invincibility in schoolboys that leads to pranks and usually ends in tears.

Fuck it, they decided, let's go for it.

They broke through the decrepit door that led downstairs from the Pit.

They almost broke their necks on the greasy staircase and found themselves in what must have been the Jesuit wine cellars beneath the Refectory.

The flames of their cigarette lighters lit the walls eerily as they explored the cellars. Underhill smashed open two bottles of claret as rats scurried away into dark corners. They gulped the wine down among the cobwebs, and eventually, in a lightheaded stupor, they found a passageway leading from the cellar to a stairway that led up to a back entrance to the Arundell Library.

This library, they knew, housed among other things an Egyptian mummy, the rope with which a Jesuit martyr had been strung up at Tyburn, an early Gnostic gospel, and a famous edition of Holbein's engravings of the *Danse Macabre*. In their first year at the College they had been shown these things on the tour of the library which was mandatory for the New Boys. Underhill had taken a particular fancy to the comic engravings that celebrated the rotting skeleton of Death taunting a series of medieval burghers, knights, clerics (Jesuits, according to Underhill), popes, peasants, paupers, tarts and royal personages, eventually leading them into the horizon in the egalitarian Dance of Death.

Beyond the subterranean stairwell that led up to the Library, the passage snaked its way to the crypt under the school church. As the evening wore on, they lost their sense of time in the dark, and moved further into the subterranean vaults which, they calculated, must have been directly beneath the sacristy—the sacristy that contained the foul secrets of the Inquisition that Underhill speculated about endlessly in the Pit.

Above them they could hear the strains of Benediction and the *Tantum Ergo*.

What they found there, as if to confirm Underhill's theories, were three sealed lead coffins laid out in a row, covered in varying shades of rust and verdigris. On one of the caskets a brass plate had the name Martin Weld engraved on it. The plaques on the other two were too old to be deciphered.

The musty air of the crypt seemed barely breathable, as if the scarce oxygen of the vault had been recently diminished by another presence. In the dark there seemed to float an indefinable perfume, as if someone had been just there before them.

TWICE NINE

"That will be twice nine, Gentlemen, if you please."

So slight and insubstantial was the whisper in the dark, that Sinclair thought he had imagined it, or that it was Underhill playing a prank.

But a sombre figure was waiting for them at the entrance to the Lower Gallery.

It was Morguer himself, standing in the snow and pale in the moonlight, looking every inch the Nosferatu.

Examining his fingernails with a frown and then picking at an invisible fleck of skin on his little finger, he spoke again, very carefully and almost inaudibly. They had to strain to hear his voice which was almost snatched away by the breeze that soughed through the trees of the nearby woods from which they had just emerged. They were both nervous after what they had seen in the crypt and had needed a smoke.

"Ah yes, our ah, so clever intellectualists, Sinclair and Underhill, out for an evening stroll, how sophisticated. Benediction must be endured by the whole school, it seems, except for you two—the Sacraments being ah, beneath the, ah, intelligentsia . . ."

Rumour had it that Morguer was an East Ender who had taken elocution lessons as part of his Jesuit training, hence his meticulously crafted and careful sentences.

The College had hundreds of windows and the many towers and other vantage points. It was inevitable that they should have been spotted emerging from the woods behind the church while they should have been at their pews for Benediction. They had probably stood out against the snow. Anyone could have spotted them. It could have been some master on sentinel duty daydreaming the evening away as he looked out of a window. It could have been any one of the boys—the school was crawling with more than its fair share of quislings eager to shop their colleagues in return for some minor blandishment or dispensation.

In the time it takes to smoke a Marlboro, someone had been dispatched to trap them as they emerged from the treeline. The odd thing was that in this case Morguer had chosen to do it himself. Normally the honour fell on the lesser Jesuit gofers like bat-faced Pottifer or Piggy Williams, or if they were not inclined or available, to the lower caste lay masters like Poof Parker or Dolly Beamish.

Twice nine was the maximum number of strokes available, very rarely ordered. A twice-nining was legendary. Twice nine was part of the package that culminated in expulsion.

This time the punishment seemed so out of proportion to the crime—Sinclair and Underhill had not even been caught smoking. They had only been out of bounds. Technically, their only crime was malingering—of having skipped Benediction.

Underhill, as was his custom, looked at Morguer in the eye and addressed him with unctuous politeness. "Sinclair and I would like to thank you for punishing us and for correcting our impious ways, Headmaster. But may we please know why we have been ordered twice nine?"

A whisper emerged from the dark, carried on a whiff of incense and chalk. "For insolence."

This was too much for Sinclair and this time he felt compelled to speak out. "But Fr Morguer, we were simply out of bounds, there was no insolence involved . . ."

"Underhill has just been insolent to me. You have witnessed it yourself."

Outrage against the blatant injustice of the ambush welled up in Sinclair and made his eyes prick, but Underhill simply smiled, having cottoned on to the Jesuitical game quicker than Sinclair. It was a game whose principal rule was that the Jesuit was always one step ahead of his pupil because Master knew

Pupil better than Pupil knew himself. It was a game which held that intent was as bad or even worse than the act itself—that just by thinking about fornication you had ensnared yourself in the tripwires of a Mortal Sin quite as badly as if you had actually had your way with the neighbour's wife. Underhill knew better than Sinclair that the Jesuits were tricky customers who did not play with a straight bat, and his grim smile betrayed a grudging admiration for their fiendishness.

Sinclair opened his mouth to protest again but in the dark Underhill squeezed his arm tightly to prevent a further outburst, and added, icily, "to which Sinclair and I can only reiterate our thanks, again, Headmaster, for your correcting us."

The Nosferatu had no answer other than to look down his nose with his undertaker's eyes at the infuriating, insolent little blond-haired cunt. With a curt nod, and a clearing of his throat, he turned and floated away on the breeze. It was then that they noticed another dark figure in the shadows, which moved out of sight sideways and silently before they could identify it.

The message had been delivered. As always it was an indirect message, but it was loud and clear. From now on Sinclair was to be tarred with the same brush as Guy Underhill—if Guy Underhill sinned, so too it was assumed, George Sinclair had sinned. If Guy Underhill suffered, so too would George Sinclair suffer. He would be made to pay dearly for being Underhill's disciple and partner in crime.

Underhill was exhilarated. He had only ever had six of the best, and for him twice nine was proof of his status as a serious outlaw. Where others would quake with fear at the legendary punishment, Underhill relished the prospect. Sinclair, on the other hand, feared the ferula. He had had six of the best back in Surrey, after the episode of the fried eggs, but twice nine was another matter altogether.

Nine strokes on each hand. They said that after twice nine the blisters remained for weeks but worse still, that the veins of the fingers often burst under the repeated bludgeoning, resulting in subcutaneous haemorrhaging which turned your palms and fingers blue. Sinclair had an aversion to blood, but far worse for him than the sight of free-flowing red blood was a horror of subcutaneous haematomes, for a bruise was nothing but trapped blood, rotting blood under the skin. And, more than the pain, he feared that he might faint at the sight of his fingers turning black and blue. And greater still than his fear of fainting was his dread of being embarrassed—of loss of face—that most Indian of phobias that his mother had contributed to his unfortunate gene pool.

In those days news of a twice-nining would spread like wildfire through a Jesuit establishment. The night that Sinclair and Underhill were to receive the ultimate thrashing a carnival atmosphere reigned in the Refectory and in the classrooms and dormitories.

An unhealthy interest had grown around the ferula, that twelve-inch piece of flexible whalebone which had probably been invented many centuries ago by some bright-eyed Ignatian zealot hell-bent on finding new ways to inflict pain on little boys. Inevitably, at the College the whole business of corporal punishment had become the subject of morbid entertainment. St Ignatius himself would have been proud.

It went something like this: the boys ranked the Jesuits and masters in terms of a) severity of the stroke, b) action, that is, the arc of the swing or whether they were the undignified type that had to leap in the air for better traction, and c) speed of delivery. The boys, on the other hand, were ranked as to quantity (a purely numerical league table) with a deduction or bonus for their ability to withstand the pain (how high they jumped up and down flapping their stinging hands in pain or how slowly or quickly they walked away from the office). Then there was the debate about remedies; whether pouring hot or cold water on the twitching hands in the Common Place, as the lavatories were known, was the more effective remedy, or whether sitting on the hot water pipes nursing their battered paws was the thing (despite the risk of acquiring piles in the process).

It was a strictly observed rule at the College that the master ordering the 'cracks' could not be the one to mete out the punishment. Furthermore, in order to increase the torment of anticipation, the punishment could be deferred for up to several days. The Jesuits had learned centuries ago that summary punishment is never quite as effective as the mock execution or the threat of delayed torment. And that the longer the victim has to think about his predicament the better.

Five evenings later, they were to report for the beating, after a supper where they were the object of much attention and speculation (there was even a small book running among the gamblers). The question was which of the two would prove to be the more pathetic victim, sly Paki Sinclair with his wagging head or that narcissistic ponce Guy Underhill, who fancied himself so much that he had no time for any of us mere mortals. Well now, we would see how much of a man he really was, and whether his smugness would withstand the devastating administration of justice by eighteen strokes of the whalebone . . . the 'Rain of Pain'.

The news got better still—Underhill and Sinclair were to be thrashed by Anthony Wyles S.J., also known as 'Spock' for his sunken cheeks and laconic manner. The fact that it was Spock's turn to administer justice was an extra treat—for four reasons: one, if you stood in the shadows of the corridor of the Upper Syntax dormitory, you had a perfect view down into his office across the quadrangle and could watch the entire proceedings; two, after Fr Cassius (whose delivery bordered on the mythical and who was only tapped to act as executioner in cases involving expulsion), Spock was widely regarded as the hardest hitter, and furthermore he delivered slowly and with style, exhibiting an elegant and economic action; three, the victims this time were Underhill and Paki Sinclair, whom Spock was known to dislike with particular intensity because of certain cartoons (which unfortunately portrayed him too accurately) that had been confiscated and had ended up making the rounds of the Staff Common Room; and four, one of the legends about Spock being that in his previous incarnation he had served in MI5 and had specialized in interrogation and psychological warfare. It was therefore likely that the physical violence of the punishment would be complemented with an element of exquisite psychological torture.

The appointed hour of 7 p.m. came and went. Underhill and Sinclair sat on the pipes outside Spock's office—otherwise known as the 'Room of Doom'—observed directly and indirectly by hundreds of eyes and ears. The tension had built up nicely. Eventually, after about half an hour of this delay, Spock's bony features emerged around the door, and his beady eyes— pissholes in the snow—lingered lifelessly over the two malefactors.

He summoned Sinclair in first, with a nod. So he had decided to warm up on the weaker of the two, so as to be able to lay into that smirking bastard Underhill with all the more ferocity. This intelligence was disseminated through the classrooms and dormitories and galleries at lightning speed. The fun had started.

Tradition required the victim to formally request the beating. The Executioner would then proceed to register the name, offence, master ordering, and quantity in an exercise book. He would then flex the whalebone and even practise his swing as Victim stood, mouth dry, heart pounding, watching, waiting. Executioner would then instruct Victim how to place his hands for maximum effect. Adjustments to hand position were often known to take place in between the strokes. The entire proceedings could be long and drawn out, and that night Spock's inclination was most definitely to take it nice and slowly. He was in no hurry that night. Nine on each hand. Not alternately, but repeatedly, down they came . . . slowly, very slowly—the Rain of Pain falls slowly . . .

Afterwards Victim (Sinclair in this case) was required to thank his tormentor. Unlike the tradition of canings at Protestant Public Schools, at the Jesuit institutions the offender was not required to shake hands, understandably, but to give thanks with a bow, and with genuine regret and gratitude in one's heart. Gratitude for the cleansing favour that had been bestowed on you— after all, as the cliché went, it had hurt Executioner more than it had hurt Victim—therefore Victim was required to feel sorry for Executioner and express sincere gratitude.

After his cracks Sinclair managed a drunken bow, his hands, which he could actually no longer feel, clamped tightly under his armpits. To the delight of the boys lurking nearby, he did indeed faint outside Spock's office after making the mistake of looking down at his numb, mangled, purple fingers. He was carted off gleefully to the Infirmary by a cheering group of ghouls, so he never did witness how it went with Underhill.

What happened in the case of Guy Underhill went on to become part of the folklore of the College. You can even hear about it today— even though the ferula has long since been abolished.

The boys who were lucky enough to have a grandstand view of Underhill's beating from the Upper Syntax dormitory say that as the cracks were delivered, ever so slowly, Underhill had stood there, unflinching. And that when the 'Rain of Pain' in the 'Room of Doom' had stopped, Underhill just stood there, with his usual slouch, as if nothing had happened. And that, unbelievably, he calmly took the ferula out of Spock's hand, brought it to his lips, kissed it, made a pontifical sign of the cross over it, and handed it back politely to Spock.

He then said something, because they saw his lips move—unfortunately there were no lip readers among them. Whatever it was that Underhill said then only he and Spock would ever know—and then they saw him laughing, yes, the fucker was actually laughing in Spock's face. They say that the expression on Spock's face was one of utter disbelief. And to make things worse (or better, depending on whose side you were on), Underhill leaned towards Spock, grasped the Jesuit's hand, shook it hard and heartily, laughing all the time, and finally, to press his point further, stepping back he clapped his hands several times, applauding Spock's delivery, before sauntering out of the office. No cold water treatment in the Common Place for Guy Underhill, no sitting on the hot water pipes to relieve the pain; he simply ambled his insolent way out through the back door to the labs and into the woods, for a quiet smoke . . . and so was born a minor legend at the College.

THE QUERENTS

It became fashionable to spend time with Underhill and Sinclair, who were now celebrated after being twice-nined. At first they shunned the attention but eventually they reached out to certain other outcasts in their year. Underhill and Sinclair invited some of their number to meet in the Pit one rainy Sunday evening.

It was a strange collection of boys—apart from Sinclair with his greasy wagging head, and condescending Underhill, there was Olatunji Ogunlesi, a charismatically criminal Nigerian who had been at the Hall with Underhill; Charles Kirkfill, a gay intellectual with a penchant for the occult, who the entire school called 'Doris' and who endured appalling bullying at the hands of the sporting mafias; the third invitee was Wanking Eddy Cayetano, a dago from Malta whose eyes, like those of a fish, were out of alignment.

Wanking Eddy was an expert in manual relief and was generally held in contempt by the world at large, being as he was a prolific masturbator and purveyor of high-quality wank mags, from which he made his living. They said that he had a supplier in London and that he accumulated vast quantities of cash from the rental of the mags. Wanking Eddy had become famous in the wanking circles, having become in fact the holder of the record for the highest number of consecutive ejaculations recorded in one sitting.

Olatunji's laugh was infectious and he exuded that powerful magnetism that Nigerian males have, and this is what drew the weak and the corrupt to him. His style of speech was declamative, destined as he was to achieve a certain political notoriety in the future. He was in high spirits that evening.

The scene, now that Sinclair thought about it all those years later, must have resembled a conclave of rival mafia families meeting for parley.

"Gentlemen, dear hosts," declared Ogunlesi, with a nod first to Underhill and then to Sinclair, who had already lit up, "dear Bwana Underhill and dear Sahib Sinclair, on behalf of your humble black servant and his sidekicks

Madame Doris and Wanking Eddy, I thank you for inviting us into your cave of guilty pleasures. *Abracadabra!*" he exclaimed, "and let the games begin . . ."

With that he brandished a half-full bottle of Jack Daniels and accepted a light from Underhill, who was squinting in the smoke with his characteristic smile.

"And you, Master Edward, chief porn-wallah," said Sinclair, wagging and wobbling his head and hamming up his Indian accent in true Bollywood style, to the delighted applause of Doris, "what brings you to the proceedings?"

"What else, dear Brothers in Christ," replied the dago, looking at Sinclair and Underhill at the same time, devoting one eye to each, every inch the furtive descendent of Arab traders, and pulling out two magazines from under his pullover, "if not two brand-new complementary editions; the Holy Book of Hustler and the Scripture according to Playboy, pages totally unstuck, for your further edification. Gratis."

"*Et Deo gratias*, Brother Edward," nodded Underhill courteously, before taking a deep pull of the Jack Daniels.

Finally it was Doris's turn. While the others had been clowning around and lighting up and reviewing the snatch in the mags, Doris had quietly produced from out of nowhere a ouija board and its plastic and glass pointer, and he proceeded to lay it out on an overturned cardboard box of bog paper.

Lighting a candle, which he placed on the box, he whispered theatrically: "Madame Doris invites the Querents to join hands around the board and seek their collective destiny . . . lights out, please, ladies . . ."

The single lightbulb was extinguished and Doris's face looked passably spooky in the candlelight.

And so, warming their buttocks on the pipes of the squalid boiler room, they proceeded to summon the dead.

G-R-A-N-N-Y-J-E-E

It was no mistake, the cursor pointed out these letters as Sinclair watched open-mouthed.

"And who the fuck is *Grannyjee* when she's not at home sucking my dick?" said Olatunji, trying to break the tension.

Sinclair was silent, and very puzzled, and probably did not hear Olatunji's remark.

"That's Sinclair's granny," said Underhill, in an attempt to embarrass Olatunji.

"Oh, I *am* sorry," said Doris, taking the opportunity to lay his hand on Sinclair's, because he secretly fancied him. "I didn't know she was dead. Oh, I *am* sorry, George."

Wanking Eddy looked alarmed and he had difficulty controlling his misaligned eyes. Perhaps this business of summoning the dead was real after all. He hadn't bargained for this.

"She's not. I mean, she's not dead, my grandmother," Sinclair heard himself say, uncertainly, fearing the worst, but then he remembered his meeting with Grannyjee on the other side of the boundary between life and death, after he had been knocked out by Jerome O'Reilly's bodyliner to the head back in Surrey. She had not been dead then either.

"Well, what does Grannyjee have to say?" ventured Doris on behalf of the Querents.

The cursor quivered again under their fingers and spelt out a message.

B-Y-E B-Y-E M-Y L-O-V-E

Wanking Eddy sniggered, but more in nervousness than out of malice. Sinclair felt very strange there in the underground room, like a sleepwalker suddenly waking in the middle of a crowd and finding himself the centre of attention.

G W-I-L-L L-O-V-E X

"What the hell does that mean, 'G will love X'?—who the fuck is X?" insisted Eddy, feeling panicky.

"Well we know who G is, anyway, don't we George?" piped in Underhill.

"Shut up, both of you," hissed Doris, "give George a chance, will you . . ."

Then the cursor started to move again.

I W-I-L-L R-E-T-U-R-N

They each took a deep breath and settled back around the board after regaining their composure, and started again. This time they did not feel embarrassment when they joined hands around the board.

Doris as always represented the Querents. "Is anyone there?" he called out.

A while passed. They heard the pipes gurgling and the sigh of the boilers but otherwise nothing out of the ordinary. Just the everyday noises and tremors of being underground in the guts of the beast. And nothing still.

Then, just as Doris was about to ask again, the candle flickered and the cursor twitched under their fingers and slid up the board to *YES*.

"Are you dead?"

This was asked to avoid the same mistake they had made with Sinclair's grandmother.

YES

"Are you happy?"

The cursor jumped, rather jerkily and they supposed, angrily.

NO

"What is your name?"

This time it was Doris's turn to frown as the cursor traced out a name that at first meant nothing to the others, but then rang a bell, a very disturbing bell.

M-A-R-T-I-N   W-E-L-D

"And who the fuck is Martin Weld when he's not at home sucking my dago di– . . . oh shit, lads, oh fuck . . ." said Wanking Eddy, his eyes now truly out of control. "Isn't that the boy at the funeral . . . I mean, the dead boy . . . ?"

B-E-W-A-R-E   S-P-O-C-K

The spirit of Martin Weld finished its visit with two messages, neither of which meant anything to the Querents:

T-H-E-Y   A-R-E   T-E-M-P-L-A-R-S
H-O-R-N-L-E-S-S   G-O-A-T

*

"When shall we five meet again?" asked Doris, still shaken but bravely trying to cheer them up after another doom-laden oracle had spoken. Underhill,

Olatunji and Wanking Eddy ignored him and sloped off out of the Pit to their lairs, heads bowed and preoccupied with what they had just witnessed. There was much to think about.

Sinclair remained in the Pit with Doris. He still could not understand the appearance of Grannyjee and the riddles she had spelled out on the board.

"She's not dead, George, don't you worry your pretty little head about her. She's only watching over you," Doris reassured him, trying to cheer him up now with a wag of his head and a little Bollywood pastiche. "All the way from Goa, *my goodness gracious me*. You are indeed blessed, *Sahib*."

Sinclair told Doris about his near death experience in Surrey, to reassure himself that Grannyjee was able to inhabit the other world without actually being dead.

Doris reciprocated with one of his own secrets, and told Sinclair that he had seen Martin Weld, the boy who had just visited them through the ouija board, the boy they had buried on their first day at the College back in 1975.

"You mean you saw him before he died? I didn't know you knew him."

"No, silly, afterwards."

"No shit, Doris . . ."

"No shit, George. It's like this: there I am in my cubicle, on our first night, after that creepy funeral, trying to have a quiet wank after lights out, and I look up and see this face peeking in round the curtain at me. I thought he was a monitor or something and that I'd been caught at it. But to my surprise he didn't say anything, just stared at me and then disappeared. Gave me the creeps. It wasn't anyone from the Hall, and next morning I couldn't recognize him as a New Boy from the other Prep Schools. He must have been from another year. Anyway, the next night, it happens again, and I tell the face to fuck off and leave me alone, but he just stares back at me and leaves eventually, in his own good time. Next day I try to spot him during Assembly but I can't see him anywhere. On the third night, it happens again and by now I'm at the end of my tether, and after the face disappears I get up and go to Fr McLintock's room to complain. He asks me to describe the boy. Large green eyes, blond hair, a birthmark on his right cheek, I say. McLintock looks at me, and doesn't say anything. He just sends me back to the dormitory. Then I tell Jerry Golding about it"—Golding was one of Doris's admirers in the year above and was also something of a psychic—"and you know what he said to me when I described the face and showed him where my cubicle was? 'Well, Doris, my dear, it looks like you've had a visitor from beyond the grave. You're sleeping in Martin Weld's cubicle.' "

TIMOR MORTIS

The day after the seance in the Pit, which was a Monday, the fates dealt George Sinclair a cruel blow. That morning after breakfast he found a blue airmail letter lying on his desk. Somehow he already knew what was in it as he opened it. It was from his mother and regretfully informed him of the death of his grandmother.

In his imagination George can see Major Sinclair standing over his mother as she pens the letter, sucking his non-existent upper lip in satisfaction as he thanks his lucky stars for the latest state of affairs, for the open horizons of a future devoid of live-in mother-in-law. As he watched his father in his imagination, Sinclair felt a twist of cold steel in his guts, as if the exquisite Elizabethan dagger of one of his Caribbean pirates was slowly ripping his insides apart.

Sinclair was light-headed with the grief of the betrayed, and then he was full of hateful rage. If Underhill hadn't prevented him he would have jumped headfirst from the window of his study onto the quadrangle four floors below. The idea was to dash his brains out on its ancient cobbles, that were slick from the Lancashire drizzle and gleamed evilly in the half-light.

Sinclair was in no state to attend double physics followed by chemistry that Monday morning and he was permitted to stay in his room for the rest of the morning, but there was to be no dispensation from games. A good dose of fresh air, the masters agreed, would provide salutary distraction from the boy's grief. Loss of a grandparent was nothing that a good scrum in the freezing mud couldn't help you get over.

At first Sinclair blamed himself for provoking Grannyjee's death by messing around with that fucking ouija board. It was Doris who pointed out to him that the letter said that Grannyjee had died two weeks before their seance in the Pit.

That night Sinclair dreamed that he saw the hooded skeleton from the Holbein engravings in the Arundell Library leading his Grannyjee away into the horizon.

MUGGINS

Grannyjee's death had a strange effect on Sinclair. The feeling of intense and explosive anger that had gripped him when he realized that he was now alone in the world didn't subside. Instead it found various twisted outlets, one of which manifested itself as a cruel impulse to torment those weaker than himself.

There was Muggins, for example. Muggins was a 'flegger'. The poor toothless sod used to wipe down the boys' trays after meals in the Refectory as he ranted and raved in unintelligible Lancastrian. The boys surrounded him and danced around him, baiting and tormenting him like a wounded bear. Sinclair, he was sorry to admit later, started participating in these tribal rituals after Grannyjee's death. Underhill, on the other hand, refused to participate and went out of his way to be civil to Muggins. But this act of decency was taken as just another manifestation of Guy Underhill's desire to be different, to stand apart from the crowd—of course he despised the semi-human trog just like the rest of us and was being kind to him just to be contrary.

What the authorities failed to realize was that by employing the slow and the retarded in the kitchens they were not doing them any favours. Like Muggins, these unfortunates ended up being teased and despised by the Men for Others when the masters were out of earshot.

The ironic thing, they later learned from Dr Tantum, was that Muggins had been a decorated special forces Royal Marine commando and had survived the most daring raids of the war, only to have half of his cranium blown off in a shooting range accident after the end of hostilities.

For most of Muggins's tormentors, this intelligence reached them late in their careers at the College. By then it was too late for them to make amends and thank old Muggins for his role in defeating Jerry and in preserving the British Way of Life, which guaranteed them their privileged education.

THE THREE FISHES

Another symptom of Sinclair's strange mourning was an intense craving for female company, but that was on the cards anyway—he was fourteen, after all. Grannyjee's death, as well as leaving him with a vicious need to hurt someone, had also left him bewildered and hungry for the warmth of female flesh. He joined the ranks of those who in their emotional starvation had the misfortune to fall under the spell of the female kitchen staff. They were local proletarian girls descended from the weird women that had once haunted the countryside around Pendle. Infatuation may have resulted in some cases from physical rather than emotional hunger, because if you returned their smiles you might well get an extra ladle of muck slopped onto your plate.

It was assumed that these leering fleggers were looking for an early marriage and a passport out of deepest darkest Lancashire. You were drawn to
them just as dogs learn to love those who feed them, or as hostages learn to
love their kidnappers. But, most commonly, infatuation was the result of glandular overload. Dear Lord, you could almost hear the boys' mothers and sisters saying in their smart London homes, those poor lads up there must want
to shag anything that moves . . .

Underhill was less vulnerable to the flegger sirens than Sinclair. When it
came to sex Underhill had a flexible disposition. Sinclair, on the other hand
was coming dangerously close to falling under the spell of the heavy mascara
and the sad puppy-dog eyes that lingered on you over the trays of steaming
brown slop in the dinner queue in the Refectory.

There was this little tart from Whalley, a village down the road beyond the
Post Office. Tracy was her name. She was heavily made-up, her face plastered
on in late seventies Gothic style, but underneath all that war paint she had a
sweet face and—it was the oddest thing—the same wry quizzical brown gaze
as Grannyjee.

Despite Underhill's efforts to dissuade him, Sinclair managed to pass her a
note as he stood before her, tumescing, in the dinner queue on a Tuesday night
waiting for his dollop of slop. She took the piece of paper, blushing deeply
beneath the Rocky Horror make-up. The delivery of the note had been noticed
by the other boys in the queue who were now whistling and jerking off with
imaginary dicks in their hands and wagging their heads *à la* Paki Sinclair.

The note had also been noticed by Tracy's colleague, an acned piece called
Molly Fletcher who was in charge of the pudding. She whispered something
in Tracy's ear that made her friend blush again, and then she leered at Guy
Underhill, who ignored her intensely. Tracy's eyes, which had before searched
out Sinclair's in the dinner queue, were now turned down modestly on the tub
of thick-skinned custard that she was administering with a ladle.

"What music do you like, then, Tracy?"

Sinclair leaned into her closely in the Three Fishes in Whalley, breathing
in her animal warmth and looking down into her budding cleavage, *lingam*
ramrod at attention and itching with anticipation. It was a Saturday night and
he had escaped into town.

"Jaasfoonk."

"You what?" He pulled on his Marlboro sceptically and took a swig at his
whiskey sour.

"Jaasfoonk."

He knew full well what she meant. She was trying to be sophisticated, poor thing.

"Oh, you mean jazz funk? Like Spyro Gyra?"

Embarrassed, she nodded into her shandy.

As with many things those days, Sinclair was caught in a limbo of ambivalence—he didn't quite know what to feel. One minute it was syrupy, pitiful love for this pretty little troglodyte with her siren's eyes—and dangerously seductive visions of future domestic bliss in the suburbs of Whalley surrounded by flegger sprogs and live-in mother-in-law—the next, simply lust for a piece of local fluff, food for his increasingly demanding *lingam*, in the manner of some Victorian gentleman experiencing lustful contempt for an East End trollop.

Later, she agreed to go outside with him, even though it was bitterly cold. In the alley behind the pub, which served as a urinal for the patrons of the Fishes on their way home, a blustery wind made their eyes water, and she let him press her up against the wall for a snog.

She was worried about being seen, had been all evening. When someone stepped out of the pub for a piss against the wall in the alley where they were hiding, she went rigid like a rabbit at the sound of gunfire. Her eyes danced wildly with fear whenever they heard a footfall or a burp.

When they were alone again his hand slipped down her neck to her shoulder, on its way to warmer treasures below, but the buttons of her blouse got in the way. Her lips parted easily and their tongues met and when he felt her finally relaxing under him after squirming like a cat trapped in a sack, he found another way in and slipped his hand up her blouse, this time to cup her warm apple-sized breast. He could feel her little heart fluttering. Each whimper from the girl was a small victory for him.

But the evening ended in tears when she pushed him off in a panic—she must have sensed a dangerous anger driving his rapist's lust when she felt his nails digging into her buttocks, like those of a housewife testing fruit. The end came when he thrust his other hand up under her leather skirt.

"I'm not a fookin' tramp, George Sinclair. Now get off with you, before I set me bruther on you. Get off with you, you fookin' paki, get back to your posh bloody schule—I'm not a fookin' tramp."

Sinclair legged it off into the alley when her voice started taking on a hysterical pitch that was bound to attract attention—and trouble, most likely in the form of the police or her brother. The last he heard of her was a child-like whimpering in the alley as he ran off into the shadows like a common mugger.

Defeated, tail between his legs, he trudged up the country lanes back to the College in the moonlight. As he walked, he smoked the last of his Marlboros and cursed himself for missing an opportunity because of his impulsiveness. He could have had her if he'd been a bit more patient and had kept fucking *lingam* under control.

Then he worried that she might report his assault. But for the time being he was glad that he was still in one piece, and every few steps he kept looking back over his shoulder at the lane to make sure that Tracy's Bro' was not bearing down on him in the moonlight with some blunt metallic weapon. Those were the days after all when football fans—and Bro' was surely a football fan— would loudly sing songs about racist murder. Bro' and his mates would have jumped at the opportunity to lay into some stuck-up rugby-playing Wily Oriental Gentleman rapist they had found wandering alone in the dark.

He passed under the massive presence of Pendle, thanking his lucky stars for avoiding a lynching at the hands of the good lads of Whalley. He'd been foolhardy enough to try it on with one of their lasses. To remind himself how lucky he was, and to dispel the dark thoughts that were encroaching on him as he passed through the witch-blighted countryside, Sinclair perversely sang the Blackburn Rovers song to himself:

> *Walkin' down the High Street swingin' me chain*
> *Bumped into paki and 'e called me a name*
> *So I swings me chain around 'is 'ead*
> *And now that paki, 'e is . . . dead!*

That Monday at dinner, Molly Fletcher gave Sinclair a long sour look as he stood before her in the Refectory queue. She ladled a gob of semolina into his bowl with furious contempt, almost cracking his plate. For once Molly ignored Guy Underhill, who as ever stood at Sinclair's side. Tracy was conspicuous by her absence.

They didn't see Tracy in the Refectory ever again, although later some wag put it about that Sinclair's girlfriend had been spotted lurking in the kitchens where she had been promoted to chief rat catcher. Sinclair's relationship with one of the fleggers was now common knowledge and it would take him years to live it down.

At the table, Underhill suggested to Sinclair that it might be in his best interests to avoid the semolina. Molly Fletcher had probably gobbed into it in a fit of righteous indignation, he said. Sinclair was profoundly depressed at the thought that flegger phlegm had most likely been a regular ingredient in his diet for many years.

Whenever he thought of Tracy he imagined a furtive creature living a troglodyte's existence underground in the kitchens, condemned to an eternity without light and surrounded by rats. He never saw her again.

GUY MAGUS

Guy Underhill became a mesmerist in their third year at the College. While Sinclair was looking for new female victims and trying to keep the demanding monster between his thighs under control, Underhill was learning about hypnosis.

Underhill later told Sinclair that he had been taught how to do it by Olatunji Ogunlesi, who in turn had been instructed by his uncle, who was some kind of shaman back in Nigeria. Underhill told Sinclair that Olatunji would hypnotize Doris and Wanking Eddy. So that was how he exacted strict obedience and devotion from these two characters and impelled them to execute his criminal commands as if by remote control.

Sinclair soon discovered that Underhill did not become a mesmerist out of academic interest. Behind Guy Underhill's professorial demeanour there lurked a very pragmatic mind. Underhill's newly acquired skill most definitely had a practical purpose, and that purpose was living and breathing, and had bones and warm flesh and blood, and it also had a name—Christopher Larkin.

Sinclair had declined Underhill's invitation to act as his guinea pig. Underhill wanted to experiment before attempting to hypnotize Larkin. He couldn't afford to fuck up his pass at the love of his life.

"Why don't you let me practise on you? You're probably worried about what I might winkle out of the murky depths of your nasty subconscious," Underhill said to him as they were sharing a joint in the abattoir one filthy rainy evening.

"Quite," replied Sinclair suspiciously, shifting his weight from one foot to the other, in between the puddles of muck on the concrete floor. "It's lucky I don't talk in my sleep . . ."

For the rest of that evening in the fetid slaughterhouse with its bloodstained walls and rusty hooks, Underhill obsessed to Sinclair about Christopher Larkin. He talked and talked until Sinclair grew tired of his obsessive talk.

"That's all very well, Guy," yawned Sinclair, looking at his wristwatch, hungry now with the onset of dope-induced munchies and counting the hours to dinner, "but it's all pie in the sky. They say he's not at all inclined your way. In fact they say he's hetero and has a girlfriend in Preston. And anyway, most of the time he's got his sodding headphones on, thumb up his bum and brain in neutral, and listening to Genesis or some other pseudo art rock trash. You might do well to forget that one, if you want my advice. Forget him. I'm sure Doris would oblige with a nice blow job in the Rat Trap if you asked him nicely . . ."

But Underhill insisted and pressed his case. "Crap. Larkin's bent, just like me, except he doesn't know it."

"Or doesn't want to know it . . ."

"And anyway, you are obliged to help me, George Sinclair. It is your solemn duty to assist a friend in need. Actually, come to think of it, I'm your *only* friend, as if you didn't know that already, and I'm definitely in need. And my need is great. If I don't have him soon, my glands will burst. It won't be a pretty sight. And you might have to clean up the mess after me."

"I'll help, but only if it doesn't involve you hypnotizing me. I've already made that quite clear . . . you can go and hypnotize Doris and Wanking Eddy, like Olatunji does, or Morguer or Spock or the fucking Pope for that matter, but not me."

"But what do you have to hide . . . from me, of all people?"

"Now that would be telling," Sinclair smirked through the smoke of the second joint. There were few secrets that Underhill was not already party to.

Eventually they settled for a compromise. Sinclair would help him find a suitable candidate and would assist Underhill in the experiment. Then if it worked, Sinclair would help Underhill befriend Christopher Larkin and would even put in a good word on Underhill's behalf, and set him up for the kill.

From the corner of his eye Sinclair noticed Underhill licking his lips, like the wolf in the fairy tale.

The guinea pig that Sinclair selected was a boy called Nick Gompertz. He was a lonely lad with bad skin who was always trying to ingratiate himself with Underhill and Sinclair and with anyone else who would listen.

"Poor little bugger, his mother must have abandoned him at birth," Underhill said with his characteristic disdain for those less fortunate than himself, when Sinclair put Gompy's name forward as a candidate.

"He's the best I can do, Guy. I can deliver him to the Pit, suitably doped and amenable. Then it's all over to you. Take it or leave it."

Eventually the day came and Sinclair had done a good job of manipulating Gompertz into the Pit. Poor Gompy and his spots—they looked particularly sore and pustulent that day—it must have been the weather. Gompy lapped up the attention that Sinclair was bestowing upon him that day for some unknown reason. Gompy gratefully gulped in the smoke of the joint that Sinclair pressed on him. By the time Underhill showed up in the Pit, Gompy was giggling and then laughing his head off at Sinclair's extraordinarily hilarious jokes—my God, he had never heard anything so funny, and shit, Sinclair's impressions of Spock and Morguer were priceless, they really were, but his lisping imitation of Dolly Beamish took the biscuit, it really did.

"Sinclair," cackled Nick Gompertz, "you're a fucking comic genius, that's what you are . . ."

To cut a long story short, that evening Underhill was able to put Gompy in a trance without the victim even being aware that he was being hypnotized. Because no one ever took the time to have a conversation with the poor little shite, Nick Gompertz gave Sinclair and then Underhill his full and undivided attention, gratefully and willingly. After all, as is well known now (but was not necessarily well known back in the seventies), hypnosis is nothing more than extremely focused concentration.

What Underhill made Nick Gompertz do, under his influence, both in the Pit that evening and then later as he whispered the trigger words into Nick's willing ear, is the subject of another story. The point is that Underhill was now sure that he could hypnotize, and hypnotize well. He was able to induce in third parties specific thoughts and actions, so long, of course, as the candidate was willing.

And now he was ready to commence his hunt for Christopher Larkin's girlish thighs.

It never ceased to amaze Sinclair how quickly and completely Christopher Larkin fell under Guy Underhill's spell. There must have been something to Underhill's theory about Larkin's latent homosexuality. To be honest, the idea of mind control and psychic manipulation did not bother Sinclair, as long as it was not *his* mind and his psyche that were being fucked with. From then on he was always careful to keep his wits about him and avoid Underhill's salamander gaze whenever he was talking to him.

The other thing that bothered Sinclair was that now that Underhill had achieved his objectives, he became inseparable from Larkin. Larkin followed Underhill around like a dumb amanuensis, and seemed to do Underhill's least bidding with puppy-like devotion. The two would disappear for hours on end. They must have found some new hiding place, because Sinclair was never able to find them—not in the Pit, not in the Rat Trap, nor the abbatoir. They must have found some secret clearing in the woods, or perhaps they pleasured themselves in one of the many priest holes of the immense building.

Underhill no longer seemed tense and on edge. On the contrary, he was now almost unbearably relaxed and laid-back, no doubt the result of glandular relief. It didn't suit him, that lack of intensity.

Sinclair no longer enjoyed Underhill's full attention, and that pissed him off.

BLACK MASS

"The Devil walks among us, Gentlemen."

Early in the morning before Easter half-term all hell broke loose. It was another scandal, for fuck's sake, and just before half-term, to make things worse. The morning bell woke them half an hour earlier than usual, and the dormitory monitors informed the boys that an early assembly of the whole school—an *Ascensio Scholarum*—had been called. And before breakfast at that. This had never happened before, not before breakfast, so the assumption was that there had been a death, a murder, perhaps or that nuclear war between the superpowers had broken out overnight, or that the plague had struck and the End of Days was upon them. It was still dark outside, and raining again. Curiosity gave way to panic and anxiety as the boys traipsed down to assembly, realizing that they were in danger of having their half-term cancelled unless this latest emergency was resolved in the next 24 hours.

They were soon to discover that what had happened was something far worse than murder or nuclear war.

With his mention of the Devil, uttered ever so quietly with his impeccable diction, Fr Morguer had struck a chill into the bone marrow of each and every boy in the hall that morning. There was a collective intake of breath, and then you could have heard a pin drop. Outside, the rain fell steadily, and the state of darkness visible persisted. On the stage, behind the vampiric figure of the Nosferatu stood his hatchetmen, the *Einsatzkommando*, the special execution squad of the Nazis' SS, as they were referred to by Underhill. There they stood, surveying the sea of hungry, puzzled faces beneath them: Spock, Dr Tantum, and the silent Fr Cassius, their faces impassive but their brains working at double speed as they geared up for yet another operation.

Sinclair watched Spock on the podium and Spock's beady eyes surveyed the audience.

B-E-W-A-R-E S-P-O-C-K . . .

Spock, like all secret policemen, knew that it didn't matter whether you lied or told the truth. All that mattered was the result, the confession. Given the passage of time and the application of pain and distress, both physical and spiritual, he could make any of the boys say anything he wanted.

After his horrid announcement, Morguer proceeded, looking down at his fingernails with regret. "Let us pray. In the name of the Father, the Son and the Holy Ghost."

He then led the Our Father and then the Hail Mary, which the boys belted out with sincere and pious enthusiasm, this time, for fear of Satan and of the possible cancellation of half-term.

"This morning, Fr Pottifer"—who was responsible for the maintenance of the various chapels dotted around the building—"as he was preparing for his daily 6 a.m. Mass, discovered that the College's entire stock of hosts and altar wine has been stolen. This can only be the work of the Devil, Gentlemen. May God have mercy on our souls."

One of the smaller boys promptly fainted and was carted out unceremoniously to the Infirmary.

After order was re-established Morguer turned the proceedings over to Spock, his Chief of Ops, who calmly laid out before the assembly the procedure to be followed for the rest of the day. Classes and games were cancelled and each Playroom was to remain at their desks under the supervision of the monitors until advised otherwise. The slightest infringement would be dealt with ferociously. It was clear that this time the authorities meant business.

With that, the school was herded down to the Refectory for breakfast, which was the quietest meal that any of the fleggers could ever remember serving.

And then it all went even quieter. It was the silence of death row as the entire school, juniors and seniors alike, sat at their desks reading their standard issue red CTS bibles. Eventually, towards mid-morning when boredom had replaced fear, notes began to be passed back and forth but returned with no new intelligence. Members of the School Committee patrolled the galleries, two by two, hands clasped behind their backs, faces suitably grim.

The suspense could not have been greater. The fate of the half-term holiday lay in the balance, as Spock, Tantum and Cassius, modern-day Van Helsings, set to work in the grim task of rooting out the Satanists.

The next thing they knew they were all on their buses or in their parents' cars or on the train back down to London for the start of half-term.

SPOCK

After the boys returned from half-term they found out that they owed their holiday to Spock and his inquisitors. To their efficiency in sniffing out evil. They were like truffling pigs, Underhill said with his usual sardonic sneer.

And then word got out that there had been a Black Mass. It was not long before the identity of the Satanists got out and spread like wildfire around the school.

The coven was made up, they said, of the following diabolists: Olatunji Ogunlesi, Master of Ceremonies and High Priest, Doris the Bender and Wanking Eddy his altar boys and acolytes, and poor little Nick Gompertz with his scabs (who would have thought he'd be into Devil worship?), the, ah, 'concelebrant', if that was the correct technical term.

For once, Sinclair's name was missing from the Devil's list, although he had in fact been the fifth participant.

All things considered, it had not really been a summoning of the Evil One, in any case, although *that* was not outside the capabilities of Doris and his ouija board, Underhill and Sinclair had joked, nervously, remembering the session in the Pit.

The five of them, excluding Underhill, who at the time had probably been engaged in some sort of physical gratification with Christopher Larkin, had met in the candlelit abbatoir, in high spirits in anticipation of the coming half-term break. They were demob happy, and we all know how dangerous that mood can be.

The fact is that at 3 a.m. or thereabouts they had simply run out of alcohol and smokes. And they all had the munchies after the several spliffs that Sinclair had supplied them with.

Gompy, eager to please as always, had volunteered to raid the chapels for altar wine and the Refectory to see if there were any scraps of bread left lying around. He was also tasked to break into the kitchens to secure more substantial fare. Olatunji made some comment about him possibly finding Sinclair's 'girlfriend' Tracy on rat-catching duty and the usual exchange of good natured insults followed. And so Gompy was dispatched on his commando mission and returned three quarters of an hour later, with his bag full of swag. It contained not only five bottles of altar wine but also several compact little brown boxes containing stacks of unconsecrated hosts. Having found the Refectory and kitchens bolted shut, Gompy had shown initiative, raiding the sacristies of the College's five chapels for bread as well as wine.

The hosts were distributed by Archbishop Ogunlesi with ornate solemnity. They were then washed down with the cloying wine, after a sermon about the dangers of gluttony and excessive masturbation, and a quick sing-song of the *Tantum Ergo* by the company. And then, their stomachs full of wafers and feeling slightly nauseous from the sickly sweet wine, they had gone to their beds. Only to be woken not two hours later by the alarum bell and the call to *Ascensio Scholarum*.

There were even rumours later that there had been an orgy as well as a Black Mass (the two tended to go together, didn't they?). Even an exorcism was mentioned, and some of the more enterprising boys even tried to sell the story to *The News of the World* in London. What they couldn't agree on was who the exorcist had been—the Nosferatu, Spock—or, most disturbing of all, the silent crablike Cassius.

Cassius was the one Underhill feared and respected most. Cassius didn't teach. He managed to get through the day without ever opening his mouth to speak. He was Morguer's *factotum*—wherever Morguer went, Cassius was not too far away, shadowing the headmaster, snooping around and delivering the hardest ferula.

Sinclair had been an outlaw for too long, a veteran of many a witch hunt, to know that it was only a matter of time before he was caught in the dragnet of Spock's *Einsatzkommando*. He simply would not admit anything. He had faith in his own skill at lying. He had also learned something of Underhill's technique of polite stonewalling. But to his cost he now knew that polite insolence à la Guy Underhill actually made things worse, because it exasperated the authorities and had already led to one set of twice nine. The problem was that he was now at the mercy of his less sophisticated friends—Doris, Wanking Eddy, Olatunji and Gompy. He had absolutely no faith in *their* ability to withstand Spock's legendary interrogation skills.

Spock's summons never came—the secret policeman's tap on the shoulder never materialized—and George Sinclair for once was not named in the plot, having escaped detection, surviving to live another day in the shadows.

Instead of feeling the heavy hand of Spock on his shoulder, something wonderful and providential had happened. He had been rescued. His *Deus ex Machina* was Guy Underhill.

Underhill informed Sinclair that he had saved his hide by a quick feat of group hypnosis in the brief interlude between the end of breakfast and the start of the day-long detention that day before half-term. He had met with Olatunji, Doris, Eddy and Nick Gompertz in the Pit. He had convinced them that under hypnosis he could fortify them against the coming onslaught of the *Einsatzkommando*. He had set about putting them under with their grateful co-operation, because they were shit scared by that stage and would even have sold their mothers into slavery to avoid the long arm of Spock's law and the sting of Fr Cassius's ferula. But instead of programming into their psyches adequate responses to the interrogations, Underhill put them under and commanded the four boys to forget that George Sinclair had ever been there in the abattoir with them.

The four dopes had nodded in agreement, because by then it was too late and by then they were well under Underhill's influence.

"You owe me one," Underhill said to him with a sly wink before sloping off with Christopher Larkin for a session in their secret love nest.

Olatunji Ogunlesi never returned from half-term because he was expelled for his role in the Black Mass. Another charge that had been pending against him was that he was suspected of having hypnotized two first-year juniors. He had apparently persuaded them to surrender all their money to him. Then he had instructed them to raid their fellows' tuckboxes, from which money had also disappeared. How the juniors had mastered the art of lock-picking was the real mystery that was never resolved, because neither of the little boys could remember how they had broken into the tuckboxes. The authorities had been reluctant to take action without further evidence against Ogunlesi. Sinclair's role in these matters, as usual, was not clear.

But now there was no question of Ogunlesi's fate. The Black Mass was the last straw that broke the camel's back, as far as the Nigerian was concerned.

"Good riddance," Dolly Beamish had sneered in the Staff Common Room, "these Nigerians are charismatically evil."

"Yes, my dear, they are. Sheer, malevolent, animal magnetism, that's what it is," Poof Parker replied. "We're to be much better off without them corrupting the weaker boys."

"*Adios* Motherfuckers! All property is theft!"

As if to prove Poof Parker's thesis, Olatunji had shouted out this slogan in defiance, punching the air with his fist in a Black Power salute. They had seen him do this as he was being marched out by Fr Cassius the day after the start of the half-term holiday to the taxi waiting at the Lions which would take him off into the uncertain future of the expelled.

Doris, Wanking Eddy Cayetano and Nick Gompertz narrowly escaped expulsion because their role in the blasphemy had been secondary and sodomy, though suspected, was never proven. The real reason that Ogunlesi had been singled out, the wags in the Staff Common Room surmised, led as usual by the cynical Poof Parker, was that Morguer and Spock didn't understand black people and feared them the way medieval folk feared left-handers—and in this case Ogunlesi's role as Satanic ringleader confirmed their fear.

The three disgraced malefactors now kept a suitably low profile after being interrogated, threatened and twice-nined by Fr Cassius. In the aftermath of the disaster the diabolists were forced to endure several extra hours of RD with Fr Pottifer every month to fortify them against the return of the Evil One. In chapel and in the Refectory the rest of the boys made sure they sat quite apart from the Satanists, as they were to be known from then on. If ever, Sinclair told himself, there was a case of that worst of Predicaments, of *Spiritual and Moral Jeopardy*, then his three friends had landed smack in the middle of its quicksand and were now in it up to their necks.

The odd thing was that the Devil Worshippers had a vague feeling that George Sinclair should have shared their punishment too. They argued among themselves about whether Sinclair had actually been there or not. It was like the memory of an event which you are not sure you dreamed or which actually happened. It was an odd thing to be unsure about, because the event was so recent, and that's why it felt so strange. Since Guy Underhill had definitely not been there, it was unlikely that Sinclair had been, because where Underhill went Sinclair went, argued Doris, who still secretly fancied Sinclair and was keen to protect him. Bullshit, replied Wanking Eddy, Paki Sinclair was there, I'm sure of it. Nick Gompertz frankly could not remember either way, but asked Eddy why, if he was so sure that he had been there, he hadn't named Sinclair as an accomplice when they had been rumbled by Spock that frightful evening before half-term.

"At the time I couldn't remember, honestly," said Wanking Eddy.

"But now, several weeks later, suddenly you can remember . . . It simply doesn't make sense to me, darling," pouted Doris

And so the interminable debate raged on between the three Devil Worshippers and, whenever the subject threatened to come up, Sinclair made himself scarce and was nowhere to be seen.

1989
QUEERING THE PITCH

AND INTO MANAGUA

" **'I'll play this one** with a straight bat,' I said to myself, Morpheus. In fact, I'd decided that I'd play the rest of my life with a straight bat, assuming I could control that daughter of mine. I couldn't afford to fuck up my first overseas posting, you see."

Morpheus has set the scene for him again. Sinclair is sitting with Ximena in the first-class cabin of an American Airlines jet that is beginning its descent over a panorama of blue cones and expanses of green water, the volcanoes and lakes of Nicaragua. He looks down at Ximena sitting beside him and squeezes her hand. She is out of sorts. She has been scowling at the stewardess all the way from Miami, because the girl has shown an over-friendly interest in her father.

Sinclair sighs and knocks back the last of his gin and tonic as Ximena smoulders beside him. He is resigned. He is excited. He feels the familiar tingling in the groin. He is anxious. Excited. He is all of these things. He has reached another fork in the road.

The Embassy put the new Third Secretary (Commercial) and his daughter in an attractive bungalow with a swimming pool in the breezy suburb of Santo Domingo, which overlooks the sweltering dust bowl of Managua. From the terrace high above that tragic, sprawling city which lies simmering in the heat by the lake, you could survey a panorama dominated by the cone of the Momotombo.

The volcano looms over its smaller clone, the Momotombito. From up there in the hills the distance and the haze of woodfires gave the volcano a purplish hue. It reminded Sinclair of Pendle Hill that lush Lancashire summer of 1979. It was a summer to be avoided, whenever he visited his memories of the College. But 1979 was a year that was difficult to avoid in Nicaragua, because it was in July of that year that the Sandinistas had entered Managua in triumph.

Sinclair and Ximena had a live-in maid called Niña Conchita. She was a square little Indian with boxer's arms who came from the town of Somotillo on the border with Honduras, a frequent target of Contra raids. She had an impassive face and a hard jaw, and she served them silently and respectfully. She didn't like to talk about Somotillo and she never asked Sinclair what he kept in the padlocked tuckbox beside his bed.

Ximena was enrolled at the American school, where Sinclair would drop her in the mornings and pick her up in the afternoons at four, depositing her under the indifferent gaze of Niña Conchita. He would then return to the Embassy or go on to debrief one of his Joes in the safe house, after spending and hour or two sanitizing his route to ensure that he wasn't being tailed by Sandinista Counter Intelligence. Most of his covert activity, including the servicing of the various dead-letter drops around the city, was conducted after dark and on the whole was pretty uneventful.

Sinclair took over only three active Joes from his predecessor, Andrew Wycliffe. Wycliffe's claim to fame was that he was an avid collector of orchids and spent his free time in the rainforests of Central America adding to his collection. He was well known in horticultural circles, as Personnel had granted him permission to publish a book on the various strains of Central American orchid.

The handover went well and was mercifully short. This was because Wycliffe, instead of spending his time briefing the New Boy, devoted himself to crating up his priceless collection and negotiating bribes and export permits for his rarities. The handover consisted of three lunches with Wycliffe and his Joes at the safe house. Two of the assets were well-placed mid-level officers in the Sandinista army, and the third was a mole in the secretarial pool of the ruling nine-man junta.

The common thread linking these traitors was money, which is the best and most credible of motives in the intelligence game, because greed is easier to control and feed than other more unstable and heady motives like revenge, patriotism or God forbid, idealism.

Soon, with the ending of the Contra war, and the coming of democracy, these agents would become redundant. That was the fear in Managua station. When your Joes become redundant, your own pink slip tends to follow shortly.

LOWLANDER

There came a time, inevitably, when Sinclair's energies shifted from learning the ins and outs of the politics of Managua Station and ministering to its undemanding agents. It was time to look for a mate for himself and for *lingam*. His motherless daughter also needed a companion. When it came to human warmth and affection, they had given up on Niña Conchita and her inscrutable ways.

The candidate chosen by Sinclair had to pass two Positive Vettings: one by the Service and one by the ever mistrustful Ximena. It took weeks of subtle hints and careful negotiation with Ximena before she acquiesced to his taking a lover. Given the disasters of the past, Sinclair sensed that without his daughter's approval new catastrophes would surely follow.

"And what can you tell me about her, father?" she asked him prosecutorially one morning, at the breakfast table, as Niña Conchita placed hot tortillas, rice and beans and melted cheese in front of them.

"Well, darling," he said, taking her little brown hand in his (an old trick, to check the girl's pulse), "you'll love Brenda. She has no children, you know, so she will love spending time with you."

"And where is she from, this Brenda?"

"Oh, she's from Holland, you know, where they have all those pretty windmills and tulips . . ."

Ximena closed her eyes and breathed in deeply, imagining Holland and its windmills and tulips. "And where, father, did you meet her?"

"At the Dutch Embassy."

"And does she know about me?" she asked.

"Oh yes, darling," he lied easily, "she knows you are the apple of your father's eye."

She closed her eyes again, and Sinclair felt her hand go limp. She was in one of her half-trances. At first he had suspected that these were episodes of the *petit mal*, a mild form of childhood epilepsy, but he had been proved wrong by the doctors in England. He had finally come to accept her real nature.

"Her . . . eyes . . . are . . . hazel . . . she . . . smells . . . of . . . flowers . . . I see her standing in a garden . . . yes . . . yes . . . I like her smile . . . ," Ximena murmured.

Suddenly she was wide awake again and leaning across the table aggressively towards him, her black eyes boring into his, in perfect imitation of her dead mother.

"Have you bedded her yet?"

He felt her pinch the flesh between his thumb and index finger. Now it was her turn to see if she could sense a quickening of the pulse in her father's hand.

"No, my love, I wouldn't dream of doing that without telling you."

"It's true, father, I know you haven't."

She let his hand free.

The fact was that Sinclair had not even asked Brenda van Kempen out yet. They had barely exchanged a pleasantry or two at the Dutch Ambassador's garden party, and then they had shared a friendly handshake, but that had been enough for Sinclair.

"You can ask her now, father . . . she will agree to be your friend."

"And yours, darling, and yours," he said, with relief.

Sinclair did manage to live up to his resolution to play things with a straight bat. Just as he had to get the nod from his daughter, so he obtained clearance from the Head Boys in London to become intimate with the candidate.

He had Brenda cleared against the MI5 and MI6 databases in London, and he even requested a loop through the CIA computer in Langley.

'Nothing Recorded Against' came back within a day. She had not been registered as a known intelligence agent and had no criminal record. She had only ever come into contact with British officials through the cocktail circuit in her previous postings in Djakarta and Delhi. The Dutch brunette with the easy smile was a rare case of a *bona fide* cultural attaché.

Service policy was that preference should be shown to British citizens when it came to hunting for a mate. However, the Dutch were on the small list of friendly countries that could be trusted to supply partners to SIS's agents abroad. If things became serious and the lucky foreigners were to have the privilege of contracting matrimony with one of Her Britannic Majesty's Secret Servants, then the candidate would be obliged to take British citizenship and would be formally indoctrinated in the ways of the Service Wife.

Brenda's clearance had come through, and this before Sinclair had even asked her out.

HER LADYSHIP

Sinclair was number three in Managua Station, designation CA/MG/3.

CA/MG/2 was a woman called Vanessa Spedding. She was a greying spinster who ran the Station efficiently and with moderate success on behalf of Head of Station, CA/MG/1. The chief was Anthony Farquharson-Jones—FJ, as he permitted himself to be known. His face was red from a lifetime of fine wines and debauchery. His Spanish was ornate and heavily accented, his English plummy and, when he wasn't having one of his tantrums, his style could be dangerously syrupy. FJ was also a middle-aged homosexual and a fellow Catholic, a legacy of the postwar days when being homosexual and a left-footer gave you an edge as a candidate. He wasn't too far away from retirement age by the time Sinclair arrived in Managua.

The buzz among the small cabal of Embassy and Consular staff who specialized in keeping an eye on the comings and goings of the Friends was that Vanessa Spedding was just waiting for her boss to slip up and break every queer little bone in his fat, nasty upper-class neck. This eagerly anticipated accident would leave the field clear for her to take over and show her *machista* masters in London what she was capable of.

Spedding was one of those females who had entered the Service late in life after a career in academia. She had been a lecturer in Spanish literature at a red-brick university, where she had acted as a talent spotter for MI6 like David Blantyre at Magdalen. She came from a family of spies—the Service likes to recruit from within families because the vetting procedure can be curtailed—her grandfather, father and elder brother having acquitted themselves with much honour during the previous wars, hot and cold. Her brother had been killed while on an undercover run against the poppy barons of northern Thailand some years earlier.

The buzz about her was that she was a pillow-biter, a bender, a dyke, or whatever it was they called lesbians those days. And a poisonous one, at that.

It was before the days of CX quotas and productivity targets inspired by management consultants. The CX coming out of Managua was sporadic and two-star at best, usually at least a week or two behind the intelligence that the massive CIA station in neighbouring Honduras picked up. Honduras, for God's sake—a whole *country* converted into a CIA-sponsored base for the Contras. The Contra boys had been harassing and worrying at the Revolution like terriers for almost ten years and were now being invited to the ballot vote by the war-weary Sandinistas.

FJ's CX rarely made the three-star category which would have propelled it into the inboxes of the decision makers. Spedding's objective was to upgrade the quality and quantity of the CX coming out of Managua Station, and for this she needed the co-operation of the New Boy. She had long ago given up on Wycliffe; good riddance to that feeble ponce and his container-load of orchids.

Now that Managua Station's performance was under review, the pressure was on Spedding to deliver the goods. They desperately needed a success to allow them to stay in business. Otherwise it was a one-way ticket back to Century House on the Heathrow express via Miami, and *adios* to the overseas allowances and the servants.

When Vanessa Spedding wanted to, she could pull out the stops and be devastatingly charming. Assuming that Sinclair's Indian blood made him susceptible to flattery, this was the tack that she decided to take with him when they had their first 'get-to-know-each-other' lunch at the Intercontinental Hotel.

The hotel is one of the few remaining landmarks remaining in Managua after the earthquake in 1972, a distinctive pyramidal structure that used to feature on the nightly news shows in 1978 and 1979 at the height of the civil war. Back in those days it was also well known as the home of Howard Hughes, who had taken over the top floor, and as the base for the legions of foreign correspondents that had invaded the country. The majority of them ventured no further than the well-stocked bar where they were amply plied with information and misinformation by the battery of CIA agents and Tacho Somoza's spin doctors.

JIMAGUA

"There are Sandinistas and there are Sandinistas," FJ had told him over lunch shortly after the New Boy's arrival in Nicaragua.

In time Sinclair would come to appreciate the difference between the Sandinista types—the sickly looking cadres of the intelligentsia, social misfits of the resentful bourgeoisie with axes to grind, and the tanned salt-of-the-earth boys and girls from the countryside, with their crude humour and endearingly foul language.

One of the former was standing before him in a garden.

Now here is a man, thought Sinclair to himself as he sipped at his tumbler of Flor de Caña rum and watched the Sandinista, who I can relate to.

The Dutch Embassy was throwing a party. Outside, in the ninety-degree heat of the garden, fairy lights twinkled in the bushes and in the palm fronds. A band was playing salsa and sporadic dancing had broken out. Expensive perfumes floated thickly over the garden. Brenda stood at his side smoking, her shoulders nicely tanned and gleaming in the humidity. She looked captivating in her black evening gown. She had just introduced Sinclair to an individual by the name of Carlos Maxwell. Maxwell was smoking a cigar. He wore the olive fatigues and stripes of a major in the Sandinista army and he was dishevelled and unshaven. There were sweat marks under his armpits.

Another hybrid enters my life, Sinclair said to himself, another dangerous mutt. He could be my twin, my alter-ego. He listened carefully to Maxwell excuse himself for not having had time to change before the party, and then start to speak about the war on the Honduran border. He had just been up to Jinotega with Daniel Ortega, the head *Comandante*, to witness the aftermath of the latest Contra raid, he told them, and he had just choppered back. He then went on to impress Brenda with a graphic catalogue of the atrocities. He seemed to enjoy the expressions of wide-eyed horror on Brenda's face as he spoke of limbs and intestines and orphans and the effects of shrapnel from the latest generation of CIA-supplied mortars.

"The Contras," he declared to the small group that had gathered around him, "are hell-bent on revenge—they know their days are numbered now that our nation's elections have been agreed in principle, and this latest slew of attacks along the border is a final vindictive push designed to inflict the maximum damage. You see, *Compañera* van Kempen," he went on, addressing Brenda preferentially, "we have good reason to believe that there is a faction in Miami that doesn't want this war to end. They feel outmanoeuvred by Washington and, quite frankly, the prospect of peace is a disappointment for them, as well as highly unprofitable."

Maxwell was amusing to listen to because he spoke Spanish like a Nicaraguan peasant and drawled his English like an Oxford-educated aristocrat. He switched between the two languages effortlessly and humorously. He also switched with ease between grisly descriptions of the horrors of war and urbane jokes about the latest peccadillos of certain members of the Diplomatic Corps, about which he seemed unusually well informed.

He makes my Brenda laugh a little too easily, thought Sinclair, irritated by a sudden twinge of jealousy. He managed to control it as the professional in him took over. He would deal with it later, he told himself, tucking the dark little emotion into one of the many operational compartments of his mind, like leading a small animal into a cage. In a second his mind was clear again and he returned to the reading of his quarry.

Maxwell was a few years older, and like Sinclair, he was an awkward mix: a light-eyed mestizo—a *gato*, as light-eyed men were called in Nicaragua— yet dark-haired. He must go down well with the women here; Sinclair had heard that a pair of blue or green or even wolf-grey eyes like his own were a passport to carnal bliss in this country of brown. Unlike your run-of-the-mill Sandinista officer, Maxwell's skin was not tanned but had the unhealthy pallor of a deskman or someone who worked only at night or in the shadows.

"He even looks like me," Sinclair mused, studying the man casually above the clinking ice cubes in his glass.

Like Sinclair, Maxwell was an intelligence officer, a rising star in the Sandino-Cuban Military-Intelligence *apparat*.

Sinclair knew a lot about Carlos Maxwell a long time before he ever met him in the flesh. In fact he had almost forgotten Maxwell's real name. The files referred to him only by his codename SNAPPER. A lot of planning had gone into that first seemingly casual encounter at the Dutch Embassy. Before making first contact, Sinclair had devoted the last two months to updating the Station's file on SNAPPER. The fact is that Maxwell had been tasked as one of Sinclair's targets for recruitment by Mackie, the 'P' officer in charge of Central America, well before Sinclair had even arrived in Managua.

SNAPPER was one of MI6's first targets to be selected randomly with the help of technology. A new cross-referencing system had just been installed in the archives of Registry deep under Century House. It foreshadowed the internet search engines of today. It allowed a tasking 'P' officer to look for new targets for his agents in the field—he had only to type in a single word, 'Nicaragua' in this case, and all sort of cross-references from all sorts of files would pop up, including the long-forgotten records of Personnel.

Maxwell was half-Scottish, like Sinclair, and half-Nicaraguan. On his mother's side, he was the grandson of one of the Revolution's first martyrs, a businessman called Luis H. Salazar who had died at the hands of Anastasio 'Tacho' Somoza's secret police in 1947 after being discovered with a houseful of dynamite. There was a footnote to the file that informed the reader that grandpa's martyrdom was not entirely altruistic or motivated by patriotism. He was just trying to get his own back because old man Tacho had stiffed him in a couple of land deals and expropriated Salazar's properties in the mine-rich interior of the country. These details were conveniently overlooked by history and the Sandinistas even named one of their more successful urban guerrilla units in his memory: the Luis H. Salazar Brigade.

Maxwell's father had been an expatriate banker and had died of malaria while Maxwell was still at school. His mother, who never reconciled herself to the never-ending tragedies of her country, the worst being the death of her famous father, followed by the earthquake in 1972 and now the war, lived a sedated existence in the suburbs of Miami.

Like Sinclair, almost uncannily like Sinclair, Maxwell had also been an overseas boy and was a Catholic. He had been educated at Ampleforth and at St Antony's College, Oxford, where he had read politics, philosophy and economics, or PPE.

Now here was the interesting part of the SNAPPER file: it was at St Antony's, known in Oxford as the 'spy college', that young Carlos had, like Sinclair, felt a discreet tap on his shoulder. Like Sinclair, Carlos had been through the selection procedure, the interviews at Darby Gardens and the Sisby but, unlike Sinclair (and here was the hook, as they called it in MI6, the axis around which the whole case turns, the crux, the *point*), Carlos Maxwell had failed to get in on the last round.

Rereading the file late one night in Registry before leaving for Managua, Sinclair had carefully memorized the reasons noted in the minutes of the Selection Committee for turning down Maxwell's application.

Intellect: Pass. Academically he had excelled (viz. ecstatic references from his tutors at St Antony's, a likely First).

Social: Pass. His social skills were good. He was personable and fluent and had the attractive and versatile personality that spies need in order to role play effectively and persuade others to break the law and put themselves in harm's way. He had also held his drink well at the cocktail party at the end of the Sisby, where he was plied liberally with Whitehall G&Ts by his eager, watchful hosts.

But sadly, it was something that was totally beyond his control that tripped him up. It was Maxwell's origins that proved to be his downfall.

Psychology: Fail. Dr Stevenson (the same grandmotherly psychologist that had interviewed Sinclair in the backrooms of Whitehall ten years later) noted a deep-seated emotional instability within candidate Maxwell. It had to do with her probing the candidate's feelings about his mixed family background, especially the murder of his grandfather and the effect it had on his mother. Candidate unable to dissociate himself fully from the current situation in Nicaragua. Candidate does not appear to be British in his core. Although the candidate is able to lie fluently, Dr Stevenson noted a disturbing evasion when Candidate was asked what nationality he considers himself.

"Despite an attractive manner on the surface," she concluded in the memo, "the centre of gravity of his personality is not solid and reliable enough for the work of Her Majesty's SIS. In short, he is not *solid* enough, not *centred* enough—not British to the core. We fear that Candidate may one day be susceptible to split loyalties and present a security risk."

In other words, the failed applicant for MI6's 1978 intake was a traitor in the making, an excellent candidate for recruitment in 1989, depending which side he ended up on. Carlos Maxwell would make the wrong type of spy.

"Not one of us," Mackie had said at their third and final tasking meeting prior to Sinclair's departure. "Not one of the spies who are recruiters and agent handlers, but a Joe, an *asset*, a *source*. A traitor."

Maxwell was a person with a character flaw that could and should be mercilessly exploited and manipulated on behalf of Her Britannic Majesty by those whose moral fibre was more reliable and less complicated.

"You chip away at that seismic flaw that runs through his personality, George Sinclair, until you undermine the whole personality. It then collapses upon itself quite nicely. You put the pieces back together again and he becomes your man. Understand?"

Humpty Dumpty. Or Frankenstein. Psychological engineering—that's how they had referred to it at the Fort. Yes, Sinclair understood very well, Sir.

There was of course no record in the files of how the candidate reacted to the rejection, but it is likely that something radical did happen in Carlos Maxwell's mind after being turned down by MI6, because the next thing that happened, the file said, was that to the horror of his tutors, he abandoned St Antony's just before his Finals (he was a sure bet for a First), left England, and never returned. A copy of his flight boarding pass was stapled in the file as proof. It was July, 1978. He had obviously snapped.

The next entry in his file was a memo dated August 1980, from the CIA station in Miami, marked Classified Level 3. Maxwell had appeared on their radar screens as an intelligence operative in the Sandinista movement. From then on, the file continued to backtrack as the analyst rebuilt the missing months of Carlos Maxwell's career from bits and pieces of secondary and tertiary sources. In the file, Sinclair saw the chits that were requests for additional data submitted to the CIA station at the Embassy in Grosvenor Square.

The CIA had had their eye on Carlos Maxwell for some time, but had not managed to identify a suitable hook with which to pull him in. What to do with Maxwell became the subject of an inter-service liaison meeting between the Cousins and the Friends in Grosvenor Square. Everyone agreed that MI6 had done a good job identifying the hook which would pull in this new source of military intelligence in Nicaragua. Maxwell had by then been codenamed SNAPPER by some fishing enthusiast in the Latin America Controllerate (and not because he had 'snapped' after being rejected by the Service). The decision to allocate the potential asset to MI6 was not controversial, and SNAPPER was soon traded for control of another asset in a neighbouring country. The Americans had bigger fish to fry those days.

Back at Century House it was felt that George Sinclair was the perfect angler to pull in SNAPPER. After all, they had a lot in common, come to think of it, being Catholics, and Scottish fathers and all that. 'All that' meaning a touch of the tar brush.

"Actually, you two should be able to get on like a house on fire," joked Mackie, Sinclair's easygoing tasking 'P' officer, during one of the many pre-mission briefings.

In July 1978, when Maxwell returned to his mother's country despite her desperate pleas, the fighting in Nicaragua was intensifying. It appeared at last that the Revolution did have a good chance of becoming reality, as it did indeed a full twelve months later. Maxwell enrolled himself at the UCA, the Jesuit-run University of Central America in Managua, and let himself become caught up straight away in the feverish euphoria of the student movement.

In no time he was acting as a courier for the *Tendencia Proletaria* faction, the urban network of the Frente Sandinista de Liberación Nacional, or FSLN. His job was to deliver hand-made Molotov cocktails and coded messages to terrified students hiding in their safe houses in Managua, Masaya and Granada. Those were the days when the anti-terrorist EEBI patrols, the Israeli-trained elite killers led by Tacho Somoza's son, Tachito, would pick you up in their jeeps, known as BECATS, shoot you in the head and dump you by the side of the road just for being young and on the streets. It cannot have been easy work.

When it became clear that he had been targeted for elimination by Tachito's bogeymen, SNAPPER managed to escape the city in early 1979 (around the time of the business with Guy Underhill at the College, Sinclair noted) and joined a column of half-starved fighters of the *Guerra Popular Prolongada*—GPP—faction in the hills of central Nicaragua, across the lake in the province of Chontales. There, they played a nerve-wracking cat and mouse game with the anti-guerrilla EEBI patrols. After months of exhaustion and near collapse, it was decided that *Compañero* Maxwell, as he became known, should return to the city.

In those days the FSLN was still a splintered and dysfunctional collection of rival factions. The interesting thing about *Compañero* Maxwell, and what bought him to the attention of the Sandinista leadership and their Cuban patrons, was that he was credited with a part in building the political bridge between the *Tendencia Proletaria* and the GPP faction. The GPP was the Cuban-backed Marxist guerrilla faction which followed the teachings of Che Guevara, advocating peasant uprisings and a long war of attrition in the countryside as the path to victory. The *Tendencia Proletaria* crowd, on the other hand, believed that the Revolution could only be won in the slums and back streets of the cities. Because he now knew both sets of Sandinistas, Carlos Maxwell took a political initiative. The message that Maxwell carried from the jungles of Chontales back into Managua was a crucial one, since it proposed a meeting between the heads of the factions, including the newly formed *Tercerista* group—the third way—with the objective of agreeing a final unified strategy, because without one, he begged them to realize, the Revolution would be stillborn.

"You're not really British, are you, Dr Sinclair?" Maxwell said, watching the dancers, when Brenda had gone to fetch more drinks. "In fact you're like me. You're an overseas boy, aren't you? A half-breed. A mongrel. A mutt, as your *Cousins* the gringos would say. I can spot a *Friend* a mile away. Takes one to know one."

Before Sinclair could digest the insider's jargon, Maxwell had turned and looked Sinclair in the eye and said, with a wistful smile, "we make the best spies, you know."

Sinclair almost choked on his Flor de Caña rum at the brazen indiscretion, and then blushed at how easily he had been tripped up.

"Don't worry, *Compañero*, no one cares what is said at parties like these, at least not at this stage of the party."

Maxwell said this good-naturedly in his Oxford drawl, nodding towards the dancers—drunk Dutch diplomats groping at their guests and sweating Americans with their crew cuts and overcooked necks dancing stiffly with sloe-eyed, honey-skinned young women on the prowl for foreign catch.

Sinclair was at a loss for words. Maxwell seemed pleased with the effect of his little joke. He patted Sinclair's arm and said, before straightening his camouflaged combat tunic and making ready to leave: "Give Brenda my regards, but there is something I have to take care of at the office."

The office? It was nearly midnight, for fuck's sake. And Sinclair knew that

Maxwell's office was in the Coyotepe, the fort that acted as the HQ of the Sandinista security and intelligence service.

"Of course," nodded Sinclair, still recovering.

"We need to talk, you and I. Granada would be best. Come to El Mango, my island in the lake on Saturday. Ask any of the boatmen, they'll find it. And bring your little girl, and of course the lovely Brenda. I'll introduce you to *my* girls. A splendid time will be had by all. Toodle pip."

It didn't surprise Sinclair that Maxwell knew about Ximena or that he had taken up with Brenda van Kempen. You didn't have to be a spy to know that. Nicaragua is after all a small country and gossip, preferably malicious, is the national pastime. Nicas are obsessed with parentage and genealogy and per-sonal relationships—Managua is a smaller community still, and the expatriate community, well, that speaks for itself.

Sinclair's relationship with Brenda was not meant to be a secret. Quite the opposite, in fact—it was good cover, totally kosher and approved by the Head Boys in London. Brenda had cottoned on pretty quickly that Sinclair was not really a lowly Third Secretary (Commercial). He had received the green light from London to endow her with 'limited consciousness'. That meant that as a trusted public servant from a friendly country, she could be made aware that he was an intelligence officer but should not be conscious of the details of his operations. She settled for this arrangement without a fuss. She was not an inquisitive woman at heart, after all.

Having Brenda and Ximena in tow enabled Sinclair to tour the country and service his dead-letter drops at weekends, and to make day trips, to make a pass at a Joe, without arousing the suspicions that he might were he on his own. This technique had been recommended as sound tradecraft at the Fort. So, as one might have guessed, Sinclair's taking up with Brenda van Kempen had not been entirely a case of love at first sight.

Their sex was kind and uncomplicated, and Sinclair genuinely liked the Dutch girl. They talked about books and films, liked food, and they both enjoyed exploring their host country and dealing with its quirky inhabitants. And the best thing was that Sinclair had found someone acceptable to Ximena, his dark watcher.

And whenever he caught Ximena watching him, he remembered the sleepy, hungry eyes of the dead Helen Henshaw, and redoubled his resolution to play with a straight bat.

*

On the drive to Granada that Saturday, Brenda and Ximena sat in the back of the Embassy's Land Rover, giggling and teasing and tickling each other. It didn't take much to amuse Brenda, and Sinclair liked the child-like side to her personality.

Ximena loved imitating other people's accents, and she did a very passable imitation of Brenda's guttural singsong Lowlander's English. Brenda's attempts to mimic Ximena were less successful. Ximena's own accent had become strange and difficult to place. If you listened carefully enough you could catch echoes of her father's Goan inflections and her dead mother's shortened Antipodean vowels. The Northern English vowels of her early childhood had almost disappeared and became less perceptible with every passing day that she was away from England.

Sinclair was pleased by how easily Brenda had been accepted by his fickle daughter. It was extraordinary how Ximena's personality had blossomed since Brenda had appeared on the scene. She laughed more, and the playful side of her personality, which in the past had strayed on the dark side of playfulness (which is cruelty), was brighter. In short, Ximena, now almost twelve and approaching the dangerous minefield of adolescence, seemed at ease with herself and with the world. Brenda, it seemed, had succeeded in distracting her from the dark side of things. The fierce black light that used to burn in his daughter's eyes in England was less apparent these days.

We'll see how long that lasts, Sinclair thought to himself darkly, as they passed the smouldering hulk of the active volcano whose massive crater is known as the Gate of Hell, on the way into the town of Masaya. If his own adolescence was anything to go by, Ximena's would be, well, to put it mildly, *interesting*. He made a mental note to check Ximena's birth chart to calculate the cycles of Saturn in her destiny, just as Grannyjee had done for him before he had been sent away from home.

They had passed Masaya, where they say that the thieves are so talented that they can steal your socks without removing your shoes.

"And what do we think of Carlos Maxwell?" he asked the girls nonchalantly, looking in the rearview mirror to catch Brenda's expression.

"He reminds me a bit of you, in fact," said Brenda, tickling Ximena. The little girl immediately burst into a flood of giggles which developed into a fit of uncontrollable hiccups.

"No, really, seriously . . ."

"Well, yes, actually he does remind me of you in some ways. He could be your elder brother," replied Brenda in her cheerful Dutch way.

"Is that good or bad?"

"Bad, father. Very . . . *very* . . . bad indeed," laughed Ximena, in between hiccups, delighted with her joke.

They were entering the outskirts of Granada, the grand old lady of Nicaragua's colonial past, known as the Gran Sultana on the lake. There was not a cloud in the sky and behind the white buildings of the city the lake awaited them. It was turning out to be a fine day.

EL MANGO

It took them a good forty minutes to penetrate deep into the archipelago of tropical islets by boat. The boatman knew exactly where they wanted to go— *"Donde el Señor Maxwell, si, así es, el Mango, pues . . ."*

The water was emerald green and thick and still. In the background loomed the less than perfect cone of the Mombacho: it had blown its top many thousands of years ago and the four hundred or so islands that littered the lake were in fact remnants of the side of the volcano that had landed in the water.

The shores of Granada receded into the heat of early afternoon, and soon the colonial towers of its white cathedral were like shimmering mirages under the massive blue vault of the Nicaraguan sky. Still not a cloud in sight. The boat passed island after island, some with spectacular mansions and yachts where Nicaragua's rich and famous had their weekend retreats, others smaller with less conspicuous cabins or shacks. More than a couple flew the Stars and Stripes—retired *gringos*, the last of the Mohicans defying the Sandinistas, the boatman confirmed.

As they passed the houses in the lake, the boatman would call out the names of the owners: *"Aquél es de Enrique Chamorro . . . ésta es de Argüello, primo hermano de la Violeta . . ."* and so on. Everyone was related in this little country. Everyone had a rich or a poor relative.

The majority of the illustrious families were now in exile in Miami, having been pushed out by vindictive young men and women, the sons and daughters of Sandino, whole families ripped apart by the Revolution. The ensuing land and property grab had been known popularly as *la piñata*, in reference to a popular Central American birthday party game. With a stick, the blindfolded birthday boy or girl smashes a hollow clay doll full of sweets and treats which rain down on you in revolutionary largesse.

Eventually they came to a medium-sized island, more like a small hillock emerging from the water, covered in thick foliage and palm trees. They heard a dog barking. Sinclair's practised eye caught an antenna and a grey satellite dish nestling among the mango trees that gave the island its name. As they moored at the small dock, they saw between the leaves a cabaña with a roof thatched with dried palm fronds, and a veranda. Carlos Maxwell and a woman were coming down the path to greet them. The dog was barking its head off and trampolining into the air on the dock, more in excitement than in menace.

The dog was a boxer called Heidi and turned out to be the gentlest of souls, despite the severe look of her snub-nosed features and the insolent challenge of her bulging eyes. She let Ximena pet her and squeeze her. She was Maxwell's girl.

"Heidi is what they call in France a *jolie laide*," said Brenda, as they sipped their coffee. "A *jolie laide* is a girl who is so ugly that that she is irresistible."

They all laughed, even Ximena.

Maxwell's other girl was Jamila. She was introduced just as Jamila, no family name, just plain Jamila from Beirut, or to be more precise, she explained in French-inflected English, from Shatila camp. It turned out that Jamila was a Palestinian, and a refugee at that, the genuine article.

As Jamila served them a second helping of thick sweet Arabic coffee, Carlos Maxwell told Sinclair that he had met her in Beirut in 1982, just after the Israeli invasion of the Lebanon. At first he neglected to say precisely what he was doing in that benighted city in the summer of 1982. However, through his oblique references to Havana and Fatah and the Fascists of the Falange, Sinclair deduced that he had been sent by his Cuban sponsors to complete his training in urban guerrilla along the Green Line and in the camps of the PLO and Hezbollah. This was genuine urban warfare and made his experiences among the idealistic boys and girls of the FSLN in the Nicaraguan civil war seem like an apprenticeship. Hands-on training, Maxwell called it, training with live rounds, which tended more often than not to be Israeli mortar shells and brick-sized machine-gun bullets which the attack helicopters of Operation Peace for Galilee regularly strafed them with. He had come a long way from the dreaming spires and the ivy of St Antony's College.

He had met Jamila in a camp run by George Habash's PFLP, where she was graduating in the black arts of the *plastique*. He hinted that she had had a hand in the explosion that killed Bashir Gemayel, and that she had connections with Abu Nidal.

Jamila, Maxwell continued, was now alone in the world. Jamila sipped her coffee and listened to her own story in silence, an inward look in her eyes. Her parents, two of her three sisters, and her idolized brother Samir were all dead, resting in the peace of the Almighty, the Merciful, after their short and brutish lives. Most of the inhabitants of the village where the family had fled just before the slaughter at Shatila and Sabra in 1982, a couple of days after the pig Gemayel had been dispatched with a car bomb, had been pulverized by the Cadillac-sized shells of the *USS New Jersey* in 1984. Jamila had been on a mission then, thanks be to Allah—he would not say what kind of mission precisely, but Sinclair could guess—and counted that as her second escape—first Shatila, now the good ship New Jersey.

Sinclair had to make a concentrated effort to keep his eyes off Jamila's body, which was athletic and blessed with many firm curves. She wore a black T-shirt above khakis with many pockets marked with the Israeli Defence Force stencil in Hebrew characters. It must have been a trophy. She also wore the red and black kerchief of the Sandinistas around her bronzed neck, which gleamed in the humidity. And, Sinclair noted for future reference, she had the eyes of a killer.

DUENDE

It was turning out to be a marvellous afternoon. Ximena was entranced by Jamila's dark, dangerous looks, and fascinated by Heidi. She was gorging herself on a mango as she carefully monitored the talk of the grown-ups. Sinclair had rarely seen her so happy.

Carlos Maxwell beamed at his new friends from his hammock. He seemed to be enjoying the attention. He told Ximena a story about the *duendes*, the little people of Nicaraguan folklore, and about magic mangoes, just like the one she was devouring.

"Did you know, Ximena, that in these parts, quite near here, there exists a forest of magic mangoes? No, I'm not joking or making it up. Up there on the slopes of the Mombacho there is a forest of fruit trees. The story goes that one day, before the Revolution, a troop of Boy Scouts set off from the Coyotepe—" this with a knowing glance in Sinclair's direction "—that's the old Spanish fort that used to be the Scouts' headquarters—for a hike on the slopes of the volcano. The problem was that they finished their rations too early. Soon it was dark and they went to sleep in their tents, without any supper. The next morning the Scouts were ravenous, Ximena, and picked the fruit off the trees. And the fruit was delicious, and they couldn't stop eating it because it was so sweet. But the Indian guide they were with told them not to touch any of the fruit on the trees, because in these parts the little people—*los duendes*—are very jealous of their fruit, the most delicious of which is the golden mango, just like the one you are feasting on right now. He told the boys that as long as they held any of the magic fruit, their path home would be blocked. And that is how it was, Ximena, the boys kept on plucking the fruit off the trees and eating it and they could not find their way out of the forest. They even say that some of the boys voted never to leave the forest anyway, because the fruit was so delicious that they could live off it for ever—a bit like the Garden of Eden, I suppose, or the Lotus Eaters."

"What are Lotus Eaters?" Ximena asked.

"People who forget their past, my dear," said Maxwell, with another glance towards Sinclair.

"And so," he continued, "they say that the troop wandered round and round in circles for almost a week, they simply were not able to find the path out of the forest. Their parents and relatives became worried and sent out search parties. Some of the old folk on these *isletas* can remember the day when it seemed like all of Granada turned out to look for the boys, combing the side of the volcano, but to no avail. Finally the Scouts were persuaded by the Indian guide to give in and each of the Scouts was made to empty his rucksack and pockets of fruit, even the boys who had become *addicted* to it. And sure enough, only when they decided to respect the property of the little people was the Indian guide permitted to find the path again and lead them out of the enchanted forest."

POST MERIDIEN

The girls were in the house preparing lunch, under the roof of thatched palms. They were getting along famously and their chatter and laughter blended in sweetly with the chirping of the *chocoyos*, a flock of miniature green parakeets that inhabited the trees of Maxwell's island.

Sinclair needed time to think. He asked to go to the bathroom. Even though the house was small Jamila insisted on escorting him.

The secrets of a house are in its bedrooms and bathrooms and cellars. Sinclair walked slowly through Maxwell and Jamila's bedroom on his way to the bathroom, scanning, registering and memorizing the contents of the room

for future reference. The bed was unmade and hinted at recent and interrupted lovemaking. Discarded khakis and T-shirts had been thrown across a
chair. An FAL assault rifle with telescopic lens was casually propped up against
the wall next to Heidi's basket. Sinclair saw black and white photos of Major
Maxwell with various luminaries including Fidel and Torrijos and Ortega and
the other *Comandantes*. Maxwell with Regis Debray, Maxwell with Jamila
overlooking a twilit city that must have been Beirut, the dog Heidi sitting
between them. That dog must have seen things most of us have not, Sinclair
thought. Maxwell with a Vietnamese gentleman. Maxwell standing next to a
very short man wearing coke-bottle spectacles.

Sinclair spotted the grey plastic extension chord that led up the wall to the
antenna on the roof. Attached to the wire he saw the short-wave transmitter
he knew Maxwell used to communicate with the Coyotepe and with DGI
Centro in Havana.

A casual observer, Sinclair stopped to inspect the contents of the book-
shelves. There were paperbacks and old hardbacks—the orange spines of the
Penguin editions of Greene, then Ian Fleming, Borges, a Simon Raven series,
Fowles's *The Magus*, Le Carré, García Márquez, the gay Sandinista novelist
Sergio Ramírez. Then there was the heavier fare—treatises by Fidel, Debray,
Ernesto Che Guevara and a hefty tome by Maxwell's master Tomás Verga,
head of the Sandinista intelligence apparat and the most influential and ruth-
less *Comandante* in the nine-man ruling directorate. The most influential
because he was the closest to Fidel.

The only concession to luxury in the room was a highly polished humidor
on the night table. It was engraved with Cyrillic script, a dedication in Russian
perhaps, and gave that corner of the room the scent of a gentleman's club.

Something made him turn and look behind him. Jamila had gone back to
the kitchen. Standing in the doorway, her head cocked, watching him with
intense curiosity, stood Heidi, Maxwell's familiar.

Maxwell stubbed out his cigar on the dirt floor under his hammock then put
his hands behind his head and gazed up at the ceiling of palm fronds.

"I've been waiting for someone like you to turn up for a while now," he said
at last in his lazy Oxford drawl.

Sinclair didn't respond. Time passed, slowly and languidly. Through the
trees Sinclair watched the afternoon clouds assembling over the Mombacho.

Maxwell had lit up again. With his free hand Maxwell was stroking Heidi
between her clipped ears. The dog slumbered under the hammock, listening

intently to the sound of her master's voice with one ear, the other cocking occasionally in the direction of the visitor, whenever he spoke or when his rocking chair creaked. The nose on her square black muzzle twitched with every change of scent borne on the lake breeze.

They were well into their second tumbler of Havana Club. Maxwell had persuaded Sinclair to try a *cohiba* from Havana.

"There's plenty more where that came from," said Maxwell with a wink, stroking an imaginary beard in a gesture well known to Cubans.

The aromatic smoke drifted lazily up into the canopy of trees that covered the little island, playing among the mango leaves and palm fronds and the *chocoyito* parakeets. Afternoon sunlight filtered down through the trees and the island seemed lost in time as they sat there in the placid green pool of Lake Nicaragua.

"This really is splendid, Carlos, what you have here. It's as if time has stopped in its tracks. The island that time forgot. It could be the 16th century. Sir Henry Morgan could be just around the corner, sailing up from Rio San Juan, to raid Granada, the Gran Sultana of the Lake. I've always been fascinated with pirates . . ."

"I prefer the 19th century, myself," answered Maxwell. "Did you know, for example, that one of these islands has a Spanish fort on it which was attacked by William Walker?"

"Ah yes," Sinclair replied, "the famous *gringo* pirate who took over the country..."

"We'll talk about Mr Walker later. There is much to be learned from his experiences in this country."

Heidi was now wide awake and licking herself without the least hint of modesty.

"*Buller licked his private parts with the gusto of alderman drinking soup,*" Sinclair said, quoting Graham Greene.

"*The Human Factor,*" replied Maxwell, "is my favourite Greene. How curious. Did you know that I met him in 1979? Was *that* in my file at Century House, by the way? He was a great friend of the Sandinistas, you know."

"And of Torrijos," parried Sinclair, not to be outdone.

"And of Fidel," Maxwell replied, stroking his imaginary beard again.

There was another interlude, as Jamila, Brenda and Ximena came back to the table with another round of thick, sweet Arab coffee. Sinclair noticed that Ximena now grasped Jamila by the hand.

PUSSYFOOTING

"Why am I being so indiscreet, George? Why was I indiscreet at the party? Could it be the rum? Could it be that in my old age I can't take my drink any more?"

"Keep talking," Sinclair replied coolly, the sly professional, holding his own drink like a gentleman. This time he was determined not to choke on it.

Maxwell puffed on his cigar and then closed his eyes. He seemed to have drifted off to sleep. All Sinclair could hear for a while was the sound of the girls laughing in the kitchen and occasional birdsong among the palm fronds rustling in the afternoon breeze. Heidi's ears twitched in her sleep.

"Well, I'm listening," he nudged. Maxwell opened his eyes again and looked into the trees overhead.

"Well, *Señor*, I'm being indiscreet because I'm prepared to cut to the chase, to cut to the quick, to come to the point, not to beat about the bush—aren't they wonderful, incidentally, all those lovely English expressions? And Heidi here is my bullshit detector. She bites if she hears bullshit. She also bites Somocistas and Imperialist Spies, don't you, my good little girl, my *jolie laide*?"

"Pray continue, then."

"We need to do a deal today, Sinclair, before we get off this enchanted island, where time has stopped, and go back to the real world. We're like mirror images you and I—twins of destiny, just two sides of the same bad coin. In Cuba, they calls twins *jimaguas*. One of us has to sell his soul this afternoon. And I really don't believe in the dance and all that pussyfooting that they train us to do. You see, in this part of the world we don't have the luxury of time. If you want proof of that, let me take you up to the border one weekend, Jinotega perhaps, so that you can see the limbs and the charred bodies and the orphans . . ."

"Sounds good. *Jimaguas*? Hmm. Interesting. But I'm still not convinced."

"I'm being indiscreet because I happen to think that one of us really doesn't have much of a choice. No choice at all, not unless one is prepared to be false to oneself. *Maktub*, as Jamila likes to say, '*it is written.*' No point trying to alter one's destiny."

"Someone I knew also used to say that to me."

"Really?"

"Yes. My grandmother. And what kind of a choice are we talking about?"

"Come off it, George, you know as well as I do. It's either you or me, isn't it? We both have masters, and our masters have expectations. We wouldn't be pussyfooting around each other if that wasn't the case."

"And how are we to decide, then? Toss of a coin? Debate? Gut feeling? Perhaps the dice? How do *you*, *Carlos Maxwell*, decide things, without being untrue to yourself? And anyway, what do you see in me? I'm just a lowly Third Secretary (Commercial)."

"I see a half-breed, like me. An outsider. An overseas boy. You may have made it to the inside of the tent, and they may have left me out of the tent, but if you really analyze it, there ain't much difference between us, is there, *amigo*?"

Silence.

"Go ahead, make your pitch, and then I'll make mine, then we'll see . . ."

Sinclair still kept quiet. Sometimes the best thing to do or say is nothing.

"Well, go ahead, I'm waiting, I won't bite, it's your job after all, that's what you are here for, isn't it. At least let's be grown up about it. It's just a game for adults, after all, isn't it, this spying business?"

Finally Sinclair replied, exasperated. The conversation wasn't turning out as he had planned.

"It's just not meant to work this way, that's all. I'm meant to cultivate you, earn your trust over time, drop subtle hints to see how you react, and pluck you when you're ripe, you know the drill . . . In fact Castro's DGI, which I understand trained you Sandinista boys, is a hell of a lot better at it than us Brits."

" 'Us Brits'. Now there's an interesting expression."

"Sarcasm will get you nowhere, *Compañero* Maxwell."

And that's precisely where they were getting—nowhere.

"Let's talk about Darby Gardens and the Sisby, then," said Sinclair, as he had rehearsed in the car that morning. "Would you like to know why you were turned down by the Service?"

Maxwell did not skip a beat. He remained rocking in his hammock, his hand dangling down and stroking the back of Heidi's ears. He answered with another question.

"Do you ever ask yourself why we cut boxers' ears?"

Foe a moment Sinclair was flummoxed.

"You know, it is extremely painful for them. So much so that it is now illegal in many countries to prune the ears of dogs—you see, the edges of the cut ear remain extremely sensitive, for all their lives. Look . . ." He ran his finger along the shiny scar tissue of Heidi's clipped ear. The dog's ear fluttered and she opened her eyes in alarm. "Why do we torture those that we love? By cutting their ears?"

"Enlighten me."

"I can't. It's so fucking cruel that I can't understand why they do it. That's the simple answer."

"I'm sorry, I don't follow you."

"The fact is I adopted Heidi. When I was in Cuba. Her owner was an Italian girl from the Red Brigades. She died, the girl, that is. Heidi is a *guajira*, a country girl from Camagüey, aren't you, *mi muchachita*? I would never have cut your ears as a puppy."

This little interlude had given Maxwell time to think and evaluate his next move in the chess game.

"Thank you, Carlos. And now, would you like to hear why we wouldn't have you?"

"Not really. I know why."

"Why, then?"

"Because I'm not one of you. It's obvious. That bitch psychologist saw right through me when she asked me what nationality I considered myself. I saw her frown as she wrote her notes."

"So what would you say," he lied, "if I said to you that the Service admits that it made a mistake in 1978, that it regrets its decision, and now wants you back as part of the team? That MI6 wants its own piece of Carlos Maxwell, of the Carlos Maxwell success story."

"Fuck them, that's what I would say, *Compañero*. Fuck MI6, and all who sail in her. Present company excluded, of course."

"They really mean it, you know, my masters. They know they fucked up. Did you know that they sacked that psychologist bitch afterwards?" My God, I am a phenomenally good liar, he congratulated himself. "They found out that she was batting for the other side, didn't they? She'd been systematically turning down any male she thought was vaguely attractive and would succeed in the Service. That just left the place full of pushy women and mediocre, ugly males like your humble servant."

"So that's how your pillow-biting colleague Spedding made it into the Service, I suppose?"

"No comment."

"I see."

There was a pause.

"Of course," Sinclair resumed, "you wouldn't be able to join us as a desk officer, in the traditional sense, like me. It wouldn't work, you're too well known already by your own side. You'd be an agent in place, if you see what I mean."

"Ah," Maxwell said, "the wrong kind of spy. The one outside the tent. Outside the tent looking in, while Dr George Sinclair sits inside the tent pissing out. Yes, I *do* see what you mean."

And then, after another pause, Maxwell delivered his decision. "I'm sorry, George, it won't work that way. Your pitch is, and I hope you'll forgive me for saying so, rather feeble. Pathetic, in fact. You wouldn't have passed the DGI training course in Havana with that one, I'm afraid."

Heidi farted, in solidarity with her master.

"Now let me make *my* pitch. I think the best way is if you let me tell you a story. It's something that happened to me at Ampleforth. I assume they told you that I'm Old Ampleforth?" Maxwell chuckled from his hammock. "*You know, the place that always used to thrash the shit out of the College at rugby . . .*"

"*Touché.* But cricket was my game, not rugger. I scored a century against Ampleforth in 1980."

"I know. Someone told us that you took five for forty-seven with your devious leg spin."

Through the haze of alcohol, because they were now on their fourth or fifth—Sinclair had lost count—Sinclair's heart skipped a beat.

Sinclair decided not to ask Maxwell who had given them this piece of information. With the mention of that cricket score the conversation had strayed into dangerous territory. There was the quicksand of intimacy, treachery afoot, something rotten . . .

Sinclair retreated and bought time. "You know, by the way, before you begin your story, what they say about the difference between Ampleforth and the College? The say that the Benedictines offer their boys the lessons of life on a plate, nicely cooked, *cordon bleu*. The Jesuits, on the other hand, provide their boys with a tin opener."

"I like that. And I think that they are right, whoever *they* are. 'Give me a boy before he's seven and I'll show you the man.' Isn't that what they say, too, your Jesuits?"

Maxwell had managed to stir up yet another uncomfortable memory from his school days—a vision of Guy Underhill in the Pit thumbing through *The Secret History of the Jesuits*. It was as if Maxwell had slipped into Sinclair's palace of memories through a back door and was now running amok in its most sensitive and tender recesses.

Maxwell caught Sinclair's frown.

"But don't worry, George, I have absolutely no loyalty to Ampleforth, nor to most institutions, in fact. Friendship is the institution that I am most loyal to. And loyalty itself. And now may I proceed?"

"Please."

"The story goes something like this: I had a friend at Ampleforth. Let's call him Jack. English as they come, Jack was. Now Jack was one of the truest friends a boy could want. He ignored the fact that I was a greasy dago—a *mestizo*—he truly liked me for what I was. We were rebellious. Neither of us could stand the Establishment, all that Catholic mumbo jumbo and religious gobbledygook, the racism and the rotten snobbishness of it all. We did a bit of drugs here and there—it was the seventies after all, what would you expect? One day they found my stash of drugs. They eventually found out that the gear was mine. But it was Jack they were really after. Need I go on?"

Sinclair, dumbfounded, thought he was dreaming. Maxwell had just invaded the most sacred room of his memory. He jumped up from his chair. Rather too quickly because Heidi looked up all of a sudden and growled as the strange man stumbled, caught suddenly in a dizzy tailspin.

"Steady as we go, old man," said Maxwell calmly from the hammock. "You know what they say about dogs, they can smell fear."

"Must have a pee . . . ," Sinclair mumbled, rushing down to the water's edge, where he forced himself to urinate into the placid waters of the pea-green lake while he thought furiously of how to play this one. This was probably the most serious delivery of the game, a true Yorker. It was worse even than Jerome O'Reilly's bodyliner which had nearly killed him at Prep School. Now how do I get out of *this* corner, he asked himself, watching the golden arc of his piss glinting in the failing tropical sunlight.

Coming back up the slope of the island to face the riddler in his hammock, Sinclair was still in a daze. He had been bowled out. Truly fucking yorked. On his way up he was intercepted by Brenda, who had seen him weaving his drunken way down to the water's edge.

"George, are you all right? It looks like you've seen a ghost," she said, rubbing up against him.

"More like the Devil," he said and continued bravely up the hill to face the sphinx.

AFRICA

"I think you've totally misunderstood me, Señor Sinclair. With that piece of intelligence I am giving you a gift. At first it may seem trivial to you. But it is something precious that you can use to advance your dastardly way up the food chain. I don't think I have to spell it out for you. Now go forth and procreate, as they say . . ."

"So you'll work for us?"

"You've misunderstood me again. Oh dear, Heidi, *what* shall we do with the drunken sailor?"

"I see, it's a token. A sign of your good faith. Of your *bona fides.*"

"Exactly. Make of it what you will. And there's more from where that came from." Again, stroking his imaginary beard. "Now, as a gentleman, I don't need to remind you that in these parts, like in Jamila's part of the world, hospitality and kindness must be reciprocated. Backs must be scratched . . ."

"I will have to get back to you on that one. So how did you know about my bowling score and my century against Ampleforth?"

"I heard it from the same person who told me about my friend Jack."

"Thank you . . ." Sinclair's head was beginning to clear. "But in the meantime, I need confirmation. The person who told you. Where does he work? I just need one word."

Sinclair already knew the answer.

"Africa."

On the boat ride back, Sinclair toyed with the word *jimagua*. Was he really Maxwell's twin? Brenda, for one, thought that they were alike.

He admitted to himself that he had reached another fork in the road. Ximena and Brenda were quiet. Ximena seemed exhausted and something had come over Brenda, a brooding look, lost in her thoughts. The boatman was silent too.

Below the darkening indigo of the sky the approaching city of Granada twinkled like fairy lights and threw tiny reflections off the oily surface of the lake.

On the drive back that evening, Ximena had fallen asleep from exhaustion on Brenda's lap. Brenda was silent and watched the falling dusk shroud the passing countryside as she stroked Ximena's hair absentmindedly.

Through the open window of the Land Rover came the smell of woodfires, the smell of Nicaragua, as the poor prepared their evening meals.

Now it was Sinclair who was lost in his thoughts, planning his next move, debating internally how to lay out the case to FJ and La Spedding on Monday morning.

As they were passing the Masaya volcano on their way into Managua, Brenda asked suddenly and without humour: "And what do we think of Jamila?"

Sinclair couldn't resist the temptation to score a petty victory: "She rather reminds me of you."

There was nothing but a bitter silence in return. He knew at once that he had walked into her trap and that his little joke had fallen flat on its face. When he looked in the rear-view mirror to gauge Brenda's reaction, what he saw instead were his daughter's watchful black eyes, quite awake now and narrow with suspicion.

Sinclair remembered his resolution about straight batting.

QUEERING THE PITCH

"The College. Magdalen. A very good provenance, my boy, excellent in fact." FJ might have been describing the wine. "David Blantyre has done us proud again," he drawled, referring to the Service's talent-spotter at Magdalen.

FJ's double-chins quivered with gusto as he spooned gravy into his mouth.

They were at La Marseillaise, Managua's only creditable French restaurant. Sinclair assumed that FJ, who was independently wealthy, would not be expensing this one. It was obvious that the lunch had a purpose other than office business: he had only to sit back and wait for the preposterous FJ to reveal his hand, and enjoy the food.

There was a pause. FJ took out a handkerchief and wiped his forehead, despite the sub-Arctic chill of the air-conditioning.

Both men ate silently and with absorption through turtles' eggs and stuffed quails, and drank efficiently through the Châteauneuf du Pape and Pinot Noir, Sinclair somehow managing to keep up with the sweating gourmand in front of him. He knew in advance that FJ took his food seriously and he went along with his host, eating steadily and with earnestness. Imitation is the highest and most subtle form of flattery, or so they had taught him at the Fort.

Apart from the food, which was first-class, lunch had been a prolonged and tedious affair. FJ had just finished recounting the highlights of his previous posting in Nairobi among the 'benighted Africans', as he called them. He was capping his resumé with a convoluted story, which he thought Sinclair might enjoy, being an anthropologist and all that. The tale concerned a houseboy who had killed a fellow servant with sorcery.

Sinclair laughed at the right times in careful appreciation as FJ knocked back the last of his Pinot.

Next came dessert, accompanied by a sweet Muscadet and another soliloquy, this time on the attributes of the African mind, from a purely post-colonial point of view, of course. While FJ continued his monologue, Sinclair's own mind was on Brenda van Kempen. He had finally managed to nail her the previous weekend on a trip up to the Selva Negra resort in the hills outside Matagalpa. This spa in the mountains had been founded by German colonists in the last century and was well known as a weekend getaway with convenient, discreet cabins and romantic walks through the rainforest.

When Ximena was snoring safely in her cot in the Bavarian cabin, and as the monkeys screamed their good nights across the trees to each other, Sinclair had lured the willing brunette into his bathtub. As FJ rambled on, Sinclair relived the soaping of Brenda's inner thigh.

He was about to visualize the next stage, which had been entirely satisfactory, when FJ said, with a slight belch, from out of nowhere: "Her Ladyship must be stopped."

Sinclair paused, a spoonful of sorbet halfway to his mouth.

In his mind's eye, Sinclair withdrew his hand from where it was going and for a moment the soaping of Brenda van Kempen's inner thigh ceased. For a split second Sinclair thought that his boss was referring to Brenda, but then he remembered that Her Ladyship was what FJ called Spedding behind her back.

FJ's face was flushed and he was sweating again despite the glacial blast of the air-conditioning. Dark patches of sweat stained his armpits.

"Indeed, FJ," Sinclair said, savouring the disloyalty of it all, especially because he'd already made up his mind that he couldn't stand the bitch Spedding either. There was definitely something worrying about her knowing looks, as if she knew things about Sinclair that she shouldn't have known.

"Of course," resumed FJ, munching on his pastry. He joined his fingers in a steeple, and affecting that look into the middle distance beyond Sinclair's left shoulder, which is the preserve of English academics, "we make a good deal less of sexual deviance these days than we used to . . ."

Sinclair let this pass in silence and merely nodded, unsure of what would follow next. FJ wasn't a man to look you in the eye, and he observed Sinclair indirectly, old fox that he was. He was the kind of man who watches his table-mates in the reflection of the silver.

"Beast with two backs, if you get my drift . . . it'll be the end of her—probably for most of us, what . . . but seriously, though, young George, she's definitely become a liability to the Service, I'm sure you'll agree. Problem is," FJ continued, addressing his cufflinks, "we need to send her home before she does any major damage. For her own good as well as ours. And for the good of the Service, of course. Look, you know, I've nothing really against dykes, nowadays most people accept them as the freaks of nature that they are. But Her Ladyship likes them off the streets, by all accounts. Imagine the consequences."

Sinclair realised that the homophobic outburst was a trifle odd coming from the likes of FJ, who, unaware of the irony, was now taking a deep draught of the sweet dessert wine. His evocation of Spedding's dry old English limbs frotting against firm, young, impoverished brown ones was proving no impediment to his appetite and the older man started on the cheese with relish.

Sinclair's interest was piqued, but he preferred to steer the conversation in another direction, temporarily, to give himself time to assess the situation. He wanted more time to savour the frisson felt by plotters the world over, because he now sensed in what direction FJ was ultimately nudging him in. It was like suddenly forcing yourself to think about mathematics or double physics on a Tuesday morning in a bid to prevent the disgrace of early ejaculation.

"Didn't I hear that she has some illustrious family connection to the Service?"

FJ masticated slowly as he ruminated on some long-forgotten memory. "Ah yes, Her Ladyship's brother, now mercifully deceased," he recalled, his mouth full of brie. "An old bore, if truth be told. Problem is, young George, death while in Service does great things for one's reputation, whether deservedly or not—not, in brother Spedding's case, I hasten to add. Her Ladyship has basked in the reflected glory of her brother for a long time, too long, in fact—the frightful bitch."

Now FJ's eyes bulged slightly and had an angry, unfocused look, as if he was inwardly reviewing a catalogue of past slights and defeats, both real and imagined.

"You mean," offered Sinclair, "the Spedding who was topped in Thailand in '76, that was her brother?"

A grim nod. FJ drew a podgy finger across his fleshy throat.

The head waiter took this as some kind of coded request and approached the table with an oily smirk. FJ waved him away.

"Decapitation. Some poppy baron sawed his head orff. With a kukri." He said this in his sweet, plummy voice, as he envisaged the blade slicing through the tough tendons of Her Ladyship's scraggy neck. But he was keen to get back to the point. "Look George, I am not a moralist, but an intelligence officer."

And a frightful bitch yourself, but never mind that, Sinclair replied sourly to himself.

"And I happen to care deeply about the Service. I know you do too. David Blantyre said we could count on you."

Sinclair tried to look as receptive and amenable as possible.

"Look, let's cut to the chase," FJ continued (my God, how many times have I been told that, thought Sinclair). "What I have to tell you may be unpleasant. Unpleasant in the extreme."

"Try me."

"No, really. Got your seatbelt on, my boy?"

"Go ahead. It takes a lot to shock me, FJ . . ."

But by now Sinclair had the stomach-churning suspicion that the bitch Spedding had dredged up some nasty career-wrecking secret from his past, and had told FJ or the Head Boys back in Century House—the drugs perhaps, or worse still, worst of all nightmares, the business with Helen, Jane, Bergsma and Aggarwal in Oxford. He felt as if the spectres of these dearly departed were lurking at his shoulder, like the waiters anxious for their tips, watching them closely as coffee was served. Between the two of them they had put away more food than a family of Nicaraguan peasants could consume in a month.

"Look, old man, I've heard it she's putting it about that she's got something on you. That your man SNAPPER is a fraud and is passing us duff gen."

He leaned back in his seat and watched Sinclair's face carefully to gauge the effects of the bombshell.

"What do you mean—you can't possibly . . . but that's fucking—" Sinclair struggled for words and then remembered Helen "— *monstrous* . . ."
Startled by this outburst, the other guests looked around at the two bad-mannered clients, one a *yanqui*, fat as a friar and stuffing his face, the other a sickly-looking young man with an outraged expression on his sallow maw, a *turco* probably.

"She brought it up at the last Ops Committee in London. Thinks

SNAPPER's too good to be true. Mackie's furious, as you can imagine. Mackie challenged her to prove it, but she said that for the time being she had no evidence. But that she was working on it. A woman's intuition, and all that. I'm *so* sorry, George, dear boy . . ."

He patted Sinclair's forearm in sympathy.

Sinclair instinctively felt for his wristwatch. The last time someone had stroked his forearm it had been to relieve him of his watch for the purposes of bewitching him. Next he instinctively felt his pocket to make sure that Madame Bernabeu's talisman was still there.

The week before, Sinclair and La Spedding had had their 'get to know each other' lunch at the Intercontinental. It had been a dismal affair, more a case of the New Boy having to present his credentials to the Headmistress. It had been tough going. Spedding was the kind of woman that made you feel dirty and guilty just by sitting there in front of her.

Sinclair had introduced the topic of FJ and how well he seemed to run the Station, but whenever FJ's name was mentioned, Spedding's fastidious mouth drooped with deep distaste, and her face twisted with annoyance.

Over coffee he had laid out his SNAPPER project and explained the case history. It was then that he had scented some sort of moral poison in the very centre of La Spedding's being. It had been difficult to put your finger on it exactly—maybe it was the way she tended to look away at key moments— maybe it was that her smile was ironic and her manner dripped with sarcasm whenever SNAPPER's name came up.

And now, with hindsight, it was obvious what it was all about.

Sinclair grasped at the decanter of brandy that FJ had been discreetly shoving in his direction. The memories of his lunch with Spedding at the Intercontinental were now starting to make sense. He had found Spedding's behaviour odd but not alarming. But now Sinclair was at a loss for words.

He felt sick. Something had soured in his stomach.

"FJ, I'm sorry, but all this talk of Vanessa Spedding—"

"—It makes you sick, I know. You *do* look a little green, if you don't mind my saying so. Talk of Vanessa Spedding usually reminds one of something nasty . . . a nasty viral infection or worse. In my book, you see, George, grown women rogering each other is one thing, but spreading nasty rumours about your colleagues is quite another matter. And very dangerous operationally. Bad for the Service."

To Sinclair, it all made sense now, especially that disturbing look in Spedding's eye at the Intercontinental.

FJ leaned back in his chair and wiped his brow. "Now what we need is proof—we have seen the smoke, now we need a fire—a situation that will result in her being shipped back to Century House and a full-blown disciplinary hearing, and then it's *'Adios, Motherfucker'* as you are so fond of saying. And if they give her her damn pension and I find out about it, I shall be the first to resign in protest. What we require is for her to be caught in an act of fundamental indecency which will result in Her Ladyship being PNG'ed out of Nicaragua by our charming Revolutionary hosts, and then PNG'ed out of the Service. You must remember that Nicaragua, after all, is a profoundly Catholic, moral country at heart beneath all the macho Marxist godlessness of our Sandinista brethren."

"Leave it to me, FJ, I beg you." Sinclair heard the Revenger talking.

FJ smiled grimly as he saw a red light come on deep in Sinclair's usually placid eyes. "You have my blessing. She's all yours, my boy. You are sanctioned to pull out all the stops. However you choose to do it, it will always be remembered that you were more sinned against than sinning. Dr George Sinclair, you are a man of honour empowered to transact dishonourable deeds. Licensed to . . . be . . . devious."

"Thank you, FJ, I appreciate it, I really do."

Lunch concluded with another blessing from FJ. "For Queen and Country. Now go forth and queer Her Ladyship's pitch, and queer it good."

Later that night, as he was slipping into the dark for his appointment with Morpheus, Sinclair remembered FJ's twinkling eyes over the coffee cup. His boss's laugh was, Sinclair remembered as the lights went out, as merry as a lepers' bell.

MONDAY MORNING PRAYERS

"Doe-eyed, but deadly, that one, oh yes, I know all about her," said FJ, munching his morning biscuit.

It was Monday morning and they were talking about Jamila. FJ was looking rosy-cheeked and well-fed that morning in his air-conditioned office after a weekend of mild debauchery.

La Spedding was absent from 'morning prayers', as FJ liked to call their regular Monday 10 a.m. meetings. FJ had asked her to fly over to

Miami to represent him at the monthly pow-wow with the Cousins.

"PLO . . . Fatah and Black September," FJ continued. "Then Hamas. Then Hezbollah and lately Islamic Jihad. Habash and Abu Nidal. The more radical and crazy and merciless the better for her. She can't get enough of terror, the bloodthirsty bitch. Her thing is bomb-making. That's her hobby—blowing people up. She is *cordon bleu* with the *plastique*. Never met her in the flesh, though, although I am told that she is a looker. Type of gal who could slit your throat and you'd still like her, she's that type, so they say."

"She *is* very nice in the flesh . . . so to speak. I don't think that Her Ladyship has come across our Jamila, has she FJ?" asked Sinclair, disingenuously, laying a seed.

"Not yet, not yet, my boy. Anyway, let's turn to SNAPPER himself. Any joy there?"

Sinclair proceeded to give FJ a sanitized version of the day at El Mango. Good progress had been made in the recruitment of SNAPPER. The estimate was good as written, he'd have it on FJ's desk for sign-off that afternoon.

"I estimate another couple of runs at him and he'll be ready to take the bait. He seemed definitely interested. I think we're on to one here, FJ."

"Money?"

"Negative, FJ. This Joe will do it because he wants to be in our tent. Just as we had assumed would be the case."

"Jolly good."

The details about school and cricket and a turncoat in Africa were conveniently deferred, for now at least. That nugget of intelligence he would keep in his back pocket until he really needed it. It could be a passport for a rainy day.

But his first priority, and indeed that of FJ, was dealing with the mortal threat that Vanessa Spedding represented to the Service. And to George Sinclair.

"Well then, young George, what of queering the pitch? Have you, ah, started . . . *queering* it?"

Sinclair outlined his plan.

As Sinclair spoke FJ's moon-face was set in concentration.

"My *dear boy!*" exclaimed FJ, when Sinclair had finished. This was the finest compliment FJ could bestow, an expression that conveyed a very British blend of surprise and admiration. "Get away with that one, my boy, and you're guaranteed a fast track in Intelligence Branch. You can count on me. I'll see to it. Personally."

Sinclair preened, despite himself. His Indian blood could never resist a spot of well-aimed flattery, and FJ knew that very well, having grown up in Lahore in the last days of the Raj. FJ's eyes were bright and gleefully alert.

Good old FJ, poisonous old queen that he was, who could want for a better boss? Sinclair was, as the Cousins liked to say, on a roll.

PNG

In the intelligence game, being declared 'persona non grata'—being 'PNG-ed'—and then sent home, is about the worst that can happen to an agent runner in the field. As long, that is, as you are safely ensconced behind a desk with diplomatic cover and have not been foolish enough to accept a deep cover posting, which is deniable and can leave you twisting in the wind.

The way it usually works after your diplomatic cover has been blown is that there is the obligatory tit-for-tat expulsion and you are sent back home, no shame in that at all, by the way. It's all part of the course, you do a double stint in Head Office (six years instead three), and when the dust has settled you are posted to a lower level embassy to restart your diplomatic cover. Or if the blowing has been sensational, they find a quiet corner for you in the General Services back-office or in Training down at the Fort, or, God forbid, in Personnel or Banking.

And as for the poor sod (or bitch, for that matter) who you have corrupted and has been discovered because of your incompetence or laziness or just sheer bad luck, that's another matter. It usually means nine ounces of lead in the base of the skull, or worse, depending on the predilections of the host Counter Intelligence operation. In Nicaragua those days, the going rate for traitors of the Revolution was a spell with the rats in the dungeons of the Coyotepe, sleep deprivation and interrogation by the Cuban experts, followed by diving lessons in a well or unconventional skydiving from a Soviet-made chopper out over the jungle.

PNG-ing is what FJ and Sinclair had in mind for La Spedding when they discussed her case at La Marseillaise. But to achieve the dark objectives they had set for themselves over lunch, the reason for Her Ladyship's expulsion from Nicaragua would have to be for more than mere spying.

The beauty of the stratagem that Sinclair had presented to FJ at morning prayers was that multiple objectives could be achieved in a single operation. In fact it might even go on to become a textbook example of planning and lateral thinking, a case study in the lectures at Fort Monckton. Case Officer Sinclair could: a) enhance his career (long-term gain); b) please his boss (short-term advantage); c) deliver a trophy—the scalp of a senior MI6 officer—to DGI and Sandinista Counter Intelligence, thus establishing his own *bona fides*; d) enhance his Joe's career prospects and thereby his *access*, the ultimate goal, *access*, that's what it was all about; and e) remove the clear and present danger represented by that horribly predatory excuse for a human being, Vanessa Spedding. Sinclair, FJ, the Service, and fuck it, the world at large would sleep easier in their beds without the jealous bitch being out there on the prowl looking for her next victim.

This ability to kill many birds with one stone was fast becoming his speciality, Sinclair realized. He remembered how elegantly he had dealt with the multiple menace of the deaths of Helen and Jane and the disappearances of Xancha Bergsma and Doctor Aggarwal in Oxford during his Positive Vetting.

That night his mood was carefree and cheerful and generous. After complimenting Niña Conchita on her dinner table, he kissed Ximena goodnight and on impulse promised to buy her a dog, after passing up her offer to inject him with his nightly dose of morphine. Morpheus could wait, for once.

He then drove to Brenda van Kempen's apartment in Los Robles. A certain melancholy had gripped Brenda since their visit to El Mango. It had something to do with Jamila. Jamila had that awful quality of making other women feel insecure. But tonight he was determined to reassure Brenda.

In the bedroom he treated her to the prolonged pleasures of French tongue-play, as he had been taught in Martinique by Madame Bernabeu.

As he came up for air from between Brenda's ecstatic thighs, he thought through his plan once again. His skills of persuasion would be put to the test, no doubt about it.

"*So . . . soooo . . . ,*" moaned Brenda, expressing so much with that small Dutch word.

To begin with, he would need the collaboration of Carlos Maxwell.

"*Ja . . . so . . . lekker . . . maar dat is heel smaakelijke . . . so . . .*"

The wild card was Jamila. Would she go for it? Probably would, if Maxwell insisted. The plan was not without risk—but, fuck, what wasn't, these days?

Back down he went. He heard Brenda gasp "*eet smaakelijke*" as she lay back and started the long journey towards the inevitable convulsed orgasm. It was always good to be appreciated, he smiled, his jaws beginning to ache. Brenda grunted and swore — "*Gott veeeerdomme*"—and Sinclair feared for the safety of the cartilage in his ears as she approached her climax.

GOING NATIVE

That weekend Sinclair, Brenda and Ximena drove to Granada again, past the smouldering volcano, the Gate of Hell. Brenda seemed to have forgotten Sinclair's ill-timed wisecrack about Jamila after their last visit, her faith in George Sinclair restored after the unbelievable multiple orgasms of Monday night. For a girl from Utrecht she had come far, and Sinclair had shown her the portals of eternal carnal bliss. She just had to hang on to him,—it wouldn't do to antagonize him and miss out on those tremendously prolonged orgasms.

They found their way to El Mango again, where, in a replay of their first visit, Carlos Maxwell and Jamila waved at them from the veranda while Heidi jumped up and down in pleasure on the dock as their pirogue approached.

"*Ahlan*, George, *habibi!*" said Jamila enthusiastically as she hugged Sinclair tightly like a long-lost relative, treating him to the pressure of her firm breasts. Brenda pretended not to notice, as she kissed Carlos chastely on the cheek.

"And darling Ximena, *ayouni*, how is the prettiest girl in Central America?" said Jamila huskily, in her French-inflected accent, her killer's eyes ever watchful. Ximena took her hand nicely. Brenda was pecked affectionately on the cheek, like a sister-in-arms.

Heidi slobbered enthusiastically all over Ximena, who announced the good news that she had been promised a dog of her own. She was congratulated by all the company.

"Just make sure it's a boy, Ximena," laughed Maxwell, watching Brenda, "because our Heidi is a very jealous girl."

Sinclair watched SNAPPER carefully during the greetings. Carlos Maxwell looked relaxed, and was dishevelled as usual in his khakis and he smoked his *cohiba*. When he caught Sinclair's eye there was something in his look. It was a wary look between professionals. It was crunch-time at last.

"Council of war time, *Señor* Maxwell. I come bearing gifts. I remembered what you said last time about hospitality and trading."

MISCHIEF AT THE COYOTEPE

Sinclair and Carlos Maxwell were putting the finishing touches to the plan codenamed Operation APACHE. They were in Maxwell's office at the Coyotepe, the historic old fort that serves as the Boy Scouts headquarters between wars. The colonial fort overlooks the Apoyo lagoon and looms over the city of Masaya and the strategic pass into Managua. Maxwell told Sinclair that the name derived from the fact that the hill-top was traditionally the home of a band of coyotes.

During the war Somoza Junior had used it as the base for his elite EEBI, who used to swoop down from this eerie in their jeeps and helicopters to terrorize the population and engage the Sandinistas as they swept up the highway to Managua in the last desperate days of the war. Now that the Sandinistas were in power the fort bristled with antennae and satellite dishes, having passed to the intelligence and security services, and its dungeons and torture chambers contained the most important political detainees. They said that Tomás Verga, the most radical and feared member of the nine-man Sandinista directorate—a *prize cunt*, as Mackie had characterized him in Sinclair's pre-mission briefing—had made the fort his home, practically, and more out of a sense of historical irony than anything else, because that is where Somoza had imprisoned him before the war.

Carlos Maxwell revealed himself to Sinclair as Verga's favourite, the son he never had, for rumour had it that Somoza's bogeymen had amused themselves by depriving Verga of his *cojones* when he was under their care down there in the dungeons.

Sinclair soon learned that Maxwell was trusted even by the Cuban secondees from DGI, who kept separate quarters and manned the banks of sophisticated Soviet-made telecommunications equipment on the top floor of the building. SNAPPER, his Joe, had been given the run of the fort and access to all of the rooms with a master key.

"The name of the game is career enhancement these days, George."

"You scratch my back, I'll scratch yours."

"Precisely."

"And you help me survive, in the process, so that I can go on to greater things, *Compita*."

"She's on to me, Carlos, I can feel it in my bones." Sinclair described to Maxwell how Spedding seemed to hover around him and pop up at the most unlikely times, as if she was surveilling him. "There was a Jesuit at the College who used to watch me and follow me around in the same way," he added, suddenly remembering Fr Cassius.

"Sounds like she's got something on you, my friend."

"Yes, I'm sick of those knowing looks. That shitweasel of a woman has got it in for me."

"It sounds like she's uncovered something unsavoury in your past, old boy."

And, to make things worse (and this he did not mention to Maxwell), Ximena had spread the cards for him the night before and had warned him that he had an enemy, a woman with green eyes, to be precise.

"There she is, father, look at her," she had said, stabbing at the Queen of Spades, reversed, with her little brown finger.

And so was born the idea of Operation APACHE.

They had drawn a series of diagrams—the decision trees and flow charts that form the basis for complex covert operations with multiple possible outcomes. The forks in the chart forecast the multiple future 'what if' scenarios. Maxwell pointed at each box in sequence, playing Devil's Advocate, challenging Sinclair's assumptions, looking for any flaw in the logic of APACHE.

They had taken a break from the tedious drill.

Maxwell had his boots on his desk, and was smoking again as he flicked through a manila dossier that contained the latest surveillance reports on the British spooks. FJ's predilections were well known and a source of constant amusement to his watchers. But so far they had not managed to get any dirt on Spedding.

Sinclair was beginning to brief him on Vanessa Spedding's routine at Managua Station when the door opened. A very small man dressed in khaki and wearing a leather shoulder holster limped in. Sinclair saw that the man wore an old-fashioned gun, it looked like a World War II Luger, under his armpit. He was wearing thick spectacles and was so short that Sinclair wondered whether he might technically be a dwarf. Maxwell jumped up and rushed to the man, grasping his outstretched hand; Sinclair thought for a second that Maxwell was going to kneel and kiss the newcomer's hand, as if he were a cardinal of some sort, which, come to think of it, he was—a Prince of the Church of Socialist Espionage. Instinctively Sinclair stood up.

It was none other than Comandante Verga, Fidel's man, come to inspect the goods.

TACHO'S LUGER

They were getting to know each other. Sinclair was explaining the rules of cricket to Verga, as Maxwell stood back and watched them, smoking. Let's see if my boss and my Joe get on.

If FJ, Mackie and theirs masters in Century House had known that Sinclair was at that moment at the Coyotepe, hobnobbing with SNAPPER and explaining the art of leg-spin bowling to Tomás Verga, they would have choked on their gin and tonics. With that one act Sinclair had broken the most basic of cardinal rules and had put his head into the mouth of the beast. But Sinclair considered that FJ had given him *carte blanche*, operationally speaking, when he had been tasked to destroy Vanessa Spedding. And in any case, if worse came to worse and they found out, he could say that he was playing the double agent, although that would be flying too close to the sun. Doubles was a game that could only be sanctioned by the Head Boys and was definitely beyond the scope of FJ's delegated authority.

In any case, how were they ever to know about Sinclair's visits to the fort, for by then Sinclair had seen the light and had sold his soul to the Devil at the crossroads.

As the sun had started its descent and the shadows lengthened across Carlos Maxwell's island that weekend, Sinclair had declared his allegiance to the dispossessed of this world—to the victims, to the oppressed bastardy of colonialism, to the hybrids, mongrels, mutts, half-breeds, half-castes, mestizos and mulattos. He was now firmly and irrevocably in the pay of Dr Fidel Castro's DGI, and his handler was to be Carlos Maxwell, an overseas boy like himself.

Sinclair's 'turning' had not been dramatic. There had been no sleepless nights and there were none of those excruciating examinations of conscience that the Jesuit Spiritual Directors at the College taught their boys to undertake before making crucial decisions. There was no sign that said *Turn Back While You Still Can* or *Abandon All Hope All Ye Who Enter Here* or *Here Be Dragons.*

Treason came easily and when he finally committed himself he felt that familiar lightness of being yet again, as if he had been relieved of an immense burden.

"It has all played out like a dream, *Comandante*," Maxwell was telling Verga. "George Sinclair is the perfect traitor, you see. He has been born to it. He and I are star crossed, you could say."

193

"I shouldn't leave you two together in a room without a chaperone, then," smirked Verga, who had a grisly sense of humour.

"And the beauty of it is," Maxwell continued, "that Sinclair is entirely willing—he has come to *papá* of his own free will. There has been no unpleasantness involved, and only minimal coercion; and even no need to bring up the business about the drugs, or what we were told about him the other day," Maxwell lied. "It's as if George Sinclair has been waiting for this opportunity all his life. I've never seen a more natural traitor in my experience, *Comandante*. And the timing is perfect. You see, the bitch Spedding has started to suspect that something is not quite right. She stopped him in the corridor the other day. 'You're not going native on us, are you George?' she said to him. That's an expression the Imperialist-Colonialists use, *Comandante*, when one of their own has begun to sympathize with the oppressed."

"Excellent, Carlos. Do go on," Verga said, caressing the Luger.

"FJ—Sinclair's boss—has now confirmed Sinclair's suspicions—that La Spedding is furious that Sinclair—the New Boy—and not she, has landed SNAPPER. And that she has started to cast aspersions on SNAPPER, doubting my genuineness. FJ has warned Sinclair that Her Ladyship—that's what they call her behind her back—is spitting blood and insists that SNAPPER's a plant, a doublecross. When FJ confirmed this to Sinclair last week, that was when Sinclair took the decision to come across to us, to his spiritual home."

"That's all very nice, young Carlos," Verga replied, "but La Spedding must be dealt with. She's a menace to the operation. As we Nicas like to say, '*a cada chancho le llega su sábado*'—every pig has his Saturday."

Saturday being the traditional day of porcine slaughter in that particular corner of Central America.

"I have found my home at last, and I will bring you Vanessa Spedding's scalp to prove it," had been Sinclair's reply to Tomás Verga as he looked directly into the little man's eyes. The *Comandante* had just asked him bluntly whether he was a double agent sent across to confuse them.

"In which case, if you *are* thinking of playing it both ways, my friend," Verga had added with a grim smile, patting the Luger under his arm. "I will not hesitate to execute you myself. I've been looking for an excuse to fire old Tacho's Luger."

Soon after his initial debriefing at the Coyotepe, it was agreed that the Sandinistas and DGI would share the bounty equally, just as MI6 and the CIA had covenanted to share all SNAPPER product. It was also agreed that Sinclair would remain as an agent in place and be played back against MI6 as a double agent. SNAPPER would in their eyes be Sinclair's Joe, and a very well placed and prolific one at that. It was all very satisfactory. The idea of playing it both ways excited him and the symmetry of betrayal appealed to the academic in him.

Sinclair was duly codenamed (he had also, like SNAPPER, been code-named well before his recruitment, but was never told his official name). In DGI tradition, he had been given the privilege of choosing his own unofficial codename. He chose SPINNER, in honour of Old Ajay the garden-wallah who had taught him the mysterious arts of leg-spin bowling and lock-picking.

SPINNER's gift to SNAPPER, his ticket to the dance, the proof of his *bona fides*, the scratching of his handler's back, as he had promised Verga, was to be the head of Vanessa Spedding. Sinclair fully understood that SNAPPER had already scratched SPINNER's back when on his first visit to El Mango Maxwell had tossed Sinclair that priceless nugget of intelligence which point-ed to a traitor in SIS's African operations.

Judging from their initial response, which bordered on the ecstatic, Maxwell, Verga and their Cuban patrons considered Spedding infinitely more dangerous than both FJ and himself combined. *La Bitch Número Uno*, Verga called her; and hers was to be the Mother of all Motherfucking *Adioses*, the three of them laughed, referring to the latest buzzword coming out of Iraq as the Imperialist Crusaders mobilized in the desert for their latest victimization of the Arab Nation. It was the eve of the Gulf War and the Mother of all Battles.

Verga proposed the Sandinista toast: "*Muerte al Yanqui, Enemigo de la Humanidad!*" The little man brandished a bottle of 25-year-old Flor de Caña that had been rescued from Tacho's bunker in 1979 (as had the Luger). Like the Luger, the rum was only brought out for special occasions.

They then toasted Dr Sinclair's homecoming to the Socialist Motherland—which, Verga said, was not a country, but a state of grace—with a hearty "*Patria Libre o Morir!*"

"And if you see us right," Verga said, his speech already slurred with rum, "I'll see to it that Fidel thanks you in person."

Maxwell winked at Sinclair and stroked his imaginary beard.

The Sandinista dream was fizzling out in Nicaragua. They had announced the elections. Sinclair had arrived at the party ten years too late. Nevertheless George Sinclair's eyes misted over because time has no meaning when you have found your home, and he was home at last.

BAITING THE TRAP

"I met a woman, Vanessa, on SNAPPER's island—El Mango."

"Yes, George, I *do* know what SNAPPER's island is called, I *have* read the file. But do go on. I haven't got all day you know."

There it was again, that infuriating condescension.

"She's SNAPPER's girlfriend. She thinks that SNAPPER is trying to recruit me, that I'm just another minor diplomat on the take. She doesn't suspect what I'm really up to with SNAPPER. I believe that we can burn her, together, you and I, Vanessa. We can get to SNAPPER through her. Then you could run her and I could run SNAPPER. Two birds with one stone. What do you think?"

"Go on, George, I'm all ears." She was noncommittal as usual.

"Well, it didn't take me long to find out how to do it. The hook is that she blows both ways. How do I know? The fact is she followed me to the bathroom at El Mango and told me that she's petrified of Maxwell—of SNAPPER, I mean. She was a bit drunk—we'd been drinking all afternoon. She begged me to help her. She's scared shitless of SNAPPER and of Comandante Verga. SNAPPER beats her, apparently. He found her in bed with a woman the other day and went apeshit, almost throttled the living daylights out of her."

Spedding didn't flinch. What a pro, thought Sinclair admiringly.

"Langley say that she's ex-mainstream PLO, ex-Fatah and now Hamas," he continued. "They say that she might even have a connection to Abu Nidal. In any case, she's been made very welcome here in Nicaragua; not only is she SNAPPER's girl, but she gets VIP treatment from our hosts because of her Palestinian terror credentials. As do most of the terrorist scum of the earth . . . oh, and by the way, she's apparently related to George Habash—PFLP. She seems to have her finger in many pies."

Sinclair watched La Spedding's face carefully to assess her reaction to the photograph that he had just pushed across the desk.

"So intense," La Spedding said, looking down at Jamila's mug shot, "those great black eyes of hers . . ."

In Spedding's own green eyes an almost preternatural light had come on. They were the eyes of a cat on the prowl for mice.

"Yes, I suppose they are . . . intense . . ."

"Very nice looking girl."

"Palestinian expatriate. Lebanon. Shatila."

"Very nice."

"I believe I can seduce her, Vanessa, I'm convinced of it. There was definitely something in the air between us this weekend at El Mango. I thought of going to FJ with it, but I couldn't bring myself to. He's not exactly the kind of person who could help, if you get my drift. Not quite a gentleman, in my book, I'm afraid. This type of 'burning' is something that needs a woman's advice, definitely, and a lot of discretion. Should I go on?"

Her eyes narrowed. Those damned green eyes that always seemed to know too much. "Of course. Do go on, George. You can count on me."

Of course he could, especially of there was shit to be shovelled FJ's way and points to be scored. Her assurances didn't fool him. There was no hint of sincerity there. She never gave anything away. She's a real operator, a real pro—wouldn't give you the steam off her turd, FJ had told him over lunch.

"I haven't come across her," La Spedding purred, "what's her name?"

"Jamila bint Samira, Samira being George Habash's cousin on his mother's side. She hasn't been here in Managua very long. She comes and goes. She seems to commute from Beirut. SNAPPER is infatuated with her. But there's a nasty sting in the tail of the story."

"Before we go on, she is to be referred to as FATIMA from now on."

"FATIMA it is then."

She raised a grey eyebrow, expecting Sinclair to continue where he had left off. Sinclair paused, swallowing hard for effect. "Go on George, do go on," she said impatiently, glancing at her wristwatch.

He started to feed her some rope. "Well, she is very attractive, our Jamila—FATIMA, I mean—as you can see from the photograph. I have become quite smitten with her myself," he smiled, looking down shyly.

"And what would your young Dutch lady friend have to say about that?"

George smiled coyly. "Well, I'll just have to sort it out with Brenda, that's my problem. But let's cut to the chase," he resumed, "I won't go into all the gory details, not just yet, anyway. The point is that FATIMA and I have arranged to see each other, behind SNAPPER's back. We are about to take the next step, if you know what I mean."

Of course she did. It was the Mortal Sin that they drummed into you at Fort Monckton. Don't get involved with your Joes, and especially with your Joannes, unless a honey trap has been sanctioned by the Head Boys, and honey traps were rare these days, more usually the stuff of Bond movies. Spedding was now successfully showing no reaction to any of this.

Now, a nice bit of play-acting, as Sinclair bit his lip and said, with adolescent anguish: "I'm afraid, Vanessa, that I've fallen in love—in *lust* more like it—with FATIMA. Head over heels, in fact. I know it's wrong, but I must have her . . ." A pause, as he let the possibilities take hold in the old girl's imagination. He fed her more rope. "But I'm not that green, Vanessa. I did a deep background check on her through ME/OPS in London, who double checked with Langley. I'm afraid she has a reputation. They confirmed that FATIMA is a lesbian, a secret one. She blows both ways, as I said. Not even her bosses know about it. Dutch Counter Espionage in Amsterdam picked her up once with a prostitute—a girl, that is. And then in Paris, SDECE said they had tailed her once over a dirty weekend, with another woman. And now it seems she's been having an affair with a Sandinista *Sub-Comandante*—who happens to be a woman— the one SNAPPER caught her in bed with the other day when he almost killed her."

Spedding was silent. For a second Sinclair feared that she might have sensed something odd about the situation, suspecting a frame-up. The old bitch was wily, and was known for her deviousness, Verga had said. Operation APACHE wouldn't be a push over, by any means. Maxwell had advised extreme caution. So had FJ, for that matter, for what the fat cunt's opinion was worth.

"Look, Vanessa, I'm desperate. But I've thought of a way out of this—a creative solution, so to speak. But I need help. *Discreet* help, because my reputation—my career—is involved. I know what I've done is wrong. I should have run it by you and FJ before I agreed to see her again. The solution I've crafted would exploit the situation and result in the turning of Jamila. The *burning* of FATIMA, to be more precise," he said.

"But you just said you are in love with her."

"In lust, I said, Vanessa—in lust."

"Even so."

"I reckon that once I've had my way with her—it's happened to me before—I get infatuated, obsessed, you see, and then I get my way, and then the hots dissipate. It starts with infatuation, then obsession, then I get my way, and then I'm cured. Their smell starts bothering me, they start to suffocate me with their dependence. And then I move on."

"So what's new?" Spedding said curtly. "Isn't that the way it always happens with men?"

Sinclair chose to ignore her. "Let me have my way with her, Vanessa. Then she is all yours and not a word to Head Office about my peccadillo. That will remain our little secret. And, as the dividend of the operation, we get insight and access—incredibly good insight and access in fact—to the nastiest of the Palestinian terror outfits. She would be a treasure trove for ME/Ops. And the Cousins would be eating out of your hand for many years to come. Think of her tradable value, for God's sake."

Again, that infuriating silence. Spedding regarded Sinclair carefully and, he feared, a touch sceptically. She tapped her ballpoint on the chrome top of her desk.

"Let me think about it. It does sound promising, though." Her tone was a little too businesslike.

"I'm afraid I need to deal with this very soon. Now, in fact. Jamila—FATI-MA—is leaving for Beirut in two days. I've arranged to see her tomorrow. We need to snag her before she leaves. I need your intervention, Vanessa, urgent-ly. I beg you. I think you would know how to deal with it. That's why I came to you, and not FJ."

Another turn of the screw and it was set. The rest was automatic. Spedding herself would trip the switch that released the trap.

TRIPPING THE SWITCH

FJ had agreed to make himself scarce that Friday, leaving the office at 5 p.m. on the dot. He was carrying a set of fishing rods out to his Range Rover, off for a nice weekend fishing up in Matagalpa, smiling sweetly as if butter wouldn't melt in his mouth. He was full of bonhomie, and even wished La Spedding a lovely weekend. Vanessa Spedding scowled back sourly. Behind her back Sinclair winked saucily at FJ.

Sinclair called home to let Niña Conchita know that he would be working late, and to put Ximena to bed before midnight. The prospect of staying up late with Spedding made his skin crawl as they sat in the Ops room at the Station and sketched out the operation, which they had christened BAN-SHEE. They used essentially the same flow charts and decision trees that Sinclair had rehearsed for his new handler at the Coyotepe. She tried repeatedly to have Sinclair defer the operation, and worried out loud about doing something so dangerous—burning is always dangerous because it is unpredictable—without adequate preparation. But Sinclair insisted, and insisted, but backed off whenever he heard himself insisting too much. His motives were, after all, totally reliable and reasonable—hell, it was the Service's well-being that they were talking about. The Head Boys were desperate for a high-level success out in the field, something big to show to the Cousins. And after all, the most inspired successes, operationally, were usually seat-of-the-pants operations, like this one, where one took the initiative and capitalized on the opportunity. Sometimes you had to take personal risks to make your employer look good.

"I know that the Service does not encourage action on impulse in normal circumstances, but there *are* times when opportunities have to be recognized and swiftly taken." He felt as if he were lecturing his boss.

Spedding was obviously a much more experienced hand than Sinclair, and she didn't like being pressured by the New Boy, as she referred to him behind his back—but his persistence worked. There was obviously that other motive, like an itch in the crotch, impelling the bitch forward too, because at the end of the day, any conscientious intelligence officer simply does not walk in and try to burn a target without weeks or even months of tedious preparation. The consequences of misjudgment or mistiming can be disastrous.

Several times Spedding got up and went for a stroll around the Embassy, to clear her head, she said.

She had been gone for a while too long and Sinclair was getting anxious that things might be about to derail. She was probably in the communications cell, on the link to London, tapping out his death warrant.

He found her in the dark, in the Library, her thin cruel face anxiously looking out into the tropical night.

He then played his trump card.

"Look, Vanessa, I'm afraid I'll have to deal with it alone myself tomorrow. I'll just have to deal with FATIMA myself . . ."

And that was that. With those words Spedding could see the enticing prospect of controlling a grade-A lesbian Joanne receding, as she imagined the New Boy blundering his way into a situation he was obviously too green to handle appropriately.

She turned to look at him. She had made up her mind there, in the dark, surrounded by books. A light went on in her green cat's eyes.

"Splendid. Leave her to me, then."

He felt the quickening of the pulse that he always felt at the start of an operation and then the tingling in the groin that he had experienced at various junctures of his career—in his first game of hide and seek with Grannyjee and Old Ajay the gardener in the gardens in Goa, and then when he had smashed Cavendish's bowling for six in the nets at school and then again when Helen

Henshaw had knelt before him in Guy Underhill's room in Goodge Street.

Sitting opposite him across the pool of light cast by the swivel lamp, La Spedding had adopted a smooth, polished, serious mien. She was after all a senior operator. Sinclair noticed that she had short clean finger-nails. A whiff of soap or men's aftershave came across the table.

Sinclair took much pleasure in assisting such an experienced officer break every rule in the book. Spedding's unseemly haste and her readiness to be persuaded was the proof of her guilt and the logic that Sinclair used to assuage his conscience, what little of it there was left. The lightness came over him again.

At first the planning for Operation BANSHEE was conceptual, and basic questions were asked, and answered by Sinclair to her satisfaction—were they sure that FATIMA would respond to blackmail, or would she laugh in their faces and call their bluff, would she call the Sandinistas and confess before she was shopped to her bosses, would her bosses really care that she was attracted to her own sex? And so it went on, into the wee hours. And then they dealt with the nuts and bolts in excruciating detail, as the operation took on a life of its own—escape routes from the house, timing of entry, weapon of choice—knife or pistol—the Station Beretta—or none at all, the best points from which to monitor the building, anti-surveillance traps, etcetera, etcetera, etcetera . . . She was extremely demanding and, Sinclair had to admit reluctantly, utterly professional in her analysis, as she devilled through all the possibilities and contingencies and traced her finger repeatedly along the lines and boxes of the flow charts. The planning for Operation BANSHEE was just as detailed, and probably more so, than Operation APACHE. In fact, BANSHEE had to dovetail with APACHE, fitting inside it like a glove. In fact, APACHE *was* BANSHEE, and overlaid it—a triumph of espionage engineering, if it worked.

And so it was that Sinclair took delight in helping Spedding devise the sequence of events by which they would trap FATIMA, setting her up for a burning and for the intelligence coup that would make Spedding's career. And, in the process, Spedding would conveniently dispatch herself into oblivion.

HONEY

Spedding walked in and aimed her Beretta, surprising Jamila in bed with Sinclair. According to the preordained sequence of events set out in Operation BANSHEE, Sinclair had been turfed out of the bed at gunpoint and told to get back to the Embassy by his outraged superior. She would deal with him later.

While Spedding spoke with Jamila in the bedroom, outside in the street Sinclair had been joined by Carlos Maxwell, and then Tomás Verga had arrived with his goons. Through their headsets they could hear Spedding speaking and Jamila sighing and sobbing intermittently. Inside, the old girl was calmly informing Jamila that her options were simple—her bosses in Beirut would be informed first, then Major Carlos Maxwell, and finally Comandante Verga, in that order—or she could be a sensible girl and co-operate with British Intelligence.

After it was all over, Jamila told Sinclair that the sequence of events was not necessarily as he had planned with Ms Spedding. For example, instead of pulling Jamila out of the bed, and instead of making her get dressed, Spedding had made Jamila stay in the bed, and had pulled the sheets off her, so as to better admire the view. She then proceeded calmly to advise Jamila of her situation, the pistol aimed steadily at a spot just above the terrorist's heaving left breast. Jamila, it must be said, was a born actress. Murder may have been her favourite hobby, but that night Jamila gave the performance of her life, showcasing a whole range of emotions: outrage, indignation, shame, fear, desperation, then hopeless surrender.

It was only after feasting her eyes on the naked girl for a good quarter of an hour that Spedding approached the bed and sat on its edge, the gun pointed casually at the terrorist's left nipple.

After another half-hour of debate and tears, threats and caresses, Spedding now lay in bed with Jamila, and they were both panting slightly, having taken their fill of honey-sweet love. La Spedding was congratulating herself in her post coital well-being for having had the courage to go ahead with the New Boy's harebrained scheme, because it had gone off like clockwork, God bless the little paki upstart. Maybe the SNAPPER business was kosher after all. Maybe she had been too harsh on him for suspecting treachery. The future was hers, and it was bright. She was already looking forward to acting as FATIMA's handler for many days and evenings to come, and savouring in advance her triumphal return to Century House. This is the asset she had been trawling for ever since she had arrived in Nicaragua. Better even than SNAPPER, she would see to that. FATIMA was the asset that would save Managua Station and make her Head after she had disposed of that clown FJ. If you couldn't find one of the Sandinistas to spy on, then spy the living daylights out of their friends, the terrorist scum that had been pouring into the country since 1979. And even if they did decide to close the Station down after the elections, FATIMA would be her ticket to a new theatre of operations. She had always hoped to get involved with Middle East Ops. What better way than to follow her new Joanne to Beirut and Damascus and Baghdad.

While the old girl daydreamed of her day in the sun, Jamila rested her head on Spedding's long breasts, and she herself daydreamed about what it would be like to cut the imperialist bitch's scraggy throat. *Allah*, the things a girl had to do for Palestine and for the Revolution.

Spedding turned and whispered in Jamila's ear that it was too quiet outside. She was starting to get twitchy. They heard a click from somewhere in the house. Spedding's eyebrows raised a fraction in inquiry. She picked up the Beretta off the night table and told Jamila to stay put. She was going to take a look around the house.

It was very quiet, almost *too* quiet. Spedding wrapped herself in the damp sheet. It was then that Jamila pressed the panic button, a dummy switch on the bedside lamp.

Whereupon the front door and then the bedroom door were kicked open by Verga's Uzi-toting, olive-clad thugs. Someone snatched the sheet away from Spedding, just as Spedding had snatched the sheets off Jamila. Spedding's pistol clanked noisily as it fell to the floor, and her hands shot up in a hilarious Wild West parody. Sinclair would have given his eye-teeth to have witnessed the scene. Jamila, Verga told him later, turned in another Oscar-winning performance, swearing in Arabic at the Sandinista gorillas. She called Verga the whoreson of a mongrel camel bitch and various other choice Palestinian insults, which they all had a good laugh about afterwards at the party at the Coyotepe, over champagne and Iranian caviar pouched in from Havana.

In the meantime, Verga stood there with Tacho's Luger pointed at La Spedding, his thick specs lending him something of a professorial look as the photographers did their work. Flash bulbs popped. Breasts, old and young, sagging and firm, swayed in the phosphorescent light of the cameras, which gave the bedroom the look of a film soundstage. Sinclair was nowhere to be seen.

Soon it was all over. Operation BANSHEE had failed but APACHE had achieved its objective. Revenger had wielded his tomahawk and collected another scalp.

MI6 AGENT CAUGHT IN BED IN LESBIAN
TRYST WITH PLO TERRORIST

AFTER THE SHITSTORM

Within a year of Spedding's downfall, FJ was summoned back to London and was forced into retirement. In a roundabout way FJ had achieved his objective, because he managed to enjoy his last few months in the field without the constant threat of La Spedding's inquisitive eye. In the end, however, his ploy backfired when the Head Boys looked for another scapegoat, as they invariably do when these operational disasters make it into the newspapers.

In Century House, Sinclair's role in the scandal was glossed over, because of the fabulous trawl he had landed. SNAPPER was the success story of the day. No one had believed Spedding when under the interrogators' lamps at the Fort she repeatedly accused Sinclair of setting her up. It was, they concluded, before dismissing her without her pension, a vicious old has-been's envy at a younger officer's success in reeling in a Super Agent. Even FJ had confirmed Sinclair's alibi. Of course Sinclair had been nowhere near FATIMA's apartment that evening—he had been having dinner with FJ at his house. Even FJ's houseboy had confirmed the story .

No one could afford to doubt Sinclair because no one could afford to doubt SNAPPER. With this single agent, SIS had uncovered the entire order of battle of the Sandinistas, not just in Nicaragua but as Castro's agents for the subversion of the rest of Central America. SNAPPER had handed Her Majesty's Government and the CIA an inside look into the workings of the *Comandantes* and their masters in the DGI—and Castro's plots to destabilize the entire region.

Sinclair's success in the field made his Controller Mackie look very good indeed. Shortly after the Spedding disaster, the traitor's information started showing up in Mackie's tray in a big way. Eventually it rolled in an avalanche of top-grade CX and Mackie had to apply to Personnel for two new analysts to help him sift through the intelligence.

George Sinclair was celebrated as the embodiment of the thrusting new blood that the Service needed to succeed in this new uncertain age.

"And good tasking is what the whole operation hinged on, they tell me. Well done, Brother Mackie, well done!" The Old Man, as C was known, leaned back in his leather chair and yawned, bestowing on Mackie the benefit of his gastric juices. It had been a good lunch.

Mackie preened. He was tickled pink and chuckled to himself. He was being congratulated by none other than the Old Man himself. He sniffed

promotion in the breeze. He could already see the new telly for the awfully
wedded one in the New Year—that should keep her off his back for a while.

"Don't recall meeting your boy," C drawled, opening Sinclair's personnel
file casually. His manner was deceptively relaxed, his eyes bland and watchful
as those of a hotel concierge."Oxbridge, you said?"

"Magdalen, Sir."

The Old Man raised an eyebrow in minor irritation and turned to look at
Mackie over his half-moon specs. That legendary obsession with detail again.

Mackie was quick enough to recover. "*Magdalen*, Oxford, of course, Sir, not
Magdalene, Cambridge."

"Thank you."

The Old Man read in silence, until Mackie decided to say something to be
helpful.

"Anglo-Indian chappie. Touch of the tar brush."

"We could do with more of them, if you ask me. Bloody effective, your boy
. . . damned good operation, SNAPPER. One of the best. Cousins eating out
of my hand now. Need more where that came from."

The Old Man had let Sinclair's personnel file drop onto his desk with a plop
and was now tinkering with his pipe absentmindedly as he looked out across
the river at the Houses of Parliament. The sun had come out from behind the
London smog and the Thames gleamed pleasantly far below them.

"As long as they don't go native on you, Sir." Immediately Mackie wished
he hadn't said that. The disturbing little thought had crept up on him and
caught him totally unaware.

C looked up puzzled, his private thoughts disturbed. "Who? The
Cousins?"

"I mean half-breeds, Sir, like George Sinclair. You don't want them going
native on you."

Mackie could have slit his own throat for his lack of foresight. It simply
would not do to question SNAPPER's pedigree. The Case Officer might be a
mutt, but SNAPPER was pure gold—*blue* blood, the genuine article, and let
no one doubt it, not for a minute.

C thought for a moment.

"Quite. Jolly good work, all the same, Brother Mackie." C had recently
taken to using ecclesiastical jargon.

A green light started blinking on the bank of telephones on his desk. C was
done, and ended the meeting with a nod.

Mackie breathed a sigh of relief and got up to take his leave.

"Now go forth," the Old Man said, with a blessing that he was to become famous for, and with which he would go on to dispatch countless secret servants, some to their deaths, "and sin again."

SNAPPER was proving to be a bloody treasure trove, Mackie would tell his colleagues. Even the most sceptical analysts at Langley, bloody killjoys that they were, could find little or no fault in the quality of SNAPPER CX. The CIA's analysts were paid to find fault and fraud and look for inconsistencies, but there was also an element of professional jealousy on the part of the Cousins at work here. With all their hi-tech gadgetry and unlimited budgets, they never came close to reeling in a source of this calibre in the whole of Central America. Not even General Noriega and all of the narcocrats of Mexico combined were worth more than SNAPPER. Good *humint*—human intelligence—had become very hard to come by these days.

"The goddamn Brits have done it again," drawled Mackie humorously through his nose in a passable imitation of his Texan liaison officer in Grosvenor Square, "scooped us, using brain over brawn, them devious cowboy motherfuckers."

The dividends for Sinclair's masters, both operational and political, were truly exceptional, and were almost too good to be true.

Like the 'magic circle' of Sinclair's supporters on the staff at the College, his progressive supporters on the SIS Recruitment Committee congratulated themselves at having stuck their necks out and voted for an ethnically sensitive candidate—touched, as Mackie so indelicately put it, by the tar brush. We could do with more of his ilk, Mackie would preach at every opportunity.

George Sinclair was one of the few officers in the history of the Service to leapfrog a grade, becoming Number Two of Managua Station immediately in the aftermath of the scandal, and then Acting Head, pending FJ's replacement, and all this at the tender young age of thirty.

PART TWO

*"Give me the boy 'til he's seven
and I'll show you the man."*
—Jesuit dictum

1979
KALI MAA

THROUGH THE LOOKING GLASS, DARKLY

"The shadows began to close in on me, Morpheus, in my penultimate year at the College. It was 1979. It was the summer term, a year after the Black Mass. There was another scandal—a drug scandal this time. What would you expect? It was the late seventies after all, and the Sex Pistols and the Stones ruled. The Cold War was at its hottest. The superpowers were going to blow the planet to Kingdom Come, and they seemed determined to do it before the end of the decade. It felt like we were living inside that song from the sixties—*Eve of Destruction*—you know the one, Morpheus? It did really feel like the world was going to end, and A-level exams were also coming up. The Pope had been murdered by the Opus Dei. Iran had fallen to the Islamists. Nicaragua was being overrun by Communists. There was trouble brewing in Afghanistan and talk of a Soviet invasion. There was this sense of impending doom, and we had to take advantage of the situation and have fun—like the street parties that people held in Europe during the Black Death."

As he tells Morpheus his story, Sinclair closes his eyes and sees before him again the woods and glades around the school. They have been turned lush and thick by the wet summer and provide ample cover for druggery and other illicit pursuits.

A stash of drugs had been dug up by the Bursar's dog, a black Labrador retriever called Calisto, under a bush in the Observatory Gardens. The drugs were not your garden-variety marijuana or ganja or weed or pot or grass or cannabis or whatever they called it back then, but narcotics of a particularly nasty variety, the kind that made you take trips and go psychedelic, and related paraphernalia such as spoons, tourniquets and syringes. The most interesting items in the cache, though, were several vials of morphine that Matron confirmed had been filched from her Dispensary cabinet.

The hush of a besieged city descended over the College once again as the

Einsatzkommando was deployed and swept through the school with the clinical efficiency that had so inspired Heinrich Himmler.

"Here we go again. No one relishes a witch hunt more than the Jesuits," Underhill declared in the Pit the evening of the disaster. "They will use the same tried and tested combination of surveillance, coercion, threats, deduction, cultivation of quislings, moral bribery, blackmail, and the 'turning' of snitches," he predicted.

They both knew that it was the same formula that had trapped the phantom egg-squasher in Surrey in 1971 and the Devil Worshippers the year before. It was only a matter of time before they were exposed.

The operation was again spearheaded by Spock, who was back in his element.

Sinclair remembered Underhill's favourite quotation about 'fear and surprise and an almost fanatical devotion to the Pope' being the best weapons at the disposal of the Society of Jesus. "Substitute the word Pope with Führer and you have the SS," Underhill liked to say, deferring as ever to *The Secret History of the Jesuits*.

Spock's finely honed detection techniques had been acquired at MI5 before he had seen the light on his personal Road to Damascus and joined the Jesuits. But now these skills failed to identify the culprit. The mass punishments and late-night grilling of suspects which had led to the quick identification of the coven of Devil Worshippers a year earlier seemed ineffective now. No one could be persuaded to own up. Doris, Wanking Eddy and Nick Gompertz were the first to be investigated but were quickly discounted as suspects. Their terror in the interrogation rooms—after being woken by the inevitable flashlight in the face in the early hours—was genuine. It didn't take an ex-MI5 interrogator to spot that.

As was the custom, the tuckshop was the first to go. They cancelled Exeat privileges for the senior boys and then they threatened to cancel the half-term holiday for the whole school, as they had done after the Black Mass, but still no one owned up. Spock and his minions prowled the corridors and galleries at night, and his shadow could be seen haunting the various chapels of the College where, it was whispered, he met with his snitches to debrief and task them under the guise of Confession or Sacristy Duty.

The isolation that Sinclair and Underhill had cocooned themselves in protected their secret. Not even Wanking Eddy Cayetano, Doris or Nick Gompertz knew about Sinclair's goodies. They may have partaken of the odd spliff with him, but morphine and heroin were another matter altogether, reserved for the Lotus Eaters. Not even Christopher Larkin had been initiated by Underhill into this darkest of mysteries, the cult of the Sleep God.

TANTUM ERGO

It may have been the stress of that desperate time, as Sinclair imagined the dragnet closing in around him; it may have been the prospect of being twice-nined again; maybe it was the likelihood of another fainting spell brought on by the sight of his pinky blue palms, followed by the disgrace of a public expulsion à la Olatunji, and prolonged social humiliation in Goa—it may have been the effect of all these accumulated fears that caused him to be taken by a fit of recurring malaria.

It happened during Saturday night Benediction, as the thurible clicked and swung, wafting blue clouds of incense over the congregation. The Nosferatu spun around on his heel, swinging the gigantic monstrance around to face the congregation of boys. Caught in the altar lights, the many gilt needles and daggers emanating outwards from the centre of the monstrous device flashed and made it look in Sinclair's febrile imagination like a divine grenade exploding. The righteous detonation of the organ made the church vibrate with its menacing bass, subliminally scaring the living daylights out of those with guilty consciences. The boys began to belt out the *Tantum Ergo* and the thurifer's censer delivered another dose of fumes towards the congregation.

The overwhelming baroque combination of sight, sound and smell must have shortcircuited some crisis of delirium in Sinclair's skull because he turned a pale shade of green and then collapsed in his pew next to Doris in a feverish convulsion.

Some of the boys, thinking back to the Black Mass, later took this to be evidence of diabolic possession brought on by the sight of the transubstantiated host. They said that as Sinclair writhed and jerked on the floor, you could see the whites of his eyes and that he was frothing at the mouth, just like the girl in *The Exorcist*.

KALI MAA AND THE NOCTIFER

Sinclair was sweating like a pig in his malarial delirium that night, half sleeping in between hideous nightmares. They were in shockingly bright colours and involved needles and intravenous contraptions hooked up to bags of brown blood, blue fingers and leaden coffins, egg yolks, black crabs and scarlet-robed monkey judges wearing wigs in a court of justice. A peculiar odour filled the courtroom. Was it incense, or something else? Was he still rolling around on the floor of the church next to Doris? A sinister macacq with the black cap and soutane of a hanging judge was about to pass sentence from the High Altar when something, most likely his own desperate panic, made him wake up.

He was on his back in the Infirmary, looking up, as though through thick smoked glass, into the dark hypnotic pools of Matron's eyes.

Nurse Bergsma, first name Xancha, was an Australian well into her thirties, and most people considered her to be a cold bitch. Rumour had it that she was part Dutch-Gypsy mongrel, part Aboriginal, which is what gave her that disturbing dark complexion. This pagan attribute created an aura of exotic dread about her. For most of the boys the idea of coming into physical contact with her was creepy. Nurse Bergsma was the antithesis of the beloved Caucasian women of the seventies—Charlie's Angels, the ABBA girls, Blondie's Debbie Harry, and Stevie Nicks—who watched over the boys from posters in their dormitories.

There were dark bruises under Matron's eyes, as if she was permanently exhausted, and perhaps that was what gave her her frightening demeanour. She had a laser-like gaze that penetrated your eyes and into the back of your skull. It was a look that would turn milk sour and easily cause livestock and crops to wither away and die.

What could be keeping her up all night to make her so tired? They said that she lived alone in a cottage up there on the exposed flank of Pendle. Perhaps it *was* witchcraft that she practised up there on that windswept fell, some of the boys said. After all that *had* been the favourite pastime of women in these parts since time immemorial.

Nurse Bergsma was known for administering drastic no-nonsense cures without compassion or the slightest hint of maternal tenderness—the BVM could take care of that. Her paranormal X-ray stare could smoke out malingerers in a matter of seconds. This explained why the Infirmary was rarely visited and lay empty for most of the year, except during the flu season. A spell in the Infirmary was to be avoided at all costs, and was anything but a cosy retreat from the classroom or from the hell-on-earth of cross-country runs or the freezing mud of the rugby pitches, so the boys stayed away except *in extremis.* The Infirmary was visited mainly after faintings or accidents on the rugby or cricket pitches, or when the overseas boys threatened to infest the school with one of their tropical diseases.

The other visitors were George Sinclair and Guy Underhill. But *their* visits were surreptitious and focused exclusively on the contents of the drug cabinet in the Dispensary.

Somehow the Infirmary was permanently suffused with a weak submarine light, and seemed to exist in a different time zone and dimension from the rest of the College. It was located in a remote wing of the building that you reached through a corridor lined with dusty vitrines full of rare stuffed animals. There were dodos, Amazonian macacqs, opossums and armadillos, the endowment of an eccentric Victorian explorer and taxidermist, an old *alumnus* and a contemporary of Darwin. On the wall before the entrance to the Dispensary, was a large, age-darkened painting of the famous Old Boy riding a cayman on the banks of the Amazon, surrounded by brown natives lurking shiftily in the tropical foliage. In a glass box under the painting sat a strange griffin-like creature, a hybrid of an eagle, an owl egret, a kestrel and a crow, and God knows what else. The dirty copper plate at the base of the exhibit labelled this forgery a 'Noctifer'. The bird's eye gleamed like a piece of polished black flint.

What happened to him in the Infirmary was one of Sinclair's biggest secrets. Before then he had two secrets: his addiction to morphine after encountering Morpheus during his near-death experience in Surrey; and the awful secret of his middle names.

Underhill also had a secret, which he revealed to Sinclair. It was that he had withstood being twice-nined by Spock by numbing his hands with pure alcohol stolen from the science labs. On the other hand, whatever had happened to him at the Hall would always remain classified, even to Sinclair.

For as long as he was to know Sinclair, Underhill would never be quite sure whether he believed what Sinclair told him had happened in the Infirmary that night—that Matron had caught him wanking. That he was the only one in the Infirmary that night and that in between bouts of feverish shivering he was masturbating away merrily under the blankets when he suddenly caught a whiff of the almond scent of skin cream. And that by then it was too late. A flashlight was in his face and he felt a clammy cold hand grab his wrist.

Before he knew it the flashlight was switched off, leaving him temporarily blinded. He felt her weight come down on him, pinioning him down. Her hand moved down his wrist, encircled his hand, then, incredibly, grasped his burning rod. Before he could yell at the cold shock of her touch, the other hand was quickly clamped across his mouth. He lay perfectly still, his heart bursting in his chest, for God knows how long.

In the dark, time cannot be measured.

Sinclair felt her breathing thickly into his ear as she hissed: "I gotcha now, you little bastard, I gotcha now . . . I gotcha now . . . I gotcha now . . ."

She repeated this mantra over and over again and Sinclair suddenly realized to his horror that she was rubbing herself against him.

Sinclair told Underhill that although he was terrified, he could not prevent the rising wave of ecstasy between his feverish thighs brought on by the rhythm of her cold hand on hot *lingam*. The next thing he knew was that her tongue had invaded his mouth and was thrusting itself deep into his throat. Perhaps it was the fever, or the disorientating effects of the dark, but he could have sworn that the tongue that probed deeply into his airways was abnormally long, cold and reptilian, like Linda Blair's in *The Exorcist*.

The image of the blue-skinned devil-goddess Kali flashed across Sinclair's mind as he lay helpless in the dark under the thrusting harpie. It was the image of the vengeful and destructive *devi*, her crimson vampire's tongue dripping with blood, the one on the Hindu icon which Grannyjee kept next to the crucifix on her dresser back in Goa. In that nightmarish icon Kali grasped several severed heads in one of her several hands, while trampling on a grey cadaver, which had now acquired the face of George Sinclair.

Sinclair told Underhill that he and Xancha Bergsma climaxed simultaneously, both convulsing together in the night as he surrendered at last to the overwhelming warmth of her dark, Aboriginal, almond-scented assault.

When she had finished feeding, the *durga* sprung off him, withdrawing as suddenly as she had descended upon him. Sinclair was left lying there exhausted, winded and feverish in the dark.

The next morning she totally ignored him as his malarial eyes followed her around the Infirmary and he fingered himself absentmindedly, reliving the unbelievable visitation that had come upon him in the dark. Perhaps it had not been her, but some succubus with an Australian accent. Perhaps there was something to the suspicions of witchcraft that were whispered about her in the corridors and dormitories. Being a witch, who had the power to invade one's dreams, she may have only violated him in spirit, so to speak. But the scent of almonds that now impregnated his pajamas and his sheets was proof that there had been nothing incorporeal about it. He had been physically set upon in the night. She had left her scent on him, marking her territory like a wolf and claiming him as her property.

Sinclair received a visit from Underhill later that day. He remembered his friend's breathless and hair-raising account of the Jesuit dragnet that was slowly and inevitably going to ensnare him—him being Sinclair. He noted that Underhill excluded himself as a target of the investigation. He also remembered that Underhill was distracted that afternoon. He was elated about something. Underhill had finally persuaded Christopher Larkin to give him a blowjob. It was a seminal day in Guy Underhill's history.

The rest of the day was spent in agonizing worry, in between fitful bouts of non-sleep. Sinclair rehearsed the inevitable disaster in his head again and again—another set of twice nine, another fainting spell, the public humiliation of expulsion, possibly a spell in prison in town at the mercy of the rapists and the nonces. But what followed would be much worse—prolonged and excruciating embarrassment at home after he had been shipped home to Goa in disgrace—the silent meals under his father's baleful stare, the tears of his mother and the shame of the whole damned extended family. But the worst thing was that it would have broken Grannyjee's poor old heart, if she had been alive, and now she wouldn't even be there to comfort him in his disgrace.

That evening Matron came and sat on the edge of the bed. At first he thought she had come in friendship to talk or explain her behaviour. Instead she gripped his wrist firmly to take his pulse while the thermometer was thrust under his tongue. She looked only at her wristwatch. Sinclair could smell her skin again, and tumescence overcame him. Without looking at her, his eyes lowered in shame, the thermometer still wedged under his tongue, he tried to manoeuvre her hand lower. She resisted and he felt her stiffen.

She turned those terrible liquid black eyes down on him, and hissed grimly. "Watch it, you dirty little bastard, or I'll have you *beaten*."

That night he dreamt that he saw Calisto, the Bursar's black dog, snatch his drugs out of his hand. Calisto wore a Jesuitical dog collar and had the face of a lesser Jesuit called Fr Pottifer. Alice-like, Sinclair chased the fleeing Labrador-priest down an interminable subterranean tunnel, which was very much like the tunnel under the sacristy that led to the crypt with the lead coffins. He was screaming his lungs out for his drugs for the love of God give me my drugs back I can't live without my drugs they are my only comfort my only source of joy and pleasure they are the key to my secret world without them I am nothing without them I cannot talk to my friend Morpheus or forget my past so give me back my drugs for the love of God give them back . . .

Just as he was emerging from the tunnel into the bright sunlight, suddenly he was wide awake and the flashlight was in his face again. It crossed his feverish mind that the incident of the previous night had never ended or had never happened or was just about to begin. Or that he was in a time warp. He must have said something because that firm cold hand was clamped across his mouth again. He froze immobile again as he felt her weight come down on him again.

But instead of arousing him again, she breathed in his ear in that Antipodean accent of hers. "Now I know you're the little bastard who's been stealing from my drug cabinet."

My God, I must have screamed out in my sleep, he thought as a new wave of fear paralyzed him.

"Now get your filthy brown hide into my office at once," she hissed, and sprang off him into the dark again.

He followed her in sheer panic, tripping over his dressing-gown cord, losing a slipper in the dark, wide-eyed with terror as his heart thumped out of control and his hands and feet went cold. He followed her into her office, expecting to see a Jesuit executioner waiting there. A night light was on beside her desk. The office was empty and smelled of disinfectant and floor polish. She was writing something on a pad on her desk, her denunciation, the verdict, his death warrant, perhaps. She took her time.

When she had finished she spun around in her swivel chair and her cold black eyes bored into him like she knew all of his secrets, past present and future.

"Kneel," she commanded, and grasped his ears.

For as long as he lived he would never be able to forget that dark forbidden taste and the scent of almonds and the pressure of her hands on the back of his head. Unforgettable too was the shudder that racked her body, and the mumbled litany of incantations in an unrecognizable language beyond time, perhaps Romany, perhaps Aboriginal, as she orgasmed again and again . . .

From then on Sinclair avoided the Infirmary even though what had happened there fascinated him in a nightmarish kind of way.

In his imagination Nurse Bergsma had become the vengeful Kali Maa, dark-faced Goddess of Destruction, collector of severed heads and mongrel bitch, and she lurked there in the Infirmary in her sub-aquatic, almond-scented lair, guarded by the hybrid Noctifer and the lunatic Old Boy on his cayman.

Then one night things took an unexpected turn. He was pulling his pajamas from under his pillow before getting into bed. He caught a whiff of that unforgettable almond scent emanating from under the pillow. He heard the tiny clink of glass upon glass and saw two vials of morphine lying there.

1986
SHAPESHIFTER

HELEN

"My past caught up with me in 1986, Morpheus. I'd been back at Magdalen for two years. I had taken my First and was well into my DPhil. And then who should come up to Oxford but Helen Henshaw. When I found out, the first person I thought of was Madame Bernabeu. Perhaps this is it, I thought, the gift she had promised me when I left Martinique. She had said that it would take time, so perhaps, despite the distance, the *gris gris* has finally worked its magic. Perhaps she has managed to deliver Helen Henshaw into my hands at last, through her intercession with *Monsieur le Bokor* in Morne Diab', just as she delivered Lucy to me in Fort de France. But, dear Morpheus, Lucy was no Helen, and Helen was no Lucy, thank God. Lucy was to ground meat what Helen was to *filet mignon*."

Morpheus chuckles dutifully.

Sinclair had found out about Helen's arrival from the list of new admissions posted on the bulletin board in the School of Archaeology and Anthropology. He would never be able to forget that day when he saw the announcement, he told Morpheus, because it was the same day that he received the news of his father's death in a car smash in the suburbs of Goa. It was the day that Sinclair officially became an orphan in this world. Grannyjee had died before that ill-fated ouija session at the College, followed not too long after by his mother, exhausted after years of resisting cancer, and now the Major was gone.

And now here was Helen re-entering his life through the revolving door of fate. What a day it had been indeed.

That summer Helen had graduated from Queen Mary and Westfield College in London and now had gained a place at St Hilda's, the all-girl college a stone's throw across the bridge from Magdalen. The list said that she was to do an MA in Hindu Mythology, special subject 'Temple Prostitution'.

"Yes, Morpheus, you may well smile, but temple prostitution is a serious and highly respected occupation. It has been so, ever since the Oracle at Delphi."

Sinclair lingered behind the ivy around of the gate of St Hilda's for the greater part of a wet Wednesday afternoon that Michaelmas term, wrapped in his cape like a Shakespearean murderer, squeezing his *gris gris* as he waited for Helen to emerge. After what seemed like hours caught sight of her profile for a split second as she glided past him on her bicycle. Some sentimental Highland gene must have been triggered by the sight of her, because in his head the plaintive wail of a thousand bagpipes erupted in all its tragi-romantic glory. The sight of her unforgettable profile also affected him physically and set his guts awash in a surge of adrenaline. The massed bagpipes of love going off in his head made the hairs on his arms and on the back of his neck stand on end. The hunt to recover the past was on.

He followed her duffle-coated back from a safe distance on his bike. Careful, easy does it George, there's plenty of time, up the High Street he pedalled, past All Souls College and the Radcliffe Camera, then past the Bodleian Library, crossing Broad Street and then along the South Parks Road up to the Natural History Museum opposite the monstrous brickwork of Keble.

The Pitt Rivers Museum is the anthropological annex of the university's Natural History Museum. Its wrought-iron roofing was designed by the Victorians to mimic the ribcages of the dinosaur exhibits and Sinclair felt like he was entering a gigantic skeleton that afternoon as he crept in behind his quarry. It was there under the metal ribs and later in the silence of the Pitt Rivers that he stalked Helen, hiding behind the vitrines and their dusty treasures.

From behind the case which houses a collection of shrunken heads, the *tsantsas* of the Jivaro Indians of Ecuador, he spied her. He saw her tap out a code—three, two, followed by three again—on the door of the Curator's office. It was next to a staircase which leads up to the second floor, near the exhibit dedicated to the African spirit cults. The door opened and closed quickly, as if she had been expected.

Sinclair impatiently killed time among the exhibits, patrolling the upper galleries of the museum, one eye on the cases, the other on the door of the Curator's office. Eventually Helen emerged from the office. It had been an hour since she had tapped her code on the door. She was flushed and was straightening her hair. Her myopia prevented her from seeing Sinclair as he watched her from behind a case of poisoned arrows.

It was then that he saw her face.

Until then he had managed only to catch its profile or a hint of her dimpled cheeks as he trailed behind her. Seen head on, her once angelic face had changed and gone were the innocence and openness that he had known when they were lovers.

Sinclair contrived the meeting by carefully walking backwards into her, beside a vitrine of South Sea head-hunters' masks. Helen spun around, and a sudden jolt of recognition brought her out of her reverie. She frowned short-sightedly, and then a shadow like the Valley of Death fell like a curtain across her face. It was as if she had seen the Devil.

"George Sinclair—"

"*Helen*, my God, what a surprise . . . Is it really you?"

But the slightly crossed, lazy eyes that had once made Sinclair's heart thump out of control were now hooded with suspicion. Her eyes avoided his, slipping away to look at anything but him. Sinclair looked down into her face and noticed mauve shadows under her eyes, the colour of melancholy. She seemed tired. Gone was the dimpled smile that used to light up her face whenever she saw him. Now she was cold and distant and her eyes kept sliding away from his probing look. She was a beautiful cornered animal, desperate to escape.

An awkward and stilted exchange followed as they emerged from the Museum into the damp Oxford afternoon. He tried repeatedly and unsuc-cessfully to persuade her to have dinner, or just a quick coffee. None of which were acceptable to Helen. She had other commitments.

"I have to finish my essay tonight for Doctor Aggarwal . . ." or "Can't, sorry, I'll miss my lecture . . .", and finally, without even looking at him, "Look George, I really must go, I'm running late, I'm sure we'll bump into each other again, alright? See you later."

Sinclair watched her cycle off, her golden ponytail tucked snugly into the hood of her duffle-coat. He watched her float away into the distance towards the Bodleian. She had left him there, standing at the doors of the Museum in front of the depressing Victorian brickwork of Keble College. A sense of emo-tional nausea that Sinclair he had not felt for many years overtook him again, like the return of an old enemy.

That afternoon, Sinclair re-entered hell, which by now was becoming a familiar place. If you had asked him, he would have admitted that he was beginning to feel at home there.

He neglected his research and he knew that his DPhil was in jeopardy, my God, how he loved that word. With every passing day that he remained clois-tered in his rooms at Magdalen, immobilized by jealousy and adolescent obsession, the quicksands of Moral and Spiritual Jeopardy threatened to swallow him up and add him to the long list of Oxford's failures. To torture him-self, Sinclair played on his cassette recorder the sugary ballads and love songs of the seventies, and most of all, repeatedly, the songs that they had played at the Great Academies Ball when he had met Helen—*The Hustle, December '63 (Oh What a Night), Silly Love Songs, It's Raining Again* . . .

He ate little and stocked up instead on drugs from his dealer on the corner of Cornmarket and doubled the morphine doses.

The trusty tuckbox and its secret compartment that housed the syringes and vials was soon brimming to capacity. It was a war chest that, he noticed miserably, was always well stocked whenever he was most unhappy.

After what seemed like weeks of notes delivered through the inter-College messenger, and many hours keeping a lonely vigil outside the lecture halls and haunting the gates of St Hilda's, she agreed to see him.

ADDISON'S WALK

"What *did* you do to Guy up there?"

There it was at last, the unavoidable question that he had been dreading for so long.

She had finally accepted his entreaties to walk with her and at least hear him out.

She had asked the dreaded question without bothering to look at him, as they strolled stiffly along the banks of the Cherwell behind Magdalen, on the far side of Addison's Walk. Sinclair watched her face with covert sideways glances as he fingered Madame Bernabeu's *gris gris* in his pocket, hoping for luck. The remains of a headache at the edge of his eyes bothered him. Not even gentle Morpheus had managed to soothe his nerves in the hours leading up to the meeting.

Helen's face was turned stubbornly away from him. The failing light of the afternoon caressed the golden cap of her hair and cast her profile into shad-ow. It was now almost autumn and a fine mist drifted across the sandstone walls of the college. The world of green leaf was slowly browning in the twi-light. The year was approaching its final season. The wind was up again and was soughing through the trees, tugging and pulling at the dying leaves. The deer in the park behind the New Buildings were twitchy, nervous even, as if some primeval disaster was about to visit the herd.

The colours of the sky that afternoon reminded Sinclair of another late summer afternoon when he had walked with her among the ruined chapels of Highgate Cemetery. Back then when they were both different people, barely children, in what seemed a different century but was in fact only less than a handful of years ago. Back then when their hands were not strangers to each other, as they were now.

His answer had been rehearsed for many weeks now but when he heard his voice recite it, it sounded hollow and deceitful and incoherent—*we were different people back then Helen I was trying to find myself and so was Guy in a way we were both victims of the Establishment Guy was sacrificed at the altar of Jesuit capitalism my father later coughed up several hundred thousand pounds they were going to get Guy anyway they made me do it as a way of punishing me and humiliating him and to make it more painful for both of us it was inevitable but they chose to torture us instead*—and so on and so on, as they walked side by side down the path.

All this seemed to go over her head. She probably wasn't even listening to him any more. They rounded the bend of Addison's Walk under Magdalen Bridge, completing the circle and heading back up to where they had begun their walk. Finally she spoke. It was as if she had not heard a single word of Sinclair's excuses, or somehow had chosen not to register what he was saying.

"At first they told me that it was a nervous breakdown. Then my parents said that he had been caught with drugs, and warned me to stay away. But there was something about the whole thing that didn't seem right. So I went to see him in Hull."

They stopped at the iron gates. She still refused to look at him. "You know, *Guy* may forgive you one day, perhaps he even has already. But *I* won't. Not ever. What you did to my cousin was totally and utterly monstrous and unforgivable. *Monstrous . . .*"

For once, Sinclair was at a loss for words. In the distance, one of the deer in the park behind the New Buildings keened as if in agony.

Sinclair begged her to walk with him behind the Deer Park. He wanted to show her the lamp-post that had inspired C. S. Lewis to write the *The Chronicles of Narnia*. Did she know that Lewis had lived in the New Buildings, where Sinclair had his rooms? Had she ever read *The Lion, the Witch and the Wardrobe*?

She wasn't the least bit interested. She had to get back to St Hilda's. She insisted. She had had enough. They entered the chill of the Cloisters.

As a Demy, or Half-Fellow of the college, Sinclair was granted certain privileges which included access to the top of Magdalen Tower. Helen reluctantly gave in to his insistence and they climbed the spiral stairway up to the top of the tower that stands as a sentinel over the southern reaches of Oxford.

From far below, the muted detonation of a shotgun reached them from the Deer Park.

They stood silently surveying the roofscape of the city beneath them. They saw the Cherwell glinting silently beneath them, and Magdalen Bridge.

The silence between them was full of unspoken, hateful things. Sinclair felt like Satan standing at Christ's side, in the desert. High above the bluish panorama of the twilit city with its spires and domes rose massively towering clouds, their edges lit by a vivid sliver of fire from the setting sun.

"We've seen this before, haven't we, Helen," he said, hoping to remind her of that special afternoon during their first half-term. They had watched a *fata morgana* forming in the clouds over the skyline of London from a bench high up on Parliament Hill. It was before their visit to Highgate Cemetery.

This did not impress her. Her steadfastness before his wiles was impressive. He did not remember this type of strength of character in her from before.

He insisted. This might be his last chance, after all. "Ever since you came up you've been avoiding me."

His voice cracked and it came out in a way that he didn't want it to, because it sounded like someone whining. It almost sounded hysterical. Now it was Sinclair who could not bring himself to look at her face. Instead he moved his hand towards hers, which rested on the sandstone of the tower's edge. She withdrew her hand instinctively, as if from an approaching serpent.

"Why does it surprise you that I *do* avoid you?" she demanded. "What you did was monstrous, truly disgusting. Can't you just try to understand that?"

That was when he seriously thought of jumping off the tower.

Before they parted at the Porter's Lodge, she had turned to him and said: "Just remember, George Sinclair, that what goes around comes around."

Sinclair felt condemned, and sadder than he had for a long time.

It was not only because the realisation was beginning to dawn on him that he would never have her again, despite the power of Madame Bernabeu's *gris gris*. There were certain situations that were too complex even for the *loas* to unravel, and this was one of them.

What he couldn't get out of his head was a resurrected memory, which he thought he had long ago safely entombed in the past. It was of the gaping expression of disbelief on the face of Helen's cousin—he couldn't bear even to say his name—as he had been snatched from the Pit and dragged down into the underworld.

Adios, Motherfucker.

THE PURSUIT OF DOCTOR AGGARWAL

Who the fuck was Doctor Aggarwal, anyway?

The evening after Helen had left him standing there like an idiot at the Porter's Lodge, he made up his mind.

He had awoken refreshed after an afternoon of morphine-induced sleep, and sitting up at his desk, he determined to attack the problem and achieve his objectives methodically. Discipline was what was needed. His dead father would have been proud of his determination that afternoon.

First things first. Who *was* this Doctor Aggarwal anyway, this eminence that she was so eager to please? What were his weaknesses and what were his appetites? After all, isn't a man most vulnerable through that which he desires the most? Knowing Indians as he did, and their desperate vanity, it would not take long to identify the good Doctor's Achilles' Heel.

He had after all decided to be methodical. He looked his new Nemesis up in the Faculty lists of the School of Archaeology and Anthropology. There he was—Doctor Prabhudas Das Gupta Aggarwal Bindrinwhale. Sinclair smiled grimly at the irony of the shared middle name. Aggarwal was a Fellow at Brasenose, an expert in Hindu mythology with several publications to his name. He also acted as Assistant Curator of the Pitt Rivers Museum. Sinclair was surprised that he had not come across him before. So what. Where did all this information get him? What could he do about the situation? He needed a way in, a foot in the door. What was the next step, where would the fork in the road take him now? Some kind of drastic intervention was required. Something quick and effective like the hexing of Lucy Kennedy in Martinique.

Then something providential happened. Fate delivered into Sinclair's hands a tool with which to further his dark crusade. He did not think twice about using it.

As he continued to stalk Helen around the city, he had noticed on a couple of occasions that she would meet a girl in a grey duffle-coat outside the Ashmolean or the Pitt Rivers after lectures. The girls would unlock their bikes, wheeling them along until they were ready to cycle together down the High Street to St Hilda's. She seemed to be particularly close to Helen and would clasp her affectionately by the arm or whisper closely in her ear, and she often made Helen laugh.

One morning when he had worked out that Helen and the mystery friend had a different timetable, Sinclair carefully knocked the girl's books out of her hands outside the Ashmolean. There on the pavement as he helped her pick the books up he released his charm and guile to seduce her. He insisted that she make him pay for his clumsiness by accepting a coffee in the Faculty Bar on St Giles.

Jane Redfern was mousey in a typically English way. The tones of her skin just a shade away from those of a classic 'English Rose'. There was a sickliness about her that hinted of anaemia or some other liverishness.

Jane just failed the beauty test—she was barely on the wrong side of the line of what separates a plain woman from a beautiful one—a matter of just millimetres between the nose and the cusp of the lip and a half-shade of skin colouring.

Her face was a wide-open book, and her smile was the type that could appear clownish in certain lights. She was like a flawed imitation of Helen. She was one of those English girls who has an eternal cold, and she sniffled into her handkerchief constantly. Her skin was very white and Sinclair imagined that his fingers would leave imprints on it that he suspected could easily turn into bruises. A girl that bruises easily, he thought, contemplating this latest turn of events and its possibilities.

Her smile at first was shy and suspicious but her interest in Sinclair betrayed itself in subtle ways.

"So what are you reading, Jane?"

"Arch and Anth."

He tried to engage her with a direct look but he could not hold her eyes, which kept sliding away in sideways glances, as if she was worried about being followed or expected to see someone she knew.

"Right," he said. "I thought I'd seen you around the Faculty . . . Oh, yes, that's it, didn't I see you talking to Helen Henshaw the other day?"

"Do you know Helen then?" she asked, wiping her nose with her handkerchief and watching the door.

"Oh, yes, we go back a long way," he said nonchalantly.

"How long?" This time she seemed genuinely interested. This time she held his gaze, leaning almost imperceptibly forward across the table.

"Since school. I was her boyfriend, I suppose."

She raised an eyebrow sceptically and blew her nose. "Oh, how funny, Helen and I were at school together in Ascot and she never mentioned you."

Outside it was starting to rain and umbrellas were opening. When they emerged into the cold September air it was slick underfoot on the pavements of St Giles. Sinclair slid his arm serpent-like and almost unnoticed through the crook of Jane's arm, so that she would not slip. They walked down Broad Street with their arms linked as if they had known each other for ever. With his free hand Sinclair wheeled Jane's bicycle along, with its basket of books, a True Gentleman. A Man for Others. A Snake in the Grass.

Autumn had finally set in.

Jane lived in a dingy flat a short bike ride up the Cowley Road. Her flatmates were two other English Mice, medical students from Northern Grammar schools.

That night Sinclair took her to the Half Moon, where they were playing Irish music, and carefully set about getting her drunk. When he was sure the Mice were gone out for the evening, he led her giggling back to the flat and into her room. There, he locked the door and then proceeded to have straightforward, beery student sex with her. Sinclair undertook this task with a lightness that surprised even him.

He found the proceedings barely satisfying, but they gave Jane's pasty skin a healthy rosy blush and a resulted in a surprisingly vocal orgasm. This pleased Sinclair because this result was entirely disproportionate to his half-hearted effort.

Afterwards, once the first round of sex was out of the way, they continued the exploration of their common interest—Helen Henshaw.

"She is not to know about us, by the way," Sinclair cautioned, "if she were to find out, her reaction may be unpredictable. You see, Helen and I had a problem a long time ago, but thank God that's all ancient history, and instead it's now me and you, Janey, my sweet dear, warm, wet Janey . . ."

They lay there in the sweaty sheets in the stuffy room with its over-active central heating. Sinclair persuaded Jane to try a joint. He taught her how to draw the smoke in, hold it in and exhale, while he massaged her inner thigh.

The drug had the effect that he had been hoping for. She didn't stop talking for the rest of the evening, and talked and talked long into the night, providing in passing some very useful intelligence.

For a start, it turned out that Jane Redfern had been a year above Helen at the convent in Ascot. It didn't take Sinclair long to get Jane to admit that she had had, and still did have, a schoolgirl 'pash' on Helen.

"Don't you worry, my sweet, warm, *sopping* wet Janey," he whispered in her ear as he stroked her, "it's entirely understandable, in fact I'd be surprised if you hadn't."

She told him, as he started to bring her to orgasm again, how it had all started.

"You see, at the convent in Ascot I was Helen's 'elder sister'. Every new girl was assigned an 'elder sister' . . . oh, George, you oriental devil, that's marvellous . . . the first time I saw her, she didn't impress me. She was very unsure of herself back then, and very plain . . . ooh, yes, more, there . . . In fact, I found her a bit mousey."

Sinclair smiled to himself behind Jane's left shoulder as he thrusted dutifully, all ears.

"I remember exactly how it happened . . . more, oh more please, George . . . I was teaching her how to hold her racquet in the squash courts . . . oh yes, George, that's good . . . very nice . . . we were both sweating from running around, and as I grasped her hand to teach her the correct grip, my lips accidentally brushed against her cheek . . ." and then, as she began her noisy climax, "oh, my God, George Sinclair, wherever . . . did . . . you . . . learn how to do . . . that . . . to a girl?"

Jane had never recovered from the thrill of that first modest physical encounter with Helen. And of course the clueless Helen hadn't even noticed and was to remain blissfully ignorant of the motives behind Jane's overfriendly solicitations. It never crossed her mind why Jane had the un-English tendency of touching and kissing and hugging her and looking hard into her eyes, whereas with the other girls she was indifferent and stand-offish.

Jane never brought herself to confess her pash to Helen, preferring instead the titillation of the unrequited crush.

"I'll do anything for her, George. Some days I just hang around with her and pretend to agree with her ramblings and theories, just for the pleasure of sitting beside her and being able to squeeze her hand and to feel the softness of her cheek when I give her a goodbye kiss."

Sinclair knew that the same modest pleasures that kept Jane going—the feel of Helen's cheek, the pressure of her hand on your arm—would be denied to him forever, like the pauper's drop of water denied the rich man's burning tongue.

"I'm jealous," Sinclair said, and he actually meant what he said this time.

"Oh, don't worry, George, it'll never come to anything . . . it's more a hobby, really, just a silly schoolgirl pash, and I have you now, anyway . . ."

Sinclair nevertheless encouraged her to go on. It was always healthy to talk about one's sexual hang-ups.

The highlight of Jane's pathetic attachment was that Helen had once fallen asleep on her shoulder after an evening of drinking, and Jane had been able to surreptitiously suck Helen's lovely, slender, unbelievable nail-chewed fingers while she slept.

Sinclair smirked into his pillow.

As long as Helen was close by, that was all Jane asked. To give her credit, though, she knew that a full blown relationship with Helen was not on the cards.

"For a start, she's healthily heterosexual. I knew all about you and her at school."

"But you said that she had never mentioned me . . ."

"I was just testing to see your reaction," she giggled, as Sinclair lit another joint for her.

"There was no reaction, you see, sweet Janey, because to me Helen Henshaw is ancient history, and what I want now is you."

"Well let's keep it that way," she yawned contentedly, as Sinclair licked her stiffening nipples.

Towards two in the morning, Sinclair was beginning to feel exhausted, but Jane's appetite seemed to increase as the night wore on, perhaps due to the effects of the weed. She begged him to continue pleasuring her. As she greedily sucked in the smoke of their fourth spliff, he complied with her request. After another of Jane's prolonged convulsions, the conversation took the turn he had been hoping for. Sinclair finally hit paydirt, because the matter of Doctor Aggarwal came up.

SHAPESHIFTING

The Mice had come home and were now safely tucked up in their beds. In the flat up the Cowley Road, in between bouts of now passionless grinding in the early hours of the morning, Sinclair kept listening. Jane Redfern just wouldn't shut up. He was able to gather from her that Helen had started to become interested in India and things Indian while at London University.

"No thanks to me, I'm sure," said Sinclair sourly.

"Well, you may actually have had some kind of influence, but minor, I expect."

Sinclair was discovering that Jane had a talent for cruelty without seeming to be conscious of it. She went on: "Back then we were sharing a flat in Highgate, near Hampstead Heath. She was at St Mary and Westfield College, reading anthropology. One day she came back, very excited about something, and told me that she had been to a lecture given by some Indian doctor at the School of Oriental and African Studies. The subject had been temple prostitution in India. Apparently that's Aggarwal's speciality. He was a visiting lecturer from Oxford. She told me that she had been fascinated by the subject and had managed to talk to him after the lecture, and that in that one conversation, he had changed the way she looked at the world . . . and then she just became more and more obsessed with his work, and she started visiting him in Oxford. I didn't like it one bit, I can tell you. Helen was always one for hairbrained schemes and theories, and vulnerable to strong personalities—the Guru Syndrome. I warned her about believing all that psycho-babble."

"Have you ever met this Aggarwal character?" Sinclair asked casually.

"I only met him up here, after we both came up from London. I felt that I knew him by then, because Helen used to go on an on about him. He's creepy. He's got these Elvis sideburns, and he's a bit of a smiler and a charmer—I think he thinks he's God's gift to women, that sort, you know? And he smells—whenever Helen used to come back to London from her trips to Oxford to see him, she seemed to have picked up this curious smell—something like a mixture of curry and incense, but with something sour thrown in, or something like that. I couldn't stand that smell . . . it's as if it had become ingrained in her clothes. I made her take her stuff to the dry cleaners, but when it came back, it still had that awful smell . . . sort of nauseating. It was even in her hair."

"Sounds like they were sleeping together, at that stage, weren't they?" he asked her, his voice carefully neutral.

"Actually, no. I could tell they weren't. Women can tell, you know. But anyway she told me—Helen has always been very open with me, you know. Her thing with Aggarwal was purely platonic at that stage. Then one Sunday night she came back from Oxford. She was positively radiant, and seemed transformed, as if she'd been charged with some weird energy."

Helen told Jane that Aggarwal had asked her to be his research assistant on his next study tour of temples in India that summer. Of course she had agreed to become Doctor Aggarwal's amanuensis.

The sun was rising over Headington Hill and soon the rattle of bicycle chains would bring Oxford out of its slumbers and the first buses would be growling down the Cowley Road.

Finally sated after their marathon session, Jane eased herself from under

Sinclair in the flat on Cowley Road, and returned to her story.

Helen and Aggarwal had arrived together in Calcutta—which, incidentally, Sinclair informed Jane was named after the goddess Kali—in the summer of 1985. They were to make their way across the Subcontinent and down to Tamil Nadu by train, stopping off at Benares to study the deteriorating condition of the funerary temples and to interview the prostitutes along the sacred river.

Aggarwal left her to her own devices for two or three days, while he visited certain associates and academics at the university.

"Or so he claimed," declared Jane as she reached across Sinclair to the night table for a hankie to blow her nose, which was dripping again. "I reckon he was up to no good."

Sinclair can see Helen now with his inner eye. She cuts a lonely but romantic figure sitting there on her balcony, tanned shoulders draped warmly in her shawl, looking out over the city as dusk falls on the reflected lights of the river. The golden light of the dying Indian sun slants nicely off her hair. A funeral procession of saffron and crimson passes by in the background, soundlessly. Flames lick up around the *ghats*, and some cadaver's skull is being smashed in by the ritual rod. In the cool waters of the river, women bathe and wash their clothes as they have done for millennia, downstream from a pier where a squatting boy nonchalantly uncoils his excrement into the slick waters of the river of life and death.

It was inevitable that Helen should become very ill in India. So ill in fact, that she had almost died. And who other to nurse her back to a precarious health than her master and guru, the good Doctor Aggarwal?

"Helen told me that in Benares, one day while Aggarwal was still absent visiting those nameless associates of his, something very strange happened to her. She had gone for a walk around the Kalighat, the funerary temple of the goddess Kali that she was obsessed with. She had been followed there by a huge black bird, it must have been a crow, it certainly wasn't a vulture. Whenever she looked up she would see the animal perched above her, looking down at her, its head cocked, its eyes looking directly into hers."

As Jane spoke, Sinclair remembered the Noctifer.

"The bird scared her so much that she fainted in the courtyard of the temple, under the midday sun. Only to be rescued by Aggarwal, who it seemed had appeared out of nowhere, providentially, because she swore that she could only have been unconscious for a few minutes."

The good Doctor had taken her back to the hostel to minister to her needs.

Sinclair sees her again.

It is later that afternoon. She has woken alone in her room, her hair a sweaty tangled mess, her brown eyes bright with fever. She lies beneath a spinning ceiling fan, which rotates slowly and inevitably like a prayer wheel, or like the karmic circle of days, or like an astrological chart of the Zodiac.

As she lies transfixed by the infinite, hypnotic rotation of the blades, an expression lodges itself in her feverish mind and repeats itself with each turn of the fan: *What goes around comes around . . . What goes around comes around . . . What goes around comes around . . .*

She drifts back into a complicated, troubled slumber.

Helen sleeps fitfully, and outside, dusk falls. Funeral pyres slowly light up along the banks of the river, like distant fairy lights reflected in the slow metallic gleam of the sacred Ganges, under a livid sunset. Chanting drifts over the roofscape of towers and aerials and *ghats* as the dead are dispatched downriver from the necropolis into the Indian cosmos and into new lifetimes.

The next time Helen wakes, she hears funeral chanting outside the window, down on the street. The fan spins on, endlessly. She is alone in the room. She wonders what it is like to die alone and how long it would take Doctor Aggarwal to find her cadaver.

"Have I died?" she wonders to herself out loud in her delirium, as the chanting goes on. "Is it me that they are chanting for?"

She hears a whisper in her ear. The voice says that she is alive but that someone she knows will die before their time, in England. She catches a whiff of incense and sulphur. Suddenly she knows that Aggarwal is there in the room but she looks around and there is no one there. Then something makes her look out of the window. The huge black bird, the same one that has shadowed her all day, sits perched on the electric wires outside her window, looking in at her.

Helen Henshaw convinces herself that she is dreaming, or that it is the sunstroke that is making her hallucinate, because she closes her eyes hard and shakes her head.

When she opens her eyes again the bird is gone.

"Now this may surprise you, George Sinclair," Jane whispered in his ear, "Helen told me that while she was sick there in Benares, she had a dream about you . . . yes, you, George Sinclair. But why do you seem so surprised?

She dreamed that she was sitting in an English garden, feeding the black bird, which she had managed to tame, when you appeared beside her. She said that you had a very long conversation about the universe, and about how time wraps around itself and that the future and the past achieve union and blend into one, engendering the present, or some gibberish like that. She told me that soon after that fainting spell she became involved sexually with Aggarwal."

Listening avidly to Jane's story, but pretending not to be that interested, Sinclair again imagines the scene: it is the waking hours before dawn, and Helen lies awake on her cot under the spinning fan, febrile, weak and drenched in sweat, remembering the disturbing events of the day before and the nightmarish bird.

Enter Aggarwal, stage left.

He places a hand on her brow. To calm her fever, Aggarwal chants a soothing tantric mantra in her ear in his captivating Indian singsong and massages her temples. Soon enough Helen is totally under her guru's spell, hypnotized, giving him her full attention, fully available.

"She told me that he helped her a lot with regressive hypnotherapy. He would take her back into past lives and he cured many of her traumas and hang-ups, and even some physical ailments, which the Doctor told her were carried over from her previous existences."

Sinclair can almost hear Aggarwal's singsong voice in Helen's ear.

"He must have done more to her than just that, you see, George, because when she came back, what she had was some kind of venereal disease. I know, because she told me, and she asked me to introduce her to my gynecologist," said Jane smugly as she nibbled on Sinclair's earlobe.

Sinclair imagines the purple monstrosity of Aggarwal's massively swollen *lingam* violating the temple between Helen Henshaw's creamy English thighs. Helen who once has been his, his virgin, kneeling before him. A young woman who has willingly shared a New World with him, who has listened to Supertramp with him as dusk fell over of London. He buries his face in the pillow beside Jane Redfern's chattering blonde head, choking back the hot tears of hate.

Helen was still very ill when she returned from India, Jane resumed. Helen had come back hollow-eyed, jaundiced and malarially thin from the three-month tramp through the Subcontinent with her guru. It was like seeing a ghost.

"I went to Heathrow to meet her. But you know, I was shocked, I almost couldn't recognize her. She had really changed, actually, literally, in a physical way. I was astounded. It was mainly her eyes, they seemed totally dead. And she wouldn't smile any more."

No more dimples, thought Sinclair as a pall of sadness covered him.

As Jane spoke Sinclair pictured a sad wintry day over the North London skyline and a dreary homecoming. Helen's profile against a taxi window. A lonely kite fluttering in the wind over Parliament Hill. The grim Sunday shop fronts of Camden and Kentish Town drifting by soundlessly under the leaden sky. The taxi pulls up outside a terraced house. Jane stepping out and paying the driver, helping the feeble Helen with her backpack. Helen wrapped in heavy scarves. Helen coughing and with difficulty lugging her bags through the narrow hallway. Helen coughing. Helen weary and looking pale. Helen coughing.

Jane said, "I made her go to the doctor and have a check-up and tests the next day. There was something definitely wrong with her blood."

Jane had also noticed a change in Helen's character. Before her trip to India she had liked to walk with Jane on Hampstead Heath and the fresh air seemed to energize her. But now, Helen insisted on being alone and took to going to Highgate Cemetery instead. She became a member of the 'Friends of Highgate Cemetery' and spent her weekends cleaning the graves and restoring the statues. She spent too much time there said Jane, it was totally unhealthy. She had become obsessed with death and told Jane about the family crypt.

"One day she persuaded me to go up there and she showed it to me. She had managed to get hold of a key. We even went inside the vault to look at the coffins. Definitely creepy, and not my idea of how to spend a Sunday afternoon."

They lay smoking. The radiator clicked and hissed. The room had become unbearably stuffy.

"She became fond of being alone. She would stare off into the distance in the middle of conversations."

"Weren't you worried that she might be suicidal?"

"For a while, yes I was. I followed her around town a couple of times to make sure she was okay. I suspected that something had happened to her in India to unhinge her. I was concerned about some sort of mental disorder. She might have been hearing voices, you see."

"Was she still seeing Aggarwal?"

"Oh yes, she would still go up to Oxford on the weekends to sleep with him. I used to see her off at Paddington and meet her when she returned."

"Did she ever mention me again?" he yawned.

"You know what . . . She did, now that you mention it . . . what was it? Oh yes, that in one of her hypnotic regressions she saw who you really were—or had been, for that matter—and that Aggarwal told her that you were to be avoided, at all costs. 'Bad for your psychic well-being, definitely bad *karma*, that Sinclair boy' "—this she said in a surprisingly good head-wagging imitation of an Indian accent—"or some such claptrap like that."

Sinclair's face, or a tensing of his body, must have betrayed him at that instant, because Jane added quickly: "Oh dear, George, perhaps I shouldn't have told you that. It seems that I've touched a nerve."

"No, no . . . it's just that it's a strange thing to say about anybody, that's all."

"Perhaps its not all quite ancient history, then, you and Helen, then, is it then, George?" she challenged, her eyes narrowing, her clown's mouth turning down at the corners as it she had just tasted bitter fruit.

He recovered quickly. "Nonsense, dear, dear, Janey," he purred in her ear, "Helen Henshaw doesn't exist, she doesn't come between us, she might as well be dead now that I have you. And I can prove it to you . . ." And with this he initiated another round of foreplay, and succeeded in derailing that dangerous turn in the conversation.

MEPHISTOPHELES AND THE TEMPLARS

Already Jane's company had become cloying and suffocating and he had fled Oxford for the day to look for someone else from his past.

It took the greater part of a Monday afternoon to track down Guy Underhill in the depths of inner-city Hull.

First he read through the student lists in the faculties on the campus, without success. Then he checked with the Registry, where he was met with blank stares and bureaucratic hostility. He was about to give up when he thought of checking the library. He sweet-talked a tired English mouse in specs, who made him wait for what seemed ages while she checked a microfiche and sipped tea out of an oversized mug with the slogan SLUT emblazoned on it.

At last, address in hand, worrying about catching the train back because it was getting late, he took a taxi into the darker side-streets of the town, further and further away from the campus and its leafy up-market student suburbs.

He worried again, this time that the cabbie had dropped him off at the wrong address, because he was standing outside a derelict semi-detached house, evidently a squat. He felt eyes watching him as he stepped through the vapours of stale piss and sweat through the half-open door and into the fetid darkness.

He picked his way gingerly through a room where a few grubby punks, gender indeterminate, were shooting up. They eyed him indifferently as he stepped over their detritus. In the shadows, something moved, and as his eyes grew accustomed to the half-light, Sinclair saw that it was another punk. The problem was that there was something very wrong with this one. It was his face. Sinclair saw that the boy seemed to be missing half his head. He heard sniggers in the room as he passed through, pretending not to notice. There were pentagrams daubed on the walls, a crude depiction of what might have been Goya's horned beast, and '666's everywhere.

One of the trolls spoke. "He's next door, his Satanic Majesty is."

Sinclair passed an evil-smelling room that probably served as their toilet or kitchen. He heard a swarm of flies buzzing fatly in the darkness, and almost gagged.

He found him in the back room.

Underhill was sitting there alone, slumped on a mattress on the floor, the cassette player next to him playing Supertramp. There was a sliver of Rizla paper in his fingers. He was rolling up. Above him someone had spray painted something on the wall:

What goes around comes around

He was reminded of Helter Skelter and of the Manson gang and for a moment he had the absurd feeling that he might never get out of that squat alive.

Underhill looked up, squinting at the visitor through the smoke. His hair was dirty and his fingernails were grimy. In the twilight he seemed to have the rheumy eyes of an old man, and his bloodless lips twitched with a faint bitter smile when he saw who had come to see him.

"I must talk to you about her, I must. Talk. Please," Sinclair heard himself croak out all of a sudden. This was desperation speaking, and it had all come out wrong. When it came down to it he could think of nothing else to say. The days of rehearsing had proved quite useless.

Underhill looked up at him vacantly before saying: "Her? You mean Helen, my cousin?"

His voice seemed to come from another dimension or from the bottom of a well.

"I must have her back. I must," Sinclair pleaded. "I need your help."

"Sit down, George. You arrived just in time. Just like you, George Xavier Gupta Sinclair, to arrive just in time. Last in, first out. Always in time for a joint. Five years now, or has it been six?"

Underhill leaned across and handed Sinclair the joint.

"How's Gran, by the way?" Sinclair said, ignoring Underhill's question, and sucking in the smoke greedily to dull the hard edges of embarrassment that were biting into him.

"Gran? Oh, she died. Couple of years ago."

"I'm sorry."

Instead of answering, Underhill smiled at him again, that same bitter smile that was more of a grimace really and seemed to cause him some sort of physical discomfort.

"So why do the punks next door call you Satan, Guy?"

"Ah, just a little joke we share."

There was silence again. The tape had clicked to a stop in Underhill's cassette-player. There was coughing from the room next door.

They sat silently in the twilit room as darkness fell.

A dog barked miles away in the city.

"Please tell your cousin it wasn't the way she imagines it. I've tried, God how I've tried, and she won't listen. Write to her, please, or call her. You must. I've no one else to turn to."

Underhill smoked, listening, watching. Watching Sinclair squirm.

"So what exactly did you say to her?" Sinclair insisted, becoming impatient with Underhill's silence.

Underhill started to say something, then stopped, and grimaced again, as if overwhelmed with the effort of remembering.

"Nothing. I haven't talked to her in ages. I think her parents found out from my parents."

He seemed exhausted.

"But she said she'd come to see you."

Another pause, another effort.

"Oh, yes, that's right. She did come. I almost forgot."

Sinclair was getting nowhere with Guy Underhill, or with what was left of Guy Underhill. As darkness fell, his old friend had become a disembodied entity, a voice in the dark, a speaking memory. Sinclair was thinking of getting ready to leave the squat when Underhill emerged from his stupor and the voice in the dark said something startling: "I will tell you why the punks next door nicknamed me Satan."

A match was struck, another spliff was lit. In the brief flash of the flame Sinclair saw that Underhill's eyes were bright pinpricks of marijuana, and as he told his story Sinclair could see from the inward look of his eyes that he was actually watching the events unfold in front of him again, in glorious Technicolor.

"I met the Devil, or at least the Devil's representative, a priest—a Mephistopheles—and he spoke to me—he made me a proposition."

Sinclair sat up. He took the joint from Underhill.

After his return from Africa following his expulsion from the College, Underhill said, his depression had deepened. He was living with Gran in Goodge Street. The visits to the court-ordered psychologist in London were not producing results and his parents had more or less disowned him. They had arranged for Gran to administer a minimal allowance to tide him over until he got his university grant, after which he would be on his own and off their books. They had turned their backs on him and would continue their selfish existence in Africa without him, he said, which was nothing new or surprising, seeing as he'd been sent away to the Hall when he was seven and they had got used to not having to deal with him. His aunts and uncles in England (that would have included Helen Henshaw's parents, Sinclair noted) wouldn't have him anywhere near his cousins. They feared that he might contaminate and corrupt them, because they were good Catholic boys and girls. News of Guy Underhill's expulsion and drug addiction had already made the rounds of the extended family and he was definitely on the family Shit List.

"I was sent to Coventry, as the saying goes, a place worse than Hull," he winced at his failed joke. "I had become the family leper."

"And what about Helen?"

Underhill looked up from his reverie, confused, irritated because his train of thought had been broken. "What about her?"

"Did *she* avoid you, like the others?"

Underhill seemed confused, failing to see the relevance of the question. "Yes. I suppose she did, now that you mention it. At first she did. She only came to see me much later."

Sinclair asked him to go on.

"Anyway, even though Gran had agreed to take me in, she wasn't happy about it, and she made sure I knew it. She could be a real bitch when she wanted to, you know, and ever since I came back from Africa she really wanted to . . . So I did something totally outrageous. I was desperate. I had no one to talk to. So I walked into Farm Street and asked one of the Jesuits to hear my confession."

"You *what?*" Sinclair couldn't believe it. Underhill begging for mercy in the nest of vipers. In the old days he would have vapourized like a vampire or broken out in allergic welts just from being in the general vicinity of the Jesuits' London headquarters.

Underhill nodded sadly and drew on the spliff. "Yes . . . amazing, isn't it? Who would have thought it? It was as if someone else had taken over inside. I used to go for immensely long walks in London to try to clear my head. I can't really remember how I got there. I remember walking through the drizzle—it was one of those filthy grey afternoons and I couldn't bear being in Gran's flat anymore. She had been taunting me all afternoon. Suddenly there I was standing outside the church on Farm Street and then before I knew it, I was inside sitting in a pew."

Sinclair saw Gran's hawk-like stare and then tried to conjure up the impossible image of Guy Underhill kneeling in a confessional.

"For a while I was the only one in the church. It was a bit spooky in there, I can tell you—I was all alone, with all those ghastly votive candles. The altar lamp was off—you know what that means—that even the Almighty wasn't at home. It felt as if there were spies or ghosts creeping around in the shadows, watching me. Then I heard footsteps and from the corner of my eye I saw a shadow step into the confessional box and draw the curtain. After a while I went in after the priest."

"Which one was it? Was it one of the priests from the College?"

"No. I'm pretty sure it wasn't. I couldn't see who it was, you see. He had his face turned away and however hard I looked through the grille I couldn't make him out. And I couldn't recognize the voice. If it had been one of the priests from the College I would have recognized him immediately. It was probably one of the locals, I thought. Anyway, let's call him Mephistopheles, because that's what he turned out to be—the Devil's messenger. He had a kind, gentle, friendly voice, with a bit of a Scottish brogue—not one of those sarcastic Borders whines, but really actually very nice and reassuring. It was strange, though, from the very start. You see, just as I was starting with the 'bless me

Father for I have sinned' routine he cut me off. Firmly but politely. You don't
know me, he said. But I know who you are, Guy Underhill. I—*we*—have been
waiting for you to come, for a while now. I know—*we* know—what happened
to you up there. And sure enough, he knew all about me and what had been
done to me at the College—like a personnel manager in a job interview walking you through your CV—nothing dramatic, all very matter of fact, non
judgemental. He seemed to know that I had been sent back from Africa in disgrace and that I was now living with Gran and that I was at one hell of a loose
end following the disaster. Then he said that he could help me. He was very
nice, very reasonable, and everything he said made sense. There were no
threats, no coercion. There was none of the patronizing hostility that they
used to throw at us at the College.

"Then came Mephistopheles's proposition. He said that I could refuse his
invitation, and that if I did, he—*they*—would naturally be disappointed but
would understand and that they would not be in the least concerned, because no
one would believe me if I revealed what he was about to tell me. For all they
cared I could go out onto Farm Street and shout it at the top of my lungs.
No one would believe me. I would simply be put away and medicated. After all
I was a drug-addict on probation undergoing psychiatric treatment and my
court-appointed psych had informed them that I was on the verge of being
diagnosed as a paranoid psychotic and that a lateral lobotomy might even be on
the cards."

"So what was the proposition?"

"I was invited to join them."

"Them? *Who* exactly?"

"The Company of Jesus . . ."

Sinclair suppressed the instinct to laugh. Underhill was obviously hallucinating but it was fascinating to witness in any case. This was surely an extension of the fantasy that he used to spin out in the Pit, of how he would join the
Jesuits in order to destroy them from within. A fantasy that he had no doubt
elaborated in the many hours of solitude in the darkness of the squat.

"But why me, I asked him. What would you want with a drug-addict like
me, a Big-Time Sinner? You know that I despise your Order, and that it has
ruined my life, you know that you have defeated me and that I still hate you.
You know that I am your declared enemy. Your mortal enemy."

So was Saul of Tarsus before he saw the light on the road to Damascus and
became St Paul, the Mephistopheles-priest had replied. And look how brilliantly successful he was. He went on to create the institution of the Universal

Church Militant, whereas he had once hunted down and slaughtered the followers of the Nazarene for a living. You see, the confessor went on, we much prefer our old enemies to join us, because they make the best and most zealous converts, just like Saint Paul. Next he went on to explain that what had happened to Underhill at school—the hate, the fear, the persecution, the betrayal by your best friend—and now the rejection by your family and your deep despair—it was all planned, you see, it was all engineered to bring you low, to bring you down into the mud, where you are crawling now. Call it 'spiritual engineering', if you like.

The priest went on to tell Underhill that from the moment they had first seen him at the Hall and later at the College, and had witnessed the depths of his antipathy, that he had been selected as a candidate for conversion and recruitment—quite a prize, he would be, if they were successful. And that the process involved the breaking of the candidate first. You have been brought down to such a low point in your life that you have even crawled into the den of your worst enemy to beg for mercy, he was told. You see, the point is that you must be made to feel as the Master felt before you can join him, so that you can truly appreciate what he had to go through and the full glory of his Way.

"You mean that I must feel the same way that Christ did when He was being scourged and humiliated before they topped him?" Underhill had asked insolently.

The priest answered with a chuckle. "Not quite," he replied. He seemed amused and Underhill could almost hear the smile on his face. "You see," he went on, "we pick you up out of the gutter of despair and suddenly, when you learn the truth, you are on top of the world. There is nothing to compare to it. It is intoxicating. It is like emerging into the light, like a rush of oxygen to the brain after you have been suffocating in an underground dungeon. We bring you through the looking glass, like Alice. From being our worst enemy you become our most jealous guardian and defender, you become a mirror image of your previous self. It is a compelling transformation, a wonderful thing. Right becomes left, good becomes bad, God becomes the—"

"Becomes the what . . . becomes who?" Underhill was suddenly intrigued.

"Now you know what I mean," the priest said. "Let's just say that we would like you to be our Saul. Saul who joined the Abhorred One."

"The Abhorred One?" Underhill replied, suddenly puzzled.

"Yes," the Mephistopheles-priest said calmly. "That's the whole point, let's not beat about the bush any longer, Guy Underhill. Under cover of the

Society of Jesus we secretly abhor Him. We serve the Luciferine Master. The Horned One. Everything we do is to his greater glory. *Ad Majore Diaboli Gloriam et Laus Diabolo Semper.*"

By that stage, Underhill told Sinclair, he thought he was dreaming or hallucinating. Sinclair tended to agree but remained silent.

"Mephistopheles went on to analyze my situation logically and calmly. He walked me through the alternatives. Turn us down and you waste away in a provincial university for a few years, then more years of mediocrity in a series of dead-end jobs and maybe one or two shallow relationships, and eventually oblivion—most probably by your own hand judging by the way you are going. But if I joined them in their enterprise, I would find enlightenment and power, more than I had ever dreamed of. To the outside world I would be a trainee Jesuit, a Scholastic doing his novitiate, spending the next few years in exhaustive Jesuitical training—in Theology and Scripture, and a spell of teaching at the College or at one of the many Jesuit schools around the world, or in the Society's house in Rome—but all the while I would be progressing through the initiation rites of the Order. In this way I would join the ranks of the Immortals and gain access to the Secret. And who knows, perhaps someone of my calibre could rise to the very top of the enterprise, and become part of the inner circle."

"*Immortals*, did you say? And what *secrets* was he talking about?" Sinclair insisted.

"He said that for the time being, he could tell me who the Jesuits really are, to whet my appetite. Other revelations would follow in due course if I accepted his invitation."

Oh no, that sounds familiar—here we go again, thought Sinclair, remembering the sessions in the Pit when Underhill expounded his conspiracy theories ad nauseam. He had controlled his urge to laugh at Underhill's dementia and was even beginning to enjoy the fanciful story. Instead he asked simply: "So who *are* our friends the Jesuits, then?"

"They are the Immortals. The Illuminati. Otherwise known as the Poor Knights of King Solomon's Temple, or Templars. Mephistopheles confirmed that the Templars were—*are*, in fact—the Keepers of the Grail, otherwise known as the Treasure of the Cathars. All of our friends, Fathers Morguer, Cassius, Spock, Pottifer—yes, even little bat-faced Pottifer—are gods compared to the uninitiated. They are Templars."

Somehow the idea of Pottifer holding the keys to the Dark Kingdom seemed ludicrous to Sinclair as he sat there entranced by the fantasy Underhill had dreamt up in the dark. Sinclair remembered Underhill's well-thumbed Bible, *The Secret History of the Jesuits*. It had all finally gone to his head and he had ended up believing the conspiracy fantasy that linked the Society of Jesus to the likes of Hitler, Mussolini, Napoleon and all the other Antichrists.

"The priest—Mephistopheles—told me how the Company of Jesus, which was officially founded by Ignatius and placed at the service of the Pope in 1540, had in fact grown out of the secret Spanish chapters of the Knights Templar. The Templars, remember, had disbanded and gone underground in 1320 after being persecuted across Catholic Europe following Philippe le Bel of France's infamous money grab. 'But the Templars were known to be in conflict with Rome,' I said, 'it doesn't make sense. They were accused of sodomy, diabolism and other hobbies such as spitting on the cross and of worshipping the disembodied head of the Baphomet. How could they possibly have evolved into the Society of Jesus? How could the fanatical storm troopers of the Vatican be heretical warrior monks?'

"Your objections are understandable, Underhill, he said to me helpfully. He seemed pleased that I knew what I was talking about. That was the whole point, he said, don't you see? Don't you see the horrific beauty of it all? What better cover than a society named after Christ—the very One we abhor— fanatically dedicated on the surface to the forces of the Vatican and the Romish Papacy, who are in fact our mortal enemies? You see, he went on, we have our own Black Pope, the Superior General of the Order—he is the Anti-Pope, the real Antichrist. And as is well known the Company of Jesus is a military order founded along the same lines as the Knights of the Temple. And Company as in a company of artillery, not as in a commercial enterprise. In case I doubted what he was telling me, he encouraged me to look at how the Jesuits were also expelled from the Continent just as the Templars had been two hundred years previously, and into how Ignatius had tried desperately to get back to the Holy Land to establish his centre of operations in Jerusalem just as the Templars had done, but that he and his followers were prevented from going there by the war with the Ottoman Turks. Ignatius in fact had travelled to Jerusalem in 1524, almost two decades before founding the Order. His intention had been to set up the Company's headquarters on Temple Mount, just as the Templars had in the 11th century."

The history lesson in the confessional box had continued. The mysterious priest had told Underhill that the Jesuits and their pupils arrived in England in the 18th century after their expulsion from Belgium. Conventional history had it that they had set up their English headquarters at the College, which in those days was an estate owned by a Recusant family that had donated it to the Order to house their school.

"But he told me that if I cared to delve a little deeper I would soon discover that the Recusant family was in fact an English Templar family. The family had gone to ground in the 14th century and had kept the estate available for its fellow Immortals for the day when they might need a sanctuary. And, the priest had said, I need not remind you of the connection between the College and the witch craze that Pendle was famous for."

By now Sinclair's head was spinning, and not just from the joint. He was suddenly caught off balance by the memory of the ouija session in the Pit, when Grannyjee had appeared. Something was scratching away in a corner at the back of his mind. Then, through his drugged consciousness, he had it, the memory, now quite clear and luminous like a spotlight, of what a dead boy called Martin Weld had told them in the Pit.

T-H-E-Y A-R-E T-E-M-P-L-A-R-S . . .

Underhill was now going on about rituals and initiations again and spinning some story involving human sacrifice. About how the blood is the life, and how each year, quite unremarked, a boy disappears or dies at one of the many Jesuit establishments around the world. About how the Order meets in grand council once a year on the 24th of June, the feast of the beheaded St John the Baptist, in one of their establishments. They meet for the Sabbatic Coven, to pay homage to the disembodied head of the Baphomet, the Horned One, the Master, and to feed him human blood.

"Why do you think the Order chose to be known as teachers?" Underhill continued. "Not for the love of educating churlish young Catholics, but because the schools conveniently provide the raw material for the blood sacrifice as well as potential recruits to perpetuate the enterprise. It's easier in Africa or Latin America, where life is cheaper. We have to be more careful and devious in Europe and America, Mephistopheles said. And so far—thanks be to the Master—no one has noticed the pattern of deaths in our schools and universities since we started the programme in the 16th century. For example, do you remember Martin Weld? In 1975 was the turn of the College to supply the sacrifice."

H-O-R-N-L-E-S-S G-O-A-T . . .

"The hornless goat?" Sinclair heard himself ask in the dark. The last of Martin Weld's riddles in the Pit was beginning to make sense in a twisted, narcotic kind of way.

"It's just another way of saying sacrificial lamb," came the explanation. "Apparently it's how the Haitian voodooists refer to human beings—goats without horns—quaint, isn't it?"

Underhill had really lost it, Sinclair said to himself through the veil of intoxication. The Devil, Mephistopheles, the Templars, Antichrists, and now voodoo and human sacrifice.

He had finally gone stark raving mad.

"Yes, that's exactly what the punks next door said at first," Underhill agreed, reading Sinclair's mind.

"So what's the moral of your story? What did you decide? Surely here was the opportunity you had always dreamt of—to infiltrate the Company of Jesus and bring about its destruction from within?"

"What do you think I decided? I wouldn't be in this shit hole if I had accepted. I told Mephistopheles to fuck off and to tell his Master and his disciples up North that Guy Underhill's soul is not for sale, and that what goes around comes around, and to watch out because one day I will come after them and I will have them."

It was now getting difficult to see clearly in the squat because beyond the window the light of day had finally failed, and there was no electricity in the house. He could hardly see Underhill in front of him. He watched the tiny glowing ember of the joint rise and fall in the darkness. Underhill was silent. He heard a rustling in the corner of the room.

From next door he heard strange noises and grunts and moans, but no words, as if the punks had started wrestling with each other silently, or were rolling around having convulsions on the floor.

"You haven't changed, George Sinclair," was all that Underhill said when Sinclair finally took his leave.

Unless he was mistaken, Sinclair thought he heard a sniff in the darkness behind him as he left the room. He had never known Guy Underhill to cry.

On the cassette-recorder Supertramp were playing *It's Raining Again*. As Sinclair left the house, a voice from 1978 came to him. It was Fr Morguer saying: "It's Guy Underhill that we want . . ."

1988
SIX

THE CLOISTERS

"There was another twitch upon the thread, Morpheus, in 1988. It was just before the final examination of my DPhil."

Sinclair explains to Morpheus, in the twilit chamber which is devoted to memories of Oxford, that he entered the secret world in the traditional Oxbridge manner. Like his banishment to England at the age of nine, the manner of his recruitment into British Intelligence had been entirely predictable, as if scripted, or as Grannyjee would have said, *maktub*.

A week before his Orals he had found in his pigeonhole in the Porter's Lodge a note from Dr David Blantyre, his tutor from undergraduate days.

> *Magdalen College*
> *Oxford, OX1 4AU*
> *June 15th, 1988*

> *George, do please drop by for a glass of sherry and a chat about your prospects.*
> *Would 5 p.m. Thursday be fine?*
> *D.B.*

The chat, in Blantyre's sunlit rooms overlooking the Cloisters, was enjoyable and informal. The fragrant bluish smoke from the don's pipe filled the room and seemed to slow down time in a pleasantly narcotic way. Sinclair was given sherry and Blantyre asked him how his DPhil was progressing and how he felt about the upcoming Orals. Then there was a pause in the conversation.

Sinclair watched the universes of dust motes caught in the diagonal shafts of sunlight that warmed the study.

After silently tamping his pipe and perfuming the room again with billows of aromatic smoke, Blantyre resumed. Had he given any thought to what he might want to do afterwards? Teaching? Staying on? And if Sinclair was so inclined, Blantyre could introduce him to some friends of his who worked in an unconventional government department that was looking for talent. It would involve work overseas. He didn't want to beat about the bush, Blantyre said, pecking affectionately at his pipe, it was intelligence work, and he thought that Sinclair might be interested given his cosmopolitan background and his language skills. If Sinclair was interested, he was to let him know, and there was no hurry, actually, and he would arrange an informal chat with his chums in London, no commitment on either side, of course. If it turned out that everybody got on, he would have to sit the Civil Service Selection Board, the CSSB or Sisby, as it was known, which was held every few months. There was a bi-annual intake. In the meantime Blantyre wished Sinclair the best of luck with his thesis and, with a mischievous wink, added that he had it on good authority that Sinclair's DPhil was as good as in the bag, and that he would soon have the honour of addressing him as 'Doctor' Sinclair. With that, Blantyre filled their glasses again, bonhomie ruled, and they downed the sherry as the bells of Magdalen Tower called the faithful to Evensong. The setting sun cast into shadow the gargoyles that lurked and watched from the ivy, keeping their ancient silent vigil over the comings and goings in the Cloisters.

Sinclair was a happy young man as he emerged into the early Oxford evening, lightheaded with the prospects of a new life that could well overtake the disappointments and horrors of the recent past. He was Kim—albeit a Kim touched by the tar brush—standing at the portals of the secret world—a player about to walk up to the crease and participate at last in the Great Game.

He tapped his pocket to make sure that Madame Bernabeu's *gris gris* was still there.

Several days later another invitation appeared in his pigeonhole in the Porter's Lodge. It was a letter bearing the crest of the Foreign and Commonwealth Office. It was from the FCO Recruitment Liaison Department, and was signed by a Mr Holiday. The letter asked him to confirm by telephone that he would be available for an interview at an address in 'official' London the following week.

The first interview took place on a Friday afternoon, at Number 3, Darby Gardens, a great white terraced building overlooking the Mall and St James's Park. Sinclair felt uncomfortable in his tie and his collar chafed, but he had stayed off the drugs the night before, to guarantee a clear head. He had strolled around the park for an hour before the appointment, nervously imagining a thorough grilling at the hands of a roomful of men in dark suits, and rehearsing answers to awkward questions—perhaps, in their omniscience, they already knew about the drugs, perhaps they had deciphered the riddle of the deaths of Helen and Jane and the disappearances of Doctor Aggarwal and Xancha Bergsma. In which case he was fucked. *Ab initio*. But if they already knew, why had they bothered summoning him? Perhaps it was a way of getting him to confess in public. But on the other hand, there were less elaborate ways to arrest him. And so on. This inner debate had preoccupied him all day on his way in on the train and as he tramped around Whitehall and the park killing time before the interview.

He rang the bell and the concierge, an old-fashioned retainer in a blue uniform who called him "Sir", checked him in. He was given a pink chit, which was to be returned after his meeting, and the old geezer asked if Sir would like to wait on a low-slung sofa under the staircase. The carpet was a deep plush red, the colour of secrecy and intrigue. So far so good. From upstairs the clatter of a typewriter floated down to him. He wasn't able to concentrate on the old editions of *The Economist* or the *Financial Times* that littered the table. He breathed in deeply to calm himself.

Eventually a lady of indeterminate age, with pearls and an impeccable accent, descended, introduced herself as Mr Holiday's assistant with a cool handshake and asked him to follow her upstairs, which he did. He felt Bondian as he appraised the elegant behind and slim legs of the glamorous Moneypenny as he followed her up the staircase, breathing in the classic fragrance of her *sillage*, as the French call the perfumed wake of a passing woman. This exhilarating feeling remained ingrained in his memory far more vividly than the interview that followed.

Sinclair was led past a typing pool of younger Moneypennys, who looked up with practised nonchalance to appraise the latest candidate who would save England and her Empire. He squeezed the *gris gris* in his pocket for good luck.

Sinclair had expected a smart, enigmatic military man like Colonel Ross in *Funeral in Berlin* to conduct his interview in a wood-panelled library. The office was indeed high-ceilinged but the furniture was grubby and bore the mark of government issue. Instead of Colonel Ross, a small man came out to greet him from behind a gunmetal desk, rather too eagerly, thought Sinclair, hand outstretched. He was balding, had an instantly forgettable face, was dressed in brown and wore cheap Cornish pasty shoes. The Man on the Clapham Omnibus, thought Sinclair.

At school, Sinclair had been taught to watch people's vowels, and in an instant Mr Holiday betrayed himself as a native of the Midlands, Birmingham most likely. Most probably a Grammar School boy made good, Sinclair concluded with satisfaction, having neatly boxed Holiday into his social niche in a matter of seconds.

Holiday asked him to take his time and carefully read a green laminated card on a clipboard, which informed the reader about the functions of Her Majesty's Secret Intelligence Service, or SIS. Sinclair was then asked to read and sign an extract from the Official Secrets Act, which he did. Holiday carefully slipped the signed document into a manila file. Sinclair remembered Dr Tantum's advice about 'estoppel' and 'irrevocable actions'. *Ab initio*. From the start. *Maktub*.

Sinclair had decided to play it as interested but not overly eager. The interview was not particularly challenging, merely a first screening. Sinclair was asked what he thought about manipulating people for a living, whether he could cope with anonymity and not being able to tell his friends what his real job was, and he was then asked to describe a person, anyone he knew, strengths and weaknesses.

"Warts 'n' all," whined Holiday in his best Birmingham.

Sinclair described Guy Underhill.

Holiday then asked him how he would persuade Mr. Underhill to commit an illegal act.

"I would play on his vanity to start with, and then play to his sense of exclusivity. It would not be difficult to recruit Underhill as an accomplice if he felt that he was inflicting some kind of harm on the Establishment, and that he was part of some secret and privileged cabal. I don't think that money would swing it with Guy Underhill, it doesn't mean much to him."

Holiday nodded blandly.

When he was asked if there was anything he wanted to let them know, Sinclair decided to be prudent and to let Holiday know up front that he was a single parent now that his daughter Ximena's mother had disappeared. Again, Holiday merely nodded and passed no comment. All in all, Sinclair was confident that he had come across as he had intended. He noticed that Holiday never noted down anything he said. The little man's hands remained folded placidly on the desk top as he listened carefully to Sinclair, head slightly cocked to one side, a perfectly bland expression on his perfectly bland face.

As he was escorted back down the staircase by Moneypenny, Sinclair passed a sweaty young man with greasy blond hair and a tight-fitting suit perched uncomfortably on the sofa under the stairs, reading *The Economist* intently. He was scratching at a sore on his face, rubbing it raw in a fit of nerves. He looked up and their eyes met, probably for the first and last time.

After he had signed out of the building to emerge into the breeze of the Mall, Sinclair could barely recall Mr Holiday's face.

But sure enough, an invitation to a second round of interviews followed a week later.

The Sisby included a series of searching interviews and interrogations in various threadbare government offices around Whitehall. There was another session at Darby Gardens with a panel of three nondescript individuals, including an elderly lady psychologist.

"What do 'X' and 'G' stand for?" the old vixen had asked casually, as if she didn't already know.

"Xavier Gupta."

For once, no one smirked when he revealed the shocking truth of his middle names, and for once he did not blush or look at his hands, and it was then that he knew he had found a home.

He had managed to persuade his landlord to let him stay on indefinitely in the flat in North Oxford. He had to pay a couple of poor students to take turns babysitting Ximena after school as he commuted into London on the bus to complete the selection rounds. The child took all this with surprising equanimity. She encouraged her father to keep going.

Finally, his appointment was confirmed, subject only to Positive Vetting. This could take up to two months, and in the meantime he was basically free until he was called up to commence training.

Now came the time for fretting. Sinclair reviewed the minefield of his recent history and in particular the events that had transpired at Oxford in the last year. He was overwhelmed by dread. All the progress so far, it could all be for naught. Now is the time for tripping up and breaking one's greasy brown Anglo-Indian neck unless one does something about it, he told himself as he watched Ximena prepare his nightly syringe.

There was little he could do about the risk of them uncovering his near expulsion from the College. But really, the more he thought about it, that episode might prove to be a plus, as he had heard that the Service actually likes to see a touch of moderate criminality in its applicants. In any case he felt confident that Morguer, Tantum and the silent Cassius would support his cause. After all, his father had bought their loyalty and the gratitude of the whole College for many years to come.

In the matter of his drug taking, which he would now have to control, he considered himself vulnerable to hostile testimony only from Guy Underhill. Apart from Helen (dead), Morguer, Cassius and Tantum (bought off) and now, of course, Ximena (unquestioning loyalty), Underhill was the only one who knew.

And so it was time to travel again to Hull to search out his victim.

HULL

"Guy Under'ill? 'E don't live here no more, mate—no, 'e didn't leave no forwarding address . . ."

After Sinclair had turned to start his trudge back to the bus-stop, the rat-faced punk turned to his friend—the one with only half a face—and whispered into his stunted ear.

Finding Guy Underhill would have to wait. If MI6's vetters did ever manage to track him down, the testimony of a drug-addicted squatter would not count for much anyway. As Mephistopheles had said in the Farm Street confessional, to the outside world Underhill was simply a narcotic-addled lunatic and certain candidate for a lobotomy.

Now there was the more pressing matter of four recent deaths to deal with. If the semi-retired Special Branch vetting officers used by MI6 cared to look closely enough, they might just connect the dots between the untimely deaths of Helen Henshaw and Jane Redfern and the disappearances of Doctor Aggarwal and Xancha Bergsma. After all, what, or more precisely, *who* did these four people have in common? The more he thought about it, the more he determined that he really did have to act in a pre-emptive fashion to prevent everything from unravelling. He had come too far now to fail. To be tripped up at the last minute by the ghosts of four very dead people.

So far no one had suspected foul play in the deaths of the girls. The Public Inquiries had returned swift unchallenged verdicts of suicide in both cases. The City of Oxford coroner was used to processing cases of student suicide. The pressure to succeed, or rather the fear of failure (socially as well as academically), routinely exacted its toll on the weaker students. And the University Proctors were always keen to avoid controversy.

As for Doctor Aggarwal, he had simply gone missing. There was a short piece about his absence buried in the back pages of the Oxford Chronicle. The article said that one of the cleaning staff at the Pitt Rivers had come forward to report seeing the Doctor at the door of his office before his disappearance. He had been greeting an Indian lady in a bright red sari.

Sinclair was convinced that it was only a matter of time before the dots were connected. As the vetting progressed, this became a monstrous possibility in his febrile imagination. He decided to take the initiative before the net trapped him. In fact, he reasoned to himself, since a link was bound to become evident eventually, why not get in there first, point out the link to them himself, and kill two (in fact four) birds with one stone?

The identity of the mysterious Indian woman in the red sari was soon established. Sinclair filed a complaint against his common-law wife, Nurse Xancha Bergsma, Matron of the College. The charge was abandonment of a minor. At the police station behind Christchurch, Sinclair was interviewed by a very helpful officer from the CID, Detective Inspector Gosforth. Sinclair stated for the record that Nurse Bergsma, the mother of his daughter, had told him that she was leaving the country indefinitely. Furthermore, he added, she had unilaterally decided to leave their daughter Ximena in his care. Sinclair also told DI Gosforth that Bergsma had mentioned to him that she had been seeing one of the lecturers at the University. He seemed to remember that it was an Indian gentleman, a name like Garawally or Godbhole or Gupta or something like that, oh yes, Aggarwal, that rings a bell, yes definitely, that was his name. And, Sinclair said, to make things worse, he had heard rumours that the same Aggarwal had been having an affair with one of his students. He thought it was that girl Helen Henshaw who had committed suicide, did they remember the case? Yes, that was it. It was a double suicide in fact. Miss Henshaw's lesbian admirer had also killed herself in her grief. Terribly sad, the whole thing, said Sinclair, shaking his head. He felt very bad about the whole thing, but when passion takes over, things tend to get out of control, don't they?

A week later DI Gosforth called in to see Sinclair at his rooms in the New Buildings. He had checked with the Royal Constabulary up in Lancashire, and yes, indeed, the Jesuits who ran the school up there had reported the Matron, Nurse Bergsma, missing. She had failed to return to her job at the College after her fortnight's annual leave.

Yes, said Gosforth as he tapped his teeth with is pencil, the disappearance of Doctor Aggarwal and Nurse Bergsma did coincide somewhat. Bergsma had vanished only a couple of weeks after Aggarwal.

"Actually, Dr Sinclair, it's not unusual for one of a pair to leave first to set things up, so that the partner in crime, so to speak, can follow later."

It was then that Ximena, absolutely unprompted by Sinclair (my God, he was proud of her), piped in and proceeded to bear expert and false witness against her dead mother. This she did with astounding skill and forthrightness. The gene of deviousness of Sinclair's ancestors—the scheming Pict in the mists of Scotland and the hungry Untouchable fighting for survival in the marshes around Goa—had found its wicked way down into this latest generation. Yes, she told the Detective Inspector without blinking, Ma had been seeing the Indian Doctor. The Doctor was very smelly. She made a show of mispronouncing the Doctor's name—it came out as "Agawa". Yes, Ma had said that she was going to go away with him to a hot country very far away. No, she told the Detective, she didn't want to go with them. She refused to go with them, in fact, because the Doctor was not nice, and he did strange things to Ma and to her.

With that explosive revelation the interview was abruptly called to a halt by DI Gosforth. He was overtaken with professional excitement now that the pieces were beginning to fall nicely into place. He requested that Sinclair and Ximena continue the deposition at the offices of the Social Services. There they could have the benefit of qualified personnel attending.

The next day, the interview continued. Upon further probing, this time by a very nice lady child psychologist, and with the aid of a book of pictures, Ximena revealed what the Indian Doctor had done to her. Yes, that's why she didn't like him and that's why she wouldn't go with Ma when she left, because Ma did what the Doctor said and she would not protect her from him.

By now Ximena was old enough to know that her eyes frightened people, so she was careful to look down and avoid the searching looks of the nice lady doctor.

The whole matter was neatly resolved when Sinclair decided to put a final nail in Aggarwal's coffin for good measure. What Sinclair did next wasn't strictly speaking necessary, because Ximena's testimony had been enough to damn both Aggarwal and Bergsma *in absentia*. However, Sinclair went through with it anyway. Instinctively he felt that it would add an extra layer of verisimilitude to the story.

The same cleaner who had reported the sighting of Aggarwal and Bergsma before their assignation in the Pitt Rivers came forward yet again. This time she reported the theft of several gold and silver artifacts from the museum. The missing pieces were ancient Hindu talismans representing *devis* and *durgas*. They had been housed in a showcase on the second floor of the museum. During one of the routine maintenance inspections the theft was brought to the attention of the Curator by the cleaner. The vitrine's lock had been picked, and expertly so, said the police technicians. They had inspected with a magnifying glass the empty spaces on the velvet where the priceless artifacts had lain. Hello, what's this then? What do we have here? A hair. A long black greasy hair. When the thief was identified, as he would no doubt be, DNA testing would establish beyond doubt how Doctor Aggarwal and his lover had financed their escape.

Soon every irregularity that had ever been committed by the museum staff was conveniently discovered, written off and ascribed to the missing Assistant Curator. With hindsight it should have been obvious to everyone that the Indian was nothing more than a dastardly embezzler, and worse.

Thus motive was firmly established and the fugitives were duly entered into the Interpol database, with theft and embezzlement now added to the charges of child molestation and abandonment of a minor. It was suspected that they had fled to India, the 'hot country' that Nurse Bergsma had mentioned to her daughter. The usual trawl through the airline and ferry records threw up nothing. That was not surprising—criminals of the intellectual calibre of Aggarwal would no doubt have travelled under false names. DI Gosforth and the nice lady psychologist said that they would let Sinclair know if they made any progress in the case. In the meantime they offered profession-al grief and abuse counselling for both Sinclair and his daughter, but Sinclair declined.

One day towards the end of the Positive Vetting period, Sinclair paid another visit to Dr Blantyre. He wanted to thank him for his referral. He also wanted to see if he could catch a whiff of any controversy that might be brew-ing. Blantyre, as might be expected, played his cards close to his chest, but gave Sinclair no cause for worry. So far so good, then.

But when he emerged from Blantyre's rooms, his veins glowing with genteel euphoria from his tutor's sherry, Sinclair encountered something profoundly disturbing. What he saw, the thing that that made his hands and feet turn cold, was a rather short man lurking at the far end of the Cloisters. Like a genie, the man suddenly stepped sideways into the shadows and vanished. Sinclair searched the four corners of the Cloisters in a panic. When he left the Cloisters and ran out into the quad in front of the President's Lodgings, he saw the man again. He was in the Lodge, talking to Arthur, the Head Porter.

Sinclair could have sworn that the man was Ignatius Cassius, S.J., except that instead of the regulation black soutane and dog-collar, the man now wore tweeds and a trilby hat. Sinclair's guts were suddenly awash in a surge of adrenaline. He decided to confront Cassius, and fuck the consequences.

As he strode briskly towards the Porter's Lodge he saw the little man step out into the High Street under the arch of the Lodge. Sinclair stepped through the doorway and onto the sidewalk a few seconds later. He looked up and down the High Street, down across Magdalen Bridge and up towards Queens, and then across the road towards the Daubeny Buildings and the Botanical Gardens. The pavements were empty, except for a herd of Japanese tourists coming down from Queens, all cameras, raincoats and umbrellas. The intruder had simply vanished, as if into thin air.

Arthur was not very helpful and shrugged off Sinclair's shrill insistence that the man could not simply have vanished as soon as he stepped onto the High Street. Arthur replied that all the man had wanted were directions to St Hilda's. It *must* have been Cassius, Sinclair convinced himself. He knew no one else who could disappear as quickly and as silently as he could appear beside you.

He strode purposefully across the bridge. It was covered with the usual vomit, blood and broken glass, the detritus of last night's revelry and a pitched battle of 'town versus gown'.

He inveigled his way past Edward, the Porter at St Hilda's. He knew Edward well. He had had to grease his hoary old palm many times before, for access as well as intelligence, when he had been stalking Helen.

No, Edward said, no one of that description had entered the college that afternoon, at least not since he had come on duty. Sinclair spent the rest of the afternoon prowling around the grounds of Helen's college. At one stage he lingered briefly outside her rooms, where she had been found dead. The thought that Helen had also stood there, at the top of the staircase, lodged itself in his mind. He was standing in the same space that her body had once occupied, he was breathing the same air that had filled her lungs. He caressed the door handle, the same handle that had felt the steady warm pressure of Helen's hand every evening.

That night Ximena calmed his fears by persuading him not to worry so much, as she pulled the curtains, unlocked her father's tuckbox and prepared the syringe for him.

Of course Special Branch became aware of the monstrous treatment that Sinclair and his daughter had suffered at the hands of Doctor Aggarwal and Nurse Bergsma. The vetting officers went out of their way to recommend to their clients at Century House that this unfortunate state of affairs should not be held against the candidate or stand in his way. DI Gosforth and the child psychologist had put in a good word for Dr Sinclair, vouching for the way in which he had comported himself. He had, they wrote, protected the interests of his daughter in a very sensitive and gentlemanly way. The Service's in-house psychologist confirmed these recommendations as appropriate to the Recruitment Committee of Personnel. Discrimination against a single-parent applicant, in this case an 'ethnically sensitive' applicant, as the head of the Committee put it, would simply not do. And so, with these loose ends neatly tied up, the whole squalid affair of Doctor Aggarwal and Sinclair's unlucky women was filed away and Sinclair's vetting came through satisfactorily.

Sinclair left Oxford and now moved into a tiny garret above a porn shop near Battersea Park. A couple of suitcases and his constant companion, the tuck-box, were his only belongings in the world. Apart from his daughter, of course.

Ximena again supported his absences stoically, with a grace and under-standing that were beyond her years and touched him deeply. Sinclair's Civil Service probationer's salary went almost completely on the rent and on food for the live-in babysitters, two scrawny girl backpackers, one Aussie, one Kiwi. He had picked them up in the pub one evening and persuaded them take shelter (and a much-needed bath) in return for menial work.

Ximena tolerated the girls, despite the echoes of her dead mother's Antipodean accent whenever they spoke to her, and she was generally well behaved. They, in turn, soon learned that the strange little 'pikkin', who always seemed to know what they were thinking, could be easily bribed with chocolate digestives. In fact, they had never seen a child, particularly a child that small, demolish a whole packet of biscuits in one sitting.

SIX

With the nightmare of Positive Vetting over, there followed a cursory medical in an office in Harley Street. There, an old duffer gave him a notional going over and declared him fit for duty. It never occurred to him to check between the candidate's toes—for it was there that Sinclair had been injecting himself into Morpheus's kingdom since Prep School.

Finally, he was in. With relief he set about thoroughly enjoying the six-month training course, the Intelligence Officer New Entrant Course, or

IONEC for short. The training included fortnightly spells down at the 'Nursery' at Fort Monckton, an old naval fort near Portsmouth, in between deskwork in London.

That year the intake was less than a handful. The cream of the universities had gone into the glamour jobs of merchant banking and advertising, which is where the money was to be made. The more politically ambitious who could not have survived unnoticed in the shadows went into the bona fide departments of the Foreign Office or the Home Office in preparation for careers in politics. Civil Service pay was generally atrocious and the MI6 pay scales were no exception.

Sinclair, another academic type from Cambridge and a backslapping ex-Gurkha officer were two to three years older than the rest of their intake. The others were graduates fresh out of Oxbridge and a couple of second-tier universities, and included two girls—a gregarious horsy type called Trish and Saskia, a classic Sloane Ranger.

They were both charming in their own way. Green-eyed Trish in particular had a hard edge about her and, Sinclair was to learn later, turned out to be particularly gifted at knife-play. She went on to make a name for herself in Covert Ops in Southeast Asia. Saskia, on the other hand, was pretty in a conventional English way, which was totally misleading as she was utterly amoral and a bit of a bitch underneath the soft exterior with that heartbreaking smile. She good-naturedly endured the covert groping of her male colleagues during the unarmed combat sessions in the gym, dispensing justice occasionally with well-placed kicks to the groin when it became a little too obvious. Saskia ended up in SOV/OPS, the coveted elite of the Service, and was able to put in a year or two of service against the Soviet Union before its disappointing collapse.

Sinclair actually came to like one or two of these individuals. They developed a camaraderie, sharing the demanding exercises and the obligatory socializing in the Probationers' Mess after a long day's work. One of their instructors was Mr Holiday, Sinclair's first interviewer, who, it turned out, despite his harmless demeanour, had done great things for the Service in Istanbul and Lagos. When his cover was blown during a disastrous one-off trip to Guyana, they had found a home for him as a recruiting officer in Personnel.

Training at the Fort was interspersed with drills on communications protocol and infiltration/exfiltration exercises in various urban settings around the country, followed by survival and orienteering training up in the

Highlands and on the Cornish wastes. The courses at the Fort included playlets where the trainees recruited each other and then interrogated each other. There were days devoted to microphotography, cipher and codes, surveillance and counter-surveillance techniques referred to as tradecraft. Then came the physical training in the black arts—unarmed, armed and in between—in the gym, under the supervision of crabby hard-as-nails instructors. There was a fair bit of classroom work as well. They were indoctrinated *ad nauseam* in maintaining communications security and in practical psychology. They learned the organizational structures and characteristics of both their adversaries and allies as well as memo writing in the style of the Service. Finally, there were after-dinner lectures from visiting senior officers.

Sinclair did well on his IONEC. He proved to be an acceptable shot with a variety of firearms on the range and he especially enjoyed squeezing off spurts of the Uzi submachine pistol in the woods. They would never have to resort to violence in their careers if they did their jobs properly and followed procedure, they were told. There were more convenient ways of eliminating threats—of killing people, that is. The gun training was more of an insurance policy and a psychological morale booster. What Sinclair lacked in terms of physical aggression he more than made up for in deviousness and he generally excelled in lateral thinking, and this was duly noted by his instructors.

He had definitely found his calling, like the boy spy Kim. He secretly thanked Dr Blantyre every night that he had not ended up in the City or in accountancy or in advertising.

A FLY IN THE OINTMENT

He had made it to where he wanted to be. But as was often the case in Sinclair's life, the way things turned out, he eventually ended up tasting the sour with the sweet. The fly in the ointment this time had a name, and the name was Simon Cavendish.

Sinclair discovered him when, against all regulations, he was reviewing the internal directory in Personnel, for want of anything better to do, one lazy Friday afternoon in between interviews in Century House.

The roster said that Cavendish's current posting was Gabarone, Botswana. He was three years ahead of Sinclair in Intelligence Branch, having joined straight out of Reading University where the list said he had gained a mediocre 2.2 in History. It is most probably another Simon Cavendish, Sinclair thought wilfully, hoping against hope that he would never see those protruding cuffs again.

The Personnel staffers were in an adjacent room celebrating some Moneypenny's birthday and the end of another dreary week of administration. They had forgotten that their probationer had been left all by his lonesome in the file room. In doing so they had broken security, and worse still, they had left the filing cabinets unlocked. Sinclair pulled out Cavendish's manila dossier and perused it at his leisure.

Further examination of the records mentioned the College, and that Cavendish had been a member of the School Committee, Captain of the Under Elevens and the College's First Eleven, an all-rounder basically, a team player, a 'chap'. What the record didn't mention, though, was his role as head of the mafia, as Inquisitor Tantum's protegé and Morguer's chief arse-licker, as Sinclair's Tormentor, the Catholic Gentleman *par excellence*. Simon Cavendish would go far in the Service, where he would have ample opportunity to further develop his skills as an anilinguist.

And now, thought Sinclair with the chill of premonition, Cavendish was his brother-in-arms. They were on the same team again.

The file contained three photocopies of Cavendish's real passport, including photograph and signature pages. Cavendish's aliases—the details of the 'legends' that had been established for him—were contained in the second tab of the file, again in triplicate.

While his colleagues were singing 'Happy Birthday' before their commutes home, Sinclair took from the file the third copy of each false passport, with its photo and signature. Finally he slipped the file back, making a mental note of its location so he could slip back on Monday after photocopying the papers.

Who knows when these may come in handy, he thought, tucking them into his underpants. Sinclair had become a true believer in taking what was on offer. For future reference.

Emerging one morning from Lambeth Underground station into the roar of South London traffic on his way into his new job in Century House, Sinclair experienced a *memento mori*.

Behind the background noise of the traffic he sensed a soft familiar sound. It was coming from the couple of tramps who he had almost tripped over. They were huddled on the stairs, obliterated by a night of meths and heroin. The ammoniac stench of stale urine that wafted up from them was overwhelming and turned Sinclair's stomach. And yet he couldn't prevent himself from looking down at them.

Expecting to see a couple of old red-faced vagrants he saw instead that it was a young man and a young woman. Both were greenishly pale and had dirty blond hair plastered down on their skulls with the grease of the unwashed. They were asleep in each other's arms, surrounded by empty bottles and syringes. They had the telltale complexions of the new generation of plague victims. The bugger's pest, someone in the office had referred to it as. Both were as thin as cadavers.

The sound that Sinclair had heard was the gentle rustle of the girl's snore as she lay curled asleep in the boy's arms, a dreamer's smile on her half-open mouth.

Looking closer he could have sworn that the faces belonged to two people he knew. Gone were the tans and the sun-bleached hair but the faces were unmistakable. In her narco-dream the girl must have been reliving blue skies and beaches and good health and days in the sun.

He remembered Lucy and Rupert asleep in the sea gorse on a beach in the French Antilles.

Yes, that's what that familiar sound had been—that delicate, female rustling snore which had lulled Sinclair to sleep in the student dormitory in Martinique.

The Man for Others stepped over his friends and hurried on.

Memento mori. Carpe diem. Ad Majore Dei Gloriam. Ab initio.

When his probation period was over, Sinclair spent the next three months completing a compulsory rotation through the support departments known as General Services, or GS . For every Intelligence Branch (IB) field officer, on average there are six GS staff supporting him, and it was deemed important that Sinclair and his colleagues should become familiar with their 'back office', as they called it, because without a solid support base even the most talented fieldman is in trouble. Sinclair learned the arcane procedures of Banking, Housekeeping, IT and Personnel in Century House, SIS's head office in Lambeth.

There followed a further three months performing research in the archives for the 'P' officers of the North African desk and then the Polish desk. 'P' officers were responsible for receipt, evaluation and classification, into three levels of importance, of the incoming Product, or CX, as the intelligence was referred to. Once the product made its upstairs, it was up to the officers of the regional Controllerates to decide how to distribute it to the clients of the Service, be they ministries, the Cabinet Office, or other friendly intelligence services, according to whatever byzantine politics or treaties ruled the day.

It was now time for Sinclair's first posting to IB; he would be joining the 350 agent handlers in the field. Before this happened he had to have another series of interviews with Personnel and various Department Heads at Century House. It was then that the success of his politicking during the GS round would pay dividends, or not. Personnel were inclined to send him to Delhi or Karachi Station, because of his ethnic background. Sinclair reminded them subtly that his DPhil had been in Syncretism and that in fact he was far more knowledgeable about Africa, Latin America and the Caribbean than about India, and that his specialist cultural insights could prove valuable in those particular theatres. Sinclair had grown up speaking Portuguese in Goa and he had picked up Spanish effortlessly at the College, where he had taken it at A-level. Another plus, he urged them to consider, was that he could easily pass for a Latino—a 'dago', as his brother-in-arms Simon Cavendish would have put it. For once, in a rare act of logic, the Postings Committee reconsidered its initial position and Sinclair's diplomatic persistence was rewarded with a three-year stint under diplomatic cover—Third Secretary (Commercial)—at Her Britannic Majesty's Embassy in Managua, Nicaragua.

Not the plummiest of postings, to be sure, but better than Darkest Africa or being shipped back to the Subcontinent. It was 1989, and the CIA-conceived Contra war against the Sandinistas was drawing to an exhausted close. There was talk of elections. Sinclair was arriving about ten years too late for the fun and games in that particular corner of Central America, but he determined to make the best of it.

The night before he left England he dreamed that he was the mad Old Boy riding his crocodile into the rainforest.

PART THREE

*"These, he said, were the mysterious groups whose gods demand
—instead of a cock, a pigeon, a goat, a dog, or a pig, as in the
normal rites of Voodoo—the sacrifice of a 'cabrit sans cornes'.
This hornless goat, of course, means a human being."*
—Patrick Leigh Fermor, 'The Traveller's Tree'

LONDON, 1999
A DISH BEST SERVED COLD

BACK IN THE LAND OF SHADOWS

"What filthy, dirty rain," he muttered to himself as the jet taxied in. He looked out through the haggard reflection of his face in the plastic porthole, as he had done so many times before. Across the runway the lights of Heathrow and its terminals were reflected in the wet black skin of the tarmac.

He winced at the memory of Gumercindo's tears. His loyal and much deceived chauffeur had hugged him and Ximena and Mem'zili in the departure area at Jose Martí. Gumercindo had wept openly under the noses of the DGI security goons who had escorted them to the airport, and under the popping flashes of the photographers. The press had been there in force to witness the expulsion of the British spy.

But at least there was a silver lining to all of this, as far as Gumercindo was concerned. Gumercindo, who had been delivering details of the initiation rites of the *abakuá* to Sinclair, had now been released of his obligation. For weeks already he had been begging Sinclair to cancel his contract, because he felt that it was just a matter of time before his brothers in the Leopard Society discovered what he was up to.

"Why should they discover you? What are you scared of?" Sinclair had insisted.

"They just know," Gumercindo had said with a haunted look in his eyes, "they just know."

At least his children, wife and mother-in-law had eaten well that hot Special Period summer.

The journey back from the tropics had been traumatic for Ximena and Mem'zili and as it neared its end it now bought back bad memories for Sinclair. Heathrow as usual was cold and damp that morning before dawn, and the fluorescent lights of the terminal gave the tired travellers from the Miami flight the spectral pallor of the undead. 'Death warmed up' was the phrase that crossed Sinclair's mind as he watched his fellow passengers disembarking that morning. Even Mem'zili's face, usually a deeply polished mahogany, looked grey in the dismal light.

Sinclair was wide awake when they stepped off the aircraft into the jetway and into the cold blast of England in mid-winter.

Ever since Sinclair had first landed there in 1971, Heathrow had existed in his imagination under heavy cloud cover and never-ending rain. The jet had come down slowly through the layers of dirty cotton wool and the grey green fields of England had eventually appeared down there. Tiny beads of drizzle had run across the porthole, making him shudder.

England was a festering wound covered by layers of dirty cotton wool, a country that was separated from the sun by thick barriers of cloud and cold metallic rain. It was the place where exiles from the warmth were sent. Now in his 37th year, Sinclair might as well have been that nine-year-old returning to Prep School from the tropical warmth of Goa. On the train into London he would again be accompanied by thoughts of suicide, as they passed the grey yellow brick of the endless rows of terraces that housed the legions of living dead of the commuter belt.

Sinclair had braced himself for the scowl on the immigration officer's face as they approached the diplomatic kiosk. Hello, who's this foreign-looking fellow in his rumpled tropical suit, followed by that insolent looking negress in a turban and that miserable looking teenager, a paki by the looks of her, with murder in her sleep-deprived eyes?

As always Sinclair was bitterly amused to see the inspector's expression of contempt turn into one of reluctant respect as his eyes scanned the passport number with its telling suffix. The officer looked up and smiled: "Welcome home, sir."

The absence of Special Branch to handcuff him as he stepped off the jetway had been a good sign. Belén had not broken. Not yet, anyway.

"And fuck you, too, *Compañero*," Sinclair replied to the Immigration officer, under his breath.

CABRIT SANS CORNES

Expulsions are dreadful, as Olatunji Ogunlesi and Guy Underhill had learned, but what follows is even worse. Even a fake expulsion like Sinclair's was difficult to deal with. The dreadful thing was the sense of never being able to return, especially if you had been banished from your spiritual home.

He was dog-tired and depressed after the trip. Personnel had assigned him a flat in Clapham as a temporary halfway home while the Service made up its mind what to do with him. The place had the dreary under-furnished feel of your typical safe house.

After showering, changing and settling Ximena and Mem'zili in, the first thing Sinclair did was to make his way up to North London. This he did very indirectly, spending half a day deploying the anti-surveillance techniques and watcher-traps that they had taught him at Fort Monckton—bus, tube, taxi, bus again, doubling back, creating little dead-ends for his hypothetical pursuers, darting in and out of shops on the way, watching for their reflections in the shop fronts, pretending to have forgotten his bag in the last shop and doubling back and watching people's feet in an effort to catch the faltering footfall that could abort his rendezvous. After several hours of this routine, he had satisfied himself that his tail was clean. There would be no need for the fallback plan today. Why would they bother to tail him anyway—he was, after all, just a sad drug-addict who had been sent back home in disgrace, another failed spook. Not worth surveilling, not worth wasting a team of Special Branch's pavement artists when they could be trailing much more lucrative targets like the shoplifting wives of Arab sheikhs on Oxford Street.

From Kentish Town Tube he walked up the hill towards Hampstead, able to relax at last. He turned up the lane that skirts the edge of the Heath.

Someone was flying a lonely kite on Parliament Hill. Sinclair could not bear to think of the hours he had spent up there on the bench with Helen Henshaw during Half Term, watching the sun set over the metropolis as the lights come on in the Post Office Tower.

He had deliberately timed his arrival so that he could have half an hour to himself in the vault.

That afternoon the Egyptian Avenue and the Circle of Lebanon were deserted and luxuriated in the Victorian gloom of the winter twilight. The huge cedar tree kept its silent vigil over the tombs. The padlock on the gate of the Henshaw vault was still there, rusted by the intervening years. It seemed that no more Henshaws had departed this world since Helen. He had it open in a jiffy, using old Ajay's tricks, God bless him—he too must be dead by now.

The crypt was set a way back from the main drag of the necropolis, at the far end of the circle, and that afternoon there were only a few people about picking among the tombs further back down the hill. He felt quite safe, confident that sound tradecraft had sanitized his route.

He sat on the ledge next to the coffin which Xancha Bergsma shared with Helen Henshaw, half expecting to hear muffled thumping and kicking from within after all those years. The casket was still white and surprisingly clean after all those years.

And it was very, very quiet.

He tried to remember his two dead lovers in the best light that he could, but he had a hard time remembering the good times, imagining instead a pair of stinking Holbein cadavers in a macabre embrace inside the coffin. He sank into an even deeper depression. It must have been the effect of the sleepless night on the jet worrying about what would happen in the next few days. Then there was the jet lag and the awful London weather. And then to cap it all, being in a cemetery. It wasn't a combination guaranteed to bring out the Sunny Jim in you.

He shivered into his overcoat as he remembered his daughter clambering down from the ledge. Surely it had all been a ridiculous hallucination, a bad trip.

He remembered his last conversation with Maxwell in Havana.

Maxwell had confirmed Sinclair's worst suspicions in the Old Havana safe house the night before Cavendish arrived. Sinclair had never seen Maxwell so embarrassed.

"Now the point is, George, you may have been compromised—remember that Belén Flores saw you with me in the Nacional that day. I told her about us. I never should have, I know. I was completely out of line, I admit it. But that day I loved you both so much for what you were doing for the Revolution. God knows what they'll dredge up out of her subconscious with all those drugs they have nowadays, poor thing . . . I had to admit to Mazariegos at G-2 that I had told Belén about you. I had to tell them, to save your skin, even though now my own hide is up for tanning. We now need to take drastic action to prevent you from being blown. It may be just a matter of time before Belén breaks up there. No one can last very long these days with the combination of the truth serum and the new techniques they keep telling us about. So this afternoon, Bermúdez—and the Committee—was instructed," Maxwell said, stroking his imaginary Fidel beard, "to decide that you are to be PNG'ed, no reason given, no questions asked."

Sinclair was calm when he should have been quaking with anger. The lightness of being had come down upon him like the Holy Ghost, shedding light and truth on his latest Predicament. And the ironic thing, he realized, was that it was not of his own making this time. It was because of Maxwell's inability to keep his fucking mouth shut. It was all because of pillow talk. Because of his need to show off to his women. This was the price of Maxwell's style of spying. A most human endeavour, he liked to say. Well, fuck him. *Ab initio.*

"If I'm to be blown, then I will defect, straight away, no questions asked."

"Negative, my friend. Defection will surely save your life but our game will definitely be over. If you defect, both SPINNER *and* SNAPPER will be blown. You *have* to understand, *Compadre.*"

"Whereas if you send me back to London, the game *may* be saved and I *may* lose my life, I see. Yes, I understand you very well, *Compañero.*"

"No one would believe that a traitor would ever agree to go back."

"Have I agreed?"

"It has been decided."

"*Maktub*, as my grandmother used to say."

Sinclair saw something painful in Maxwell's eyes. Carlos Maxwell was an admirable liar but this time his concern seemed totally genuine.

"Yes, *Compay*, the solution definitely has its risks. But if we had not taken risks, there would have been no Revolution. In Cuba. Or in Nicaragua, for that matter. But look on the bright side, old man. Who knows, Belén may well hold up until the safety net that I have woven for you is in place."

"Safety net?"

"Remember what I told you about Africa, that time in Nicaragua? At El Mango?"

Sinclair could already see the net being woven.

"And, *Compadre*," Maxwell continued. "I am sure that whatever, or whoever, has guided you to this fork in the road will see you right."

There was a barely audible footfall in the portal of the tomb followed by a whiff of cigar smoke.

"They've been burning the midnight oil in Havana for you, *Compañero* Sinclair," said Carlos Maxwell. He was carrying a bouquet of cemetery flowers. He too looked spectral in the failing English light.

He sat down opposite Sinclair on the ledge next to the coffin and produced a cigar, a match and a flask from the folds of his Russian greatcoat.

"You'll find the envelope under the flowerpot behind Karl Marx's grave—I thought you'd like that little touch. And here is a bunch of flowers for you to arrange in said flowerpot as you service the cache. And do cheer up, old man, you look more than a little browned off, if you don't mind my saying so. Cheers."

"And what about Gabarone?"

"All under control. The logbooks were in good shape. It's all come together rather nicely—a nice little operation we cooked up there, *Compañero*, Operation COÑO, if I say so myself."

"And Geneva?"

"All done, don't worry. It will go like clockwork. Our Zionist friend has done us proud again."

"I do appreciate what you've done for me, Carlos. I know you're sticking your neck out to help me." Sinclair said this without irony. He knew that Maxwell was now on the blacklist at every British and American airport.

"Come on, George, don't be so modest. Take some credit. It was you who took the initiative and nicked that copy of Cavendish's false passport when you were still a trainee. Without that bit of foresight, Operation COÑO would not have been possible. Now that you've had time to reflect, you have to agree that it's in Centro's best interests to deflect suspicion from you and from SNAPPER. And from what I hear, this Cavendish is a sharp cookie. He'd be bound to rumble us eventually. It would have just been a matter of time."

"So Operation COÑO kills two birds with one stone, then, *Compay*?"

"That it does, *Compita*, we get rid of Cavendish, a *coño*, a real-life living and breathing cunt on two legs (he tried to kill you once, didn't he, with a cricket ball?) and at the same time we preserve the integrity and credentials of SNAPPER, long may he prosper, and all those gullible parasites who sail in him, like that little turd Mackie . . ."

LEGOLAND

On Monday morning, Mackie was to be the first officer to interview him. Poor Mackie had had to argue with Personnel, who was in a filthy mood, for the right to be the first to debrief Sinclair. Personnel had been at his most disagreeable that weekend.

"Another officer gone native, another fucking disaster and another fucking weekend lost, dedicated to fucking damage control," Personnel had muttered darkly into his tea.

Sinclair was waiting for Mackie in the interview room on the ninth floor of the new space-age headquarters building on the river at Vauxhall Cross. When Mackie came in, his eyes were watery and seemed pained by the light, as if he had been drinking. He avoided looking directly at Sinclair (no surprise there) and certainly did not offer his hand to be shaken. Mackie looked defeated in his pinstripe, which was shiny with over-use, and his bloodless mouth had a twisted bitter look to it. He has probably gnawed away the inside of his mouth with worry, Sinclair found himself thinking. He did not look like a man who had slept well. No wonder, because for the poor dumb bastard the downfall of George Sinclair could very easily turn into his own downfall. After all he had been Sinclair's senior tasking officer and mentor. The only thing that poor Mackie clung on to for dear life, the raft of salvation in the tempestuous sea of George Sinclair's disgrace, was SNAPPER.

Mackie sat with his back to the window which gave out on to the doomed panorama of South London and the forlorn lower reaches of the Thames. Sinclair could only see him in silhouette. Sinclair's failing eyesight was becoming more of a problem every day, and since his return to England it had worsened. He had the feeling that every room he ever set foot in had had its lights purposefully dimmed, just for him, just to rile him and make his life miserable. And so he could only really see Mackie's grey bulk against the light of the dreary London afternoon.

The little man spoke in that high-pitched Scottish whine of his disappointment and of wasted opportunities. Especially because SNAPPER had been, and *continued to be*, he insisted, looking at Sinclair intently, such a supreme intelligence coup. "How could you throw it all way, George, *how could you?*"

Sinclair was not expected to answer.

He sensed that Mackie was petrified that there might be bad news in the offing about SNAPPER, that Sinclair's fall would in turn bring the whole SNAPPER operation tumbling down around his ears. Like the Tower card in Ximena's Tarot pack, which showed a little man falling to his death from a burning tower that had just been struck by lightning . . . a little man with Mackie's face.

And it was definitely SNAPPER's continued well-being and productivity that Mackie wanted to talk about that morning, not Sinclair's drug problem or his 'bizarre obsession with voodoo'. That was none of his business. Personnel and, perhaps, the psychologist would have to deal with that can of worms. His priority now was keeping SNAPPER on his well-deserved pedestal.

"SNAPPER has left a message saying that he will not meet with your replacement under any circumstances."

"So would you if you were SNAPPER," said Sinclair, calmly, looking down at his nails.

"And what, pray, is that supposed to mean?" snapped Mackie bad-temperedly.

"That in this game you only deal with those you can trust. Do you not? Come off it, Mackie, you know that very well. I don't know about *you*, but it's the first thing they taught *me* at the Fort."

"And why on earth should SNAPPER not trust our Simon? I mean, for God's sake, he trusted you, we all trusted you, and look how, well, how untrustworthy, yes that's the word unfortunately George, how *unworthy* of his trust, of *our* trust, you proved to be."

Sinclair let this pass in silence for a moment and watched the rain clouds stacking up above the ugly roofscape of South London behind Mackie's head. Now it was time to act.

"I have bad news for you, Mackie, I'm afraid, and for the Service."

"How can it can get any worse?" the Scotsman whined, sensing a new disaster about to overwhelm him, like a deer suddenly aware of the mountain cat watching him. Shit, there was a limit to what a man can do to weasel out of trouble, especially trouble created by unreliable third parties. Mackie imagined a new series of late-night grillings and admonitions from his implacable bosses in the crisis room on the twelfth floor. That's where he seemed to spend most of his time these days.

"Unfortunately, yes, Mackie, it can. Much worse."

Mackie seemed to be bracing himself, and he folded his arms over his chest as if getting ready to deflect a mortal blow. It was amusing to see how quickly seasoned fieldmen like Mackie forgot the lessons about body language that they had drummed into them at Fort Monckton.

Now the moment has come, thought Sinclair, the moment that he has been dreading all along, the thing with no name that keeps him up at night. The thing that induces panic attacks at three in the morning. The revelation that SNAPPER has been the doublecross of the century, that all that priceless intelligence that has the Cousins eating out of his hand is artfully concocted chickenfeed, nothing but mere chickenfeed.

My Mackie can already hear the knives being sharpened in Personnel. He can already see his sorry demoted self walking in through the front door of his semi in Surbiton, his tail between his legs, to own up to the wife. Wife is a hatchet-faced vixen who has taken to the gin bottle in recent months. Hatchet-faced and a gin fiend. Hell on earth. Mackie already inhabits one of the outer rings of hell, Sinclair thought, pictured Mrs Mackie's booze-addled face and suddenly feeling sorry for his boss. He sees Mackie as the Ten of Swords in Ximena's Tarot, the man with ten swords sticking up out of his back. Sinclair had an empathetic ability to step into the shoes of other people, especially when they were in trouble.

"Yes, Mackie, very bad news," Sinclair resumed, suddenly discarding his sympathy like a soiled rag and relishing again the tortured expression on his boss's face. He took a manila envelope from his briefcase and pushed it across the table to his boss, who was by now looking very sick indeed.

Sinclair felt that lightness again, the same lightness of being that Milan Kundera's hero experienced as he casually betrayed those around him.

"In there you will see proof that things are much worse than they appear. Drugs and voodoo, well, yes, I admit that those aren't nice hobbies for Boy Scouts and good Secret Servants, and I'm quite prepared to face the music on both counts. But treason, well, I don't think treason is a nice hobby either. I could have told you if you'd given me half a chance before shoving me and my family on the plane like common criminals. But take a look, go on, go ahead, take a look for yourself, you have all the time of the world, now that the damage has been done . . ."

Mackie's face had acquired a dreadful pallor and his bloodshot eyes were now dark with worry. Sinclair thought that Mackie was going to vomit into the envelope as he opened it, with such reluctance and distaste that it might as well have contained a dose of the bubonic plague.

Sinclair watched the little Scot's face, which had drained of the last drop of colour in the last few minutes, as he scanned the papers which he held in his trembling hands.

And then a look of enormous relief came over him.

"My God," he breathed, loosening his tie, the colour returning to his face, "for a moment I though you were going to tell me that SNAPPER was a fraud. These papers appear to be about someone else, a Donald Sullivan, who-ever he is."

"Fortunately, for you, Mackie, SNAPPER is not a fraud. Believe it or not, he does care about the Service, even though we never saw fit to bring him into the tent back in 1978. He still believes in England. That is why he has given us this information."

Sinclair walked around the table and fanned the papers out in front of

Mackie, and proceeded to walk his boss through the treasonous story they represented. What the papers had to say had still not sunk in with Mackie, because they contained only text and numbers, and sometimes Mackie was pretty slow on the uptake, despite the fact that he had scored very high marks in the analytics part of on his entrance Sisby.

What Sinclair had laid out for him were photocopies of a series of cheques made out to Donald J. Sullivan, with accompanying deposit slips from various branches of Crédit Suisse in Johannesburg, London and several European capitals. The individual amounts were in the thousands, the total well over $150,000, US, the dates spread over a period of two years or so, all neatly consolidated in three pages of bank statements. The cheques had been issued by a Panamanian company called Globe Financial Services and had been countersigned by two people with Spanish-sounding names. There were also account-opening forms at the Crédit Suisse in Geneva signed by the account holder and countersigned by the client executive assigned to him. The account executive being a Swiss Jew who was in the pay of DGI through an elaborate false flag operation through which he was made to believe that he was helping out Mossad.

"The Panamanian company, you will no doubt have your girls confirm in due course," said Sinclair, "is a shell trading company set up by our friends at the DGI. The signatures belong, according to SNAPPER, to none other than Antonio Cagundio Sánchez, the Head of Africa Division, and to Marcelito Irigoyen Cabrera, Second Secretary of the Cuban Embassy in Gabarone and Donald J. Sullivan's paymaster and handler."

"And who is this gentleman, Donald Sullivan?"

Sinclair was really enjoying himself now, as he led the blinking Scot down the path to a really nasty surprise.

"Well, if you care to look in the archives, Mackie, you will see that Donald Sullivan is the Southern Africa correspondent for a well-known periodical, which as you know is run by a very good friend of the Service. Donald Sullivan is also one of the approved legends of one of our own brethren."

"Well who the fuck is it then?" glowered Mackie, turning on Sinclair with panic in his eyes as he felt the thin ice cracking under him again.

Sinclair had saved the best for last.

Take it easy, don't overdo it, Maxwell had advised him during their secret rendezvous in Highgate Cemetery, don't appear to gloat.

From his jacket pocket Sinclair now took out a folded photocopy of the photograph and signature page of a British passport. The photocopy bore the stamp of the Crédit Suisse, Geneva, and showed that the applicant's passport had been laid carefully alongside the bank's signature card by the Jewish account executive, to match the signature and verify the identity of the account holder (a nice bit of sleight of hand by DGI's forgers in Havana—a photocopy of a photocopy made to look like it was the actual passport itself on display).

Sinclair unfolded the piece of paper and laid it out in front of Mackie, smoothing it out with his hand, revealing the face of Donald J. Sullivan, alias Simon Cavendish, SIS's former Number Two in Botswana. Now, thanks to SNAPPER's information, it was clear beyond all reasonable doubt, that Cavendish was a proven DGI agent and fully paid-up traitor. The man who Mackie had just sent out to replace George Sinclair and to take over the running of MI6's star asset in Latin America.

THE RUBBER ROOM

You didn't want to end up in the Rubber Room.

Sinclair had been instructed to report to a basement beneath the Dorchester Hotel in the West End. The basement is owned by MI6 and its officers refer to it as the 'Rubber Room'—it is basically your standard interrogation chamber with one-way mirrors and recording devices, but this one has padded, rubberized walls.

Another underground room in a series of underground rooms, Sinclair thought, remembering the Pit and the crypt under the College church, and the cellars under his houses in Haiti and Cuba. And now the Rubber Room. Was it all going to end here, underground?

It was a kind of halfway house. It was here that renegade officers, rogue agents, traitors or those suffering from nervous breakdowns, those who had flipped and lost it or who needed a bit of active chemical intervention or sleep deprivation to jog their memories, were sweated or calmed down, ministered to, and then observed, recorded, sweated, threatened, and observed. And recorded again, possibly for the last time, before being shipped down to the Fort for a more permanent course of treatment. It was where they bled you like a pig, sucked the marrow out of your bones until there was none left, scoured every corner of your soul. What was left of you by the time they had finished squeezing out the juice was not worth much—a husk, a shell, a gibbering wreck perhaps.

Sinclair was asked to sit in a windowless waiting room. The experience reminded him of sitting outside Spock's 'Room of Doom' waiting to be summoned for his twice nine. There was a soft hum in the background from the ventilation system. It was like being at battle stations in a submarine many fathoms beneath the surface of the ocean.

Sinclair remembered the Pit again and then dwelt on the memory of Dr Tantum's words, recommending him to break away from the malign influence of Guy Underhill and come up to the surface for air. This is where bad apples like George Xavier Gupta Sinclair could well end up unless they played their cards right—in airless underground rooms with limited possibilities.

Sitting there, Sinclair analyzed those possibilities. The most likely scenario, he tried to convince himself, was that he'd been summoned there to bear some kind of witness against Mackie, who was probably a strait-jacketed dribbling vegetable by now, judging from the way he had flipped when Sinclair had finished explaining, with the help of the forgers in Havana and the Zionist bank clerk in Geneva, that Donald Sullivan and Simon Cavendish were one and the same gentleman. Sinclair relived an anxious moment when he feared that Mackie was about to burst a blood vessel and go apoplectic on him.

A darker possibility had been lurking under the surface since he had been summoned to the Rubber Room. It came up to the surface like a bubble of fetid marsh gas. He had managed to keep the downside out of his thoughts ever since his expulsion from Cuba, but only barely. Perhaps Belén had broken at last, perhaps they had seen through the stratagem of Operation COÑO. Perhaps they were going to grill *him*, perhaps the game was up and he had finally been forsaken and deserted by his *orisha*. Perhaps Elegguá had run out of patience with his wayward son at last and had closed the gate on him once and for all. Sinclair felt his pulse quicken as he imagined the routine to come—the straps, the tourniquet, the pinprick in his inner arm, the kind words of the interrogator. But then why had they taken the risk of allowing him to walk in on his own. Why hadn't he been bought in in cuffs by Special Branch?

A split second before the door opened Sinclair felt a minute change in air pressure on the back of his neck and he braced himself.

OXFORD, 2002
THE SATURN RETURN

MORPHEUS

"**It was a Saturday** afternoon in early June, Morpheus, not so very long ago, when it all started to unravel—do you remember? It was almost three years since our return to England and my dismissal from MI6. By then, what had happened in Cuba seemed like a half-remembered opium dream. Haiti and Nicaragua were even vaguer hallucinations. I might as well have never set foot out of Oxford, because for all I knew the whole damn business with MI6 had been a fantasy conjured up during one our trips together."

"Not likely, old boy," says Morpheus, his usual agreeable self.

Perhaps, Sinclair insists, as he remembers the events of that Saturday afternoon, he will wake up and it will be—God forbid, the recurring nightmare that haunts all university graduates—just before Finals. He will be totally unprepared with only ten minutes to revise the entire three-year syllabus.

Morpheus chuckles.

Sinclair was never called back to the Service or asked to continue meeting SNAPPER. He had eventually stopped worrying about Maxwell's failure to contact him, and the puzzling silence from Havana. He had settled into the routine of his new life, or half-life, more like it—teaching at Magdalen, writing and researching under the supervision of David Blantyre. The Oxford University Press had finally published his *Comparative Analysis of Afro-Antillean Syncretism* and it was selling modestly but steadily.

And at home in the long evenings and empty weekends, with the help of Ximena and Mem'zili, he paid homage to his memories in the company of Morpheus.

That afternoon Oxford seemed deserted. A veil of drizzle covered the domes and steeples of the city like a shroud. In the front room of their semi-detached house in North Oxford Ximena lay curled asleep on the sofa, dark and catlike.

275

She was twenty-two years old, and had chosen not to leave her father's side. Instead she had pledged herself to watch over him during the difficult years that followed their sad return from the tropics. Sad, yes, Sinclair acknowledged, but not entirely disastrous because at least he was free and his family was safe.

He heard coughing from upstairs. Deep, bronchial coughing. Poor Mem'zili had never adjusted to the climate.

My God, where have the years gone, thought Sinclair, drawing the curtains of his study to shut out the view of the steady, interminable rain soaking the world outside. With trembling fingers he placed a record on the turntable. The hum and scratch of the record player filled the room, followed by the opening of *Riders on the Storm*, all dreamy piano and doom-laden rain.

By the light of his desk lamp, squinting because his eyesight was still failing and had become more unreliable than ever, Sinclair rolled his sleeve up, flicked on a vein and deftly injected a half-vial of morphine into his inner arm. There was no need to do it between the toes any more—because there was no one left to hide it from.

In the room next-door his daughter sighed in her sleep. From upstairs he heard another cough and the muffled tread of Mem'zili.

Waiting for the drug to work its magic, Sinclair settled back into his reading chair and squeezed Madame Bernabeu's *gris gris* in his pocket. He intoned the mantra that accompanied and comforted him like a talisman whenever he moved through the passages of memory that lead to the most tender or dangerous recesses of his past: *What Goes Around Comes Around . . . What Goes Around Comes Around . . . What Goes Around Comes Around . . .*

He closed his eyes and waited until he could see the pulse of the music threading its colours between those of his magic words. The music led him like a mythological thread through the vaults of his mind. Synesthaesia, the French poets used to call this fusion and confusion of the senses, they had been taught at the College.

Feeling the warmth of the drug blanket him, he again fingered the *gris gris* that he had always carried in his pocket and thought kind thoughts about Madame Bernabeu and her pleasant skin and the delights of her gardens in the shadow of Mont Pelée. He thought of his dead women. He thought of Helen. Of Jane. He thought of Martina Mendieta. He tried not to think of Xancha Bergsma.

Soon it was time to surrender to the merciful balm of the drug that bathed his consciousness in a soft rising wave.

The last image, half dreamed, half imagined, that he saw before stepping over the threshold into the past, was Carlos Maxwell's face.

The reliable words of his mantra, like the Abracadabra code in *The Thousand and One Nights*, have worked like a charm. Soon he finds himself standing before a door, about to begin the exploration of one of the many chambers of his past. He steps through the door and begins the slow and careful retreat into his memories, as if stepping backwards into the dark still waters of a sacred pool.

Because his fortieth birthday is almost upon him, that afternoon the theme of his exploration is to be the cycle of the planets and the passage of astrological time and their influence on his coming of age and on what happened to him afterwards.

He dwells for a while on the accident of his muddy skin and on the cruelty of English schoolboys. He then steps back and, evoking an image of his dead grandmother, he considers the bigger picture. He considers the position of Saturn, the Great Malefic, in the horoscope that was cast for him in a hot country halfway around the world. Saturn, whose awful shadow, as Grannyjee had predicted in 1971 and as Martina Mendieta had further confirmed on a bench overlooking Havana Bay in 1998, had re-entered Gemini in August of 2000, after an absence of 29 years.

The voice of the dead Jim Morrison and end-of-the-world music of the Doors reached him from a time and a place many years and miles away from where he was now floating. His friend Morpheus, who this afternoon had the face of his friend Carlos Maxwell, had appeared at the steps of the pool to welcome him back into the familiar country of the past. Sinclair sank deeper into the warm sacred waters, and just before he was totally immersed, he saw that his friend had been replaced by the manifestation of a Yoruba god. It was, he was sure, Elegguá, the God of the Crossroads, because he it had taken the form of a thin Afro-Cuban boy. The child held a crooked stick and who was staring down at him intently from the edge of the pool, his eyes bright with mischief.

In the astounding clarity of the narcotic dream that followed, Sinclair's eyesight was restored to perfection. He was a feathered beast roaming the skies above Northern England. A full moon illuminated the immense blue panorama of fells and fields far beneath his wings. His predator's eyes focused in below on a towered building which was surrounded by woods and lay under the distinctive curved silhouette of a massive hill. He glided down to the place, the black feathers of his gigantic wings rippling on the powerful northern breeze; soon the movement of his wings subsided as his talons came to rest on the granite ledge of a dormitory window on one of the upper floors of the building.

Sinclair, feral-bird-of-prey, the bearer of the night, looked in through the window and saw a small dark boy shivering in his cot.

TU ES GUY

There was a knocking at the door, another twitch upon the thread. The Doors had finished performing their album a long time ago. It was now dark outside and raining steadily. The record had run its course and the needle now bumped up repeatedly against the spindle in a rhythmic, crackly thump.

Ximena appeared from her bedroom, rubbing the sleep out of her eyes. She stood at Sinclair's side as he emerged from his own slumber.

"A man comes, father."

Before Sinclair could make sense of where he was, Mem'zili had come downstairs and her ageless mahogany face looked around the door into the study. After a fit of rachitic coughing, she announced in her deep hoarse voice that she would see who it was.

Mem'zili greeted the stranger with caution, frowning at him with undisguised scepticism. He was asked to stay right there on the doorstep, out in the rain, as she announced the visitor in Creole. These days it was very hard to get her to speak English.

Guy Underhill stood there in the study, his mac dripping with rain, surrounded by Sinclair, Ximena and the sceptical nanny. Sinclair squinted at him, unable to make out the features of the tall thin man who stood there, smiling down at his family. "Damned eyesight, gets worse every day . . ."

It took Sinclair another second to compose himself and say something. He had not laid eyes on Guy Underhill for many, many years, not since he left him curled up on his mattress in a squat in Hull in 1988.

"Guy, my God, is it really you?"

"The one and only, I'm afraid. And who is this charming young lady?" he purred with a smile and a courtly bow in the direction of Ximena.

Mem'zili had retreated and scowled at the visitor from her corner, arms wrapped around herself as if caught by a sudden chill.

"My name is Ximena Sinclair. And you are . . . ?"

"Guy Underhill, at your service."

Sinclair couldn't deny it, it was really him, with that same sad, charming smile. It was an older and more fragile looking version of the wreck he had left sobbing in the squat.

Underhill was thinner and paler than he had been as a boy. Time had turned his golden locks sandy and dull, and his skin was now oddly translucent. Delicate blue veins haunted his temples. But what had not changed were those infuriatingly blue eyes of his, eyes that looked you directly in the eye, always teasing and challenging. Now there was something hungry-looking and insistent and wolfish in Underhill's stare. Sinclair looked away, remembering Underhill's fondness for hypnotism.

Sinclair was still flabbergasted. "I'm so sorry, Guy, old boy, but my eyes are going. I wasn't sure it was really you, and this damned light doesn't help . . . but do come in, come in, you caught us all napping, I'm afraid . . . My God, it's been so long, is it really you?"

"No trouble, George, really, I was just passing through, I couldn't really not drop in, being in North Oxford and all that. And they said that I simply had to meet your lovely daughter. And it is your fortieth birthday soon, after all, on the eleventh if I'm not mistaken. You know, mine was last December—beat you to it, methinks a little celebration is in order."

While Sinclair looked at his hands, trying to figure out what to make of this latest turn of events, Underhill's blue hypnotist's eyes sought out Ximena's black psychic gaze.

CABRIT AU CURRY

That evening Mem'zili pulled out all the stops and treated them to her speciality, a fine dinner of *cabrit au curry*—curried goat, candied yucca and boiled plantains.

Underhill's refusal to eat made her even more suspicious of his *bona fides*, and Ximena also was taken aback by their guest's bad manners. Mem'zili whispered to Sinclair in the kitchen, while Underhill sat at the table watching Ximena suck the bones clean, that something about that man—Underhill— was not quite right.

"*Attention, M'sié George, attention . . .*"

*

They had stayed up late in Sinclair's study after Mem'zili had cleared away the dinner table. She had asked Ximena to help her wash up and there was a hushed conversation in the kitchen, which Sinclair and Underhill pretended not to notice. Eventually Ximena came in and said goodnight, pecking her father affectionately on his forehead but avoiding Guy Underhill's insistent gaze. She went upstairs like a good girl. Butter wouldn't melt in her mouth, thought Sinclair grimly. He was ill at ease and did not relish the prospect of spending time alone with Guy Underhill.

Underhill settled back into the sofa and after a while, as if choosing his words carefully, joined his fingers in a steeple and asked: "Do you remember a certain conversation we had in a squat in Hull, about Mephistopheles, the Knights Templar and the Society of Jesus?"

"Yes I do, and I remember that you told Mephistopheles to fuck off."

"And do you remember the fate that Mephistopheles said would befall me if I rejected his invitation?"

"Something about your being condemned to a life of mediocrity and shallow relationships?"

"Quite right, George, you have quite a memory."

Sinclair did not answer. He lit up a joint.

"Well, his prediction proved uncannily accurate," chuckled Underhill, accepting the joint that Sinclair offered.

Sinclair remained silent, his intelligence training taking over once again—let them talk, and you just listen, listen, listen, because humans love to talk and they will reveal their hand eventually. Give them enough rope.

"One detail that Mephistopheles failed to mention, however, was that they would watch me—keep me under surveillance, if you like—if I didn't accept. And this is what in fact happened. They have stalked me and spied on me and trailed me and harassed me ever since my 'Confession' at Farm Street. I know what you're thinking—'do they know you are here?'—well, you'll be pleased to know, I managed to give them the slip. I confused them at Reading station on the way here. I could be anywhere in the British Isles by now, as far as they're concerned."

My God, Sinclair told himself, he's still deluded after so many years. And what stamina to keep the fantasy going for so long!

"And now, and here is the real reason that I am here, dear George, you may also recall me telling Mephistopheles that what goes around—"

This time Sinclair did speak, finishing off Guy's sentence: "—comes around. And that *you* would come after them."

"Precisely."

A weird light lit up Underhill's unblinking gaze.

Sinclair watched the tiny embers of the joint rise and fall as Underhill smoked. It could have been 1988. They could have been sitting in the same squat in Hull for all he knew.

The following day Mem'zili refused to accompany them on their journey, insisting that her cough was getting worse.

They were to spend the week, including Sinclair's fortieth birthday, at the Bergsma cottage up in Lancashire. And from that base they would execute the stratagem that they had agreed upon the previous night.

THE GATES OF HELL

And so it was that the three of them, Sinclair, Ximena and Guy Underhill, were standing at the entrance to platform twelve at Euston station in North London, waiting for the three-fifteen slow train. Even though it would have been quicker to go up north from Oxford, via Birmingham, Underhill had insisted that they travel back down to London to get the train up.

"It wouldn't be right to do it from Oxford. It must be done from Euston."

And now they stood there at the entrance to platform twelve, with their tickets, waiting for the announcement to board.

"Platform twelve, welcome to the Gates of Hell," Sinclair imitated a British Rail announcer and chuckled, winking at Ximena.

Underhill's pallor had taken on a greenish tint, his glaucous eyes seeming to blend in curiously with the dirty turquoise marble floors of the concourse. The kiosks were now garishly brighter than twenty years ago and sold CDs and DVDs and croissants when before they had sold only inky newspapers, tinned beer, cigarettes and sausage rolls. Outside a grim London afternoon was underway and the muffled roar of the traffic barely made it across the plaza and through the thick glass walls of the station.

The station itself had not changed that much, Sinclair observed. He reminded Underhill of the places where they used to smoke before catching the school train. He pointed out what used to be the smoky British Rail bar under what was now an enormous digital clock. That was where they would tank up furtively before their escorts showed up to herd them onto the train.

Underhill nodded without enthusiasm and was oddly quiet that afternoon.

Weakened by something, he was uncharacteristically unsure of himself. Perhaps it was the effects of the whisky and the dope that that they had taken late into the night. It certainly wasn't Mem'zili's *cabrit au curry* because the man simply didn't eat. He seemed to live off alcohol, drugs and cups of tea.

Walking down the ramp to the train Underhill started telling Ximena that this was precisely where he, her father and their friends used to gather at the beginning of term way back in the seventies to start the long journey northwards and back to the College.

"I know, Mr Underhill," she replied curtly, "Ma told me the same thing, because this is also where we used to catch the train back up North whenever we came to London."

The tone of her reply worried Sinclair. Every time she spoke to Underhill it was to put him in his place, as if she needed to establish that her relationship with him was not to be that of uncle-niece. There seemed to be some subliminal conversation going on between them, and it made Sinclair uncomfortable.

"Yes, Guy," he said, "Ximena used to make this journey all the time, when she lived with her mother up there."

When they were settled into their compartment, Ximena unwrapped their lunch and poured coffee for them from her flask. Underhill refused to take anything.

"Suit yourself, Mr Underhill," she said, unwrapping a packet of chocolate digestives which she proceeded to work through systematically, demolishing them one after the other, munching angrily.

Outside, the dark industrial outskirts of London receded and were soon a memory. They gave way, despite the summer, to wintry back gardens and allotments and finally to the muted grey-green of the countryside speeding silently by.

Underhill whispered to Sinclair that he had never seen a packet of digestives disappear so quickly in one sitting.

Ximena heard him. Nothing escaped her—she had an unnaturally sharp sense of hearing.

Underhill cleared his throat.

"May I ask what became of Xancha?" he said with a sideways glance at Ximena, who seemed lost in her thoughts again and was munching away on her biscuits as she watched the countryside slip by into the past.

It was as if Ximena had not heard the question. Far from it, thought Sinclair, nothing escapes her.

He answered: "She died several years ago, Guy. She is buried in Highgate Cemetery, in fact, quite close to Helen Henshaw, your cousin."

"I'm so sorry for you and Ximena . . ."

"No need," the girl said, to the countryside.

"In fact, Guy, Ximena's mother is always with us," said Sinclair.

"That's a comfort, indeed, I'm glad you see it that way . . ."

This time she did turn.

"And what way would that be, Mr Underhill?" she challenged, her tone in danger of turning ugly.

"I mean, that she is with you in spirit."

"Actually, Mr Underhill, for your information she is closer than you think," she said, taking out the *nganga* from her overnight bag and placing it between them on the plastic-topped table.

Afternoon gave way to evening as the train sped northwards through the Midlands, and the darker it became the more animated and charming Underhill became, as if drawing energy from the coming of the fleeting northern summer night.

To recreate the journey as authentically as possible, they caught the green bus at Preston station. It was pretty much deserted that Thursday evening. The bus, which from the look of it had to be one of the original ones that they had ridden all those years ago, was also almost empty—the last passengers had got out several stops before their journey's end.

Old landmarks emerged in the twilight, as the bus rattled its draughty way through winding lanes lined with endless dry walls, surrounded by deserted fields and stunted trees.

"Remember what we used to say about the countryside, Guy?"

"Fit only for witches."

Ximena scowled with disapproval.

When they passed the war memorial they knew they were on the final approach through the single street of the village. It led to the top of the Avenue, and it was where the pubs were, and the cigarette shop where they used to buy their tobacco from old Ma Hill.

"Ah yes, Ma Hill. No doubt a good six feet under and pushing up the daisies these many a year," Underhill winked at Ximena, his nocturnal humour returning.

Suddenly, to Ximena's reluctant delight, as if on cue, her father and his long-lost friend spontaneously began to chant a Pythonesque litany as they passed the first of the pubs:

Blessèd be the Bird and Brat
Blessèd be the Eagle and Child
Blessèd be the Three Fishes
Blessèd be the Bailey Arms
Blessèd be the Tickled Trout
Blessèd be the Shireburn Arms
Tantum Ergo Sacramentum
Veneremur cernui
Et Antiquum Documentum . . .
Blessèd be Old Holborn
Blessèd be the Rizla
Blessèd be Brother Marlboro
Blessèd be Ma Hill
Aaaaameeeen!

The bus left them at the top of the Avenue before turning back and roaring away, belching a black cloud of diesel. Soon it was eerily silent.

"Like the coach in *Dracula*, it will go no further," observed Sinclair.

Underhill liked that and smiled. Ximena ignored them.

The three of them were left standing there, under the statue of Our Lady perched on the globe of the earth and the horns of the crescent moon.

There was still enough light for them to see, a good mile down in the valley below them, at the foot of the Avenue, the twin pools gleaming in the moonlight. The water reflected the few lights in the huge dark mass of the building.

Sinclair turned cautiously for a sideways look at the expression on Underhill's face. His eyesight, which really was getting worse by the day, let him down once again. A shadow seemed to hover permanently over Underhill, as if he was perpetually situated in Sinclair's 'blind spot'. Strangely, in the moonlight, Underhill seemed to fade away whenever a cloud moved across the moon.

ON PENDLE

An hour later they were unpacking their bags at the Bergsma cottage and, although it was midsummer, Ximena was lighting a fire in the grate to expel the damp.

They had walked up the spine of the Pendle Hill under a full moon, which some would say made them particularly vulnerable to the preying witches of the fells, but the hike was uneventful. Ximena had unlocked the door of her mother's home for them, and then opened windows to let the mustiness out, while Sinclair reacquainted himself with the house.

An exceedingly faint scent of almonds lingered in the rooms of the cottage. It became more noticeable in Xancha's bedroom, whose walls and ceilings had once been so familiar to Sinclair. He realized that the tear-drop paisley patterns of the pale blue wallpaper had lurked undisturbed in one of the rooms of his subconscious during the intervening years, because they were all of a sudden so intimately familiar. He must have memorized those patterns as he had lain there on that same bed with her, exhausted after her silent but demanding tutelage, all those years ago. A particular summer afternoon in the bedroom came to mind. Oddly enough what he remembered was not the lesson in tongue-play or the contortions from some chapter of the Kama Sutra. What he did remember, as if it were yesterday, was the trembling shadow of the leaves of the tree outside the window, playing on the sunlit blue wallpaper.

He felt wistful as he breathed in the atoms that his daughter's mother had left behind. They must still be floating in the air of the room.

Ximena took charge of the proceedings, allocating sleeping quarters efficiently, to the secret pleasure of Sinclair, who was suddenly overcome with tenderness towards her. She had so much of her mother in her. She was silent and businesslike as she dispensed the dinner of tinned sardines and pitta bread and uncorked a bottle of wine for her father.

"I won't offer you any, Guy Underhill, seeing that you don't care to eat with us."

Sinclair noticed that it was no longer 'Mr' Underhill.

"Just a drop of wine, my dear, then, to keep you company." Underhill said this with a stolen, wolfish glance at the girl.

After dinner a familiar craving came over Sinclair and he refused Underhill's invitation to stroll with him in the woods around the cottage. He preferred to spend some time alone, if no one minded. With barely disguised reluctance,

Ximena agreed to show their guest the garden and the view from the edge of the hill. From there you could see far below the twinkling lights of the College squatting massively before its rectangular ponds and, beyond it, the gleaming pewter thread of the moonlit river flowing between the trees.

"Watch out for the weird women out there in the woods. You're taking your life in your hands if you insist on wandering around on Pendle when there is a full moon," Sinclair joked.

Underhill smiled as he trembled with theatrical fright but Ximena did not find this at all funny. She had never found the persecution of witches amusing, and she had made this plain to her father and to her mother before him, whenever the subject of the Pendle witches came up. It was as if she had some hidden affinity with those poor executed wretches from the 17th century.

Sinclair again refused Underhill's invitation. He was just not up to it, thank you very much, and tomorrow would be a long day.

"But it's such a glorious night," Underhill had insisted. "Look at that wonderful full moon, what a beauty . . . hanging there over the fells and fields like . . . like . . . a piece of Stilton cheese."

Underhill was talkative and seemed energized by the moonlight. Sinclair half-expected to hear the howling of wolves in the valley and Underhill's ecstatic exhortation to listen to the melody of the Children of the Night.

From the window of Xancha's bedroom Sinclair watched them stroll along the treeline in the blue light of the moon. Again he noticed that irritating trick of the light, aggravated by his failing vision, of Guy Underhill's odd transparency whenever he crossed a shaft of moonlight or a moonbeam fell on his gaunt frame.

Underhill was gesticulating and seemed to be explaining something to Ximena, who walked beside him, holding her *nganga*, which she caressed absentmindedly, her head cocked as she listened.

At one point, before they stepped into the woods, Sinclair saw them stop in their tracks and saw his daughter turn and look up at Guy Underhill, a sceptical expression on her face, as if she was having a hard time accepting something important Underhill was telling her.

ABO

While Underhill and Ximena walked in the woods around the cottage, Sinclair lay on his dead lover's bed and flicked on a vein in preparation for another meeting with Morpheus.

The drug found its well-trodden path through his blood vessels and into the capillaries of his brain. He followed the same routine as always, carefully and methodically testing and half-opening the doors of the many chambers of his mind, before making his decision and stepping in gingerly to explore a particular vault of his memory.

What Goes Around Comes Around

He recited his mantra to himself as the morphine worked its subtle magic.

What Goes Around Comes Around

This evening it is clear, he says to Morpheus, in which direction the exploration will lead him. His friend and guide is now standing faithfully at his side again at the threshold, his hand on the door.

He wakes beside Matron. His eyesight is restored to perfection. It is 1980 and they both lie exhausted under the blue patterns of the wallpaper. They have just emerged from a particularly vigorous session and are catching their breath.

Xancha Bergsma was anything if not methodical. She had introduced a regime that required that they devote each session to one part of the anatomy, and on that particular afternoon, Sinclair remembered, they had concentrated exclusively on exploring the surprisingly versatile attributes of the nipple.

Her rules were simple: total obedience, no questions unless she invited them, and she was a stickler for hygiene. In return, she purged him of all his adolescent angst and appointed herself his venereal teacher. She had chosen him, and him only, and although she rarely spoke to him or showed him any real affection outside of the bedroom, he felt more secure and increasingly confident in himself under her dark watch than he had ever felt before, even with Helen Henshaw. They never spoke about Helen Henshaw, although Sinclair was sure that Xancha knew about her.

Xancha Bergsma was a puzzle, and unpredictable as the Lancashire weather that summer. Sinclair had a wilful suspicion that behind the granite façade there was a friendly spirit yearning to get out, but it was like pulling teeth and he was most certainly not in control of the relationship.

That afternoon something gave him the courage to break the rules. It was perhaps the illusion of intimacy that was created when she permitted him to lay his head on her brown chest and listen to her heartbeat as they recovered from their exertions. The pulse of her heart and the warmth of her skin reminded him that she was after all only human, despite the aura of mystery that surrounded her. That afternoon he was taken with a feeling of tenderness and a potent desire to know what lay behind the enigma of those black eyes.

He asked her how she had come to be at the College.

He was surprised when she agreed to tell him her story, at least the bare bones of it, because he had hardly heard her ever put more than two sentences together. It was one of the few times that she had ever opened up to him and answered his questions.

Her story went something like this: She had been born in Australia, at least that's what she had been told. Since she could remember, they had told her that her father was a Dutchman who was really a Gypsy, an itinerant seaman who had broken away from a tribe of Romany that haunted the back roads of Friesland and made its sad trailer parks its home.

"I never knew the bastard," she said. "They said he was killed soon after I was born. Bled to death on the floor of some bar in Melbourne. All he left me was the name Bergsma."

As for her mother, now this was the interesting part: her mother was an Aboriginal prostitute operating out of the back streets of the port of Melbourne. For whatever reason, only God knows why, she said, the child had been allowed to survive the pregnancy and had been given up for adoption at the local Roman Catholic church. And for some strange reason, for the ways and reasons of God are mysterious and, well, illogical, the Jesuits ran that inner-city parish and specialized in paying particular care to dysfunctional and discriminated Aboriginal families. They had permitted the orphan to keep the name she had been born with instead of assuming some Irish or Italian or Spanish Saint's name.

The story became even more intriguing. She remembered the orphanage, which was an annex attached to the church, and she described it for Sinclair. The cold showers, the tropical heat of the classrooms, periodic delousing, chasing lizards on the whitewashed tombstones behind the church, the walls of the church blindingly white in the sun, the hard cots. The attitude of the Jesuits towards the dark Abo children, the abandoned spawn of immorality, was unpredictable. One day they were kind and tender, one day oppressive and irritable. Most of the abandoned children, like her, were the discarded half-breed offspring of drunken white Aussies, sailors, sex tourists and the sick and drug-addicted prostitutes of the port. Her earliest memories were of standing in a sunlit church holding a bunch of posies, and handing them to one of the priests. He was a short silent man, a Scot, and his name was Ignatius Cassius, S.J.

He had been there in her life from this first memory. It was Cassius who had watched over her as she grew her sullen and resentful way into adolescence, and it was he who supervised her studies and encouraged her to go into nursing. She became a Registered Nurse at the Melbourne Royal Infirmary, financed by the Jesuit coffers, and was then put to work in the Infirmary of the orphanage. She observed the Catholic rites, took the sacraments and complied with the regime of the Jesuits on the surface. She helped them dust and clean the Sacristy, and tended to the flowers of the church, while secretly rejecting it all as mumbo-jumbo, the claptrap of the male-dominated club of the Church, the price of accommodation and three meals a day.

And when his time came up, it was also Cassius who persuaded the Provincials of the Order to allow him to take her with him back to the UK, where, he argued, improbably, that there was a shortage of qualified nurses at the Jesuit houses. The ability of a Jesuit to effectively adopt a stray orphan and then to persuade the authorities to permit her to accompany him seemed extraordinary to Sinclair, but he did not press the point with Bergsma, as he listened to her. He assumed that Cassius must have had access to some special lever to achieve that extraordinary feat.

After a year or so of acclimatization in London, where she fell ill from the cold and almost died of pleurisy, and where Cassius arranged for her to help out in the Jesuit Infirmary at Farm Street, her silent protector took her up to the College. There she joined the staff, almost unnoticed, becoming one of two junior nurses assisting Mrs Malvinas-Growler, the Head Matron who ran the Infirmary in those days. Yes, dear old Mrs Malvinas-Growler, May She Rest in Peace, a wily, gin-addled chain-smoker with a moustache who, Bergsma said with her habitual smirk, looked like the grizzled Lauren Bacall in her hoary old age. That was ten years ago, more than half a lifetime ago as far as Sinclair was concerned.

There was a pause in the story. When Sinclair tried to steer her towards telling him how she felt about Fr Cassius, she dried up. She pushed him off her and instructed him to go and wash his genitals and return to the College.

LANCASHIRE, JUNE 11, 2002
BACK INSIDE THE BEAST

BACK INSIDE THE BEAST

"The College was deserted, Morpheus, because it was half-term. Ximena had warned us as we came down the slope of Pendle that even though the boys had gone home there would be Jesuits about. And that some of the kitchen staff—the fleggers, she called them—would have stayed on to feed their masters. We approached the black hulk of the building with its towers and cupolas under the full moon from across the cricket flats, where Helen and I had pledged ourselves to each other in 1979. There were only a few windows lit against the huge mass of the building."

Sinclair had paused and looked up at the big fat moon, which was careering through the clouds. Stilton cheese, indeed. He would not have been surprised to see the silhouette of a Pendle witch riding across it on a well-greased broom on her way to a Sabbatic coven over the wood, in the abattoir perhaps, or the Rat Trap.

"If anyone happened to be looking from the building they could see us coming," Sinclair whispered to Guy Underhill and Ximena. "We must stand out in the light of the moon."

A flashback suddenly hit him. How in 1977 he and Underhill had been caught out of bounds before being twice-nined.

Then another as he turned to look towards the cricket pavilion, half-expecting to see the sideways movement of that silent shadow which had disturbed him when he had kissed Helen for the first time at that very spot over twenty years ago. It was a presence which he suspected of having followed him halfway around the globe, like a bad conscience.

A recollection of Helen's lazy and wilful brown eyes made him shiver.

Striding purposefully ahead of her father, Ximena shrugged off his paranoia. Guy Underhill said nothing. He lagged behind them, and whenever Sinclair looked back to check that he was still with them, the tall figure looked insubstantial, if not positively translucent, blending in and out of the background in the difficult half-light which was made worse by Sinclair's declining eyesight.

They crept around the side of the building, keeping to the pitch-black shadows that the moon cast under the walls. Soon they were standing outside a door in the wall; it was the door that led from the back of the building into the Infirmary.

Ximena pulled out a key and slipped it in the lock. The door opened without a sound, as if someone had greased the hinges in advance, and the girl led them in, stepping through the gloom confidently. She could have been walking through the front door of their semi-detached in North Oxford. This place had been her home too, after all, Sinclair reassured himself, and there was no reason for them to have changed the lock after so many years.

The smell of iodine and disinfectant carried in it a flood of half-memories and sensations that made Sinclair's guts churn in a panicky wash of adrenaline.

"Isn't it amazing," whispered Sinclair to Underhill, "how easily Ximena finds her way in the dark, after so many years away."

The two of them stood in the Sick Bay with its rows of beds as Ximena reconnoitred the corridor beyond the Dispensary. By the moonlight, which bathed the place in that sub-aqueous luminosity that Sinclair remembered so well, he led Guy Underhill by the elbow and showed him the bed where Xancha Bergsma had first come down on him.

"Look how narrow it looks now, how ordinary, a boy's bed, no more than a cot really. Shocking to think that so much, so many matrices, threads and forks in the road had flowed from that single encounter in the dark all those years ago."

Sinclair then led his friend to Matron's little office, which happened to be locked, because it contained the drug cabinet.

"That's where we used to nick the morphine, remember?"

Next door to Matron's office was a smaller room with a single bed, where she would sleep when on overnight duty.

"That was the room," Sinclair told Underhill, without looking at him, "where I convalesced after my penance and where Bergsma took care of me at the end of that hideous summer term."

They found Ximena at the entrance to the Dispensary, looking dreamily at the stuffed black bird, the Noctifer, in its glass cage, her head cocked as if listening to its instructions.

She stands with one foot in this world, one in the next, her father told himself as he watched her.

Above the fake bird, as he knew it would be, was the painting of the Old Boy riding his crocodile into the rainforest.

In the dark, the Upper and Lower Galleries of the College seemed more immense than in his memories, now that they were empty and were lit only by shafts of blue moonbeams that slanted down through the stained glass high up in the windows. The heads of the African trophies and the tribal masks that lined the walls of the Lower Gallery were infinitely more sinister now, with their devil horns and watchful eyes. The weapons on the wall seemed heavier and more pointed now, their edges sharper and more lethal than he remembered them.

They found themselves at the entrance to the Refectory, at the foot of one of the many staircases. There, the walls were covered in rows of old school photographs. They were long pictures of the entire assembled school of more than five hundred boys and staff. In each photograph the boys stood in five rows, each of the five Playrooms with its own row, with the front reserved for the staff, who were seated. These photos had been taken with delayed timers that swept the camera lens from one end of the assembly to the other, left to right, over a period of half a minute or so. The theory, which apparently had been successfully tested once, was that you could appear twice in the same shot, by having your image taken at one end of the line then running round the back of the assembly faster than the sweeping lens, so that you could be taken again at the other end.

Ximena directed her father and Guy Underhill to the five photographs of their generation, which ran from 1975 to 1980. As you progressed through the school, you would have seen yourself in a lower row every year, your face maturing with the passing of each year. Eventually you ended up in Poetry, the last Playroom, standing behind the masters and the Jesuits who sat in the front row, flanked by the handful of Rhetoric boys who were preparing for the Oxbridge exams. There sat Morguer, Morguer's shadow Cassius, Spock, Dr Tantum, Pottifer, Dolly Beamish, Poof Parker and the other lesser denizens of the College.

Sinclair, Underhill and Ximena looked at the 1979 photograph. The significance of that year was not lost on any of them.

"Look, there is Ma," whispered Ximena reverentially, pointing out the unmistakable piercing eyes of po-faced Nurse Bergsma. She sat with her arms crossed defensively on her chest, at the right hand edge of the front row.

"And there he is, Ximena, Yours Truly . . . ," said Underhill, pointing out in the half-light his own face in middle of the fourth row down. "Gosh," he went on, "look at those hairstyles—and look at those tie knots, bloody enormous they were back then. Double Windsor, mine was, by the look of it. I daresay most of us were wearing flares, and platform shoes too, by God."

Underhill was in a good mood and directed all of his comments at Ximena for some reason but she made no secret of ignoring him.

Sinclair peered closer, cursing his eyesight, barely making out Guy Underhill's smirk and the unmistakable V sign—the 'fuck off' sign, not the 'V for Victory'—which his fingers made at the camera as they rested on his forearm.

"And where, Ximena, is your father?"

They looked and they looked, running their fingers repeatedly along the rows of familiar faces, each face igniting memory cells that had lain dormant for decades. They searched again and again, but George Sinclair was nowhere to be found, not in 1979 at least.

They double-checked against the other photos. In every year from 1975 up to and including 1978, George Sinclair and Guy Underhill had stood together, descending through the middle of each row regularly and on schedule. But 1979 was a problem. That year, Guy Underhill, with his gesture of defiance, stood quite alone.

"Where on earth could I have been?" Sinclair wondered aloud. "I don't remember ever having missed a school photograph."

It was truly a mystery.

They speculated, before they moved on to where they were heading, that he must have been ill in the Infirmary the day of the school photograph.

What was not a mystery, though, was the reason for Guy Underhill's own absence in the final photograph, taken in 1980.

THE DANGERS OF DRUGS

They came upon Dr Tantum in his study off the landing of Upper Syntax dormitory, in the very same room where in 1979 Sinclair had been interrogated and 'turned' by his Playroom Master.

The room had not changed. It was suffocating inside, and Tantum's halitosis had not improved in the last twenty-three years. When Sinclair and Ximena entered, Tantum looked up suddenly, because they had not taken the trouble to knock. Twenty-odd years had not done much damage to the

Australian's features, not that they could have deteriorated much anyway. Still, the goatee was streaked with grey. Those same puffy masturbator's eyes peered up at the intruders with suspicion.

"I'm sorry, I didn't hear you knock . . . hello, *you* look familiar," he said, as the penny dropped, his predator's gaze narrowing as he looked upon his Nemesis, and then at Ximena, who was standing there next to Sinclair, holding what looked like some kind of gourd.

"And aren't you Ximena, Nurse Bergsma's girl?"

"I am. And this is my father, George Sinclair."

"George Xavier *Gupta* Sinclair, spin-bowler, drug-addict, Catholic Gentleman and Traitor. *Ab initio*. At your service, Dr Tantum."

Sinclair took his old place in the hot seat in front of Tantum's desk. This time, however, he trained the anglepoise lamp back into the Playroom Master's eyes, so that Tantum squinted like one of his interrogees.

"This is what is called turning the tables," Sinclair said, to no one in particular, perhaps to the Gods of Vengeance hovering over his shoulder. Sinclair recalled the rituals in Haiti and Cuba where he always had the feeling of supernatural entities assembling to watch over the proceedings, and now he felt certain that he was being watched.

Tantum shifted uneasily in his chair. Looking out of the window for inspiration, he seemed to wince with some kind of premonition.

I'm afraid it's too late to do something about those haemorrhoids, thought Sinclair nastily. You're a pig whose Saturday has finally come, he thought again, remembering that wonderful Nicaraguan proverb. But there would be no quick and easy *coûp de grace* for this gasping little piggy.

When Ximena had finished fastening Tantum's ankles to the legs of his chair, Sinclair pushed a small brown package across the desk towards his Playroom Master.

AN ACCIDENT WAITING TO HAPPEN

"A stake through the heart," said Guy Underhill, "would be the appropriate method for dispatching the Nosferatu."

They had found Fr Morguer in the sacristy of the Sodality Chapel, laying out his vestments in preparation for his own private Benediction. The monstrance sat on the ledge under the cupboard, next to the vestments, its gems and spikes and blades gleaming dangerously in the candlelight.

When he saw the intruders at the door, Morguer instinctively took a pace back into the dark recesses of the sacristy.

At first Underhill had refused to enter the sacristy with them, as if he risked vampiric evaporation, but Ximena had given him a sharp shove from behind and he now stood behind the Revenger.

"I'm behind you all the way, old man," he whispered into Sinclair's ear.

Sinclair was looking into the depths of Morguer's soul.

Morguer ignored Underhill's comment, as if he simply wasn't there, and instead looked back at Sinclair with his hooded eyes. You could almost hear the blades and gears of his brain grinding into action. This one might not prove to be so easy, thought Sinclair, as he watched Morguer advance, the memory still fresh in his mind of how compliant Tantum had been when given the choice of swallowing the lethal cocktail of hallucinogenic drugs or of being thrown head-first out of the window into the quadrangle.

Morguer was an old man now but he squared his shoulders like a boxer and turned to face Sinclair. The years had been undeniably unkind to him. Sinclair noted the wizened bags under the eyes, and he could see the skull beneath the paper-thin skin.

But when Morguer saw the object that Ximena was caressing, there was a sharp intake of breath and he instinctively crossed himself, his back arching as he took a step backwards like a vampire presented with a crucifix. It was then that he knew what he was up against.

The next phase in this silent ballet of to-and-fro was when Sinclair took a step forward towards the priest and spoke in a low voice as he bowed ironically at his old Headmaster: "George Xavier *Gupta* Sinclair, Father. Traitor, voodooist, lock-picker, drug-addict, Man for Others, headhunter, at your service. *Ad Majore Dei Gloriam.*"

And then, while Sinclair engaged the Jesuit in an awkward, halting conversation, Ximena had quietly grasped the enormous gem-encrusted monstrance (it seemed almost as big as her) off the sacristy shelf and had lain it quietly on the floor behind Morguer, its blades reflecting the red glow of the altar lamp.

They hadn't really planned it, but such is the genius of improvisation—for father and daughter were now a highly effective and intuitive team—that Sinclair knew what to do when he saw his daughter drop down on all fours just a few inches behind Morguer's knees. He raised his fist and stepped forward, with menace, and Morguer stepped back, and that was that.

TREMENS

The last of the Unholy Trinity to be dispatched was Ignatius Cassius, S.J.
This time Guy Underhill insisted on waiting outside Cassius's door in the
Jesuit wing. The only thing he said to Sinclair, whispering it in his ear as
Sinclair pushed the door open, was the word *"Mephistopheles . . ."*

It was as if the little priest he had been expecting them, because he was
quite, quite calm, and did not resist when they burst into his room nor when
they settled him into a chair in the corner, or when Ximena thoughtfully tied
his shoe laces together.

For the first time ever, George Sinclair heard Cassius speak. The hard
man's voice was strangely and unexpectedly soft—kind even—and reminded
Sinclair of his own father's Scottish brogue.

An old memory which had been teasing at the edges of Sinclair's mind,
something about a kind voice and a Scottish brogue, now became a name—
Mephistopheles, the tempter of Underhill.

And like Sinclair's father, Cassius appeared to speak without moving his
lips—it was rumoured that his tongue had been surgically removed—hence
Underhill's failure to identify him as Mephistopheles in the confessional in
Farm Street all those years ago.

From his chair in the corner of his spartan cell Cassius addressed Ximena,
who stood clasping the *nganga*. She stared back at the little priest with her
black eyes firing on all cylinders, with that look—the 'with menace' look—
that usually heralded the coming of drastic behaviour. Sinclair heard a low
feral growl, barely audible, emerge from his daughter's side of the room.

Perhaps because he must have known what was coming, Cassius's monologue had the recapitulatory feel of a last will and testament.

"Ximena, you should know that your mother Xancha was *my daughter*.
Now, *her* mother was a whore from Melbourne. That may sound bad, but
your grandmother was a very special person, with many special powers, which
it seems you have inherited. Your mother never knew I was her father. She
went to her grave, wherever that may be"—with a dark look across to
Sinclair—"thinking that her father was a drunken Dutch Gypsy." He turned
back to Ximena. "So that makes you my granddaughter, and if I beat you it
was for your own good."

Sinclair looked anxiously across the room to Ximena, who stood silent and
dark and glowering at the old man.

"Yes, father," she said to Sinclair, almost spitting it out. "He *did* beat me.

With the ferula. Again and again, because Ma said that he enjoyed it. She said that he used to do it to her as well when she was a girl in Melbourne."

Cassius's head sank, perhaps with fatigue, perhaps with shame, it was difficult to tell which. He held his head in his hands, his fingers rubbing his scalp between the short grey stubble. Sinclair noticed a tremor in the priest's liver-spotted hands.

Cassius looked up at Sinclair from his corner and asked with the philosophical calm of a death-row inmate resigned to his fate. "Do you know that in some parts of the world they say that the children of priests are were-wolves?"

With that wistful observation Cassius unknowingly satisfied an itch that head been bothering Sinclair ever since the shadow of Cassius's daughter had fallen upon him. Cassius had found the right word to describe Xancha Bergsma. Ever since she had first thrust herself into his life in the College Infirmary over twenty years ago, Sinclair had searched in vain for the right word to describe Bergsma, Cassius's daughter: Amazon, harpie, *lamia*, succubus, energumen, black seraph, witch, vampire, valkyrie, virago, wraith, harridan, Kali, predator, sphinx, bitch, dominatrix. But now, here it was, a word that reflected her preternatural and predatory nature perfectly. *Werewolf.* The daughter of a priest.

Cassius now moved on to the matter of George Sinclair himself, setting his eyes again on the girl.

"Now let me tell you about your father. This man," the bullet head nodded in Sinclair's direction, "who is your father, is truly a son of the Devil. He is wicked. He is a thief. He lies. He picks other people's locks. He is addicted to drugs. He betrays people. He is a Devil Worshipper. He is a voodooist. He killed your mother, as well as other women. I warned your mother about him. I never approved of her choice, but she insisted that he was to be the one. I couldn't stop her. By then she was beyond my control, you see, totally obsessed, infatuated. And as for you, my dear granddaughter Ximena, I have watched over you all your life. I have tried to protect you from him, if only because he kills people. I kept watch over you in Oxford. I followed you to Nicaragua. I followed you to Haiti and then to Cuba. I was at all those devil-ish voodoo seances that your father made you go to. Did he ever tell you that he participated in a satanic Black Mass here at the College? Ever since then he has been dealing with the Powers of Darkness. But that's not the worst thing that your father did here.

"I did my best to have him removed from the Secret Intelligence Service,

Ximena. I told the Cubans about your father's drug addiction and what he did to Guy Underhill here at the College in 1979, so that they would use the information to get him expelled from Cuba—that way you could come back to England and be closer to me. So what does he go and do, your father? He manages to twist certain facts and fabricates others so that this information is seen to have come not from me, but from someone else, from a man called Simon Cavendish, who was a fine upstanding Catholic Gentleman and an Old Boy of this College."

Sinclair let the old priest have his say even though he was tempted to interrupt and set the record straight in front of his daughter, because there were so many inaccuracies in Cassius's version of history. The family gathering would all be over soon enough. The little man stopped talking at last, seeming to have run out of steam in the face of Sinclair and Ximena's silence. And Ximena didn't seem to be about to change her mind anyway, she knew that her grandfather had got it all wrong, especially in the matter of who had killed her mother and her father's other women.

Where is that bored look of contempt now, eh, Father?

Now it was Ximena's turn to speak and she stepped forward with the *nganga* and looked her grandfather in the eye with that prosecutorial look of hers, as if passing sentence.

"My mother, your daughter, Xancha Bergsma now lives inside this gourd, which is called a *nganga*. She is *mpungo*, an enslaved spirit. Sometimes she comes out in the form of a scorpion. She does whatever I tell her to. She is my servant. She hated you as much as I hate you."

His granddaughter's final bizarre gesture took the wind out of Cassius's sails. He blinked stupidly at her, and then looked up at Sinclair with hollow eyes. He seemed very old all of a sudden.

Sinclair touched Ximena's arm gently as she was unstoppering the *nganga* and suggested that there was a more appropriate way of dealing with her grandfather. She stepped back, corking the gourd up again. She was willing to humour her father. It was his day, after all.

"Are we ready, then, Ximena?" asked Sinclair.

She nodded grimly.

"On your feet, Father," said Sinclair.

Revenge is a dish best served cold.

The little man stood up out of his chair arthritically, almost tripping over his shoes, because the laces had been tied together. His age was now truly showing.

He glared at Sinclair. *I will come back to haunt you,* his look seemed to say.

Sinclair was holding something black in his hand. Cassius looked at it uncomprehending. He must think, Sinclair said to himself, just like I did over twenty years ago, that it is a cosh, or a ferula. And then it could be a gun. But no, it is a scourge.

Sinclair thrust it into Cassius's hand, stepped back, placed his hand on his daughter's shoulder, instructed Cassius to remove his shirt, and nodded at the priest for the proceedings to commence.

PIT

"For old times' sake," she said, leading them behind the kitchens into the dirty inner courtyard and down into the Pit, after they had watched the messy spectacle of Fr Cassius flaying himself to death with the cat o'nine tails. It had taken them a while to wipe themselves clean of the little man's blood and now Sinclair was more than ready for a smoke.

His daughter never ceased to amaze him. Sinclair kept on having to remind himself that as a little girl Ximena had roamed the building during the holidays. It was her home too and she probably knew all of its nooks and crannies better than he or even Guy Underhill ever had.

Down in the subterranean boiler room, it was as if the intervening decades had been an illusory fancy, insubstantial as the blue smoke of a joint. The same yellowed pressure gauges and pumps and valves and the same fat rusty pipes were there in their time warp. Everything now existed in the weak light of a single light bulb, but the effect may have been because of Sinclair's worsening eyesight. The floor was as filthy as they remembered it. In the corner was the same old door that they had broken through on their way down into the Jesuit wine cellars. It was through that door that Underhill had been dragged by Fr Cassius at the start of his journey into the underworld.

Ximena asked them to sit, and they found their old niches. She had prepared a joint for them back at the cottage and now she took it out and lit it for the two friends, solemnly and with her habitual air of ceremony. She passed it to her father first, who gulped the smoke down greedily to calm his nerves, because he *was* nervous, however much he would have denied it. The sight of spurting blood and the whole jerking mess of Cassius convulsing on the carpet, the skin falling off his back in ribbons, had unnerved him deeply and he had been lucky not to faint. But in reality he was more nervous about having to relive the night of Underhill's abduction from the Pit, and of having to confess his biggest sin in front of his daughter. He felt that what was coming was to be a trial of sorts, staged by his own daughter, who would act as both prosecutor and judge with those unforgiving black eyes of hers.

He passed the joint to Underhill, who squinted in the smoke and smiled in satisfaction in his own inimitable way as he took a deep drag. By then Ximena was perched high on a transversal pipe, cradling her *nganga*, gazing down at them from on high like the Cheshire Cat in its tree in Wonderland, or like an Old Bailey judge from a bench high above the condemned. It was hard to imagine what was going through her head as she watched them smoke in silence. She had brought them this far, now that vengeance had been exacted, and Sinclair felt a sense of finality about this meeting of theirs underground. It was as if she was now waiting to witness the final act in the reconciliation between George Sinclair and Guy Underhill, now that those responsible for their tragedy had been dispatched.

Sinclair gulped, ready to deliver his opening statement, and opened the batting. "Ximena, my dear," ("M'lud", he had almost said), preferring to address her rather than Underhill, who was watching him intently through the smoke, "this is the place where we used to play the ouija board . . ."

Ximena nodded slowly, like prosecuting counsel, waiting for the witness to incriminate himself.

With this topic he hoped to defer the inevitable discussion of his first act of betrayal, his biggest sin (*"monstrous"* Helen had called it), that had happened down here in the filth of the Pit in 1979.

"…with our friends Doris, Olatunji and Wanking Eddy, who are dead, all dead now," Underhill finished the sentence for Sinclair.

"Which leaves my friend Guy here," Sinclair resumed, "and Yours Truly as the only survivors of the seance. You see, Ximena, another spirit came to us that night, after Grannyjee and Martin."

"You mean that Grannyjee appeared here, in the Pit, father? And who was Martin?" Her interest had been piqued now that the discussion had moved on to the dead.

"Yes, Ximena, this is where your father's grandmother appeared, through the ouija board, that is. She said that she would return, didn't she, George? She came to us after she had died, didn't she, George, but before you had been told."

Sinclair nodded, and added, changing the subject, which was still raw to him: "And then the dead boy, Martin Weld, came to us."

"Oh, *yes*, the boy they have in the crypt down there," she added with a nod at the door, with such enthusiasm that Sinclair couldn't help but gape at her in surprise.

"But you mentioned another spirit, that came *after* Grannyjee and Martin Weld. Who was *that*?" she demanded.

"Well," Underhill replied, "it was an *angry* spirit. He swore at us and he said that he was a dead priest, and that we shouldn't be playing with the dead. He said that all forms of divination were forbidden in the sight of God. He was very annoyed with us for having disturbed him. He threatened us, didn't he, George?"

Sinclair nodded and picked up the thread: "He said that he had died on his fortieth birthday because he had broken God's Law—for disturbing the dead. Just as we were now doing."

What happened in the Pit that evening in 1977 after the puzzling riddles of Grannyjee and Martin Weld had been spelled out on the ouija board went on to become another of the legends of the College.

The fact is that of the five Querents, the majority did not live long enough to experience the dubious pleasures of middle age.

Olatunji, who had become a radical activist, was hacked to pieces while riling up a crowd of angry machete-wielding Islamic anarchists in the city of Kano in Northern Nigeria in 1997.

Wanking Eddy Cayetano went on to become a cultist in California and was one of the thirty-nine suicides who joined the Heaven's Gate Mothership coasting in the wake of comet Hale-Bopp, shortly after his 37th birthday.

Poor old Doris never saw the new Millennium. He bled to death on a London pavement in 1999, after being ambushed and stabbed in the kidneys by a jealous lover.

After the deaths were reported in the College Association newsletter, certain alumni remembered that Olatunji, Eddy and Doris had been known as the 'ouija boys' and recalled their role in one of those witch hunts after a scandal about something to do with blasphemy and a Black Mass. It was then easy then to put two and two together, and so the legend was born: that at the ouija reading in the Pit that afternoon, the soul of a defrocked priest or some vengeful Catholic archangel had predicted in no uncertain terms the untimely death of each of the Querents.

"So he told us that like him, *we* would all die before we reached forty, the spiteful sod," Sinclair said.

"A curse, how interesting, father, I wonder what Mem'zili would make of it," Ximena said, leaning forward on her pipe and stroking the *nganga* as she always did when she became excited. "And so how old were Doris, Olatunji and Wanking Eddy, then, when *they* died? Don't tell me, let me guess."

"That's right, my dear, they were all under forty, no doubt about that," said Underhill.

"And *you*, Guy Underhill," she demanded, looking down at him, magisterially, from her inquisitor's perch, "how old are *you*?"

"My fortieth birthday was last December, the 17th to be precise."

"How curious," said Sinclair, "I had forgotten that your birthday is on the feast day of St Lazarus, of Babalú-Ayé."

A memory of that disastrous *toque* in Guanabacoa on the Saint's feast day flashed across his mind. He saw his possessed daughter standing still in the circle of candles, but he quickly banished the vision.

"And father . . . ," she said from her perch with a weird smile. "Yes, tomorrow father is"—with a flourish—"*forty years old.*"

"Unless he perishes this evening," said Underhill, with a hideous grin that in the half-light of the Pit looked like the rictus of a death's head. It gave Sinclair the chills even though he knew Underhill had to be joking. Christ, though, his sense of humour was as sick as ever.

"Now *that* is spooky, don't you think, Guy Underhill?" she said, ignoring her father. "But it remains to be seen, doesn't it, Guy Underhill? Perhaps we should go down there," she challenged him, nodding towards the door that led to the crypt, "and pay a visit to Martin Weld—the goat without horns, *le cabrit sans cornes*, the boy that the Templars sacrificed in 1975. What do *you* think, Guy Underhill?"

Then she said brightly, hopping off her perch. "Shall we, father?"

By then, as the three of them moved stealthily in the underground passage through the cobwebs and the rat shit and the broken glass on the floor of the wine cellar, Sinclair was beginning to suspect something complicit between his daughter and Guy Underhill. It was as if the conversation in the Pit, and now this journey into the Underworld, had all been rehearsed.

OXFORD, 1987
DEVI

XIMENA

All of a sudden, out of nowhere one Sunday afternoon, while the bells of Magdalen Tower were tolling for Evensong, his past caught up with him again.

There she was, standing on his doorstep in the New Buildings: Xancha Bergsma.

You can't escape your past, George Xavier Gupta Sinclair, her black eyes seemed to say.

An insistent knocking at his door had woken Sinclair out of a deep narcotic sleep. He now stood stunned and paralyzed in the black hypnotic stare of his first lover, like a deer caught in headlights. The X-ray gaze pierced straight through to the back of his skull.

She still smells the same, that same balmy scent of almonds was the only thought that occurred to him.

He blinked hard to make sure that he wasn't dreaming and that this was not a case of her succubus invading his dreams. He gripped Madame Bernabeu's *gris gris* in his pocket to ward off the Evil Eye of Xancha Bergsma.

She was po-faced as usual. Something moved next to her skirt. Sinclair looked down and noticed that she was holding a child by the hand. The girl must have been five or six. She was dark-skinned and she looked up at him with the same penetrating gaze as her mother, a mini-Xancha. But there was something else about the child that was disturbing and yet familiar at the same time.

"Come in, my God, come in."

"You don't have to say anything. Your daughter wanted to meet you, that's all. She's been insisting on seeing you."

Sinclair was reeling. "My God . . ."

His head was spinning.

"Her name is Ximena."

He took the girl's tiny dark hand in his, and looked into the black eyes of his daughter—she had inherited her mother's penetrating black look, which scoured the interior of his cranium. As her eyes bored into his, a connection was made that was to change his world forever. A flood of visceral tenderness overwhelmed him. He moved down to hug her, but the child withdrew.

"She's not like that, George, she doesn't like hugging."

"Does she talk?"

"Only when I have to," answered the girl matter-of-factly in a tiny imitation of her mother's voice, while she sized up her dishevelled father up with those unavoidable eyes. So this little person was the fruit of their covert love-making on Pendle.

"She has been insisting and insisting that now is the time to meet her father."

And then, as an aside as she walked into the room, she whispered something in Sinclair's ear. "The little bitch has almost driven me mad."

And then later, when the tiny girl was safely out of earshot, busy exploring the nooks and crannies of Sinclair's bedroom and study, and methodically going through his drawers as if in search of evidence, Xancha Bersgma declared: "She is psychic."

"How do you know?"

"She sees what you do. She knew what you were like before she ever met you. And lately she has been telling me about a woman from your past."

While the little girl rifled through the notebooks on his desk, Sinclair told Bergsma about Helen Henshaw and Doctor Aggarwal and how Aggarwal had turned Helen against him. He was careful not to mention Jane Redfern.

This news did not seem to have any effect on Bergsma. Her only reaction was to say: "Yes, I know, that same little vixen you used to wank about at College . . ."

She let the subject drop, adopting an expression of extreme boredom.

Bergsma told Sinclair, in case he was interested, that she was still the College Matron, and that she lived alone with Ximena in her cottage on Pendle. The Jesuits had turned a blind eye to her pregnancy and had then found a temporary replacement for her before it became too obvious and the boys started talking.

And that when Ximena was older, in the holidays the child had taken to roaming the corridors and passageways of the College. She knew the names and histories of all the rare stuffed animals in the collection near the Infirmary.

"Her favourite is the Noctifer, that silly forgery outside the Dispensary, God knows why."

"I know the one," said Sinclair.

Bergsma ignored him.

For the rest of their time together that day, Sinclair was to learn that the child was wise beyond her years and had an old head on her shoulders. And that there was no love lost between mother and daughter, despite the fact that Bergsma addressed her as "my pet". Knowing Bergsma as he did, this endearment was no doubt ironic, more like the way a witch might refer to her familiar.

Sinclair imagined a bleak upbringing for his darkling daughter in Lancashire under the strict regime of Nurse Bergsma.

At one stage, Sinclair, still emerging from the confusion of morphine-induced sleep, experienced a mild panic attack and had blurted out: "It all seems like a dream. I can't believe it. Now what do we do? What are we going to do now?"

"Nothing. She just wanted to meet you. We are going back on the train at five. I have a job to do. And she has to go back to school."

"My God, no, no you can't . . ."

Just as they were about to argue, for the second time that afternoon there was a knock at the door. It opened, revealing Jane Redfern's blonde English head peeking into the room. She stood there in the doorway running a hand through her hair as she gawped at them.

She did her best to hide her surprise, bless her, but her frown and her mouth gave her away. Her eyes pricked, settling first on Bergsma and then on the little girl, and then the shocking resemblance between Sinclair and Ximena sank in like a stone dropped into a dark pond. She stood there, her arms now hanging limp at her sides. She seemed about to burst into tears.

Xancha Bergsma's mouth was a cruel hard line and she stared malevolently at Jane with the eyes of a cobra. Ximena took her place next to Sinclair, grasping his hand for the first time, and followed her mother's cue, looking the intruder directly in the eye, defiantly, but silently—'with menace', as a prosecutor would have put it.

The co-ordinated onslaught of the two pairs of dark eyes was such that Jane was forced to look down as she backed out from the room.

"I'm . . . I'm sorry, I'll come back later, George, if that's all right, sorry . . . so sorry . . ."

Sinclair did not say anything or try to prevent her leaving, but stood there stupidly, amazed at the awesome display of hostile psychic power that his two women had unleashed on poor Jane. Without even saying a word.

"I rather hope you haven't been dipping your little brown wick in *that* mouse," said Bergsma, as if she didn't care, anyway.

"Not a chance. Definitely not."

There was silence—what else—from his brown women.

"Cup of tea?" he offered.

"Yes, but with chocolate digestives," insisted his daughter.

The next thing he knew they were on the platform at Oxford station waiting for the five o'clock train bound northwards. They would be back on Pendle Hill by ten, with Ximena snugly tucked up well before midnight.

By now Ximena had attached herself firmly to her father's hand, which she gripped intensely, and she stood fast and close to him.

Xancha moved towards him, for what he thought was a goodbye kiss. Sinclair felt Ximena's hand tense as her mother approached. Instead of the kiss, Bergsma embraced him and he felt her familiar breath in his ear as she whispered: "I'd like to come down on you again, George Sinclair."

With this Xancha and Ximena Bergsma took their leave.

"Father, I will be back to see you. I like *Olfox* very much." She looked up at him, complicity in her eyes, as if inviting him to read between the lines.

That was all his beloved Ximena said, as her mother pulled her away from Sinclair and they mounted the grimy blue train for the journey back up North. Sinclair would never forget the wistful, knowing gaze of his daughter from the train window, and her heartbreaking child's wave, as the train pulled away.

Soon all that was left in the breeze that wafted through the desolate platform was a vague scent of almonds mixed with diesel.

Not since the days after Grannyjee's death had Sinclair felt the heartbreak of separation so keenly. He felt disorientated and stunned, like some ancient Briton after his camp has just been decimated by a raiding party of frenzied blue-faced Picts emerging out of the mists of the North.

REVENGER

Like a Grand Master seated on a throne from the pages of some Masonic novel, Doctor Aggarwal was waiting for him.

"I have been expecting you. I knew that you would come."

As he said this, the good Doctor blinked and looked the visitor standing at his door up and down, with the contempt that certain expatriate Indians reserve for one another.

Sinclair had an instant before tapped out Helen's secret code—three then two followed by three again—on the door of the Curator's office in the Pitt Rivers Museum. And yes, there it was, that curious sulphuric smell that Jane Redfern had described. Sinclair fingered Madame Bernabeu's *gris gris* in his pocket and invoked the memory of her blessings for protection.

Behind the thick spectacles Sinclair could see that the Doctor's eyes were now dangerously liquid and mischievous. The Doctor had recovered from the surprise of seeing him standing there in his doorway.

A sly smile distorted his face as he asked: "And how can I help a fellow Indian scholar?"

Sinclair stood there at the door looking down at the Doctor who sat illuminated in a pool of light behind an immense desk piled high with dusty tomes and manuscripts. For the first time Sinclair looked directly into the face of his Nemesis.

It is probable, thought Sinclair, as he squeezed Madame Bernabeu's *gris gris* in his pocket for protection, that in my mind I have magnified him into someone mysterious and monstrous, someone—or some*thing*—more dangerous than he is in reality. He is no Doctor Dee. He may be able to shape shift and hypnotize people, but these are tricks, and he is not superhuman. He is an Indian who eats, sleeps and shits (and ruts—he added as an afterthought), whose hobby just happens to be hypnotizing and fornicating with English Roses like my Helen. He is just like the rest of us. I have to demystify him somehow, in order to fear him less. I have to take him off the pedestal that my hatred and jealousy have placed him on, in order to defeat him, and then Madame Bernabeu's *gris gris* will do the rest.

It was then that he remembered Lucy Kennedy's parting words to him and thought that they applied quite nicely to Doctor Aggarwal, thank you very much, dear Lucy: "a turd with eyes and two legs." Yes, this is how I will think of him from now on, a turd with eyes. I will demean him by dehumanizing him.

When Sinclair failed to answer again, a shadow of concern muted the mischief in Aggarwal's eyes. He blinked rapidly. "Well, speak up, Mr Sinclair. I *do* know who you are, you see."

Then, a little impatiently: "Well . . . ?"

Sinclair looked at the Doctor again, this time directly into the vortex of his eyes, but carefully (as he used to look at Guy Underhill at the College), mindful as he was of the Doctor's fondness for hypnosis, and he tried to imagine the stratagems forming inside his inscrutable head. He saw a sardonic sneer of contempt transform the Indian's face with a dark light.

Sinclair did not wait to be asked to sit down. Instead he plopped himself into the visitor's chair, slouching insolently in front of the Doctor. There's no way I will stand there like a naughty schoolboy in front of the Headmaster.

"I see that your parents have not been successful in teaching you good manners. Well, I suppose, given your background, that's not entirely surprising."

Sinclair held his ground and held his gaze steady on the Indian. Let him have his say, stay calm, don't take the bait.

"As they like to say here, cat got your tongue?" demanded the older man.

Yes, this is how I will win this battle. My silence will shame him and force him into a sortie, exposing himself.

Aggarwal continued, mixing his metaphors, a defect common to Indian Anglophiles: "Well, then, if you are unwilling to open the batting, *I* will kick off."

Sinclair nodded.

Before he started, Aggarwal's face again split awkwardly and Sinclair heard an unpleasant sound. It was laughter, braying and nasal. "For a start, I know why you are here—I expect you are here to hear it from the horse's mouth, so to speak. So let me tell you why I find you such unsuitable company for young Helen and why I have told her as much. You see, Mr Sinclair, I have done a fair bit of research on you, I have lifted up several rocks and what I have found underneath has a nasty sour smell to it."

No match for the sulphurous stench that emanates from your every pore, answered Sinclair in his head.

Aggarwal's face was contorted again by that sick smile as he pulled a manila folder from a drawer of the desk and placed it in the circle of light cast by his reading lamp, smoothing out the papers in front of him with the fussy tidiness of an academic about to expound his latest theory. He licked his forefinger with a brown tongue and turned a page.

"Ah yes, here it is. Let us start with your provenance. Family 'Fernandes'. Catholics, well, of course, and that explains a lot of the pathology of your case. Did you know, for instance, that the Goan Catholics are no more than a tribe of Untouchables that was bullied and tricked into submission by the Jesuits in the 16th century? Easy pickings for the Company of Jesus, they were. There was no way such a genetically weakened strain of Dravidians, subhumans almost, could withstand the Stormtroopers of Holy Mother Church. And please don't get me wrong, Mr Sinclair, these are not the ramblings or inventions of some lunatic Brahmin academic with a grudge, these are scientifically proven facts. You see, the Jesuits offered both spiritual and temporal sustenance and salvation to these pathetic wretches. It was the only way for these mentally and physically debilitated outcasts to progress out of their *karmic* misery, by adopting the myths and lies of an alien religion—crutches for cripples, if you like—that gave them the semblance of some sort of social worth, and a few extra grains of rice a day at the mission house. If Ignatius's Soldiers for Christ—led by Xavier, after whom you are named—had not shown up, the tribe would probably have vanished over time in some Darwinian holocaust. A strain that, should it have been left well alone under its rock, would have simply gone the way of all anomalous and dubious genetic strains—into the merciful dust of oblivion, or to be reincarnated as bugs or snakes or vermin. But now, we see, thanks to early colonial manipulation, that particular genetic pool has survived into the present day, in the form of families such as Fernandes and DaSilva and Xavier, of which you, George Xavier *Gupta* Fernandes Sinclair, are a prime specimen."

To be honest, Sinclair was having trouble following his self-imposed strategy of silence, because, as Aggarwal spoke and had fully intended, Sinclair could think only of his mother and of Grannyjee—*sub-humans almost*, Aggarwal had called them. Sinclair was not a violent sort but he was barely managing to resist the impulse to stretch across the desk, grab the speaking turd warmly by the throat, and repeatedly slap his taunting, wagging, racist Brahmin head. And to make things worse, the turd knew that his middle name was Gupta. But before he could examine the implications of this disturbing fact any further, Aggarwal continued.

"So then, for starters, as I hope I have proved, on the purely genetic level, you are unsuitable stock for our dear friend Helen—you are disqualified from her Aryan gene pool, like a Southern Negro in the United States is barred from the country club. Are you with me? Good. Now let us move on to the next item."

Again the brown serpent's tongue darted out to lick a finger and a new page from Sinclair's dossier was selected. "From the purely genetic hypothesis we now move on to the physical manifestations of your flawed genetic inheritance. In some, this might be evident through various degrees of autism or certain forms of imbecilism—Downs Syndrome, if you like, but in the case of your good self, the gene—mitigated somewhat as it has been by the aggressive intervention of your father's chromosomes—has manifested itself through a propensity to addiction—and not only substance abuse as my colleagues would call your well-known drug addiction these days, but emotional addiction which manifests itself in various forms of masturbation—physical, mental (*well*, intellectual, if you like)," this with another sneer, "and emotional. Such non-productive, dead-end pathology also disqualifies you from having a fruitful relationship with the likes of Helen Henshaw."

This time Doctor Aggarwal did not even bother to look up to make sure his pupil was following, but moved on to the final magisterial exposition of his thesis, carried away as he was by his own grandiloquence.

"And now, finally, moving onto the moral plane, there seem to be some very serious flaws evident in Mr Sinclair's character, Your Honour," this with a nod to an imaginary judge and with an Indian's fondness for litigation, "which are no doubt linked to his genetic debilism. For instance, the Subject does not think twice about betraying those closest to him in order to save his own skin. Not the kind of suitor to be recommended for fine upstanding English girls looking for long and mutually fruitful relationships, such as Helen Henshaw, M'lud . . ."

Aggarwal blinked rapidly and then looked up with that awful grin, having finished tidying the dossier in front of him, a self-satisfied barrister resting his case. Aggarwal's eyes were now thoughtful and amused, anticipating his opponent's next move.

Sinclair stood up slowly. His voice was furiously controlled and he prayed that it wouldn't quaver and betray him.

"I only came to tell you that I know what you have been doing to Helen. And that I will have you, Doctor Aggarwal, I *will* have you. And I *will* have Helen Henshaw back. Goodbye, Doctor Aggarwal."

For the second time that Hilary Term he felt physically sick as he stood in the cold air outside the Museum of Natural History. His head was spinning, he was feeling nauseous and dizzy in front of the vertiginous brick work of Keble College, this time as the result of Doctor Aggarwal's psychic assault. Every one of the Doctor's words had been designed to wound, and wound they had, deeply, like little thrusts of a razor-sharp kukri. It was death by a thousand cuts. Sinclair's stomach heaved and he almost vomited on the doorsteps of the Museum.

For the rest of that week, after his humiliation at the hands of Doctor

Aggarwal, Sinclair walked around like a ghost—in slow, submarine motion, with great effort, like a *zombi*, just like he had when he had been hexed by Madame Bernabeu in Martinique in 1983.

But it did not take him long to pick himself up, dust himself off, and metamorphose yet again into the Revenger. He had no intention of succumbing to Aggarwal's psychological warfare.

When he looked back at the interview, Sinclair surprised himself by the degree of self-control he had shown in the face of Doctor Aggarwal's wiles. No self-respecting *full-blooded* Indian would ever have been able to countenance such monstrous insults and humiliations. If anything, Aggarwal had just made things worse for himself, revealing to Sinclair a truly Nietzschean racism that he had not come across in the flesh before. This gave a sense of legitimacy to what the Revenger had in store for him—the same kind of moral justification that Mossad's hitmen must have felt when hunting down the Black September terrorists across Europe after the massacre at the Munich Olympics.

Doctor Aggarwal lived in North Oxford. He lived alone on the top floor of a semi-detached house in the upper reaches of the Woodstock Road. Sinclair had now found his new vocation in life, the latest dark grail of Revenge, and he trailed his quarry religiously, sticking to him like a shadow over the next few days. Tracking his movements, he noted down the smallest details of his routine in his Revenger's notebook: tutorials, lectures, meal times, duties of the Assistant Curator at the Pitt Rivers, committee meetings of the South Asian Society, the occasional trip up to London on the train for a lecture at one of the colleges or museums there, it all ended up in Sinclair's notebook.

Aggarwal in fact cut a rather comic figure as he cycled his awkward way around the city, his bulbous nose stuck in the air under those thick coke-bottle specs and with those ridiculous sideburns. When he wasn't sitting on his bike with his bum stuck in the air, he had a rather pathetic shambling gait which Sinclair supposed endeared him to silly gullible girls like Helen Henshaw. There is nothing like a vulnerable little genius to bring out the worst mothering and smothering instincts in a woman.

One afternoon Sinclair was watching the Doctor's house as he pretended to fix the chain of his bicycle, when he spotted Helen Henshaw. She was in her duffle-coat, gliding up to Aggarwal's front door on her bicycle, as if floating in on the air, her basket loaded with textbooks. This was the first time that she had come to his house for a tutorial, as they normally met in the Curator's office at the Pitt Rivers.

Sinclair felt a stabbing metaphysical pain in his heart—Aggarwal's razor sharp kukri thrusts again—when he saw Helen run her hand through her hair and straighten her blouse under the duffle-coat and then take out a pocket mirror to check her hair again, before ringing her guru's doorbell.

He was cycling back to his rooms at Magdalen. His loins ached from another marathon debriefing session with agent Redfern. As he pedalled, Sinclair continued to obsess about Helen Henshaw and her own obsession with the devilish Doctor Aggarwal.

Sinclair's encounters with his spy Jane Redfern had been successful, from an operational point of view, because she kept him supplied with a steady stream of intelligence about Helen. But all this was at a price—hours of loveless grinding and rutting, Jane's cloying emotional dependence and her ever-present suspicion about Sinclair's true motives.

Nothing in life is a coincidence, and sure enough, as he negotiated the heavy traffic on the roundabout at the foot of Magdalen Bridge which acts as the crossroads of South Oxford, Sinclair saw out of the corner of his eye the familiar colour of a duffle-coat and the gleam of golden hair in the sunshine. It was Helen on her bicycle, on her way back to St Hilda's, the basket on her bike jammed with her textbooks.

Opportunities like this rarely came his way these days.

It was almost an instinctive decision that he made as he squeezed the *gris gris* in his pocket for luck and then deliberately took his other hand off the handlebars, knocking himself into the side of a intercity coach returning from London and promptly falling off his bicycle onto the pavement not ten yards from where Helen was, perched on her saddle and about to kick off for the right turn onto the road leading to her college.

He broke the fall with his forearm, protecting his face as he had seen it done in films, and when he had rolled nicely across the pavement in her direction, he pretended to lie quite still, face down, as he heard a woman scream and then the familiar English Rose voice of Helen Henshaw asking someone to call an ambulance.

He pretended to come to, and when he uncovered his face and looked up, affecting puzzlement and confusion, he was gratified to see Helen's hand shoot up to her open mouth and her startled brown eyes looking down into his.

"My God, George, it's you. My God . . ."

Somehow he had managed to persuade her and the onlookers that he had no need of an ambulance. After getting to his feet shakily and dusting himself off, he waved the terrified coach driver away and insisted, like the true gentleman he was, that he was fine. It had just been a tumble, nothing was broken, nothing serious, only slightly shaken, he was terribly sorry—he imitated the amusing habit of the English, apologizing profusely to the coach driver for having been knocked down.

Soon the little knot of onlookers dissolved and went its way, disappointed at the lack of blood and grey matter splattered on the street. He was now left alone with Helen on the pavement.

She had no option but to offer him a cup of tea in her rooms at St Hilda's. Sinclair, shaken but not stirred, reluctantly accepted and wheeled his bike along with her to her rooms, apologizing all the while for inconveniencing her and causing such a fuss. But she insisted. Despite her desire to be rid of him she could not refuse to help him. She must have assumed that in his vulnerable state he could be no threat to her. Sinclair's split-second calculation on the roundabout had proved to be spot on.

And now he was in. He had penetrated her lair.

Easing himself onto the threadbare sofa in her study, he pretended to swoon and dropped the teacup in a very convincing way, creating a nice little mess for her to clean up. The trick worked nicely because soon enough he felt the coolness of her hand on his brow and felt her warmth close to him as she bent over him and tried to make him sit up on the sofa again. His eyes still closed, he sensed under that unbelievably nostalgic Helen-scent that she gave off a disturbingly bitter aftertaste—the smell that Jane Redfern had complained about and which he had detected in Aggarwal's office—the sour scent where the Doctor had marked his territory.

Pretending to come to again, this time he redoubled his apologies and offered to make his offensive self scarce immediately. She had to restrain him as he giddily made to pick up his coat. He thrilled at the pressure of her hand on his shoulder.

"Oh dear, Helen, I'm ruining your day. I'm so sorry. Just let me help you clean up that mess and I'll be on my way. My God, this is so embarrassing. Of all the people to be knocked down in front of . . ."

"That was quite a knock you took. I'll arrange for a taxi to take you up to the Radcliffe Infirmary. You can't be too careful after a concussion like that."

Sinclair was convinced he could see genuine concern in her eyes, a slight echo, a flicker of the old honey of love that used to captivate him when they were children.

"Absolutely not, Helen,"he insisted. "I can make my way up there on my own. I've wasted enough of your time. I'm so sorry." He affected a look of hideous embarrassment.

"Alright then. But drink your tea first, then you can go."

He thought he detected a sense of relief as she said this. He was sorry but he was going to have to disappoint her.

He settled himself back onto the sofa and watched her pick up the teacup and then wash it in the basin and plug in the electric kettle again. While she was busy doing this, he took the opportunity to look around at her room, to try to get a sense of this new unavailable version of Helen Henshaw, the woman he had not stopped fretting about for so long now and who haunted his every waking moment.

He saw a built-in wardrobe, batik wall-hangings and Indian miniatures on the wall above her bed, and then something caught his eye. It was a small shrine on her desk by the window. He saw the many arms of a familiar bronze *devi* dancing above an unlit votive candle and joss sticks and some dried flowers the colour of saffron, which Sinclair identified immediately as a funerary garland, a souvenir from her exploration of the *ghats* along the River Ganges. This was the chance he had been looking for, to engage her in a real conversation now that the fainting performance was over. He had to say something that would make her want him to keep talking.

"I like your Kali shrine, by the way."

She did not turn, continuing instead to fuss nervously over the milk for his tea, looking for a teaspoon and the sugar. "Yes . . . thank you."

"You must have picked her up at the *Kalighat* in Benares. While you were researching your thesis on temple prostitution. Before you fainted in the sun."

This time she did turn, alarmed, her eyes forcing themselves to look at him despite their natural inclination to avoid. She looked sick, as if she had just swallowed some unpleasant tasting medicine.

"How . . . how did you know that I was in Benares?"

He had to avoid answering to keep her intrigued. "And the garland, it's from a funeral. I know."

"But how—?"

This time it was Helen who seemed unsteady on her pins as she came towards him and gave him his tea, very unsure of herself.

She must be cursing herself for having picked me up off the street, he said to himself bitterly. This boy—this *wog*—is nothing but trouble, she must be saying to herself.

He noticed her fingernails, chewed to the quick as ever. Her hand on the handle of the cup had a yellowish tinge to it—a sign of malaria, of too much quinine. Or of a more disturbing disorder. Jane had mentioned that something was wrong with her blood.

"I'm sorry, Helen. Perhaps we should talk about this another time. To be honest, I'm still feeling a bit queasy. I'm really not up to it. We have so much to talk about . . ."

But she blocked his exit by setting herself down on a sequinned pillow in front of him. She sipped nervously from her own mug of milky tea, keeping her eyes down. He watched the crown of her head and the centre parting of her hair and the shadows under her eyes as she drank. When she did eventually look up at him, he was overwhelmed by the memory of their first lovemaking, when she had knelt before him like a supplicant in Guy Underhill's room in Goodge Street.

"So how did you know about Benares?" she insisted. It obviously pained her to have to deal with Sinclair, but her curiosity was getting the better of her—just as he had planned.

Again he avoided the question.

"By the way, if you don't mind me saying so," he said in reply, "*you* don't look at all well."

"I'm not. I'm not well." She looked down again and whispered into her tea: "No, not well at all."

"Perhaps I can help you?"

She started to say something, to protest, but he cut her off, gently.

"Look, Helen, I know you despise me. I *am* despicable, I realize that now. I know that what I did was monstrous, as you keep reminding me. But now I only want to help you. As a friend. Look, I've learned to put all of our history behind us, I accept that, it's been hard, but I do. Now I just want to be your friend. And it worries me that you look so ill these days. That's all. I'll go now if you like. I'm sorry."

He heard himself deliver these lines impeccably. The tone, the weariness, the sincerity, were all perfect, all Oscar material.

She sighed and looked at the wall this time, inspecting a framed miniature with unnatural interest, as if struggling with some complex inner dilemma.

It was now or never.

"I know about Doctor Aggarwal, you see. I know what happened after you fainted in the *Kalighat*."

She turned on him, pale and alarmed.

315

"What do you mean by that? What's to know? It's none of your *fucking* business anyway, George Sinclair."

He had never heard her speak like that before. But he had to persevere, to press on, however painful the result was. There was no going back now that the genie was out of the bottle.

"What's to know? Well, for a start, I know that he has made you sick. Believe me, Helen, I know."

She stared at him, an expression of horror and disgust disfiguring her face.

"How *dare* you!"

"I *dare*, Helen, I *dare*, because I care for you, Helen Henshaw. As a friend, as a friend—"

She snatched the empty teacup from his hands, sprang up off her cushion and headed for the basin. Sinclair thought for a moment that she was going to throw up in it, but instead she let the cups drop in the sink with a clatter, and turned on him again. The expression on her face said that the interview was coming to a close.

"Yes, well, for your information I do *love* him. I *love* Doctor Aggarwal. There. I've said it. And I *sincerely* hope it hurts you to hear me say it, George Sinclair. Taste of your own medicine. See how it feels to be rejected. To be betrayed. What goes around comes around, remember?"

"No it doesn't hurt, Helen, because I don't love you anymore," he lied. He never thought he would ever hear himself say those awful words.

She parried: "Doctor Aggarwal was right. He warned me about you, George Xavier *GUPTA* Sinclair."

"Yes, I know what he has been whispering in your ear about me," he replied. Each time he fucks your brains out, he continued to himself.

She was furious now. She started to say something but then a thought must have crossed her mind and her face twisted in disgust again. But the uglier that her hatred of him made her look, the more he loved her, there were no two ways about it.

"No . . . just get the fuck out of here, you shit. Once and for all, before I call the Proctor."

Sinclair got up out of the sofa. "Yes, I'm on my way out, Helen. In a minute I'll have left your life forever, for the very last time. But before I leave just hear me out."

She stood frozen, her hands at her throat, as if expecting a physical attack at any time.

"Your Doctor Aggarwal is a vampire. And I don't mean one of those psychic vampires people talk about. I mean a real vampire. One that shape-shifts. One that follows you around temples as a huge black bird. One that drains your energy *and* drinks your blood and makes you have bad dreams. One that hypnotizes you and controls you and drugs you so that he can have his way with you." And then, turning back her own word on her, he added: "What your Doctor Aggarwal did—what he does to you—is *monstrous*. How can you love such a . . . such a . . . *monster*?"

He could see that she was terrified now, because she knew that he was telling the truth.

Now as he gripped the door handle, it was time for the *coûp de grace*, it was now or never, and he knew that the memory of her face twisting in outraged incredulity at what he said next would remain imprinted in his psyche forever. He delivered the final thrust without mercy.

"A monster that can't love you because he has another lover."

She looked winded, as if her breath had been knocked out of her. But she did manage to croak something as was closing the door behind him on his way out, entombing her with her nightmares.

"It's *you* that's the monster, George Sinclair . . ."

DEVI

Xancha Bergsma looked stunning in her crimson sari. She had even painted a scarlet bindi on her forehead. The Third Eye, she called it.

More like the Evil Eye, if you ask me, Sinclair commented cheekily to himself as he appraised his old lover with new eyes.

"Yes, it really suits you, Matron," he said with genuine admiration.

The colour of the silk draped over her shoulder lent warmth to her complexion and set off her brown arms exquisitely and the gold bangles on her wrists jangled pleasantly as she sat before a mirror passing a sandalwood comb through her hair.

They were in Sinclair's rooms in the New Buildings. Ximena sat on the tattered sofa munching a chocolate biscuit, watching her father and mother in this parody of domesticity, a curious expression on her little face. She was silent as usual as she observed and munched.

Bergsma instructed him to rub some fragrant oil into her hair. The little boy in Sinclair remembered spying on Major Sinclair doing this for his mother in her boudoir in Goa many years ago.

Bergsma's hair was black and heavy and fine in his fingers and it gleamed with the oil.

They rehearsed once more the next steps in the plan and Sinclair coached her in the right accent to adopt and the right things to say if you were from Benares. His hands moved through her hair and down to the warmth of her neck, which he proceeded to knead and massage, as in the old days on Pendle. Her proprietary almond scent mixed pleasingly with the aroma of the oil, and the animal warmth of her body was like a catalyst fusing the two together with what threatened to be devastating results. He was beginning to feel the effects and stole a covert glance at Ximena, but she had not taken her eyes off them.

At least Bergsma's perfume would mask the sulphurous fumes of Aggarwal's lair, he thought, nastily.

"When it's over, you will owe me one, George Sinclair. And I fully intend to collect, this time."

"Is that a threat or a promise?" Sinclair asked cheekily.

Lingam stirred with old memories

She grunted, staring at her new self in the mirror.

"Of course, Matron. It will be a privilege," he added quietly.

He felt her stiffen then relax as his hands slid from her neck down beneath her collar bone.

Ximena, well into her second packet of chocolate digestives, surveyed them gravely from her seat.

Everything went swimmingly, like clockwork.

Sinclair had laid the groundwork of the operation in detail before Bergsma and Ximena had arrived in Oxford.

A letter had been received by Doctor Aggarwal from a Mrs Anudartha Vasudeva Chowpatty, visiting from Benares. The lady was interested in the illustrious Doctor's research into temple prostitution. Being a devotee of Kali, Mrs Chowpatty claimed to have in her possession an interesting piece of information about certain tantric practices involved in Kali worship. She claimed to have been recommended to the Doctor by a very nice young English girl called Helen Henshaw whom she had bumped into by chance in Benares the summer before. Since she would be in Oxford next week, would the good Doctor be so kind as to accept her visit to discuss the above in person?

It was an offer that Sinclair knew that the good Doctor simply could not refuse. And sure enough the Doctor's note agreeing to the appointment was duly delivered to the concierge at the Randolph Hotel, who agreed to pass it on to Mrs Chowpatty when she checked in. Sinclair himself had shadowed Aggarwal as he cycled down from North Oxford and down St Giles to deliver it personally to the concierge at the hotel, a beatific smile on his face.

An hour or two later another note appeared in Miss Henshaw's pigeonhole in the Porter's Lodge at St Hilda's. It was a typed memo bearing the crest of the Curator of the Pitt Rivers Museum, and it begged Miss Henshaw to come for an interview at his office in the Museum. A position had recently become available for a long-term research project in India sponsored by the Museum.

The trap was baited, the wires stretched, the springs compressed.

In the Pitt Rivers, Sinclair held Ximena by the hand as he took up his favourite watcher's position behind the case of Ecuadorian shrunken heads. He looked at his watch.

Ximena was fascinated by the doll-sized heads with their long shiny hair and the pretty coloured threads that hung from their lips and eyelids. Sinclair was daydreaming about how Doctor Aggarwal would make a decent-looking *tsantsa* when, at the appointed time, he felt a familiar scent wafting between the vitrines of the exhibition hall. He turned to catch Xancha Bergsma glide imperiously through the museum on the wings of her red sari, leaving in her wake a musky scent of sandalwood and almonds and the admiring glances of visitors and staff alike. Striding by, Bergsma gave a wicked wink in the direction of where Sinclair and Ximena were lurking and this made Ximena erupt in a fit of giggles.

The devastatingly attractive Indian goddess stopped to ask a cleaning lady directions to the Curator's office, and then Sinclair saw her tap on the door. It opened immediately and closed quickly behind her, as if someone had been standing behind it waiting for the knock.

Time passed slowly, as it does when you are waiting for good things to happen. Give her a few minutes to do her thing. Discipline, that was the order of the day. Sinclair thought of his father. He then amused his daughter with stories about the little people of the rainforest, the pygmies, and about Grannyjee's tree-dwelling fairies in India.

After checking that the coast was clear, Sinclair and Ximena emerged from their hideout and approached the door, the little girl on tiptoe, enjoying the game of hide and seek enormously. Both put their ears to the panelled wood.

Sinclair heard muffled noises. Xancha Bergsma talking in a passable Indian accent, the Doctor responding in a silky purr with words that Sinclair could not make out. A question, an answer, and then some kind of chanting, first in the Doctor's voice, and then in Xancha's, and then in unison. Then there was laughter. Then a bump as if someone had knocked a knee against a piece of furniture. A grunt. Then silence.

Another glance at the watch and Sinclair and Ximena withdrew to their vantage point to watch the next stage of the game unfold.

On cue Helen Henshaw walked in. She was a little breathless after he bicycle ride up from St Hilda's. She looked drained and not at all well. Father and daughter spied her as she unwound her scarf and took out her pocket mirror, and, as she had done in front of Aggarwal's door in North Oxford, looked at herself in the glass critically and dabbed powder on her cheeks. It was true; as Jane had said, Helen's face had acquired an unhealthy pallor since her return from India.

Ximena tugged on her father's sleeve. She had something urgent to say. When he bent to listen to her whisper, he heard these words.

"I saw that woman last night in my dream. She will pay for what she has done to you, father."

Mrs A. V. Chowpatty, her hands pushing hard against the Assistant Curator's desk for traction, her legs astride like those of a criminal being frisked up against a wall by the police, was bucking and moaning under Doctor Aggarwal, who had entered her smartly from behind, in honour of Blessèd Kali Maa.

They had not even had time to unwind the crimson sari in their unseemly haste.

The Doctor had got caught up awkwardly in the folds of the sari and at the same time was chanting his favourite tantric mantra to the *devi*, so it was no wonder that he didn't hear the tapping on the door. The door, which, again in his haste, the good Doctor had neglected to lock behind his irresistible visitor.

After the incident, the first thing that Sinclair had to do was to pay his dues to Xancha Bergsma in his bedroom at Magdalen, as he had promised. It was awkward and difficult to concentrate with Ximena there and they had had to lock the bedroom door. Bergsma had had to shout at the little girl who insisted on scratching on the door as Sinclair was made to pay his price.

"I know what you're doing," the little girl whimpered. "I know what you're doing in there."

After they had cleaned up, Sinclair had taken Bergsma and the sulking Ximena straight to the station and had seen them onto the train.

When he returned to Magdalen he was teary because he was already missing his daughter. He knew that they had wounded her. He noticed that his rooms and his clothes and his sheets were impregnated with Xancha's sandalwood and almond perfume. Territory had been marked. Something palpable about her still lingered in the air, as if she had left a charged energy behind to watch over him.

Instead of elation he felt a curious lassitude. Instead of stalking Helen and Aggarwal, he decided to let nature take its course. He had set a train of events in motion and whatever happened next would happen whether he watched or not. He put himself to sleep that night with a well-deserved dose of high-grade morphine from his pusher on Cornmarket and chatted amiably to his friend Morpheus about the events of the day before lights out.

What Goes Around Comes Around . . .

Indeed it does, comments Morpheus, always so polite and helpful, in the halfway world where they always meet. Revenger smiles to himself as the lights go out slowly in his palace of memories.

The weekend after the operation in the Pitt Rivers, he allowed himself the luxury of relishing every detail of the aftermath as recounted by agent Redfern, whom he was debriefing in his bed in the New Buildings.

There had been an anxious moment when Jane had noticed the curious smell in his sheets and she had accused him of seeing another woman. For a moment Jane seemed panicked by the notion that it might have been Helen Henshaw, but she then discounted it. The other candidate was Sinclair's ex, that dark Gypsy piece from up North. Jane knew about Xancha Bergsma and Ximena. How could she forget the daggers in their eyes when she had first met them in Sinclair's room? She harboured a deep-seated suspicion that the dark women, the Amazon mongrel and her miniature clone, with their aggressive stares, still had an unhealthy hold over Sinclair.

Sinclair was becoming good at thinking on his feet by then. He explained the smell away with a fluent lie by admitting that yes, he had had Ximena stay over for a couple of days because her mother had been taken ill up in Lancashire. And that these days the little girl had taken to dousing herself heavily in perfume, God help us, not yet seven and already into perfume and make-up. This seemed to satisfy Jane, at least for a while. Stranger things had been known to happen. As usual, though, Sinclair knew exactly how to take her mind off things and make her relax.

In between and during the prolonged bouts of copulation and oral gratification that followed, Jane told Sinclair how puzzled and disturbed she was about Helen's behaviour these days. She told Sinclair that she had looked in on her friend in her rooms at St Hilda's the day before and that Helen had refused to let her in. Why had Helen refused to talk to her and why had she said something about disloyalty and betrayal? Something catastrophic seemed to have happened in Helen's life, Jane said, going down on Sinclair with her usual enthusiasm.

He made a good show of appearing to be only mildly interested in his ex-girlfriend's latest crisis. Without betraying too much interest, he made Jane repeat the reports about Helen's rage, about Helen in tears, Helen in despair, Helen inconsolable, Helen hell bent on revenge, Helen on the verge of suicide, Helen refusing to tell her what the matter was. Jane had never seen her like that before. Not even at school in Ascot or at University in London afterwards. What on earth could have happened to make her so emotional? No idea, Sinclair offered, tapping Jane's inner thigh open with the back of his hand and preparing to dive again.

From that day on, Jane told Sinclair as he entered her for the fourth time that evening, Helen's face had that walled-in look, a look of utter despair.

THE WARDROBE

Two days later, Jane Redfern was paler than usual and a little the worse for wear, he thought—definitely green around the gills—when she showed up on Sinclair's doorstep. Mouse must have been drinking, thought Sinclair to himself cruelly, catching a whiff of gin on the breeze.

"It's Helen . . ."

As she said this her voice cracked, and she walked into Sinclair's arms, hiding her face in his chest.

"What about Helen?" Sinclair tensed as his words came out, expecting another onslaught of jealousy, another accusation.

"I found her in her room at St Hilda's. She was in her wardrobe."

"What on earth was she doing hiding in her wardrobe?"

For half a second Sinclair had a ridiculous notion of Helen trying to escape into another world through the wardrobe like Lucy in *The Lion, The Witch and the Wardrobe*. He remembered the C. S. Lewis's description of Lucy looking back into the empty room from Narnia.

"She must have done it last night, because she was cold and stiff when I found her."

"What—?" It was beginning to sink in.

"With her scarf."

"My God. What . . . was there a note?"

Jane shook her head.

"Did you call the police?"

She nodded. He could feel her hair on his face. Sinclair felt peculiarly numb.

She started crying again. She cried silently and jerkily into him.

When she had finished, Jane sniffled into Sinclair's sleeve, then blew her nose noisily into her handkerchief, and pulled him into his bedroom and on to the narrow student bed. She undressed carelessly and lowered herself onto him and in her inconsolable grief, which was spiked with intermittent bouts of wild-eyed insane laughter, she proceeded to provide him with an hour of unrestrictedly lustful and potent sex.

That unexpectedly erotic episode revealed an intriguingly bipolar side to Jane's character. Sinclair now became genuinely interested in further developing his sexual relationship with her. He was devastated by Helen's death, no mistake, but at this stage only in a theoretical way because the monstrosity of the death had not yet sunk in, and in the short term, *lingam* and not his heart ruled that day. Swollen in his jeans, he determined that he would seek out Jane for a change and suggest some kind of experimentation to her, something tantric perhaps, like that stuff that Helen and Aggarwal had been in to.

He timed his visit to coincide with the absence of the Mice. He knocked and knocked again and rang the bell of the flat on Cowley Road, but there was only silence. He went into the alley down the side of the house and jimmied open the window of the downstairs loo, and was soon inside the flat. Upstairs, the door to Jane's room was open, but the bedroom was empty. Her clothes were scattered on the bed. He moved to the bathroom, which is where he noticed that pink fluid had overflowed in buckets from the bathtub, making the chessboard lino of the floor slick and dangerous. He slipped and when he got back to his feet, he saw her.

Poor Jane was chalk-white, drained totally of the last drop of blood. She sat alabaster-naked in the red water. Thankfully her eyes were closed and she looked peaceful. By the time Sinclair found her the water had stopped flowing, and the deep slashes in her wrists, distorted under the water, looked like pink bracelets under the marble of her curled fingers. Her palms were turned upwards, as if she had been watching the blood seep out of her wrists into the warm bath.

On the dresser next to the bathtub Sinclair saw an empty pill container and a note in Jane's neat italic handwriting. Sinclair had seen too many films to know that he was not to touch anything. He managed to read the note.

She could no longer live without her friend Helen Henshaw.

He took his desert boots off before he stepped out of the bathroom, so as not to leave wet footprints on the floors of the flat and, retracing his steps, he exited the way he had entered. He carefully wiped down the window sill, puzzled yet at the same time unaccountably ruing the missed opportunity for an interesting sexual encounter. And so he left his dead friend Jane Redfern to the Mice.

CAPUT AGGARWAL

Three days after Jane's suicide, Xancha Bergsma and Ximena appeared again on Sinclair's doorstep in the New Buildings.

Ximena had brought her father a gift. With a flourish she presented a little box covered in blue velvet to Sinclair. A playful mischief animated her eyes. Xancha Bergsma sat smirking at them from her armchair in the corner, watching as Ximena made a fuss of unlocking the casket with a tiny brass key. She then pressed it gingerly into Sinclair's hands with an extravagant sense of ceremony. After making sure that he was paying attention, like a conjuror she opened the lid for her father. A scent of formaldehyde rose up and stung him in the nostrils, almost making him retch. He looked in.

Inside the casket, placed on a miniature red velvet cushion, sat the severed and shrunken head of Doctor Prabhudas Das Gupta Aggarwal Bindrinwhale, *quondam* Assistant Curator of the Pitt Rivers Museum, Helen's guru and hypnotist, and Sinclair's Nemesis.

The *tsantsa* was very small indeed and bore a remarkable resemblance to the head of one of the macacqs that haunted Sinclair's malarial nightmares. The

Doctor's thick black gleaming hair had been well oiled and carefully cut into a miniature pomaded quiff, with Elvis-like sideburns, and had been combed delicately. The empty eye-sockets had been sewn shut with red thread, as were the swollen purple lips. The Hindu's bulbous nose, which was now strangely out of proportion with the highly polished features of the tiny face, had taken on the look of a tapir's snout.

"How on God's good earth did you—?"

"We won't bore you with the details, Dr Sinclair," sneered Bergsma from her corner. "Suffice to say that he hardly felt a thing. Being a registered nurse does help sometimes. But my gosh, the bloke had bucketfuls of blood in him, he did . . . now *that* was a bit tricky, getting all that blood out," and with a nod to Ximena, "but we managed, didn't we, my pet, without making too much of a mess."

Ximena nodded matter-of-factly as she gazed lovingly at their handiwork.

Bergsma continued, cosy in her armchair, her legs tucked beneath her: "I read up on the method used by the Jivaro Indians. It took Ximena and me a whole week to prepare it for you."

Sinclair looked down at the little brown horror in the casket and Bergsma recited the process and Ximena giggled with glee at their achievement.

"What a to-do with the Doctor's head, right, pet?"

Ximena nodded happily as she combed the hair of the thing.

Bergsma spent the next few minutes describing in excruciating detail the tedious process of levering the eyeballs out of their sockets, of liquefying and pulling the brain out through the nostrils with a knitting needle, of the boiling and reboiling of the skin of the face off of the cranium (it just slipped off, didn't it, pet, just like boiled chicken off the bone?), its treatment with herbs, oils and waxes, followed by more boiling and finally another lengthy treatment involving hot stones. The sewing up of the eyelids and lips with the traditional red thread had been Ximena's treat, and her tiny fingers had been proven to be very nimble at that task.

"And the hair-style was actually Ximena's idea."

"And guess what, father? The hair will keep growing." His daughter seemed to find this hilarious.

Ximena giggled again as she continued combing the gleaming hair of Aggarwal's *tsantsa* with a tiny doll's hairbrush.

THE CIRCLE OF LEBANON

On the fifth day after Helen Henshaw's funeral, Sinclair, Xancha Bergsma and Ximena, all three elegantly clad in black, came into Paddington from Oxford by train. Ximena carried a small bunch of posies and was quiet and solemn. Bergsma's face had acquired a semi-permanent smirk of self-satisfaction since Sinclair had told them about the double suicide of Helen and her friend Jane.

In Paddington Ximena made a fuss about wanting a cup of tea, so they had to go and sit in the fetid fumes of the British Rail café. Bergsma graciously brought Sinclair his coffee and watched him drink it, and Ximena slurped her tea and nibbled on an oversized chocolate digestive biscuit.

From the Tube station on Highgate Hill they walked down Swain's Lane past the gates of the cemetery. A good ten yards further on Xancha asked them to stop, and she began picking the lock in a door in the wall. Once inside the graveyard, they wended their way up the hill along the same avenues and vistas of tombs and chapels, under the gaze of weeping angels, that Sinclair and Helen had frequented that half-term, ages ago.

Sinclair had a curious feeling of being watched and being followed as they made their way up the familiar path. At one point he even thought he saw out of the corner of his eye a small dark shadow dive out of sight and into the vegetation behind a baroque tomb. Perhaps it was one of the foxes or other feral creatures that make the undergrowth of the cemetery their home.

Up the Egyptian Avenue they went, past the black doors of the mausoleums, and around the track of the Circle of Lebanon in the shadow of the cedar tree, until they were standing in front of the moss-covered walls of the Henshaw Family crypt. The chapel door was locked with a huge brand-new padlock and chain.

"No worries," said Bergsma as she produced a hatpin from out of nowhere and expertly picked the padlock.

Sinclair felt queasy and loosened his tie.

Inside there was a dank chill and a pervading smell of dead lilacs. As their eyes adjusted to the darkness, they made out several metal caskets, some of which were clearly ancient and encased in lead, laid out neatly on shelves. The newest casket was shiny and white—a virgin's coffin—and was topped with garlands and floral tributes.

Sinclair stepped closer to read the cards on the wreaths. One in particular caught his attention; he pulled it off the flowers and read it in the light by the portal; it had familiar handwriting on it, spidery and blue. It was a message from Guy Underhill to his cousin.

Dearest Cousin,
What Goes Around Comes Around . . .
Forever,
Guy

Sinclair's heart skipped a beat as he scanned the scrawled words and he suddenly felt dizzy. His heart fluttered. This time the nausea seemed physical.

Ximena made him read the card out loud.

"Whatever does it mean, father?" she asked, as if she already knew the answer.

Sinclair had trouble answering. His mouth was dry. He ended up shrugging his shoulders, at a loss for words.

"We tricked her good, didn't we, my pet?"

Bergsma winked at Ximena with a crooked smile, from across the vault.

Ximena nodded, her expression still solemn and respectful, as she ran her tiny fingers along the gleaming white metal of the new casket, hesitating to play with the latch, and then stood on tiptoe to smell the flowers.

"Well, we did," Sinclair heard himself say, remembering the scene at the Pitt Rivers Museum, "but who would have thought it would end like this . . ." He was having trouble swallowing.

Bergsma was speaking again. She was telling him that a couple of days after the incident in the Pitt Rivers, Ximena had knocked on Helen's door at St Hilda's, pretending to be lost and that Helen had taken her in and given her a cup of sweet tea, more like Indian *chai* really with lots of cream and honey, just how she liked it, and some digestive biscuits but not chocolate ones.

Sinclair was confused. He did not remember visiting Helen with them.

"She had been crying, father," whispered Ximena, gently, and with some emotion.

"You mean you went to see her? But when? I don't . . ."

It didn't make sense. Directly after the incident in the museum Sinclair had put Bergsma and their daughter on the train.

He heard Bergsma say that she had shown up at Helen's rooms at St Hilda's half an hour after Ximena. She had pretended that she had lost her daughter on a tour of the college. At first Helen didn't know who she was, probably because of her shortsightedness, and because Bergsma was wearing a hat, coat and dark glasses.

But as soon as Bergsma removed her glasses and made herself comfortable on Helen's bed, next to Ximena, Helen realized who she was—the sari-clad arse-fucked seducer of Guru Aggarwal.

"She didn't struggle much, did she, Ma?"

"Surprisingly little, in fact, my pet, almost as if she welcomed it."

"But it did hurt, didn't it, Ma?"

"I suppose it did, just a little bit, my pet."

When Bergsma had finished her work, with a little help from Ximena, Helen had been left hanging neatly in the wardrobe next to the coat hangers and her party frocks and duffle-coat, looking for all the world like just another student suicide.

"So much stress, these Oxbridge kids have, especially the girls," chuckled Bergsma evilly.

"And then we did that Jane Redskin, or whatever her name is," Ximena piped up brightly.

In Jane's case, the nurse's training had come in a treat. Bergsma assured Sinclair that unlike Helen, poor Jane had felt absolutely no pain. In fact it was probably quite a pleasurable way to go, in warm bathwater and all that, just like the Roman emperors. She had just drifted off, quite nicely thank you and without a fuss.

Sinclair felt queasy again and tried to speak out in disgust but his tongue would not do what his brain wanted. He moved in slow motion, as if walking under water. He couldn't lift his arms even.

"Damn it, you've . . . *drugged* me . . ."

"We made her write the note," Bergsma said, anticipating his next question.

"But . . . how?" he heard his voice croak a long way away.

"Your clever daughter held the razor blade to her throat while I dictated."

"And then Ma made her take the medicine."

Bergsma took Sinclair by the hand and made him sit on the ledge next to Helen's coffin. He moved slowly and obediently. She kissed him full on the mouth, deeply. Ximena watched, a strange expression of disapproval crossing her face.

When he turned his head, in slow motion, to see what all the noise was about, he saw that Bergsma had knocked all the floral tributes from the top of the coffin onto the ground. She was at work again with her hatpin, this time worrying away at the latch under the lid of the coffin. She finally managed to push up the heavy coffin lid, with a grunt. The all-too-familiar smell of formaldehyde, but now mixed with the sweet stench of incipient decomposition, filled Sinclair's nostrils. He could not resist the impulse to look in.

Inside, it was bigger than he would have imagined. The dead girl seemed small and lost among the heavy silk pillows and thick padding of the casket. They had dressed her in what looked like a virginal bride's white gown, God knows why. Helen's face was now grey and swollen, a caricature of the face that Sinclair had once worshipped, and there was a bluish tinge around the nostrils and lips. The mauve shadows under her eyes had turned brown. A frilly white collar covered her throat. Rosary beads had been threaded through her fingers, which grasped a bunch of dead roses. The fingernails were chewed as ever, and the fingertips were beginning to acquire a shade of aquamarine blue. It was hard to imagine that he had once loved the thing that lay there.

"It's a big, big coffin inside," said Ximena, impressed. She was now standing on the ledge looking into the casket.

Suddenly Sinclair heard her cry: "Oh Ma, oh Ma, I dropped my posies inside . . . please, get them . . . there, they fell in behind Helen's head."

"Where, you silly child, I can't see them."

"There, Ma, there, Ma, lean in a bit more, you'll see . . . You can't see from there . . . here. On this side . . . look."

"Nonsense, you silly little cow, there's nothing there. My God, what a stench, George Sinclair. To think you once took your pleasure with this beastly, stinking pile of skin and bones."

"But there it is Ma, there it is, lean in a bit further . . . you'll see . . . behind the head . . . yes a little teeny-weeny bit further . . ."

How Ximena managed to trip her mother up, push her off-balance and at the same time lever her into the coffin, making her fall on top of the dead girl, was something that would never cease to amaze Sinclair. As time went by, he would ask himself whether the whole episode had been a hallucination.

By now he was immobilized and fascinated at the agility of the trick that his wonderfully clever and gifted daughter had just played. He saw, or thought he saw, Bergsma's brown legs flailing in the air, and her black stilettos disappearing into the casket, and then he definitely heard and saw the heavy coffin lid slam down behind her, cutting off Xancha Bergsma's scream of horror.

Ximena hopped down off the ledge, a serious look of intent on her sweet little face. And then her tiny fingers did something clever with the same latch that her mother had so expertly picked a few moments before. The child had inherited her lock-picking skills from both sides of the family, it seemed.

Breaking in to other people's boxes had turned into the family hobby *par excellence*.

Sinclair sat on the ledge, watching his daughter pick up the flowers from the floor. Soon all that he could hear were muffled cries, which must have been threats and curses, and then whimpers, followed again by stronger sounds, and a vague thumping from within.

The sounds were becoming weaker as Ximena led him out of the crypt by the hand. At the doorway she asked her father politely to lock the chain behind them. Which he did, diligently although with clumsy fingers. He then followed her obediently like a *zombi* around the Circle of Lebanon and down the Egyptian Avenue again, and eventually out of the cemetery onto Swain's Lane, holding her tightly by the hand.

On the train back to Oxford Ximena matter-of-factly explained to her dazed father what had happened after they had bid him farewell on the platform at British Rail Oxford after their last visit, when Ma had had her meeting with Doctor Aggarwal in the Museum.

She and Ma had simply got off the train at the next station—she thought it was called Didcot—and had taken a taxi back into the city, where they had holed up in a bed and breakfast in North Oxford. From that base mother and daughter had trailed Sinclair and had tracked him tracking Helen and Doctor Aggarwal. That's how they had discovered his furtive assignations with Jane Redfern.

In her tiny, cute grown-up's voice, Ximena explained what happened next. "Ma called Helen a bitch and said that she had to go. And that Jane Redskin, which is what Ma called her, was a disgusting creature. We were sad that you had kept that a secret from us, father. Ma said that you should have had better taste, and that Jane was just a sad Mouse. And then we finished off Doctor Aggarwal, 'to close the accounts', Ma said."

Sinclair, as usual, was at a loss for words.

"And now, father, it's just you and me, *Contra Mundum*. I don't know what that means but Ma used to say that to me before she brought me down to meet you. So now it's just us, father, just the two of us."

"It means 'against the world', my dear."

"I like that, father, against the world, just you and me. That's very nice."

The spires of Oxford were coming into view and the train creaked slowly into the station. Sinclair was emerging from his trance.

"I like Olfox very much, father," Ximena said, squeezing her father's hand in friendship and anticipation.

In the taxi up to North Oxford, they held hands, Ximena's hand tiny and brown and cool in Sinclair's sallow fingers. She hummed a childish tune and cheerfully swung her legs under the car seat. Sinclair noticed that she still held in her other hand the posies from that morning, and for some reason this seemed to comfort him very much.

When he was tucking her up in her bed in the spare bedroom later that night, Sinclair managed finally to ask: "And why did you lock Ma up in the coffin with Helen?"

Ximena smiled at him sadly. "Because she did not belong between us any more, father. She has served her purpose."

Sinclair was puzzled and asked her to explain what she meant. She refused.

"Do you miss her?" he insisted.

"Not really, father. She was never nice to me. She was beastly to me." And then, before she asked Sinclair to switch her bedside light out: "And father, by the way, please don't keep any secrets from me again."

"Never again, I swear." He really meant it.

With a squeeze of her hand, she sighed contentedly in the dark, "we will do great things together, father, you and I. *Contra Mundum*, then, father?"

"Yes, *Contra Mundum*. God bless, sweet dreams, my dear, dear sweet child."

At last the shocking day was over. Sinclair went back downstairs to the living room to gaze at the trophied head of Doctor Aggarwal.

After he had packed up the box and placed it back on the mantelpiece, he went to look for the comfort of deep sleep in the realm of Morpheus, where he was always welcome. When he entered his study to prepare his syringe he noticed that someone had left a book-shaped package wrapped in red silk on his desk. It looked familiar. He unwrapped the package carefully to reveal a set of Tarot cards.

The card at the top of the pack was the Papess, otherwise known as the High Priestess.

"Where did you get these?" he asked his daughter the next morning.

He already knew the answer.

"They were Ma's. But they're mine now."

1979
THE SWEET WITH THE SOUR

THE TURNING OF GEORGE SINCLAIR

The end came, inevitably, as he knew it would. But it was not to be the end of George Sinclair at the College, as he had anticipated. They had selected a much more sickening punishment for him than twice nine followed by expulsion.

When it came, it was in keeping with time-honoured Jesuit witch-hunting tactics. Sleep deprivation, as we all know, ensures maximum disorientation and totally destroys your self-confidence. Just as he was drifting off to sleep Sinclair had been dragged out of bed after being woken by a flashlight in the face. He felt a vice-like grip pincering his arm. A small but powerful black-robed presence yanked him out of his bed and frog-marched him into the study of Dr Tantum, the Playroom Master responsible for him and the other ninety boys in his year. In the airless study stood an unholy trinity: Tantum, the Nosferatu, and Morguer's hatchetman, Fr Cassius, the small grim-faced Scot who administered the hardest ferula in the school and never spoke, hence the legend of his tongue-less silence. Cassius's other quality was that he would suddenly appear beside you, without notice; his method was to approach from the side, crabwise and silently.

Tantum was an Australian with putrid breath and teeth that looked like he had had a serious disagreement with a bus. In the suffocating study, an anglepoise desk lamp trained into his face, a wave of nausea overcame Sinclair.

But it was the Nosferatu who spoke first.

"Let me come to the point quickly. We know it was you but it's, ah, Guy Underhill that we want. He is a far more dangerous threat to the school than you. We need evidence. Co-operate or it's a one-way ticket to, ah, Goa," whispered Morguer as he addressed his fingernails.

Underhill's father was a lawyer associated with some development agency in Africa and was therefore suspected of supporting left-wing causes, hence the need for evidence. Sinclair's father, despite his less than perfect pedigree—he was a convert—was already a proven benefactor of the College with considerable financial clout at his disposal, and future endowments were at stake. It all made sense.

"We now leave you in the good hands of Dr Tantum. Dr Tantum is, as you know, your Secular Advisor. You will be expected at Confession tomorrow at 6 p.m., in the Sodality Chapel, with me. I am personally replacing Fr McLintock as your Spiritual Director from now on."

With this, the two black robes melted into the shadows beyond the door. Morguer's familiar, Cassius, appeared to float silently after his master, leaving in their wake a faint smell of chalk and altar wine.

Which left Sinclair staring at his hands as he sat in front of Tantum's desk, wallowing in the pestilence of the Playroom Master's full attention.

Tantum, with his ridiculous Trotsky beard and those beady rapist's eyes, was a failed Jesuit. This is the type of man who relishes interrogating dirty little Anglo-Indian drug peddlers like me, thought Sinclair, mindful of the many traps that the evening had in store for him.

The interrogation that followed had been carefully rehearsed, and was laced with all kinds of sophistry and casuistry. It started like this: Tantum told Sinclair that he, and certain other enlightened masters, whom he termed Sinclair's "friends and supporters on the staff", considered Sinclair to be one of the most brilliant and gifted boys of his generation, just like Brendan Cowey, Head of the Line and destined for an Oxbridge scholarship, or like Simon Cavendish, already Captain of the First Eleven. But that unlike these gentlemen, Sinclair's gifts of leadership were being callously and wilfully thrown away by his association with Guy Underhill. Now Guy Underhill, well, he was a poisonous snake of the most insidious kind, Sinclair's secret enemy, a bad apple and the worm in the apple itself, envious of Sinclair's obviously superior intellect and talents and anxious to drag him down with him. What 'they' were worried about, Tantum confided, was that Guy Underhill was likely to corrupt the rest of the boys just as he had corrupted Sinclair.

"We think it's time that you surfaced, George Sinclair. You have nothing to fear in the sunlight," said Tantum as he shifted his weight on his ample buttocks.

Sinclair was told that he could redeem himself and honour the promise of his talents and live up to his parents' sacrifices, get his scholarship to Oxford and go on to a brilliant career *Ad Majore Dei Gloriam*. He could, despite this setback, take his place at the high table with the best of the Catholic

Gentlemen of the College. He could still live up to Ignatius's ideals and become a man for others.

"But everything in life has a price, Sinclair," Tantum said unctuously, grinning slyly, narrowing those sexual predator's eyes.

Please don't smile that grisly grin, said Sinclair to himself as he hugged himself tightly and another wave of nausea overcame him.

Just as he was wondering whether to throw up all over Tantum's desk, something was said that knocked the wind out of Sinclair. What came next was worse than being punched in the solar plexus by the bullies on the rugby pitch when the ref was looking the other way.

'They' knew, Tantum revealed, that it was Guy Underhill who had convinced Sinclair to import the drugs into the College. And furthermore, they had good grounds for suspecting that Guy Underhill had been at the Black Mass, and that Underhill had in fact had been the prime mover behind the blasphemy. Never mind that they had never caught him and that the culprits had never named him as a participant. But now, with Sinclair's co-operation, Guy Underhill, like Olatunji Ogunlesi, had reached the end of the road and the College could be rid of him.

Sinclair begged the master not to make him do this to his only friend.

"Don't grovel, Sinclair, it doesn't suit you," came the reply. "And he isn't a true friend. You know that deep down."

Sinclair insisted for what seemed like hours, at times even matching Tantum in the interminable argument. At one stage Tantum accused Sinclair of having attended the Black Mass with Guy Underhill. This Sinclair denied repeatedly and tearfully, imagining his father's cold grey eyes upon him.

Tantum backed off for a while. But the horrors of that evening were not over yet. Tantum now accused him of having been in league with Olatunji Ogunlesi and of having stolen money from tuckboxes. As the tears flowed again, Tantum sensed that victory was in sight, but then Sinclair would summon some inner strength and hold his ground, and Tantum felt that after all, perhaps, Sinclair would not break.

Another deadly body blow was delivered to restore things to their desired state: "And they are not even throwing in your attempted rape of Matron in the Infirmary. You see, I've been able to persuade Nurse Bergsma not to press charges if you co-operate."

That was to be the first and last reference to Xancha Bergsma during the whole proceedings. Sinclair was shell-shocked.

But still he resisted.

Towards three in the morning Tantum became impatient and delivered the ultimatum in plain Australian: "Deliver Underhill's head and you will be spared. But make no mistake, George Sinclair, even though we like and admire you, your friends and supporters may not be able to save you from 'Them' if you don't play the game. 'They' will not hesitate to send you home, and possibly to the police, if you waver from your commitment. You will go down, believe me, and then you may never be able to get up again—it's up to you . . ."

Sinclair again noted the 'us and them' theme that Tantum had been deftly weaving into his arguments since the beginning of the interview.

With this ultimatum began Sinclair's slippery descent into the secret abysses of betrayal. To say that Sinclair was in hell is an understatement.

By the time he emerged from Tantum's study in the early hours of the morning, in a lightheaded kind of way Sinclair felt that was coming up to the surface. Into the fresh light and clean air of a clear day, after captivity in the sunless blue submarine world where he had been trapped. Perhaps he was beginning to agree that others—Guy Underhill—had held him back down there, and that as Tantum said, he had never ever really belonged down there. Tantum appeared to have exorcised the rebellion and non-conformism out of him in a matter of hours. To give him credit, Tantum was not a great believer in the ferula—fucking with his boys' minds was far more effective and enjoyable.

Outside Dr Tantum's window the watery glow of dawn was about to wash over the witch country. Whatever creatures and their familiars that had wreaked havoc and had their way in the shadows under Pendle were no doubt scurrying back to their lairs with the coming of the light.

THE SWEET WITH THE SOUR

Things are never straightforward in life, especially when they are going badly. Life, for certain individuals, has the habit of tripping you up and piling up complication upon complication, like a game of three-dimensional snakes and ladders.

The thing that plunged Sinclair back into hell despite the sense of release he felt after that first session with Tantum, was that he finally met Underhill's cousin Helen Henshaw and became hopelessly infatuated with her.

According to the custom of the College, the Jesuits permitted an opening of the school in the middle of the summer just before it disbanded for half-term. It was an event known as Great Academies, when parents, sisters and cousins converged on the school for three days of dinners, exhibitions, cricket matches and entertainment, including the school play. It all culminated with the Academies Ball. This last event was held under a vast marquee outside the east wing of the College, beneath the windows of the library.

It was at the Ball that Underhill introduced his cousin Helen Henshaw to Sinclair and it was there that they fell in love. Or at least where Sinclair fell in love with the fair-haired, peach-skinned, brown-eyed Helen, only two years his junior. She was gorgeous, with her blonde hair and brown eyes and dimples. She reminded Sinclair of Stevie Nicks—slight, pretty, with something of the hippy and the non-conformist about her long skirt and high boots. The way her sleepy brown eyes lingered on you under the golden cap of her hair, above the blushing peach of her dimpled cheeks, was absolutely unforgettable. Helen had a slight unfocused crossing of the gaze, a venereal strabismus, which gave her a lazy but hungry look, a look that was bemused and aroused at the same time. Sinclair later discovered that her eyesight was terrible but that she avoided glasses for vanity.

Compared to the dark pits of Xancha Bergsma's eyes, Helen's sleepy eyes were alive with the glowing honey of love.

Sinclair would always remember their first kiss. He could still taste it many years later, and feel the pounding of his heart in his ribcage. How different this was from the obscenity of Matron's Kali-tongue.

Years later he would still be able to close his eyes and see Helen's drowsy gaze and relive the freshly washed scent of Helen's hair and hear Helen's sweet words in his ear as he and Helen danced at the Ball to the nostalgic love songs of the schoolboy band. How he loved to say her name, which he would later take to repeating again and again like a secret mantra.

After the slow dance, they managed to slip away from her parents and from Underhill, who was at the other end of the marquee trying to persuade Christopher Larkin to fellate him in the Common Place. Out of the marquee they went, into a warm summer night full of stars, into a New World. They pledged themselves to each other on the cricket flats under the starlight as music from the Ball wafted from the glowing tent, and in the distance the purple flank of Pendle loomed in the splendid northern night. Sinclair kissed her nail-chewed fingers and her dimples in the summer night. He adored her. She smiled her sweet dimpled smile and he was born again.

After the covert horrors of Xancha Bergsma, Sinclair felt as if he had landed on the pristine beach of some New World like his beloved pirates. Filled with the possibilities of a fresh start, and redemption, he felt that he could be purified by the nobility of pure love. He would dedicate himself entirely to this innocent creature with the slow brown eyes and dimpled smile, devoting himself in self-sacrifice to her well-being and adoration.

But even as they kissed, Sinclair felt in his intestines the worm of nausea gnawing slowly away, a worm that grew fatter each day, as the Day of Reckoning approached, nourishing itself on his guilt.

In his private hell, like Lazarus, Sinclair fantasized that he would be redeemed him from his Predicament. Helen would save him. He would wake up one day in their New World, which was peopled only with the innocence and beauty of Helen and other Helen-like humans. He would become a devoted Helenist. He would forsake the drugs, corruption, the cynicism of Underhill, *beedis* and Marlboro and Winston and Old Holborn, Rizlas, cheap booze, dirty forced sex, and best of all, the monstrous act that was looming in the horizon would evaporate in the golden sunlight which was a halo around his beloved Helen.

They stood hand in hand on the cricket flats, listening to a popular ballad drift over from the marquee, comforted by the massive, familiar presence of Pendle in the background. But then Sinclair's blood froze as he saw, or thought he saw, a small dark shadow moving sideways into the darkness of the cricket pavilion, out of the moonlight. And he could have sworn that he caught a whiff of almonds on the breeze.

HALF-TERM VIRGO

That half-term in London after Great Academies, Sinclair and Helen officially lost their virginities in Gran's flat in Goodge Street. Sinclair never told Helen that his real virginity had already been forfeited in the College Infirmary.

The delicious horrors of the Infirmary seemed like the something out of a bad trip, but the memory of Xancha Bergsma's tongue continued to disturb and fascinate him. Now, the shy mewings and the small gurgling sounds that Helen made when she orgasmed under him were sweet compared to the disturbing Aboriginal chant that Matron intoned each time she came down on him Up North.

Underhill had made his bedroom available and had excused himself for the afternoon, so that 'nature could take its course', as he put it. They both agreed that Underhill was the best friend a boy could ever have and the best cousin a girl could ever wish for.

Helen had given herself to Sinclair in a cool and self-possessed manner. This pretty girl, who could have had anyone, had chosen to offer herself to a half-caste, to her cousin's best friend. Like the good Convent School girl that she was, she had bathed herself for the occasion and had started the proceedings by kneeling before him on the carpet, gazing up at him with her mouth half-open, like a communicant seeking the holy wafer.

Afterwards, they lay on the futon in Underhill's room sharing the proverbial post-coital cigarette and listening to Supertramp. The lovers watched the reflection of headlights drift across the ceiling. They lay waiting for him to come back, listening to the muffled roar of London traffic outside the window as dusk and then night fell over their New World. Supertramp sang *It's Raining Again*.

She fell asleep in his arms. It was all as it should be, highly satisfactory. As long, that is, as he did not think of the other thing, his Predicament. He lay watching the lights drifting across the ceiling. Then he turned and caught a glimpse of himself in the wardrobe mirror—and he saw two lupine eyes watching him back in the twilight.

THE EGYPTIAN AVENUE

The day before the end of the half-term holiday, Sinclair discovered a morbid streak in Helen. They had spent the afternoon snogging on a bench on Parliament Hill, high above the skyline of London, watching the changing colours of the sky over the Post Office Tower and describing to each other the faces and animal shapes that the clouds made. Now they were hurtling along the Underground in the dank filth of the Northern Line, on their way back to Goodge Street, when something occurred to Helen. She was suddenly animated, taken by an idea.

"Promise me you'll say yes?"

"Depends," said Sinclair.

"Forget it, then," she said, pretending to sulk.

"Go on, then, I promise. I'd do anything for those dimples."

"Promise you won't laugh?"

Sinclair nodded, sucking Helen's nail-chewed fingers as a blue-haired woman frowned disapprovingly in their direction from over the pages of *The Daily Telegraph*.

"You have to keep your eyes closed until the last minute."

Helen enforced the game strictly, blindfolding him with her red cashmere scarf and pinching him when he tried to peek. She led him off the train at the next station and through the labyrinth of passages of the underground station until he was thoroughly disorientated. She led him onto another train eventually.

Between a gap in the scarf he saw the station names each time the Tube worked its way back up the top end of the Northern Line, past Euston, Camden Town, Kentish Town and still northwards. He knew where they were as she led him up out of the underground, still blindfolded, and up the steep stairs that lead out onto the chill winds of Highgate Hill.

A few minutes later, after a brisk downhill walk, they stopped and Helen pulled off the scarf. They were standing at a door in the wall, in Swain's Lane, a few yards beyond the wrought-iron gates of Highgate Cemetery.

Helen produced a key and before he knew it she had opened the door and they were inside.

Hand in hand they picked their way through the rows of gothic chapels and crypts and legions of fantastic Victorian angels that wept and glowered at them from their perches above the overgrown, vampire-infested necropolis.

At the top of the hill of the eastern section of the cemetery, which is the older, Victorian side, you come upon the mock ruined walls of a structure called the Egyptian Arch, bounded by two enormous columns with lotus leaves carved at their bases. If you walk through the Luxor-like gate, and up the Egyptian Avenue past heavy black doors behind which lie the exclusive ossuaries of wealthy Victorian families, you emerge at a curious structure called the Circle of Lebanon. So called because at the top of a roundabout of overground vaults there grows a monstrous cedar tree.

Sinclair and Helen walked hand in hand halfway around the circular path, past the doors and gates of the private crypts that had been built under the tree. She stopped and pulled him to her. Sinclair saw that she had become melancholy. He felt a shiver in her embrace. They kissed in the shadow of a lichen-covered chapel and Sinclair felt the frisson of stealthy love, of being alive, very much alive, among the dead.

After they kissed, they held each other tightly and Helen whispered in Sinclair's ear: "When I die I will be buried here."

Not I want to be buried here, but I *will* be buried here. George thought she was fantasizing. But an impish smile on her face disturbed him.

She pointed upwards, like one of Leonardo's Blessed Virgins.

George raised his eyes to the lintel over the entrance to the vault and saw the words 'Henshaw Family' chiselled into the granite.

DIES IRAE

After half-term, the separation anxiety of adolescent love was added to the cocktail of hormones and conflicting emotions that Sinclair was drowning in. His life became unbearable. One evening he considered walking off the window ledge into oblivion, but imagined the mess that his dashed-out brains would make on the cobbles of the courtyard, and then he thought of drowning himself in the pea-green soup of the ancient indoor swimming pool. One evening he came within inches of opening his veins in one of the grime-encrusted marble sarcophagi that served as bath tubs. He sat in the tub contemplating the blade of his trusty lock-picking Swiss army knife for almost an hour before deciding that the mess of the blood would be too disgusting. He would probably faint before managing to slice through both wrists, at the sight of the blood. He made himself dizzy just imagining it spurting forth in an uncontrollable dark brown pulse, like a newly tapped oil well. Then he considered running away from the College and so he placed a call to Ascot. He persuaded a puzzled but willing Helen to collaborate from her convent school, fixing a time to meet her at the gates of her school in two days time, only to cancel the arrangements at the last minute.

It took another late-night session in Dr Tantum's suffocating lair to restore his resolve to face up to it and put the whole business to rest before the end of term. Tantum did a thorough job explaining to Sinclair that in the short term the unpleasantness of betrayal would be outweighed manifold by the long term benefits of Sinclair's re-entry into the fold. The ends would justify the means. And anyway, he said, turning the argument on its head in the classic Jesuitical manner, is it really betrayal if it is he who has really betrayed you by pulling you down, by keeping you down in the shadows where you don't belong? Sinclair could not afford to let Guy Underhill's treachery hobble a brilliant career, starting with Oxford. Did Sinclair really think he could ever forgive himself if he took the wrong path now? Could he imagine how he would feel sitting in some second-rate provincial red-brick university a couple of years from now? And, the argument turned in on itself again, he would in fact be doing *Guy Underhill* a favour by forcing him to face up to his true, horrid nature, because no man or boy is beyond redemption.

"Take it from someone who really does have your best interests at heart," breathed Tantum in the marrow-churning miasma of his den.

"There are times," he continued, "and situations in one's life upon which one's career spins on an axis, the crux of the matter—from which derives the word 'crucial', by the way. If you get it wrong, make the wrong choice, the top stops spinning, you fall off and you are nixed. Once you fall off the axis, you can't get back on and restart spinning. To use a legal phrase, you are *estopped*. *Ab initio*. From the very beginning, no argument. Do you understand me, Sinclair? It means that if you screw up now, then you throw away your whole future. You can never ask for a second chance. You forfeit your whole future. You are estopped from arguing your case ever again. It's now or never. *Ab initio*, George Sinclair, remember that phrase, *ab initio*."

THE DARK SIDE OF THE MOON

One evening towards the end of June, after Evening Studies were over, they sat in Sinclair's study listening to *Dark Side of the Moon*. Sinclair was day-dreaming about kissing Helen in Highgate Cemetery. Underhill slouched in the armchair, rolling a fag. He seemed deeply worried about something.

"They've given up trying to find the owner of the drugs. Something weird is going on, I can feel it, something is definitely not right . . . There's something bad in the air. Something foul is afoot, something rotten in the state of Lancashire. All of a sudden they call off the interrogations and the mass punishments, but they haven't caught you yet. Do you really think you've got away with it, Sinclair?"

Sinclair shrugged carefully. He noticed again that Underhill did not include himself as a target of the investigation. It was Sinclair, not Sinclair and Underhill, who had got away with it. How curious. Perhaps there was something to what Tantum had said about him, after all.

"It's like the silence before the storm. They must have something up their sleeves," observed Underhill.

"I expect so," Sinclair nodded miserably.

*

The endless summer term was finally drawing to a close. They were in exam season and for a while even the tedious anxiety of the year-end exams provided Sinclair some welcome relief from his Predicament.

But the sword of Damocles that had been hanging over Sinclair's head for several weeks was now hanging by a very thin thread indeed, and would soon fall and decapitate him if he did not act.

The sly glances of Tantum, the silent Cassius, and even Morguer in his direction, pregnant with menace, reminded him that the clock was ticking. Sinclair remembered one hellish Sunday Mass when Morguer had looked down at him directly in the eye from the pulpit while he intoned the nightmarish verses from the Book of Revelation.

The deal was that when he was ready, he was to ask Tantum for a small ration of the confiscated drugs with which to spring the trap. That was all it would take to sell his soul.

One awful Saturday, memories of his sweet dead Grannyjee overcame him and made him cry like a seven-year-old behind the derelict abattoir with its brown bloodstains and rusty hooks, as he stood in the mud and sucked on a miserable rollie.

And later, as the wretched, mourning, lovestruck, Helen-sick, soon-to-be traitor skulked around the College avoiding cricket and other school activities, Cassius had at least on three separate occasions silently appeared beside him. He had come out of nowhere, and stood there unspeaking, like a bad omen, before melting back into the shadows.

The last of Cassius's visitations was the most hair-raising. It was getting dark and Sinclair sat alone smoking inside the abbatoir when he felt the evening breeze on his neck and he knew that Cassius had entered. He had been stalking him all day. Sinclair froze where he stood, barely letting the smoke out of through his nostrils. He felt rather than saw Cassius stop and turn. Something moved at the corner of his right eye. Sinclair turned his head and found himself looking directly into Cassius's eyes, which were dull and bored.

The rollie burned Sinclair's fingers and he let it drop.

Nothing seemed to surprise the little Scot. Cassius nodded curtly and he came a step closer and lowered his head as if readying himself to ram Sinclair in the stomach or deliver a head butt.

Sinclair tensed for the impact.

At the last moment the little Jesuit looked up and he met Sinclair's eyes indifferently. He raised an index finger heavenwards as if to invoke some higher authority, in a gesture that bizarrely reminded Sinclair of Leonardo's painting of St John the Baptist, and then bought it down slowly, levelling the finger at Sinclair's temple, like a pistol. Sinclair closed his eyes, more in embarrassment than fear. When he opened his eyes again Cassius had vanished.

They had him in their sights was what Cassius meant to say with his gesture, that was all. And that the time was coming to pull the trigger.

RAT TRAP

It had been a muggy term. The Lancashire countryside was green and humid and had acquired an almost obscene tropical lushness that summer. Sinclair, now deprived of his stash of drugs, was reduced to long tramps into the overgrown, steamy woods, sometimes with Underhill, sometimes with Underhill and his sex slave the grinning idiot Christopher Larkin in tow, to share a wretched cigarette or maybe a swill of cheap gin among the gnats and the mud.

The hellish quality of his Predicament hovered over his head like his own private storm cloud. It was only occasionally pierced by rays of sunlight when he talked to Helen on the telephone.

The worst thing was that he could not confide in his victim. Instead he would interrogate Underhill endlessly about his cousin, her school, who her friends were, what music did she actually really like, did she really like Pink Floyd or was she just being polite, was it true that she had read all those Graham Greene novels, did Underhill know of other boyfriends, present or past, do you think she might take something stronger than a joint, might she be persuaded to experiment with heroin later on, or a dose or two of morphine, and so on?

One evening in the woods Underhill said to Sinclair. "I just don't understand what you see in her. Yes, she has brown eyes, and dimples. But don't be fooled by all that sweetness and light. Things with Helen are not always what they appear."

This irritated Sinclair no end. "Sour grapes, it sounds like to me, Guy Underhill. You can't stand to see me happy and in love. I expect it's all because your own fling with Christopher has come to an end. Oh, yes, I *have* heard . . ."

It was true. Underhill was experiencing the anguish of unrequited love again. He told Sinclair, as they smoked in the woods now without the pleasure of Christopher's company, about his past for Philip de Vries, a boy in the year above, and about his many unsuccessful passes at the unsuspecting lad. Philip had replaced Christopher Larkin as the object of Underhill's carnal attentions. Sinclair nodded impatiently and moved the subject back to Helen before Underhill could start one of his interminable eulogies of Philip.

Another afternoon they were smoking at the Rat Trap, which is a filthy toolshed in the woods not far from the abandoned Abattoir. Carried on the breeze were the strains of the choir singing the *Dies Irae* in the College church.

Sinclair decided to tell Underhill about a recurring dream that had been worrying him for weeks. In his dream there was always a monumental storm brewing and that it was always night time. That he was invariably woken by the wind crashing through the trees in the garden outside the window and the drumming of the rain on the roof. That he was in the Tropics somewhere. It could even have been Goa, though he doubted it, because it felt like another country, somewhere he had never been before. The air-conditioning had been turned off and he had gone to sleep with the windows open, but now the sheets were damp with sweat. Through the windows, in the dream, Sinclair could see frenzied palm tops possessed by the wind which came in off the ocean. He lay in the darkness listening to the storm settle over the coast. He heard a sigh in the darkness and turned to look at the profile of the woman lying next to him in the bed, a profile set off against the twilit blue of the wall, a woman who was Helen but yet was not Helen at the same time. As if sensing his gaze, she opened her eyes and turned to him. She moved closer to him and he felt the scent of her hair as she laid her head on his shoulder. She looked up at him and he felt her warmth and was caught off-balance by her slightly cross-eyed gaze. Her sleepy brown eyes were dull in the twilight. She said in a child's voice: "I was dreaming about you too . . ."

"But the odd thing," Sinclair told Underhill, "was that she said this to me in a strange language, not English."

"So how could you know what she was saying, if you couldn't recognize the language?"

"I just could, that's all. The dream is very real, Guy, very real, like a lucid dream, when you know you are dreaming . . ."

But, as with everything else in Sinclair's life in those days, the dream had a sweet and sour quality to it. At some stage in the dream, and this part he never mentioned to Underhill, their lovemaking would be disturbed by a scratching on the floorboards, as if some small black crustacean or scarab, he couldn't tell, was scuttling into the corner of the dark room, and a scent of almonds would invade the room through the open windows.

PIT

As the days went on and the end of term approached, the clouds on the horizon continued to sulk there and hour by hour the air become heavier with their threat. For days the heat was moist and heavy, while the stormclouds lurked angrily like a massed army on the horizon of the witch-infested fells, as if waiting for the moment to move in for the kill.

On the second night before the end of term, there was thunder and lightning, but it did not clear the air.

Finally, the night before the end of term, Dr Tantum's hand pushed a small brown package across his desk towards Sinclair.

There was thunder outside. Then there was sporadic rain dashing out of the dark and spitting and scratching against the glass of the window of Sinclair's study as if some Pendle witch were desperately trying to claw her way in.

And there was Underhill sitting in the armchair next to the door. Sinclair sat at the desk rolling a joint.

"Where did you get *that*?" asked Underhill.

"I've had it in reserve for the grand finale."

"Now that's a strange thing to say," said Underhill.

At last, the storm broke in a titanic apocalypse. The vaults of the building amplified the claps of thunder into mythological thunderbolts which heralded the End of Days. The heavens opened and sent shockwaves of sound and light through the corridors and dormitories, frightening the younger boys in their cubicles, because they had committed Mortal Sins and thought that Judgment Day was finally at hand.

The stormburst did finally clear the air and the sky, and the next day's sun dried out the cricket pitches for the carnival of matches that marked the end of summer at the College.

And for George Sinclair, the Day of Reckoning was finally at hand.

As the First Eleven opened the batting against Ampleforth, Underhill and Sinclair lit up their last joint in the Pit.

Somewhere high above them, in one of the dormitories, a radio was playing *Shine On, You Crazy Diamond*.

It was unbearably hot and stuffy in the boiler room. Underhill sat on a fat rusted pipe beneath a row of yellowed meters, one of which was labelled *Perfection*. Next to it was one that read *Pressure*. How apt, though Sinclair miserably. Underhill lit up the joint, squinting in the smoke, gulped in the smoke as Sinclair had taught him to, and smiled.

Over the years Sinclair had learned to love that expression of pleasure on Underhill's face. But now, very soon, Underhill would be gone.

Suddenly the lights went out in the Pit.

Something Wicked This Way Comes, he heard Grannyjee chanting in his head.

"George . . . ," whispered Underhill in the dark

"Don't be frightened, Guy."

A rat scuttled among the dry leaves and Rizla papers that littered the floor. Perhaps I have a bout of malaria coming on, thought Sinclair in the dark, as a cold tremor gripped him.

They felt a chill at their backs, as if someone or something quite evil had entered the room and was standing close to them.

"George, I can't see you."

This time there was a desperate edge to Underhill's voice. This time Sinclair did not answer him.

The lights were on again soon enough. They turned and saw a small bullet head emerging up the stairs and through the door that led down to the wine cellars. Like a bat swooping in for the kill the black gown and grim pitted face of Ignatius Cassius, S.J., invaded the underground chamber. He silently and expertly snatched Underhill off the pipes and pulled him away, walking backwards with Underhill's head in a head-lock towards the door to the Underworld from where he had just emerged.

Underhill's face, as Sinclair watched him, transformed into that universal, open-mouthed mask of disbelief worn by the betrayed since the beginning of time.

Perhaps there is something I should say, said Sinclair to himself. Spellbound, he watched the grotesque sight of Cassius pulling Underhill backwards down into the subterranean tunnels, like a sand-crab on the beach backing into its hole with a sardine grasped in its pincers.

Sinclair crouched trembling in the far corner of the Pit among the cigarette buts, broken bottles and rat droppings.

"*Adios*, Motherfucker," Sinclair heard himself whisper in the dark.

But by then, Guy Underhill was underground and belonged already to the past.

PENANCE

The evening of Guy Underhill's expulsion Sinclair sat alone in his study contemplating the empty armchair that his friend used to lounge in. A curious lightness had come over him, as if what he had just done were some mere trifle, as if it didn't really matter in the grand scheme of things. Instead of agony and guilt he felt the lightheaded relief of a deep-sea diver coming to the surface.

Later that evening Sinclair was summoned to have his final Confession with his Spiritual Director before being discharged for the end of term. In the candlelit gloom of the Sodality Chapel, Sinclair whispered a litany of venal sins that he had invented for the occasion. But his Confession with the usually laconic Morguer was to be anything but a formality.

For once the Nosferatu's whispered responses from behind the grille contained a note of emotion, which took Sinclair aback.

"Don't even *think* that you can come in here and recite a laundry list of meaningless sins at me."

This was said with some venom. Sinclair suspected that Morguer had been drinking.

Venal sins did not interest him. What he was after was the real thing—a Mortal Sin—like a truffling pig.

"You know full well what you've done, but you don't have the guts to confess it. And don't think that with Underhill's departure it's all well now between you and us. You owe us, George Sinclair, you *owe* us."

"Yes, Father."

A pause, an eternity, then, the voice behind the grille resumed. Sinclair could imagine Morguer's nose wrinkling in disgust as he spoke.

"And for me personally there is nothing more repulsive than the stench of a traitor. But what we did we did for the good of the community. In your case the ends justified the means. Unfortunately for us we depend on benefactors like your father to keep us going."

"Yes, Father."

"And don't think I don't know about what you tried to do to Matron. The sins of the flesh are almost as repulsive in the eyes of the Lord as treachery. You are to report to Fr Cassius's office tonight for your penance, because penance you must do. And you are not getting away with three Hail Marys this time, I can assure you."

After a perfunctory absolution Morguer growled, a little too loudly for comfort, as there were other boys in the pews waiting for Confession, "And now, do me favour and fuck off."

"Yes, Father."

Later that night, after a joyless supper of grey stew and something brown which the fleggers seemed to take an inordinate delight in serving, Sinclair knocked on Fr Cassius's door in the Jesuit wing. Cassius opened it and with a silent sideways nod of his bullet-head ushered Sinclair in. He locked the door and proceeded to place a towel along the bottom of the door for soundproofing.

Sinclair took the opportunity to look around. Cassius's cell was spartan.

When the little Scot turned to face Sinclair, he held a dark instrument in his hand. For a moment Sinclair thought it was a gun. And then he thought it was a ferula. It was thrust into Sinclair's trembling hand. Sinclair looked down again and saw that it was a flagellum, thick and black and greasy—the genuine article with lead beads on the end of nine leather thongs, a cat o'nine tails, the same scourge that had been used to mortify the Flesh of the Redeemer.

"Thank you, Father," croaked Sinclair. It crossed his mind suddenly that Cassius was inviting him into one of those sado-masochistic rituals favoured by the Jesuits—the ones that Guy Underhill used to speculate about, and for an instant he had a freakish vision of him lashing Cassius's back with the scourge as the little Scot quivered in ecstasy.

But then, when Cassius failed to come any closer, a spasm of fear knotted his bowels and for a hair-raising moment he thought that he might literally shit himself there where he stood. Then enlightenment again—he was always falling for the Jesuitical trap. That was it, that was the whole point, humiliation, rather than violence, which is secondary. The Jesuits excelled at mind games and took their pleasure in psychological warfare. The threat of violence was enough, *that* was their game. The mock execution was worse than a bullet in the head.

But this time he was badly mistaken.

Cassius nodded and looked at Sinclair with that cold, bored look. He then stepped back two paces and with arms crossed, looked again impassively at Sinclair. He nodded once more, and waited for Sinclair to initiate the proceedings.

A SCENT OF ALMONDS

When he woke he was in an unfamiliar room. It must have been a private room in the Infirmary, judging from the antiseptic smell of the place.

He must have lost a lot of blood because he felt weak and light-headed, and his back was wracked with pain. He did not recall passing out. The last he remembered was Cassius's bored eyes watching him as Sinclair raised the scourge and brought it down on himself and the shocking insult of pain as the flints bit deeply into the skin of his back. Then there was nothing but a vague memory of a black chamber full of echoes, followed by a warm darkness seeping in through his back, and finally silence.

A bedside lamp glowed weakly by his side, but there was no clock and someone had removed his wristwatch. It was still dark outside. The headlights of a car swept across the wall in between a gap in the curtains as it tuned onto the mile-long Avenue on its way up to the Lady Statue. The first of the boys were already going home.

He heard a click as a key turned in the lock and the door opened.

Her scent preceded her. This time there were no flashlights in his face. Instead, a cool brown hand was placed on his brow and the black eyes look down at him. This time the smudges under her eyes were less livid. She looked healthier, as if she had recently fed on the blood of some small animal. There was a gleam in her eye and the hint of a smile haunted her dark lips.

"Ah, it's you again. So we made it through our ordeal, did we?" she whispered, in what could have been taken for kindness.

She stretched over him to turn off the bedside light, her fragrant black hair brushing softly against his face. In the blue light that gleamed weakly through the chink in the curtains he saw the nurse's kit slip silently off her shoulders and he beheld the dark Amazon in all her glory at last. The sheets were pulled back. Her hands were cold. This time she came down on him gently, lowering herself slowly and taking extreme care not to put pressure on his shredded back.

As he was enveloped in her warmth he felt a sensation of extreme kindness emanating from her body and it crossed his mind that what had occurred had probably been some form of initiation or rite of passage, like those of the secret societies that so obsessed Guy Underhill. Extreme pain had to be endured in order for the candidate to be allowed to enter the Mystery and experience extreme delight.

In the twilight Sinclair heard once more her breathless, whispered, guttural incantation in that prehistoric language that seemed to emanate from an endlessly undulating red desert on the other side of the planet . . .

In the dark he heard a child's voice say: "Thank you Matron, thank you for all you have done for me . . ."

LUCIFERINE

"Let me make it absolutely clear," Morguer hissed in the confessional. "There is to be absolutely no further communication between you and Guy Underhill. Not while you are here or when you are in London, for that matter. Is that understood? You will report any approaches from Underhill to me personally. You should expect threats and perhaps even attempts at revenge. You are to let me know if you do. And for good measure you are to avoid any and all contact with Helen Henshaw, Underhill's cousin. Oh yes, we know all about her. She is also unreliable, mischievous, and is quite likely in league with Underhill."

Before Sinclair could protest Morguer cut him off, saying: "I am quite prepared to dispatch Fr Cassius to London and even to Ascot to deal with any trouble should it occur."

Sinclair knew this was no empty threat. And Cassius had back-up in the capital, based at the Jesuit's London headquarters in Farm Street. The nest of vipers, Underhill had once said.

Sinclair managed to keep track of what happened to Guy Underhill after he was led in handcuffs from the school that summer evening and into the panda car that waited at the Lions, its flashing lights casting an eery red glow across the stonework.

The next morning, as the boys lugged their trunks out to the buses, Sinclair read the terse announcement on the noticeboard. Guy Underhill would not be returning the following term.

Later he was to learn from Dr Tantum about the quick arraignment at

Preston Crown Court, a guilty plea, probation and, he imagined, Underhill's solitary train ride down to London and Goodge Street, and then, as she opened the door to her grandson a full day before he was due, the frown of perplexity that would complicate Gran's fierce face when she didn't fully understand what was going on,

Dr Tantum could have proudly pointed to this as the fate that could have befallen Sinclair, but for the enlightened intervention of the magic circle of 'friends and supporters'.

That end of term it was out of the question that Sinclair would be able to lodge at Gran's flat in London as usual before his flight home to India. Instead Dr Tantum personally arranged for him to fly out of Manchester and connect at Heathrow, two days after the end of term, so that his back could have a couple of days to heal in the Infirmary. And heal it did, or at least the healing process began, quite nicely thank you, under the soothing balm of Matron's ointments.

During the holidays in Goa, Sinclair probed his parents with subtle questions to test their knowledge of the incident, but they remained blissfully ignorant. His back continued to heal, the itching a sign that the scars were cauterizing nicely, as Matron had said they would, and there was no reason for his parents to see his back or hear about it. Things had turned out satisfactorily after all and despite several sleepless nights at first, probably from the jet lag rather than from guilt, he reassured himself, he had the long summer holidays to look forward to. And, in time, the worm of guilt that had grown fat and lived in his intestines during the Predicament would eventually wither away and die . . .

During the holidays, in the large airy house on the coast, in between pleasuring himself with the memory of Matron's kindness, Sinclair was able to devote himself to mourning Grannyjee's absence. It was something that he had not been able to concentrate on in England since her death. And yet he felt so light and carefree that he even sought out his father's garden-wallahs in an outburst of *joie de vivre* and organized day-long games of cricket on the lawn.

Masterjee had grown into a fine young cricketer, the wallahs agreed. The rumour was that he would soon be going to Oxford, which old Ajay advised them as he looked up from the padlocks which he was mending with his now arthritic fingers, was the best university in the world.

And then, one evening towards the end of the holidays, Major Sinclair made a proud announcement at dinner, to the glowing approbation of his wife, who was to die shortly afterwards. The College authorities had decided to name one of the modules of the new science laboratories the 'Sinclair Wing' in recognition of his generous endowment. Sinclair picked at his curry and gazed at Grannyjee's empty chair.

GLORIA MUNDI

Sinclair enjoyed the fruits of full rehabilitation, or almost full. It was not surprising, given recent events, that he was passed over for membership of the School Committee.

That next summer, a year after the business with Guy Underhill, Sinclair made it back into the First Eleven. For a while he even enjoyed the reluctant approbation of Simon Cavendish and his mafia, at least on the cricket field.

Sinclair avoided Doris, Wanking Eddy Cayetano and Nick Gompertz. His ex-friends now maintained a low profile after their narrow escape from expulsion after the Black Mass. Fresh in their minds, like a ghastly turd on a fine carpet, lay the memory of interrogation at the hands of Spock and of being Ferulaed to Kingdom Come by little Fr Cassius. The nagging doubt persisted about whether Sinclair had been there that fateful night or not. They lurked pathetically in the shadows and eyed Sinclair with suspicion, like sick puppies, fearful to confront him without their protector Olatunji, long expelled. Doris withdrew into himself even further, Eddy continued to prosper quietly in the mag trade, while Gompy looked for new friends.

Sinclair maintained contact with Helen through clandestine phone calls placed from the phone booth by the Post Office on the road to Whalley. Happily Helen didn't seem to know what had really happened because she had asked Sinclair whether it was true that Guy had been expelled for drugs.

Through these calls with Helen he periodically tracked the sad declining trajectory of Underhill's luciferine fall from grace: a brief spell in Africa with his parents, special tutorials in London, a botched suicide attempt in his grandmother's flat in Goodge Street, visits to a psychologist, and later, about a year later, Underhill's retreat into obscurity started with the news of two middling A-levels and banishment to a minor red-brick university.

During that final term, in between heroic spells at the wicket, including an unforgettable century against Ampleforth, Sinclair went on to take four brilliant A-levels and a coveted Demyship in Archaeology and Anthropology to

Magdalen College, Oxford, the finest university in the world as Old Ajay had said. The magic circle of Sinclair's 'friends and supporters' was duly complimentary. In the Staff Common Room Dr Tantum was feted and congratulated on his ward's spectacular results and its effect on the Oxbridge league tables. Another Catholic Gentleman had been saved from himself by deft and sensitive handling by a brilliant educator and mentor. *Ad Majore Dei Gloriam et Laus Deo Semper!*

It seemed that except for Tantum, the Nosferatu and his silent amanuensis Cassius, no one knew of the events that had culminated in Underhill's expulsion, not even Spock. At least no one ever mentioned it overtly to him again. It was as if by sorcery the whole incident had been erased from the space-time continuum—it could have all been an unpleasant hallucination brought on by bad dope—save for the absence of Guy Underhill, but this grew less unbearable with each passing day.

Sinclair no longer avoided the Infirmary. He took to taking long solitary walks after dinner. Some of the boys said that on late summer nights that final term, when the northern sun set very late, his lonely figure could be seen working its way in the gloom up the spine of Pendle Hill.

And many years later, on lonely nights, the memory of what they did up there in Matron's cottage on Pendle, her cold brown hands and the Aboriginal lullaby that she hummed as she readied his syringe, would lull him to sleep.

VALETE—ADIOS MOTHERFUCKERS

The Preston bus collected him at the Lady Statue that stood guard over the Avenue, perched on the globe and the horns of the crescent moon.

Sitting in the back seat of the bus as usual, Sinclair lit up a rollie for old time's sake. He turned to look out of the rear window for a final glimpse of the cupolas and turrets that had been the backdrop of his coming of age. He was startled by a lurid sunset of purple, orange, scarlet and gold that burned above the twinkling lights and the towers of the College and was reflected in the rectangular ponds in front of the building. In the distance, under the enormous banks of storm clouds that seemed to go up forever high above the glorious apocalypse of the sunset, loomed the unforgettable shape of Pendle Hill, dominating the witch country of the fells. A large dark bird, it must have been some kind of bird of prey, given its wingspan, circled high above the landscape. Probably my friend the Noctifer, he fancied.

353

A door had shut in Sinclair's life and he had come upon a fork in the road. Further down that road, a new door, a low door in the wall surrounding an enchanted garden, would soon come into view.

HAITI, 1993
BARON SAMEDI

THE CRUX

"The wave of history, Morpheus, had turned in my favour. It was 1993 and my posting to Nicaragua was coming to an end. By then, you see, I had an inkling of what I was looking for, and it was time to move on and find it. But in the end it found me. It was something larger and more powerful than spying or sexual obsession and it was pulling me in to its vortex, into my own version of the Heart of Darkness. And I let myself be pulled in, like a gratefully drowning man."

It had been agreed that MI6's Managua Station would stay open to service SNAPPER, but they all knew that SNAPPER's days in Nicaragua were numbered. After the scandal with Spedding, FJ, the previous Head of Station, had returned to the UK in disgrace. An air of weary resignation pervaded the Station. The Friends had been reduced to three: just two junior cipher clerks reporting to Sinclair, who was now Acting Head of Station.

The country had been left exhausted after the Contra war, and now the defeat of Fidel in Nicaragua and the coming of peace coincided with the departure of SNAPPER and SPINNER from Managua. Democracy was definitely not conducive to good spying, and Sinclair and Carlos Maxwell were not the only spooks to pack their bags.

And so it was that Sinclair's posting in Nicaragua came to an end after the coming to power by the anti-Sandinista government of Violeta Chamorro and her following of crypto-Somocistas.

The Sandinista intelligence service under Tomás Verga continued to function as a state within the state, for a while at least. Inevitably, however, the influence of the new government made itself felt in the internal politics of the intelligence apparatus. Although the armed forces remained stubbornly in the Sandinista camp, soon it was the Somocista Contra boys with MBAs from Miami and then inevitably the CIA advisors who were lurking around the

355

corridors of the Coyotepe, and not the Cubans. Verga withdrew from the day to day operations, some say to assemble his own networks with trusted Sandinista operatives, a shadow service of the official institution. Most of the Cubans were recalled, but not before leaving behind a handful of sleepers to keep watch over what was going down in the post-Sandinista era and to report to their puppet master, the little man Verga, whose own strings were still pulled from Havana.

The Head Boys in Century House were in a panic. The problem was that SNAPPER had vanished completely off the radar screen and, Sinclair was *terribly* embarrassed to admit, he had not left a forwarding address. The first thing that SNAPPER had promised before going to ground was that he would return, and the second thing that SNAPPER insisted on, and which Sinclair modestly passed back to Head Office, was that in future SNAPPER would accept no handler other than Dr George Sinclair. It was an ultimatum. No Sinclair, no SNAPPER. Several people's careers in London, not least Mackie's, were on the line if SNAPPER disappeared for good.

Sinclair suggested that he take his annual leave abroad pending SNAPPER's reappearance. He did not want to go back to England. He had neglected his research in Nicaragua. He needed some time to himself.

The continued well-being of SNAPPER was so important that Sinclair's application was accepted without the usual weeks of wrangling and In- and Out-Tray battles between IB and Personnel. They say that C himself made the ruling.

Sinclair's extended break seemed an entirely reasonable solution. After all, it was well known that Sinclair was also an academic, specializing, of all things, in Afro-Antillean religions—or voodoo, to the ignorant. They knew that he was writing a book. The Service was full of people with oddball hobbies, like Wycliffe, Sinclair's predecessor in Managua, with his obsession with orchids. One of the Deputy Controllers for West Africa was a mildly successful novelist plying soft porn and detective plots under a pseudonym, with the blessing of Personnel.

Sinclair was given permission to take his leave in Haiti, a sabbatical for a maximum of up to six months. He could research his book and do whatever he pleased, on the condition that as soon as SNAPPER surfaced, Sinclair would follow his Joe wherever he went, even if it turned out to be Moscow or Timbuktu or "the fucking Vatican", as Mackie put it. And there was to be no hanky-panky on the side in Port au Prince either, Mackie had warned him, although if he came across anything of interest he should let Mackie know before doing any serious sniffing. Haiti after all had no MI6 Station and was CIA turf. The Cousins occasionally allowed SDECE in but they would not take kindly to a wandering Anglo-Indian Brit sticking his greasy nose where it did not belong.

Mackie had spent many bullets to get Sinclair this package, including a generous accommodation allowance. It simply wouldn't do to be let down, Mackie whined down the encrypted phone line. He had it on good authority, he told Sinclair, that changes were coming. There was talk of a new regime waiting in the wings to take power in London. They were antic-ipating a bloodbath, and Stations would definitely be closed if they did not produce. It would all probably coincide with the move from Century House to Vauxhall Cross, where they were building a monstrous space-age HQ. And in the meantime, a lot of people's careers where riding on the continuing suc-cess of SNAPPER.

While the wave of history lifted Sinclair's academic career, it drowned his relationship with Brenda van Kempen. Brenda had become addicted to Sinclair and had made certain demands on him. It may have been because of that feeling of desperation and finality that grips those coming to end of their overseas postings. Brenda was scheduled to return to the Hague and Sinclair steadfastly refused to discuss marriage. There were tears and difficult conversations and more tears followed by teary lovemaking but in the end she accepted reality like the brave Dutch girl she was. Ximena watched the sad little drama wistfully from the side lines, but sided as always with her father, who was under her protection.

Brenda's efforts to stay in touch with Sinclair were unsuccessful and did not survive long after she was transferred back to the Netherlands and he to Port au Prince. After all, they had just been two ships passing in the diplomatic night.

When they were in Haiti Ximena often asked her father what had become of Brenda. She told Sinclair that she could see Brenda sitting at a window, looking sadly out at the tulips and the windmills and the slow steady rain of the Lowlands. Sinclair knew that his daughter had become very fond of Brenda. He assured Ximena that Brenda was a friend who would always be welcome in their house. This seemed to assuage Ximena's melancholy, but not for long. It was cold comfort for a girl who missed a mother figure and soon Sinclair became concerned when his daughter took to sitting for hours on end under the trees of their new garden in Pétionville, high in the hills above Port au Prince. He would often find her there talking to her pet lizards and her imaginary friends, some of whom appeared to have acquired sinister characteristics.

As the days passed, he saw in her the same destructive inward-looking sullenness that he had adopted as a boy at Prep School in 1971, when he had declared himself an exile from the warmth.

THE GODDESS OF LOVE

Mem'zili joined the Sinclair household a few weeks after their arrival in Pétionville. It was taking Sinclair a long time to find a nanny for Ximena. He had become exasperated, because all the applicants, young and old alike, had fled terrified at the sight of Ximena and her hypnotic gaze, crossing themselves and spitting for protection against the Evil Eye of the child.

Erzulie was the last in a long line of candidates. When she walked into the living room that torrid Saturday afternoon late in September, Sinclair had felt in his bones that his search was at an end.

Erzulie was a big-boned African, tall and erect, age indeterminate. She came from Dessalines, which is a poor village on the south coast of the island known as a centre of the *petro* cult. The inhabitants of Dessalines are treated with utmost respect, if not fear, by ordinary Haitians. She had been named after Erzulie Freda Dahomin, the Goddess of Love. When Sinclair interviewed her, he immediately recognized in her direct look and proud bearing the pure strain of the Nago people from Old Dahomey, now known as Benin. From his research Sinclair had learned to how place the descendants of Caribbean slaves, who came from the West of the Dark Continent, in their respective ethnic groups— Yoruba, Igbo, Kongo, Fon, Ewe . . .

As the heat of the afternoon wore on, sunlight filtered through the palm fronds and played on the walls of the living room and the smell of overripe guavas wafted through the house. Ximena had stopped playing with her lizard and now started to circle her father and the candidate cautiously, all ears, sniffing the air suspiciously, while Sinclair questioned Erzulie about her knowledge of the *loas*, their attributes, feast days, offerings, food and other preferences. Erzulie answered cryptically but confidently, was knowledgeable about herbal remedies, but refused to answer Sinclair's probing questions about the *petro*, one of the most secretive of the Afro-Haitian cults. Nevertheless,

Sinclair knew that she would be a valuable asset in his research as well as a suitable companion and role model for his motherless daughter.

To Sinclair's relief, Ximena also seemed to approve of the tall Dahomean princess. Erzulie faced the child without fear and took Ximena's brown hand in hers and inspected the lines of her palm slowly. When Erzulie looked up into the girl's black eyes, Ximena was smiling down at her. Erzulie smiled back. Perhaps it was the fact that Erzulie was a practising *mambo* under the direct protection of the Goddess of Love. Perhaps it was the fact that Ximena had seen the coming of this black woman in the Tarot. In any case, it was clear that Erzulie understood Ximena's nature.

Ximena told her father that she liked the way Erzulie's polished skin gleamed in the sunlight, the clean pink palms of her hands, and that she smelt pleasingly of coconut oil. By then Sinclair knew his daughter well enough to know that Ximena liked Mem'zili for other reasons. That was enough for her to be invited to sign up with the Sinclairs.

Eventually, as time passed, Sinclair and Ximena addressed their new companion as "Mademoiselle Erzulie", "Mam'zelle Ezili", then "Mem'Ezili", and eventually, as they came to love her, "Mem'zili". Sinclair imagined this would have had Xancha Bersgma spinning like a dynamo in the cramped confines of her coffin in Highgate Cemetery.

Since that day Ximena had grown up under Mem'zili's watchful care speaking a curious mixture of French, Goan-inflected English, and now, to complicate matters, Haitian Creole. The Australian/Lancastrian accent inherited from her mother would eventually become hardly noticeable.

To the Haitians, 'les Saint-Clair', *père et fille*, made an odd pair of *blancs*. For a start they were not really *blancs*, even though the father, who looked sickly like the 'Turks' who controlled commerce in Port au Prince, was said to work for *Zanglais*. As for the girl, who was a shade darker than her father, she could scare the living daylights out of you just by looking at you. And when the tall priestess from Dessalines moved in with them, the rumours started, quite predictably, but that wasn't surprising. It was not the first time that a *blanc* had taken a live-in mistress from among the local population. The French had started that practice centuries ago and, by the 20th century, half the country consisted of many shades of fine-looking, stiff-backed mulattos and the most spectacular mulatresses of the Caribbean.

It was not the first time either, whispered the more knowledgeable observers of this strange trio, that foreigners had taken to dabbling in *vodoun*.

PAPA LEGBA

Underground again, Sinclair found himself standing in front of an altar that belonged to a horned god. The altar and the figure representing the *loa* had just been drenched in the blood of a goat. The altar was illuminated by the flames of many votive candles which reflected off the sheen of the blood that covered the head of the idol. The atmosphere was stifling in the underground room. Old offerings surrounded the shrine—rotting bananas and bottles of rum in which dark things floated, flowers, corn and a sticky mess of molasses. The dead eyes of the goat looked up at him incuriously from the foot of the altar, where its severed head had been placed.

This time he was not dreaming. Beside him, a hand on each shoulder, sponsoring him before the deity who was Legba, stood Mem'zili and the *bokor*, a sorcerer of the *petro* cult.

As his sponsors intoned the litany before the god on behalf of the supplicant, Sinclair thought of his friend Guy Underhill kneeling in the confessional at Farm Street, calmly discussing the sale of his soul to his Mephistopheles, and he thought of Doctor Faustus, who had once had his own Helen.

They had warned him in advance that Legba carries within him a devilish attribute, and that it all depends on the state of your heart, as you stand in supplication, whether what you invoke with your implorations is the dark side or the side of light.

Deeper and deeper she led him into the *petro*.

There were sessions with the *bokor* that lasted for hours and then he was handed over to the women, for days of ritual bathing and prolonged divination as cowry shells were cast and analyzed and then thrown and read again and again to confirm the answer. When it came, it was the same answer over and over again, despite the many different ways in which the question was asked, and despite astronomical odds.

The slightest mistake in interpretation of the *loas'* instructions, Mem'zili reminded him whenever he complained about the tediousness of the rituals or got twitchy and felt like going home to Ximena, can have disastrous results.

For the best part of a week he slept at the house of the *houncis*, a group of women novices, newly initiated, who were supervised by a *mambo* priestess much more senior than Mem'zili in the secret hierarchy of the religion. In fact, Sinclair noted for future reference, Mem'zili would bow her head and touch the big woman's feet whenever she entered the room to come and see

Sinclair and report on Ximena and to help him with his injections of morphine.

Entrails were read and a seemingly endless procession of pigeons and chickens were slaughtered, their blood fed to the gods who inhabited the corners of the *houncis'* house as they watched over Sinclair's initiation. Then came the more substantial sacrifices of pigs and goats, a lamb and even, to Sinclair's horror, a black cat followed by a black dog.

The slaughter was interspersed with cleansings administered by the *mambo* and her women. Inevitably, this took Sinclair back in his mind to the *hounfor* in the hills above Fort de France, where Madame Bernabeu had once danced around him in the firelight.

ZOBOP

"What can you tell me about the *zobop*?"

The wickedest people in the world, he knew full well, were the *zobop*.

Mem'zili glanced at him askance, centuries of African scepticism and a touch of raw fear in her look.

"But *m'sié*, we have just been on a very long journey into the *petro*," she replied, as if that wasn't enough for her insatiably curious employer.

"Yes, but is it not the *zobop* who deal with the *cabrit sans cornes*?"

She was pretending not to understand but he persisted. He knew full well, Sinclair lectured her, that the *petro* was an aggressive offshoot of mainstream *vodoun*. It had developed during the slave uprising that had expelled the French colonists, when swarms of militant and often violent African spirits had been recruited in the struggle for independence.

The *zobop*, on the other hand, he knew, were the wickedest of the Bizango secret societies of Haiti, and they went a lot further that the *petro* in their necromancy, drawing their arcane powers from the upper reaches of the Congo river rather than from Dahomey, where mainstream *vodoun* originated. He knew that the *zobop* preferred to work with the dead rather than with the *loas*.

"You know what I mean. You know very well, Mem'zili, that the *zobop* are under the protection of Baron Samedi. And, yes, I know that the Baron is the Nemesis of Legba. And you know very well what the Hornless Goat is and why it is offered."

This time Mem'zili avoided his hungry, wolfish look, and Sinclair knew when she looked away that he had touched a very sensitive nerve. He had reached the crux of the matter, the axis, the centre of things around which all else revolves. He had suspected it all along, and now, after years of research, after years of hacking through the undergrowth, he had come upon a clearing in the jungle. He had finally come across the wellspring from which all of Haiti's dark mysteries spring.

But would he be prepared to drink of its dark waters? Would he be prepared to erect the Baron's black cross in the cemetery?

This could end in tears, Mem'zili thought, and crossed herself.

LONDON, 2000

FOOD FOR THE GODS

In the Rubber Room, behind the mirror, a figure was huddled in a foetal position in a padded corner, hugging himself. The man had an incipient sun tan from an all too brief stay in Havana, but now his skin looked a sickly yellow under the unforgiving fluorescent strip lighting.

A minute earlier the door of the waiting room had sighed open and a beaming Mackie had come in and greeted Sinclair like a long-lost friend, pumping his outstretched hand. Unlike the last time he had seen him on the ninth floor of Legoland, Mackie was the picture of health and he was wearing a new suit. He chatted amiably as he led Sinclair to a room behind a one-way mirror and sat him down next to the transcribers behind a bank of recording devices and sliding switches that reminded Sinclair of a recording studio. Sinclair was handed a mug of tea and a biscuit and he settled back and looked into the Rubber Room.

"They've been bouncing him off the walls all night, George," Mackie whispered confidentially. "He insists on seeing you. Says he won't talk unless you're present. We pulled him out of Havana just in time. Thank the Lord"—it appeared that Mackie had found religion since his last ordeal—"that SNAPPER never agreed to meet with him."

"But he must have read SNAPPER's file before he came out to replace me. He must know who SNAPPER is," Sinclair ventured.

"Thank God again, we did our job well, for once."

Mackie ran his hand through his hair in a curiously vain gesture that Sinclair had not seen him use before. "You see, young George, only *I* have the whole SNAPPER file which contains the background on Carlos Maxwell. It is safe and under lock and key in my office. And as you well know, Havana Station, or any other Station for that matter, never has any reference to the true identity of any of its Joes in its files on site. In fact I was going to fly out next week to initiate Cavendish in the mysteries of SNAPPER myself. But our Dear Sweet Jesus must still love us."

This last comment was made without the least hint of irony. Sinclair noticed how quickly 'our Simon' had become 'Cavendish' and how the Good Deity was now routinely invoked.

"Cavendish swears he didn't tell DGI about SNAPPER," Mackie continued. "In fact he swears he is not a DGI agent at all and that he has been framed. By you. But the final confirmation came through just today—you are now, I am glad to say, in the clear, and Cavendish is dead meat. And it turns out that you were right—all of Cavendish's trips out of Botswana and the dates and places of the bank deposits were a perfect match. No question of a frame up there. And how could one of his fake passports ever find its way into the hands of DGI, anyway? Whenever they aren't being used, these documents remain in Personnel under lock and key and all copies that were ever made are still there in his file. We're quite sure about that, the logbooks confirm it, and all copies ever made were registered and are accounted for. And furthermore all the Moneypennies who had ever been in charge of the filing cabinets in Personnel have been accused of treachery, interviewed at the Fort, threatened, and they have all passed their polygraph tests with flying colours. No, a frame-up is quite, quite out of the question. SNAPPER has saved our bacon yet again, thank the Lord."

Later they gave them five minutes on their own. They had restrained Cavendish, strapping him to his chair for fear that he might attack Sinclair and bite his face off in the manner of Hannibal Lecter.

On the contrary, Cavendish was quite calm now, partly because of the drugs, and partly because he had by then realized that his situation was hopeless, and that Paki Sinclair had finally outwitted him and had won the game. Like he had with the business of the Stilton cheese that Sinclair had planted in his tuckbox in Surrey. Like he had when Cavendish had failed to keep him out of the First Eleven at the College. If only Jerome O'Reilly had bowled that body liner a little bit harder in the nets in Surrey, then things might have turned out quite differently.

While Cavendish droned on about these defeats, Sinclair savoured the memory of his enemy opening and closing his mouth soundlessly like a fish washed up on the sand, gasping for breath, as he had been led off in utter disbelief to be beaten by Gollifer—nothing more than a petty thief, the proof: ten pounds of rotting Stilton in his tuckbox. For a while back then in Surrey, this Establishment creature's world had been turned upside-down. And now it was happening again, but this time with infinitely more serious consequences than an appointment with Dr Ferula.

Unfortunately, because everything that was said or done in the Rubber Room was recorded, Sinclair could not tell the human wreck in front of him what was really on his mind—about the immense pleasure he felt—and therefore he could not enjoy his revenge to its fullest extent. But you can't have everything in life, can you?

Cavendish was now shivering intermittently. It could have been with fever from the truth serum, but more like it from fear or anger.

"They've a-a-agreed to have Fr M-Morguer come down from the College and say M-Mass for me. Then he will hear my Last C-C-Confession."

"How nice for you. Do give the Nosferatu my best wishes."

They could have been two friends chatting on the pavement after Sunday Mass at Farm Street.

Suddenly Cavendish was gripped by a spasm of shuddering and he told Sinclair about the anal probe and the indignities of how he had been treated when they plucked him out of Havana. Sinclair barely prevented himself from making a comment about humiliation.

"They've ask-k-ked me to do the 'd-decent thing'," Cavendish managed to stutter, looking at Sinclair with the eyes of a drowned man. "They will take me down to the Fort and tonight after d-dinner they will hand me a Walther with one bullet in it and invite me to b-blow my brains out in the bathroom of the IB Mess, after being so kind as to tie a towel around my head to k-keep things t-tidy."

"*Ad Majore Dei Gloriam*, Simon, old boy. Remember that it is all in God's hands now and everything that will happen to you is To His Greater Glory, as Fr Morguer taught us. Oh, and by the way, *Adios, Motherfucker.*"

For some reason that was the only thing that occurred to him to say as he stood up to take his leave. Because he was sitting with his back to the camera, however, he had managed to get away with a sly wink at Cavendish, who was crying silently again, his gaping mouth soundless and fishlike again, as if he could feel the oxygen of his life petering out.

Revenge is a dish best served cold, after all, Sinclair thought, as he left the Rubber Room and that wonderful lightness descended on him again.

"It's always a shame to see a young officer lose it," sighed Mackie, packing up his briefcase for his commute home and an evening with the Awfully Wedded One, having again narrowly sidestepped a career-wrecking disaster.

"He *is* getting a bit delirious in there, you know, poor old Simon. He said something ridiculous about having to blow his brains out tonight," said

Sinclair, making sure Mackie noted his concern for a fellow agent, even though in this case the agent in question was treacherous scum and was not long for this world.

Mackie ignored his remark. "You were at school together, weren't you?" he asked. "Is that what he meant when he was burbling on about tuckboxes and cheese and the nets and the First Eleven? And what was that thing you said just before you left?"

"Oh, that was our school motto. The Jesuits used to make us write down the letters A.M.D.G. before we wrote anything. *Ad Majore Dei Gloriam*. It means 'To the Greater Glory of God'. It reminds us that everything we do is done to the greater glory of our Maker."

"But did I not hear you say the word 'motherfucker' as you left him?"

"Oh, that," he laughed sadly, "that was a common term of endearment between friends back at school. Did you know that we were best friends back then? Very close we were. So you can imagine how it breaks my heart to see him lose it. He of all people, I still can't believe that he could betray his country."

That night—it must have been after the hour of reckoning, after Lights Out for Simon Cavendish, who must have been sleeping the sleep of the worms in his body-bag—for the second time in his life Sinclair laughed himself to sleep, thinking about Simon Cavendish.

TROUT

Now that George Sinclair had been cashiered out of the Service in disgrace, the debate over what to do about SNAPPER and who should handle him raged on at Legoland and in more recondite corners of Whitehall. A whispering campaign had started in the bars around Vauxhall Cross. In the CIA annex at Grosvenor Square, the Cousins had come on aggressively and were making a pitch to take him over.

"Over my dead body," Mackie would insist at those interminable meetings that always ended in deadlock. Once he even thumped the table, forgetting all about English phlegm. He was a Scot, anyway, for fuck's sake, forget about English decorum. That was the problem with the English, Mackie confided to himself, always drowning in their own phlegm. All wind and pish, the English, all fart and no shit. There was a lot at stake here. A lot of people's careers depended on the well-being of SNAPPER.

The problem, the dilemma, Mackie repeated, was that SNAPPER still insisted on dealing only with Dr Sinclair. He had even refused to meet with Mackie himself.

What Mackie didn't know was that by then he himself had become the subject of a secondary series of meetings held out in the country houses of the more senior officers of the Service. His loss of control at the last pow-wow with the Cousins in Grosvenor Square had been noticed.

"It's too big for him," C had drawled to his Chief of Ops as they fished for trout (which C pronounced as "trite") in his estate up in Scotland. "He'll choke on it."

There was an almost imperceptible pull on C's line and then the delicious tension of something trapped tugging at the end of it.

C's nostrils, C/O/Ops noticed for the first time, were extremely furry, and they now twitched and widened as they scented the impending death of a small creature.

And then, as if hit by a thunderbolt of enlightenment, C had turned to C/O/Ops in the stream and declared: "I've got it. Know what, old boy? Let's do nothing. That's it. Doing nothing is usually the best way forward. See what happens. Let events take their natural course. Don't force it. Do nothing. That's it. That's settled, then."

Now that that was settled, C/O/Ops turned his attention to the good-sized trout that C had just landed and which was beginning the slow agony of its death throes on the river bank.

Personnel arranged through David Blantyre for Sinclair to return to Magdalen as a Junior Fellow. The Service's custom was to help discharged officers, whether honourably or dishonourably discharged as Sinclair had been, to find work in the City, academia or as Prep School masters. What SIS's top management fears the most is the rogue agent willing to spill his guts out to the press after being sacked, so they are inclined to bend over backwards to help even those who are no longer of any use, the detritus of the secret world.

Finding a place for George Sinclair back in the real world was a fairly straightforward task given his background and the College's ties with the Service. They were still worried about Sinclair and his potential for mischief making—who could trust a drug-addict and a voodooist after all—so having him close to Blantyre made them feel better.

At their farewell lunch in a tapas bar not far from SIS's building by Vauxhall

Bridge, which Mackie had lately taken to referring to as 'Ceaucescu Towers', Mackie told Sinclair that the SNAPPER issue had still not been resolved. He told Sinclair that he had been authorized to ask him to remain on call.

"It's 'anything can happen time' again, you see, young George. You may still be asked to return, or you may be asked to continue handling SNAPPER, perhaps even if to the world you have been discharged from the Service. Stranger things have been known to happen. I don't need to tell you that things are not always quite what they seem. And the second option may be the more effective one, in many ways. For many reasons which I am *not* authorized to discuss with you."

Mackie went on to give Sinclair the pleasing news of the demise of Robin Ruskin in Havana.

"Very strange, the whole business. By the way, did you know that he had applied to join the Service?"

"I did not, Mackie," Sinclair lied, popping a peanut into his mouth.

"They said that he caught some kind of leprosy out there. One of those tropical flesh-eating diseases that eats you away while you are still alive. Haemorrhagic dengue, that's what they call it, I think. He literally rotted to death. Quite gruesome, by all accounts." Mackie shivered theatrically as he reached for his Vermouth.

"Poor sod," said Sinclair, draining his third glass of Merlot and remembering Ruskin's pink crablike hands picking at his face. He silently toasted the efficiency of Ximena Sinclair's *nganga* and the thing that lived inside it.

"Misery loves company," Mackie waxed, philosophical.

"When it rains it pours . . ."

"Where I come from, North of the Border," Mackie went on, "the old women say that deaths come in threes. Cavendish, Ruskin, and . . . ?"

He couldn't imagine who the third might be. Mackie wasn't thinking clearly by then.

But it has been more than three, in my case, many more, Sinclair concluded, munching on a handful of peanuts.

Mackie, slightly tipsy by now, noticed that Sinclair was lost in his thoughts and was counting something on his fingers.

First Grannyjee, and then the news about his mother, before he had left the College. Then his father in that car smash on the day that he learned Helen had come up to Oxford. Then came Helen herself, then Jane Redfern, followed closely by Doctor Aggarwal. Seventh was Xancha—what a way to go, that one, he shuddered into his wine. And then, he couldn't quite remember when, he had heard that his school mates Doris, Wanking Eddy and Olatunji Ogunlesi had all met premature ends. Dead, all dead.

He remembered Doris's face in the candlelight of the Pit. Eddy's suicide was more surprising than Doris's murder, but then nothing coming out of California should surprise anyone these days, least of all news of mass suicide under instruction from a lunatic guru. He wondered if Eddy was happy now in the Mothership that followed in the wake of comet Hale-Bopp. And multiple strokes of the machete in Olatunji's case. Never really cut out for a long life, poor Olatunji, despite his charismatic personality.

Lately, in Cuba, there was Martina Mendieta, victim of a scorpion. Victim of the *lamia*, of his daughter's *mpungo*, more like. He did not count Major Mendieta among his dead, because they never told him what finally happened to the poor sod. Probably still rotting in the dungeons under the Morro.

And now Simon Cavendish. The delicious demise of Simon Cavendish was now followed by the light dessert of Robin Ruskin. Quite a tally. He had run out of fingers. Thirteen corpses, and still counting . . . he wondered whether thirteen stiffs to your name was average for a man not yet forty. Might well be. Some kind of world record. Cheers.

They drank in silence.

"Sounds like something karmic, in my humble opinion," said Sinclair, at last.

"You what?"

"*Karmic*. It's something my Indian grandmother taught me. It means that that poor bugger Ruskin must have fucked up royally in a previous life to be treated in this one to such a slow, lingering death."

"Oh, right, George," Mackie shuddered again, "I forgot you were into that sort of thing. Cheers."

He has finally done it, he tells Morpheus at the crossroads that night after his farewell drinks with Mackie. Morpheus listens courteously, as he always does when Sinclair reports his achievements.

Simon Cavendish was my *cabrit sans cornes*, you see, my Hornless Goat.

The *zobop* in Haiti do it.

The *abakuá* in Cuba do it.

The Templars did it to Martin Weld, according to Guy Underhill.

You have to feed the god, you see, dear Morpheus.

Cavendish was my supreme offering, Morpheus. Through him I was able to fulfil the vow I made in Haiti. *Human sacrifice*, Morpheus, that's the name of the game. It had to happen that way.

What goes around comes around . . .

Morpheus, always so understanding, nods kindly as Sinclair slips under. It is time for lights out again. Morpheus is always so understanding, so obliging, the best of friends. Only someone like Morpheus, who knows our George so well, can understand how dispatching Simon Cavendish is not murder, or even revenge for that matter, but propitiation, a gift, food for the gods.

JUNE 11, 2002
DANSE MACABRE

TAROT

Gulping in the last precious atoms of rank air in the coffin where his daughter and Guy Underhill have trapped him, enlightenment suddenly arrives in the form of a crystal-clear recollection of another seance, this time presided over by Xancha Bergsma.

It was a summer Saturday at the end of June, after an afternoon of victorious cricket. Sinclair's last term at the College was coming to a close. The spectre of the betrayed Guy Underhill was receding quite nicely thank you and the future was bright and full of possibilities.

The evening was splendid, and even God's little creatures, the birds, were singing, celebrating His Greater Glory and another victory for the First Eleven. Sinclair was flushed and glowing and sweaty in his cricket whites after his tramp up the slope of Pendle Hill. He was extremely pleased with himself. They had trounced Ampleforth comprehensively and he had taken a respectable five for twenty-seven and scored a century before being LBWed (deservedly, he was big enough to admit) to an in-swinger.

His lover was waiting for him with her table set with wine and food. All was well with the world. Even Simon Cavendish had taken the time to congratulate him. What more could a lad want?

"What's the occasion?" he asked, as always a little lacking in confidence and off-balance in front of her. He suspected that it might have something to do with his exploits on the cricket pitch, because good news travels fast.

That evening Xancha Bergsma was to surprise him with a new aspect of her enigma

"Tonight your future will be revealed." She said this without the least hint of drama, as if it were a part of the syllabus to be covered in Double Physics on a Tuesday morning. It was to be just another part of his education.

Outside the wind had started up again.

They ate their dinner silently. She wasn't interested in hearing about his exploits on the cricket pitch. Sinclair listened to the wind in the trees and watched her as she ate and drank. She watched him back.

Then there was the obligatory session in her bedroom. That evening they explored each other's backs after she had read out the relevant chapter of the Kama Sutra to him.

Finally after their exertions she led him back by the hand through the darkened cottage and lit a candle.

They now sat at the table buck-naked like Devil Worshippers. Her black eyes reflected the single flame of the candle like obsidian. Outside the wind had died down and it was at last silent on Pendle. It must have been late because the northern summer sun had gone down at last. The isolated house on the now darkened fell, the eerie quietness, in fact the whole damned setting, he remembered, gave him the creeps.

Sitting before his naked mistress he suddenly saw an image of Doris's face in the Pit as he laid out his ouija board in the candlelight. He would not embarrass himself in front of Bergsma the way he had when Grannyjee had appeared through the ouija board that night in the Pit in 1978.

He had never dared to ask her about the rumours of witchcraft or about her Gypsy background. He was apprehensive that night when she set a book-sized packet covered in a red silk handkerchief on the table and then proceeded to carefully unwrap a stack of large, well-thumbed cards with pictures on them. He had seen this type of playing card before, but only in books, with their unsettling gothic pictures of hierophants and priestesses and towers and devils and suits of swords, golden cups, coins containing pentagrams, and staffs—these, he was to learn later, were the Major and Minor Arcana of the Tarot.

It is all so obvious to him now, as he lays in his tomb, next to the cheesy mortal remains of Martin Weld. He is running out of air, and as the buzzing is starting in his ears again he begins to hear familiar voices calling to him from far away. Yes, it is all so obvious now, with hindsight, the significance of the cards that Xancha spread before him that summer evening.

Even though his knowledge of the Tarot was limited, he had shuddered at the preponderance of reversed cards, which was never a good sign.

"That one, the Fool, is you, George Sinclair, the Querent, the Seeker—the Fool, ambling along the edge of a cliff, looking upwards, an idiotic smile on your face.

"The Chariot—you will travel but you will always return.

"The King of Spades—a dark man, older, hostile to you, will pursue you for the rest of your life wherever you may travel.

"Look, there is your Helen, the little vixen—the Queen of Hearts, reversed.

"And yes, there is Yours Truly, the Darkie—the Queen of Spades, in opposition.

"The Page of Spades—a dark young person, dear to you, but treacherous . . .

"Ah, yes, here it is—Betrayal—the ten of swords, see the ten swords sticking into the man's back?—yes, that is your friend Guy Underhill, lying face down, stabbed in the back. And there will be others.

"The Tower, destroyed, and reversed—the end of hearth and home.

"The Lovers, reversed—the end of love.

"The Devil, reversed.

"And finally, Death.

"Reversed . . ."

THE MAGIC CIRCLE

Just before he is about to give up and go under for the last time like a drowning man, lying there on top of the putrid remains of Martin Weld, a rib jammed awkwardly into his cheek, and just as the buzzing of countless voices like a swarm of flies is roaring in his skull like ten thousand chainsaws all cranking up simultaneously, Sinclair finds within himself a hidden reserve of energy. He kicks up with all his might, first with his knees, then levering himself down with a force so maniacal that with a sickening crunch he collapses downwards through poor old Martin's rib cage into his abdominal cavity. He kicks up now with his feet. Suddenly there is a rush of cold dank air and the lid of the coffin is off him and clattering loudly on the stone floor. He springs up out of the casket, his poor lungs bursting with life-restoring oxygen, and the next thing he knows he is running down the subterranean passage looking for Underhill and Ximena, who, he now realizes to his horror, have betrayed him.

Now he stands at the foot of the staircase that leads up to the Arundell Library. He hears voices coming down from the top of the stairs. He follows the murmur of the voices up the stairs, as if drawn by an invisible thread, like a sleepwalker. Behind the heavy nail-studded door he hears Ximena and Guy Underhill laughing amidst the chatter of a crowd, as if there is a cocktail party going on in there. Or some other gathering like a wake or a packed court room. Once again, silently blessing old Ajay, he starts to pick the lock but the door is already unlocked. The massive slab swings open on its hinges with a theatrical groan.

The room is alive with the din of conversation. It is brightly lit and crowded with a fancy dress party. Everyone is wearing what at first looks like the costumes of the Venetian carnival. However, when Sinclair looks more closely he realizes that the gaudy medieval costumes are from the engravings of the *Danse Macabre* that hang on the walls of the Library.

He sees the scarlet robes of a cardinal, the gold braid of a bishop gleaming in the lights, the black gown of Death, the helmet of some Conquistador, and a kilt swinging from a woman's shapely hips and several conical hats and hoods. He sees macabre facings, pentagrams on chains, and curiously knotted lanyards. He even sees the occasional pair of boots and spurs and the brightly coloured strips of campaign medals of a regimental best. He sees a cloven hoof.

He does a double-take. The Devil's hoof turns out to be the two pointed boots of a witch.

There seems to be some sort of poetry recital going on.

"A spy in the house of love . . . ," a girl's voice sighs, to chuckles from the gathering.

"And death shall have no dominion . . . ," someone else chants, to scattered applause.

Cheering breaks out from the back of the room.

"And the Gates of Hell shall not—," a familiar voice starts to declaim, but stops in mid-sentence as Sinclair's entrance is noticed.

Cigar smoke and various dizzying perfumes, including incense perhaps, hang thickly in the air. The company falls silent.

George Sinclair steps into a magic circle.

They stand around him in their own little clusters, like groups of friends or professionals at cocktail parties, refusing to mingle.

A dishevelled man wearing a rusting breastplate and the plumed helmet of a medieval Knight is the first to speak up.

"*Compañero* Sinclair, welcome to our little gathering. We were beginning to wonder when you would show up."

"My God, Carlos Maxwell, not you, surely, surely not you . . . ?"

The presence of his handler and friend affects Sinclair very deeply.

"Yes, I'm afraid so, *Compadre*. That little *coño* Tomás Verga shot me in the head with Tacho's Luger, remember the one he used to wear under his armpit? It happened at El Mango, not long after I returned from London, after our final debriefing at Highgate Cemetery. By the way, it was naughty of you not to tell me whose crypt we were in, don't you think? But never mind, there are no secrets here in the Afterlife. You do remember El Mango, though, *Compita*, don't you? The island that time forgot? Well, what happened is that we—Tomás Verga and me—got drunk on Flor de Caña rum and, as is inevitable in Nicaragua when men drink together, there was an argument. Verga accused me of being a double agent and of spying for MI6. He accused me of being *your* agent and playing it both ways, and he never forgave me for telling Belén Flores about you. But now, with the luxury of hindsight that being dead gives you, I began to suspect that there was more to it than that. Some murky business with the Cubans, I thought at first. Then I thought that perhaps he was worried that I was becoming too successful, and that I was beginning to make him look ineffective. But being dead, you see, reveals things to you that you would never have suspected when you were alive. It turns out that Verga was SIS's man all along. I was topped because I was beginning to suspect that all that chickenfeed, the SNAPPER CX that I was feeding MI6 through you, was in fact not chicken-feed but the real gen, provided courtesy of Comandante Verga. And that Verga was handled personally by C himself. And that by extension they knew about your treachery all along—you and I were mere conduits, and totally expendable. You might even be tempted to conclude that you were recruited by those wily Brits *precisely* because you had the profile of a traitor, which is what they needed. And yes, I can anticipate your next question: they *were* prepared to sacrifice your friend—your enemy—Simon Cavendish in order to keep the deception going. A real wilderness of mirrors, as it turns out."

Maxwell's ghost sighs regretfully, and pauses, his friendly gaze resting easily on Sinclair.

"But all is well now," he continues, "because none of that matters any more. It was all a game, anyway, a game for grown-ups—the Great Game, as the Brits used to call it—and now I'm reunited with my girl Heidi, which makes me an immensely happy ghost."

Sinclair looks down and sees Heidi's cocked head and bulging eyes watching him. They have put the monstrous nail-studded collar of a medieval War Hound on her for the party. The truncated nub of her tail wags enthusiastically as Maxwell's pale fingers fondle her velvety ears.

"And he is reunited with *me* . . ."

Sinclair cannot immediately place the voice. He does recognize the shy but insistent gaze of a woman called Belén Flores, codename SABRINA. She is wearing the habit of a Nun.

"Did Carlos tell you what the people you call the Cousins did to me at Quantico?"

Ever hesitant and lacking in confidence even in the Afterlife, the shade of Belén Flores looks to Maxwell for confirmation. Her Knight nods grimly, looking down at his War Hound, still stroking Heidi's ears.

"They executed me at the base after they had got all they could out of me, after I had confessed everything, or almost everything. They told people afterwards that I had committed suicide in my cell. But I never betrayed you, George Sinclair. Although we only met once, remember—at the Nacional—I always remembered you and I never told them what Carlos told me about you, because he always thought of you as a brother. That is the truth. But the strange thing is that during the interrogation they never once asked me about you. Perhaps there is something to Carlos's theory about it all having been a set-up. I suppose they already knew about you, so why bother asking?"

She says all this rather hesitantly, looking up shyly at Sinclair from under her cowl in the doe-eyed manner of Lady Di. But then her eyes light up when she tells Sinclair that now she has all eternity to play with Heidi, the dog she never had. The dog who contributed so much to the Revolution.

"And he is also reunited with me," he hears another woman say, and then that intimate Arabic greeting: "*Ahlan*, George, *habibi*!"

This time it is the husky voice of Jamila—codename FATIMA—Maxwell's girlfriend, the Palestinian girl with the killer's eyes who had helped out with the business of La Spedding in Nicaragua. She stands back respectfully, behind Maxwell's left shoulder, like the second wife. She is wearing the traditional black *burka* of a Bedouin Nomad. She unwinds the veil off her face and in an inviting gesture runs a hand through her luxurious curls.

"The Israelis," (which she pronounces *ezra-ilis*), "captured me in Jenin three years ago, just after Carlos had come to see me in Beirut. You were in Cuba by then, I think. I was training one of our girls how to recruit suicide bombers when two Jews of the Shin Bet walked in. I won't tell you what they did to me, not in public, anyway. Before they shot me they said that they had picked me up because of information that an MI6 agent in Nicaragua had given them about me."

"Most probably the MI6 agent in question was Yours Truly, old man.

Happened to need a chip to bargain with after they called me back to HQ, you see."

The speaker is plate-faced FJ, wearing, as you might expect, the Franciscan garb of Friar Tuck. His red face is flushed with wine-induced bonhomie. The massive folds of flesh under his chin wobble like gelatin as he remarks that he died quite happily and painlessly, thank you. Cause of death, an embolism, as he slept next to his catamite in his retirement home in Málaga, having gorged himself on his favourite meal of quails' eggs and pheasant. His last happy memory before dying was telling his Moroccan lover how they had set up the bitch Spedding, *La Bitch Número Uno*, "as I understand you and your Cuban friends called her. Nice way to go, by the way, embolism, highly recommended."

He winks good-naturedly at a whey-faced woman with grey hair and green cat's eyes. The woman is dressed in the scarlet gown of a Queen and is scowling back at him venomously.

"Her Ladyship still refuses to talk to us, even now. She overdosed after she was dishonourably discharged from the Service. Without her pension, I'm glad to say."

Another one who refuses to speak, and who stands next to FJ and Spedding in the MI6 contingent, glaring resentfully at Sinclair will red eyes, for he has been crying, is Simon Cavendish. Like La Spedding he is also pasty-faced. Whey-faced and lily-livered, dressed as an Altar Boy in scarlet and white. The burn from a gunshot is still visible on his temple. Simon Cavendish—he of the gaping fish's mouth.

"Do not shake your gory locks at me," says Sinclair to himself, barely overcoming the impulse to cross himself and spit, to ward off the Evil Eye of the dead cricket god's stare.

Sinclair is shocked to see Brenda van Kempen's smiling face there among the dead. She is dressed in the garb and wooden Dutch clogs of a Milkmaid. He feels genuine sadness that the life of this pleasant young woman has also been cut short, for she too must have died prematurely to be part of this select gathering. Despite her story, her open Lowlander's smile is testament to her nobility. And although it is a sad story, Sinclair enjoys hearing her throaty Dutch singsong again after so many years. What she says she says without bitterness, and perhaps even with an undercurrent of wry Northern European amusement.

"You see, you changed my life for ever that night in Managua. I became addicted to oral sex because of you, and I couldn't get enough of it, so when I

377

got back to Holland after my tour in Africa I resigned from the Diplomatic Service and took up with some KLM air hostesses in the red light district in Amsterdam—we set up a little co-operative."

The girls had set up their practice along a neon lit canal behind the railway station. Each had a speciality—Brenda's was oral gratification. It was in there, in 1993, in their cosy little *grachthuis*, that she was murdered by one of her tricks, a psychopathic bank manager from Barclays in London on a quick swing through Amsterdam branch. She has become another of the red light district's statistics.

Sinclair begins to tell her that if at all possible, if regulations permit here in the Netherworld, he would very much like to make it up to her. In any way she might chose, if she knows what he means.

Before she can answer, Sinclair is distracted by the absurdly bright, parrot-like headgear of a Jester.

For next it is the turn of the Cuban contingent, who are gathered in a small intimate knot, drinking *mojitos* in honour of Sinclair's homecoming. It seems that it is always Friday afternoon for them here at the portals of the Afterlife. For the next few minutes Major Alvaro Mendieta, a.k.a. LAZARITO, a.k.a. MARTINET (who it turns out is the unfortunate clown dressed in the harlequin diamonds of a Jester), his delicious wife Martina (an Astrologer with an astrolabe and stars on her hat), Gumercindo (grinning and looking delightfully incongruous as a Black Pope) and Robin Ruskin (a Leper in purple rags like those of Babalú-Ayé, holding a little tin bell) make way politely to allow Sinclair to step into their little sub-gathering. They are reminiscing in Spanish, doling out complaints or compliments to Sinclair as the case may be, according to their various fates.

For instance Gumercindo advises Sinclair that his meddling into the affairs of the *abakuá* was discovered and that he was suspected of giving away the Leopard Society's most sacred secrets to his boss the white spy. For which he was ritually slaughtered by members of the local chapter in Matanzas, where he had been born. Skinned alive then rolled in salt and brine, the required punishment for snitches in the arcane regulations of the Calabar. Gumercindo's ghost flinches at the memory.

As her husband drones on and on interminably about his wife's betrayal, Martina Mendieta edges closer to Sinclair. She seems sad and has a wistful look in her Helen-like eyes. She stands so close that he can smell the scent of her hair. It makes him remember the blue walls of their love nest in Cuba.

Interestingly enough, just as Martina is about to slip her hand into

Sinclair's, a rather jolly fat man with a sweating face, smoking a cigar and dressed as a Burghermeister, joins the group. Sinclair does not recognize him. He shakes his outstretched hand, which is plump, soft, friendly, but very, very cold.

"My name is General Mazariegos. I don't believe we ever had the pleasure of meeting, not face to face, at least. I was Colonel Adalberto Bermúdez's boss in G-2. I knew you, through him, by your code name—SPINNER."

He speaks of inter-departmental skulduggery and rivalry between the DGI and G-2. Sinclair would never have suspected that such petty turf wars were possible in a Revolutionary Paradise such as Cuba. The General recounts how he was one of the victims of the purge that hit G-2 following Tomás Verga's execution of Carlos Maxwell in Nicaragua.

"All hell broke loose in the Department—no pun intended, given the circumstances. It was a terrible disaster, because Maxwell was a rising star. Fidel was furious. He demanded a head on a plate. So they came down on me like a ton of bricks, *coño*, I mean someone had to be blamed for the loss of *Compañero* Maxwell—he was DGI's brightest boy after all—and I was the one who was made to pay for it, even though I had nothing to do with Nicaragua. I was getting long in the tooth anyway, and they needed a scapegoat. So here I am, associated with you in one way or another. Our paths did cross, at least indirectly. I am pleased to meet you at last. I did hear so much about you," with a nod towards the knight, "from our friend Maxwell."

Good or bad he does not elaborate and Sinclair is in no mood to ask.

Sinclair takes his leave, for now at least, and resumes his rounds. He comes upon a group of women. When he sees who it is he is startled to discover that adrenaline still rushes in his guts even though he is already dead.

It is Helen's turn to speak. She is holding a broom and is dressed sexily in black. Her unforgettable venerean strabismus is cast in half-shadow beneath the broad peak of her conical Witch's hat. The broomstick looks as if it has been greased for the Sabbat, and she caresses it with her unforgettable fingers, the nails as ever chewed to the quick. Hers are the pointy stiletto boots that Sinclair has previously mistaken for the cloven hoof of the Devil. When Sinclair recognizes her, his heart gives an involuntary somersault.

Staring at her hungrily he has a vision of this most beloved of witches skimming the treetops on her broomstick, crossing the moon and banking in low cloud.

In the Afterlife she still bears a striking resemblance to the young Stevie Nicks, her shortsighted gaze aroused with what looks to Sinclair like carnal intent. He is smitten, drowning in the sea of love. Perhaps there are opportunities for forgiveness and reconciliation here in the Afterlife, thinks Sinclair, *lingam* stirring, watching her much-remembered lips as they part to address him in that sleepy English Rose voice.

"I was telling Jane here that they say you never forget your first love. Well I never did forget you, George. Never will, even here. That thing with Doctor Aggarwal, I see now, that was not right. I should have stuck with you, even after what you did to my cousin Guy. I was horrid to you. I feel so bad about the way I behaved. The whole business made me feel squalid and dirty and guilty, like a pair of wet knickers. Perhaps I deserved to die. In fact I seriously considered suicide after I discovered Doctor Aggarwal with your Matron, but your women beat me to it."

"Crap," says her friend and admirer Jane Redfern, garbed as a medieval Serving Wench, as she tugs at Helen's hand in rebuke. "He's a bastard, he screwed me to get at you, he's low life and you know it, Helen Henshaw. I can't believe the crap you've just said."

But this has no effect on Helen, who still looks on Sinclair with longing tenderness. Jane casts a bitter look of reproach upon Sinclair, then glances back at Helen with a worried expression on her face, as if expecting trouble. "I just can't *believe* the two of you . . ."

But Jane is interrupted by the nasal tones of another girl's voice, a plaintive Northern voice.

"But *I* were your first love, weren't I, George Sinclair?"

Sinclair sees the painted white face and sad eyes of a girl called Tracy whom he vaguely remembers. He cannot see her clearly because she is tiptoeing up behind Jane Redfern's shoulder, straining to get a glimpse of Sinclair. She seems to be wearing the cap and apron of a Cook.

"I topped meself after what you did to me behind the Three Fishes in Whalley. You see I was in love with you, but all *you* wanted was to have your way with me. That's why you never saw me serving you again in the Refectory. I expect they didn't even bother to tell you."

Sinclair is starting to relive the memory—his fingers slipping between the girl's panties and her warm buttocks in the darkness outside the pub in Whalley, when yet again someone interrupts his reverie.

"My goodness gracious me, you don't seem to have a very successful track record with your women, do you, George Xavier *Gupta* Fernandes Sinclair, in the sense that they don't seem to last long after they cross your path. After your shadow has fallen upon them."

This voice he certainly recognizes—the sardonic singsong of the Indian accent, but he cannot see the good Doctor's face.

Helen and Jane then stand aside, like parting curtains, revealing the unlikely sight of a headless Fakir standing there in his ballooned trousers and pointed slippers. Like a circus trick, he holds a glass of sherry in one hand, and tucked under his other arm is the *tsantsa*, the tiny severed, turbaned head. The brown face of the little disembodied head speaks again, as Doctor Aggarwal addresses a bemused Sinclair.

"If I had a head to do it with, I would take my turban off to you. Honour is given where honour is due. I can only admire your guile and dedication, the best serpent in the grass I ever had the pleasure to be bitten by. A most thorough job you did on me. You are truly the Revenger, the personification of revenge, which is, as you know, being a fellow Indian, the most delicious curry ever known to man, best served cold with much turmeric and coriander, better even than a good mulligatawny. Or a vindaloo with a papadum."

Sinclair nods politely, acknowledging the compliment. He wonders whether Aggarwal is hallucinating because his mixed metaphors are threatening to break down into incoherence. Perhaps that is what decapitation followed by headshrinking does for one.

"I very much wish," says Sinclair to the ex-inhabitants of his Oxford days, "that I could stay and chat with you more." He feels a tug on his sleeve. He is the busy host whose attention is eagerly sought by other dear friends and enemies. He looks longingly once more at Helen's lips and her dimpled cheeks before taking his leave.

Pulling at his sleeve gently is a slim pale young man who looks as if he could be playing Hamlet, for he is dressed in the elegant black tights of a Cleric. He directs Sinclair towards yet another little sub gathering, which, it turns out, consists of the denizens of the Sinclair's Martiniquais adventure. It is none other than Rupert, who raises his hand in a casual gentlemanly wave, and smiles his Gentleman's smile, greeting Sinclair with the distant familiarity that is practised by Englishmen of his class and background.

Sinclair is not at all pleased to see Lucy Kennedy in the frock of a Barmaid, nor is she necessarily pleased to see him, judging by the evil scowl with which she greets him. She does look appetizing, though, quite edible, because her suntan and her sun-bleached hair are as he remembered them and she no longer has the tell-tale scabs of the bugger's pest.

"You sad paki fart, you put a hex on me and fucked me over for your own self-gratification, and then you drove me into the arms of Rupert, and look where that got me."

With his impeccably good manners, Rupert raises his G&T in a silent toast at Dirty Luce, as he used to call her behind her back in Martinique. Rupert looks much better than he did on the stairs of Lambeth Underground station, where Sinclair last saw him wasted and dreaming his acid dreams.

Madame Bernabeu's smiling nut-brown face is a welcome change from Lucy's sour features. Madame is dressed like the Papess of the Tarot. She takes his elbow, as she had done in the sugar-cane press in Martinique many years ago, and confidentially whispers her Creole breath, fragrant with *maracuja*, into his ear: "*Monsieur le Bokor* at Morne Diab'—remember him?—he told me to beware of you, that you walked in the shadows with Baron Samedi, with the Ghédé. I ignored him, and I paid the price. He said that I should never have given you the *gris gris*. As a result I lost my powers and in no time all of my *maléfices* turned back on me and I died, very quickly, leaving the Professor a widower. But I do nor regret our time together," she chuckles, with an impish wink that produces a stab of lust in Sinclair. "Especially our times in the cane press and under the mosquito net."

And finally, his College friends greet him. They stand in a close circle, wearing shiny black cloaks and hoods which look as expensive and soft as bat wings. They are sporting on chains the silver pentagrams of Devil Worshippers. Even in the Afterlife they have obviously not managed to shake off this ill-deserved reputation. As Sinclair approaches each of them in turn, they let the black capes slip off their shoulders, revealing other costumes.

And first, speaking of friends, is Doris. There he is, looking out demurely from beneath the muslin veil of a conical headdress. He is magnificently enrobed like the Princess he has always longed to be, and his arms are draped around the shoulders of his Page Boy.

"I don't believe you ever met Martin, not in the flesh, at least."

The Page Boy is a blond-haired boy of about thirteen with a birthmark on his right cheek, just as Doris had described him when as a ghost the young lad used to haunt his dormitory at the College. Martin Weld, the original *cabrit sans cornes*, nods cordially, acknowledging Sinclair's arrival. The fact that not half an hour ago Sinclair was sharing the same coffin with him does not seem to bother him. While Doris paddles Martin's neck fondly, he eyes the ghost of Rupert slyly, casting a simpering look in his direction as he plots his next move.

Wanking Eddy as usual is looking shifty. Wearing a burnous, he looks every inch the Arab Trader. He fixes one roving eye upon Sinclair, the other upon Olatunji Ogunlesi, whose Cardinal's robes rival in finery the gold brocade of his chauffeur Gumercindo's papal vestments.

As for Cassius, Morguer and Tantum, the most recent of the dearly departed, they are there too. The trio stands in a tight knot, newcomers to the party. They are still draped in their burial shrouds and redolent of formaldehyde, looking for all intents and purposes like victims of the Black Death. They eye Sinclair with suspicion, for they bear no love or friendship towards their executioner, unlike some of the other guests, who have had time to think and have found it in their hearts to forgive. It is far too early in the karmic process to expect forgiveness from the Unholy Trinity.

To Sinclair, this resentful trio seems to have become one amorphous person—Sinclair sees a silent sideways movement like a crab's, and remembers the flesh peeling off the little priest's back in short strips. He hears the East End inflections of someone with a satanic face who can no longer be bothered to hide his provenance because here there are no secrets. He sees the bags under the Nosferatu's cheekbones and he sees him pushing back his cuticles furiously with a paper clip. He catches a whiff of decomposing flesh, but he soon realizes that it is the putrid exhalation that accompanies a few disjointed and nonsensical words uttered in Australian. Dr Tantum, eyes bulging, is still having psychedelic visions under the influence of the mind-altering drug that dispatched him in his office a few hours ago.

And who then is this splendid soldier dressed like one of the Pope's Swiss Guard? He stands pike in hand, guarding the Unholy Trinity like a bodyguard. Suddenly he steps forward and salutes smartly. It is Muggins—but instead of the stuttering idiot flegger with half a cranium, he is now dressed immaculately in his highly polished helmet and breastplate and ceremonial regimental garb. On his breastplate are multi-coloured medal ribbons from various military campaigns, some well known, others secret. He looks like a new man with his new set of teeth.

"You see, Master Sinclair," he says, not without irony, "here on t'uther side, the virtuous are restored to their most pristine condition. I now have the whole of me head back and I can wear all of me medals proudly and I don't 'ave to wipe your fookin' trays, not now."

Sinclair looks away, ashamed of having tormented the noble Muggins when he was a boy. As he turns away he catches a scent of almonds in the air.

And there she is, in all her glory, dressed as Kali Maa—she is even wearing a necklace of tiny skulls—her face made up in indigo blue. She moistens her blue lips with her tongue, which is a livid scarlet, before she holds forth. She speaks of how tiring it is being her daughter's servant—an *mpungo*—and of spending the majority of her time in a *nganga*; of the challenges of shape shifting into a scorpion; she speaks of the awfulness of suffocating in a coffin, and of lying on top of a decomposing corpse; and then, finally, after she has all of these complaints off her chest, she speaks of love: "I tried to love you in my way. I knew you were a killer, a Malefic person. I felt so much pity for you but I could never express my love for you."

Uncharacteristically, she pauses, looks down, and swallows hard with emotion. "My father," she nods at Fr Cassius, who is watching her carefully from across the room, "always taught me to be strong. And it is true, he did warn me about you, and yes, it is true that I ignored him and insisted on having you. And now I hate him for it. You see, it's not all love and kisses and cuddles and forgiveness here on the other side, whatever they taught you at the College. We are like the Greek Gods—although we are dead and immortal in our way, we are still subject to lust and hate and jealousy and spite and envy and desire and we are still nourished by revenge, which we look for and feed off whenever and wherever we can find it. It's the same with the *orishas* and the *loas* that you are so fond of. For those of us who remain enslaved by these feelings, it will take many more rounds of reincarnation to break away from them. The process is called karma. My karma, at least until our daughter decides it is time to release me from that fucking gourd, is to be her agent, her wraith of vengeance upon the world."

As the blue *devi* addresses him, Sinclair himself is taken again by that infuriatingly ambiguous emotion. Is it love or pity or fear or hate that he feels for this werewolf of a woman? Even in the Afterlife she is bound to remain an enigma to him. He will never understand her.

A smirking cadaver in Death's black cowl has been watching Sinclair silently since he first entered the Library and all the while as he has made the rounds of the deathly cocktail reception. He watches Sinclair and at the same time is engaged in earnest conversation with an old lady.

An old lady. Sinclair's heart pounds wildly in his ribcage as he hopes against hope that the grey hairs of the lady are those of his long-lost Grannyjee, but his hopes are dashed when she turns from talking to her grandson Guy Underhill who, it turns out, is the one garbed as the Grim Reaper. It is Gran, Underhill's grandmother, in a Tart's mini-skirt showing off her legs, which are

surprisingly sturdy and well-muscled for an old lady. She does not smile at
Sinclair, but regards him with the same bewildered expression that he remembers her greeting him with when he used to turn up with Underhill at her flat
in Goodge Street for the half-term holiday.

A combination of disappointment and irritation leads to an ill-tempered
outburst from Sinclair as he finally addresses Guy Underhill.

"And Underhill, Guy Underhill, since *you're* not dead, what the fuck are *you*
doing here in the middle of all these fucking ghosts? What are *you* doing
dressed as the Grim Reaper, for God's sake? What are *you* doing with that
enormous fucking scythe? So fuck off with you—go and haunt some other
dead fucker. *You* said *you* turned forty last December 17th. So *you* must have
survived the ouija curse."

"I did not."

"You fucking well did." Sinclair is losing his temper now.

"Did not."

"Did!"

It is then that he hears Ximena intervene.

"What Guy Underhill *did* say, father, if I am not mistaken, is that his fortieth birthday was last December 17th. But he did not say that he was actually
alive on his fortieth birthday—did you, Guy Underhill?"

By this stage it is all getting too much for George Sinclair, too ridiculous.
He rubs his eyes and feels like weeping. He has become, as the saying goes,
tired and emotional.

"Correct, my dear," said Underhill with a mocking smile, addressing
Ximena and deliberately ignoring Sinclair. "In fact I died back in, back in, ah
. . . it must have been in the mid eighties, just after your father George came
up from Oxford to visit me in the squat in Hull. You see it was his indifference
that got me in the end. I had survived his betrayal, just barely, but when he
turned up asking only about my cousin, well that just broke my heart. So after
your father left, I asked the punks in the squat to inject me to Kingdom
Come."

And sure enough, as if to corroborate Underhill's version of events, a
deformed creature wearing a Bishop's mitre and crozier steps into the magic
circle to testify. It is the punk with half a face, the major part of his cranium
missing, who announces to the company that he also died from an overdose
but not on purpose, like Mr Underhill here, and in 1987, not 1985.

Guy Underhill speaks again, this time addressing Sinclair directly: "You
may remember something that was written on the wall of the squat? *What*

Goes Around Comes Around . . . Well," he says, turning away, "that's all I have to say."

There is someone special missing from the proceedings. It is someone who Sinclair has been longing to see and who continues to elude his gaze as it wanders searchingly over the familiar faces of his dead friends, lovers and enemies. It is someone, perhaps the only one, who can rescue him from this abominable hallucination. Someone who can whisk him off and travel with him, showing him the way home to Shiva.

He thinks of asking his parents, who stand apart from the rest of the crowd. Major Sinclair looks stiff and ill at ease as he sips his sherry, spine ramrod-straight and looking no worse the wear for the car accident that claimed his life while Sinclair was at Oxford. The Major's wife looks down at her hands, refusing to look at her son in the eye. Standing respectfully behind his masters, Old Ajay the garden-wallah salutes Sinclair with a cricket umpire's gesture. He holds his arthritic index finger up before his nose, signifying the Sinclair has been bowled out—dismissed—and must begin the long trudge back to the pavilion.

"*Where* is Grannyjee?" he insists.

Grannyjee, who has been dead for years. Who had been the first of all these people to die.

Grannyjee—who after all has been known to appear to him even when she was not yet dead—is nowhere to be seen. And when he needs her most. Her absence is beginning to infuriate him.

There is a note of desperation in Sinclair's voice as it cracks into the embarrassing high-pitched whine of a lost boy looking for his granny. The circle of the dearly departed begins to close in on him.

"Here I am."

But it is not Grannyjee's voice.

He spins around frantically, looking for the loving eyes of his grandmother, who will surely save him from this aggressive crowd of undead. Instead he sees, for the first time in his life, a loving smile in the black eyes of his daughter Ximena.

"If only you had eyes to see, father . . . I am still disappointed that you never recognized me when you had the chance. It's me, you see, here I am. *I* am Grannyjee. Didn't I say that I would return to watch over you, didn't I?"

Things can't get more bizarre. He turns to face the company, apologetically. The Company of the Dead.

"So many deaths, so many of you. In my forty years I have been involved in many deaths. I have so many deaths to answer for. More than I ever imagined."

More at least than the thirteen he had counted at the tapas bar at Vauxhall Cross on his last day as a spook.

It is again Ximena-Grannyjee who solves the mystery for him.

"The problem is, father," she explains patiently, "that you happen to have a Malefic Saturn in your Twelfth House. In India they say that men with Saturn in the Twelfth are to be feared, because they walk with death, whatever they touch dies, they infect others with mortality. They are the King Midas of death. In Cuba and Haiti and Martinique, like Madame Bernabeu says, they also saw you for what you are, a son of Baron Samedi. Such men are their own worst enemies, because the Twelfth House is also the house of self-undoing, and Baron Samedi is a treacherous patron. Why do you think I had to come back to watch over you? Why do you think I cried so much when they sent you away from me in 1971?"

"But then why did you lock me in the coffin with Martin Weld? Why am I dead . . . or am I?"

"You are dead, father. And I did it because soon there would only be me left for you to hurt. Look around you. I am the only one alive here. Look at all the dead, even Guy Underhill is dead. I am the only one left who you can still infect with your mortality. Each one of these dead is a *cabrit sans cornes*. A human sacrifice. It wasn't just Simon Cavendish who you sacrificed. They *all* died for you. They died because of something you did or because they had something to do with you or because you crossed their paths—or, as Doctor Aggarwal put it, because your shadow simply happened to fall upon them. Each one of these dead people was a human sacrifice. Each human sacrifice enabled you to survive another day, another year, to make it to your fortieth birthday. You infected them with premature death. If you could so callously betray your best friend Guy Underhill—like his ghost told me you did, while you were shooting up and we were walking in the woods around Ma's cottage—you could also do it to me . . ."

"Please, please, then, my love, even if I am dying, tell me once again that *you* are alive, that you don't belong here with this crowd."

"I am alive, father. But I live in both worlds. You should know that by now."

Sinclair is suddenly fantastically tired. Something in him wants to bring the whole absurd phantasmagoric proceedings to a close, once and for all. He is ready to move onto the next phase, whatever that might be. Oblivion hopefully, but knowing his luck and Grannyjee's secret doctrine, more likely some unpleasant karmic reincarnation. A frog or a stoat, perhaps. Knowing his luck, that is what he will return as because of his misdeeds, the evidence of which he has just reviewed in the form of all of these fucking ghosts assembled in the Arundell Library.

After all, he thinks irritably, death can't just be an interminable fancy-dress cocktail full of past life reviews with your nearest and dearest. So they have all made their point: Sinclair is a Malefic bastard. Now what? This state of affairs cannot persist, surely. There must be some finality to whole bizarre situation, must there not?

"So where is he, then? Where is the Devil? Or Baron Samedi or the Ghédé for that matter. They're one and the same, aren't they? Isn't the whole point of this ridiculous gathering that after the past-life review—which each of you have been so kind as to assist me with—his Lordship is meant to appear and drag me down kicking and screaming into the fire, like Faustus?"

As if on cue, the whole circle of ghosts erupts in a collective fit of laughter. Sinclair sees FJ pointing at him as he rocks on his heels in mirth, and Belén Flores puts her hand over her mouth, permitting herself a shy chuckle. Even the surly spies Spedding and Cavendish seem to have been cheered up by Sinclair's joke. Gumercindo's teeth flash and even the poor Leper Robin Ruskin is holding his belly in almost painful merriment.

It is Helen who finally lets him in on the joke. As if playing charades, her fingers form of a pair of horns growing out of her forehead and then she points at Sinclair. That is when he looks down at himself for the first time and realizes that all along he has been dressed in red and black, an elegant crimson cape draped over his shoulders, and that in his left hand he holds a red pitchfork. He raises his hand to his temple and feels a goatlike horn.

He hears the rustling of cloth behind him.

"Welcome home, George Xavier Gupta Sinclair."

He turns just in time to catch a flash of light glancing off a blade. It belongs to the enormous scythe that black-robed Guy Underhill, in keeping with his role as the Grim Reaper, is bearing down upon his head.

*

The scythe splits his skull, trepanning his brain like a hot knife through butter. Sinclair breathes his last.

He is still in Martin Weld's coffin in the crypt where his daughter has locked him. Or is he? For a split second, as his brain starts to shut down, he wonders whether he is not in fact still in his study in North Oxford, and whether his return back up North has just been another bad trip.

The buzzing of the chainsaws is back again, and he is being sucked back into the spinning vortex. It's always the same story, he says to himself, the same vortex, the same tunnel, over the ages, following each of my many deaths. But the thing is, he continues, that you only ever remember it when you are in the tunnel.

In the dark he searches in vain for the thread of golden light that once had once almost led him to Shiva and looks for the kind warm hands of his grandmother.

But this time Grannyjee is not there to greet him on the other side, since she is back in the Land of the Living again and is a girl called Ximena Sinclair.

He looks back down the vortex that has swallowed him countless times through the ages and he fancies he sees a man sitting in an armchair in a little house in North Oxford, an arm thrust out, a livid vein turning blue, an air bubble travelling up an artery, a syringe on the table beside him.

In the distant gloaming, in the direction of what seems to be a crossroads of some sort, a figure is waiting to greet him.

In the heavens, in the outer reaches of the solar system, Saturn is coming to end of its massive and inevitable foray through the sign of Gemini. Many millions of miles above an unlikely circle of ghosts assembled in a musty library in the middle of nowhere in Lancashire, the Great Malefic has finished his work in the Twelfth House.

The ghosts, who appear to have been celebrating some kind of Danse Macabre, are disbanding, melting back into the walls and bookshelves of the Arundell Library.

And Morpheus, whose other name, it turns out, is Baron Samedi, has wrested control of the crossroads from the man-child Legba.

It is the second week of June, 2002.

On the first day after half-term, there was a funeral service with full choir, incense, gem-encrusted black funeral vestments—the works. It was officiated by Spock, the new Headmaster, and it was being held in memory of the dead;

the dead being Fathers Morguer and Cassius, and Dr Tantum. They had, it was reported, all died coincidental but natural deaths during the half-term holiday. No one believed it for a minute.

The three coffins lay in a neat row under the monstrous gothic altarpiece. Prayers were also offered for the soul of an Old Boy of the College by the name of George Sinclair (1975-1981) who had passed away in Oxford recently. The rumour going around the Staff Common Room was that he had died of a drug overdose. Some of the older masters remembered him. Dolly Beamish, overdue for retirement, and bat-faced Pottifer, also well past his sell-by date, reminded each other of what they had always said: that "that Sinclair boy was nothing but trouble and that it would all end in tears".

2003
EPILOGUE

BENEDICTION

At the College, it is time for Benediction. The late September evening breathes a chill, moist air over the moonlit countryside, with its fells and the dark shape of Pendle, countryside which is fit only for witches and their familiars.

The new Assistant Matron, who they say is the daughter of a previous Matron who had served at the College some years ago, sits at the back of the church. She scans the congregation with outrageously dark Gypsy eyes, as if looking for someone.

They say that she lives in a cottage up on Pendle Hill with an old black crone who keeps house for her. Some of the boys (and not a few of the Staff) are fascinated and repulsed by her at the same time.

It is unusual to have anyone in the Infirmary so early in the new term. Miss Sinclair sits on the side of the boy's bed in the Infirmary, grasping his wrist as she takes his temperature and feels his pulse. She looks only at her wristwatch.

"What's your name, boy?"

The child looks familiar. His hair is a dirty blond and, unlike the others, he dares to look her directly in the eye.

He replies, awkwardly, because the thermometer is still wedged under his tongue.

"Underhill, Miss. *George Underhill.*"

A week earlier the bus from Preston (by the look of it probably the same one that had carried George Sinclair away in 1981 and had bought him back to meet his fate in 2002) had disgorged a new generation of Catholic Gentleman—Men for Others—and their trunks and tuckboxes, in front of the Lions.

It was dark and the lights of the building's many windows promised warmth within, out of the polar wind that made the flags snap loudly overhead.

A New Boy, his eyes watering in the cold blast, had looked up beyond the massive façade at the eagle-topped cupolas. He seemed rather small for his age, with his mousey blond hair and rosy cheeks. He had stood there grasping his cricket bat, ready for the game.

He had been destined to stand in that place from a time well before he was even a lustful twinkle in his father's eye. He had been registered at birth. The building had been waiting for him for centuries.

L . D . S .

AN EXTRACT FROM CHAPTER ONE OF
'A COMPARATIVE ANALYSIS OF
AFRO-ANTILLEAN SYNCRETISM'

ELEGGUÁ

In the Afro-Cuban *regla de ochá* or *santería*, as it is more commonly known, Elegguá is the God of the Crossroads and the Messenger of the Gods. This *orisha* is the deity that opens and closes the way, the gatekeeper, and therefore this opening chapter is dedicated to him.

Elegguá is the owner of doors and of the road, of crossroads and of opportunities, and he has twenty-one paths or avatars. He is also the cosmic trickster and revels in malice.

This duality may be explained by the tradition that says that Elegguá walks alongside, or is a derivation of, a much older, more sinister and devilish Yoruba deity called Eshu (viz. Exú below).

Elegguá is, with Oggún, Ochosi and Osún, one of the four powerful *orishas* known as the Warriors, and is commonly depicted as a cement head with cowry shells for eyes, ears, nose and mouth. A nail and a rooster feather protrude horn-like from the crown of the head, which sits in a clay dish surrounded by offerings. The shrine is placed behind the front door of the devotee's house. The requirements for his shrine are fishmeal, tobacco, rum, toys and sweets, with which he must be propitiated on Mondays. Elegguá must be appeased and fed constantly by his children. His favourite food is the blood of a young black goat slaughtered by the sacred knife. He should be wafted with tobacco smoke and sprayed with rum.

In the rituals of the *lucumí*, who are the descendants of the Yoruba in Cuba, he is invoked with the sacred *batá*. These are the three doubleheaded hourglass-shaped drums which are themselves inhabited by spirits called *aña*. The gatekeeper has his own proprietary rhythms which act like a code to communicate between the world of humans and that of the *orishas*.

He is always the first of the divine horsemen to be invoked, and the last deity to leave the proceedings, the alpha and the omega of the *regla de ochá*. In the various *lucumí tambors*, otherwise known as *toques* or *bembés*, the *akpwon*, the singer-priest, starts the ceremony by insulting and taunting the god in order to attract his attention and dislodge him from his parapet in Yoruba heaven. This is necessary in order to make the deity take an interest in the human world and come down and mount his horse—one of his devotees who has been led into trance by the sacred code in the drumbeat. His attributes include the *garabato*, a hooked stick with which he clears the undergrowth between his world and ours. Without his permission and intervention, the paths between the Upperworld and the Underworld will remain closed. In Cuba, the God of the Crossroads syncretizes with St Antony of Padua, St Martin of Porres and the Christ Child of Atocha, and, in some traditions, with the Archangel Michael, equivalent of the avatar Elegguá Agongo, who is invoked by the bewitched to help turn the evil spells cast by their enemies back upon them. The devotees of this saint are forbidden to eat eggs, are likely to live on or near crossroads, tend to be born on Mondays and are advised to avoid firearms.

Every person's head is owned by an *orisha*, whether they know it or not and whether they like it or not. The *omo Elegguá*, or the child of Elegguá, is a person whose life is marked by mischief and constant ambivalence. He can be best described as a 'tricky customer'.

In Haiti Elegguá is known as Papa Legba and in *vodoun* this *loa* is associated with St Peter (who controls the entrance to heaven); he is honoured by tall drums called *asoko*. He is referred to as *Met Kafou (Maitre Carrefour)*. The Haitian rites always begin with the following incantation:

> *Papa Legba, ouvrez barrière pou moin passé!*
> *Papa Legba open the gate so that I may enter!*

Legba's Nemesis is Baron Samedi, the dark *loa* who takes care of the dead and also haunts the crossroads, the place where the spirits cross into our world; the Baron feeds on the dead, the Ghédé, and is the guardian of the cemetery and the master of shapeshifting. His symbol is a black cross on a tomb. (In *santería* the Goddess of the Cemetery is Oyá).

In the Brazilian *candomblé*, Elegguá or Legba is Exú, and is summoned by drums called *atabaques*. In Brazil, this *orixa*, whose attribute is the trident—the pitchfork—is commonly mistaken for the Devil, but in fact Exú is to be feared only because he restores equilibrium by administering justice to the wicked.

In other world traditions, Elegguá has been associated with Hermes, or Mercury, the Messenger of the Gods, the restless Trickster God of the ancient Mediterranean. He is also associated with goat-like Pan, the horned God of Mischief, half-man half-goat, the cloven-hoofed faun, who is said to be the son of Hermes.

To the Egyptians he was Anubis, the jackal-headed guide of the dead, who shows the dearly departed the pathways to the 'undiscovered country' and guards their tombs, which are the gateways to the Afterlife.

To the Hindus, the archetype is manifested as Hanuman, the playful Monkey God who, like the Warrior Elegguá, is also a martial figure, a general of the celestial army in the service of Shiva the Destroyer, of whom he is a favourite, much as Elegguá is the favourite of Olofin, the Almighty.

In the European tradition, a playful incarnation of the archetype is the Elizabethan *Puck*. But perhaps the most troubling and distorted manifestation of Elegguá in Europe can be found in court records of the 14th century. During the persecution and trials of the mysterious Knights Templar, it emerged that members of the Order were accused among other things of worshipping the disembodied head of a horned god called the Baphomet, otherwise referred to as the Sabbatic Goat, and whose image appears to have found its way into the popular imagination via the Devil card of the Tarot.

Finally, in Western and Vedic astrology, this disturbing archetype is undoubtedly manifested in the planet Saturn, the Great Malefic, the Lord of Karma, and in the Zodiac with the two-faced quicksilver sign of Gemini, which is ruled by the planet Mercury (see Hermes above).

Whatever the derivation or manifestation of this deity, the point is that when Elegguá comes, he comes to test the human heart.

(From chapter one of George Sinclair's 'A Comparative Analysis of Afro-Antillean Syncretism', Oxford University Press, 2001)